11/22/11

To Dwell among Cedars

Books by Connilyn Cossette

OUT FROM EGYPT

Counted with the Stars
Shadow of the Storm
Wings of the Wind

CITIES OF REFUGE

A Light on the Hill
Shelter of the Most High
Until the Mountains Fall
Like Flames in the Night

THE COVENANT HOUSE

To Dwell among Cedars

THE COVENANT HOUSE 1

To Dwell among Cedars

CONNILYN COSSETTE

BETHANYHOUSE
a division of Baker Publishing Group
Minneapolis, Minnesota

© 2020 by Connilyn Cossette

Published by Bethany House Publishers
11400 Hampshire Avenue South
Bloomington, Minnesota 55438
www.bethanyhouse.com

Bethany House Publishers is a division of
Baker Publishing Group, Grand Rapids, Michigan

Printed in the United States of America

Library of Congress Cataloging-in-Publication Data
Names: Cossette, Connilyn, author.
Title: To dwell among cedars / Connilyn Cossette.
Description: Minneapolis, Minnesota : Bethany House, a division of Baker
    Publishing Group, [2020] | Series: The covenant house ; 1
Identifiers: LCCN 2020029206 | ISBN 9780764234347 (trade paper) | ISBN
    9780764237881 (casebound) | ISBN 9781493428090 (ebook)
Subjects: LCSH: Ark of the Covenant—Fiction. | GSAFD: Bible fiction.
Classification: LCC PS3603.O8655 T6 2020 | DDC 813/.6—dc23
LC record available at https://lccn.loc.gov/2020029206

This is a work of historical reconstruction; the appearances of certain historical figures are therefore inevitable. All other characters, however, are products of the author's imagination, and any resemblance to actual persons, living or dead, is coincidental.

Cover design by Jennifer Parker
Cover photography by Mike Habermann Photography, LLC
Map illustration by Samuel T. Campione

Author is represented by The Steve Laube Agency.

21 22 23 24 25 26   7 6 5 4 3 2

For my Grandma Ruth,

whose love for Israel and unwavering support for its people inspired my explorations of the roots of my faith, and whose insistence on standing four-year-old me on a piano bench to sing beloved hymns for her annual holiday gatherings was the foundation of my love of music. "If they won't listen to you sing, Conni," she used to say, "then go tell your story to the rocks. Jesus will hear you." Her memory is a blessing to me and all who knew her, and I cannot wait to worship beside her in the world to come.

The Great Sea

Tyre

Acco

ASHER

NAPHTALI

Mt. Hermon

EAST MANASSEH

Sea of Kinneret

ZEBULAN

WEST MANASSEH

ISSACHAR

GAD

Shechem

EPHRAIM

Shiloh

Beit El

Ramah

BENJAMIN

Ayalon

Mitzpah

Jerusalem
(Jebus)

DAN

Ashdod

Ekron

Eshtaol

Kiryat-Yearim

REUBEN

BethShemesh

Ashkelon

Gath

JUDAH
(Yehudah)

Hebron

PHILISTINES

Gaza

Salt Sea

SIMEON

Be'ersheva

MOAB

Jordan River

Part One

In those days there was no king in Israel. Everyone did what was right in his own eyes.

Judges 21:25

Now Israel went out to battle against the Philistines. They encamped at Ebenezer, and the Philistines encamped at Aphek. The Philistines drew up in line against Israel, and when the battle spread, Israel was defeated before the Philistines, who killed about four thousand men on the field of battle. And when the people came to the camp, the elders of Israel said, "Why has the LORD defeated us today before the Philistines? Let us bring the ark of the covenant of the LORD here from Shiloh, that it may come among us and save us from the power of our enemies." So the people sent to Shiloh and brought from there the ark of the covenant of the LORD of hosts, who is enthroned on the cherubim. And the two sons of Eli, Hophni and Phinehas, were there with the ark of the covenant of God.

As soon as the ark of the covenant of the LORD came into the camp, all Israel gave a mighty shout, so that the earth resounded. And when the Philistines heard the noise of the shouting, they said, "What does this great shouting in the camp of the Hebrews mean?" And when they learned that the ark of the LORD had come to the camp, the Philistines were afraid, for they said, "A god has come into the camp." And they said, "Woe to us! For nothing like this has happened before. Woe to us! Who can deliver us from the power of these mighty gods? These are the gods who struck the Egyptians with every sort of plague in the wilderness. Take courage, and be men, O Philistines, lest you become slaves to the Hebrews as they have been to you; be men and fight."

So the Philistines fought, and Israel was defeated, and they fled, every man to his home. And there was a very great slaughter, for thirty thousand foot soldiers of Israel fell. And the ark of God was captured, and the two sons of Eli, Hophni and Phinehas, died.

1 Samuel 4:1–11

One

Arisa

1070 BC
ASHDOD, PHILISTIA

"Lukio!" I screamed, as a wave crashed over us and yanked my brother's small hand from mine. He disappeared under the surface, and I lunged into the foamy surf, gasping with relief when I caught hold of his tunic, then gagged as brine hit the back of my throat. My fingers stiff from fear, I pulled upward until he emerged, sputtering seawater. Tightening my grip, I curled my toes into the shifting sand as I fought the insistent pull of the sea and dragged us both to the beach, fighting my exhaustion and the weight of a seven-year-old who stood a head taller than others his age. When we were finally free of the current and the earth was once again firm beneath us, we flopped our sodden bodies on the sand, chests heaving and eyes on the pure blue canopy above.

"I told you not to go out so far," I panted, squinting against the glaring sun.

"But I saw the biggest shell, Risi," he said, his voice small and

9

contrite. "It was rolling out with the waves. I couldn't let it get away."

"And you should drown yourself for a shell? You have plenty, Lukio, a whole collection."

"But—"

"No. You must listen to me and not wander off," I said, hoping I sounded enough like our aunt Jacame that he would take me seriously. "You might have been dragged out to sea had I not seen you go under." Angry tears burned the backs of my eyes.

Lukio was silent. His wide eyes—one green, one brown—watched me as I railed at him and the shock of what had nearly happened caught up to me.

"We only have each other," I whispered, digging my fingers into the gritty sand. "What would I do without you?"

With a sob he flung himself over me, his arms winding around my neck. "I'm sorry, Risi! I only wanted to get the shell for you. It was a purple one like you like—" The rest of his explanation was lost as his tearful apology muffled against my wet tunic.

I sat up, pulling him into my lap and gripping his sea-soaked body tight against me. I kissed his head, salt on my lips as I took a deep breath and reassured myself he was safe. The sea hadn't taken him. We were together, and we were both safe.

A shadow moved over us, and I looked up to find Jacame frowning at us. "If the two of you are quite finished playing in the water, there are baskets to carry home."

"We weren't playing—" Lukio began.

"Of course," I interrupted, not wanting my aunt to know I'd been closing my eyes and humming through the song I'd learned from Azuvah instead of watching my brother. I'd been trying to practice the strange melody and the words in the foreign tongue our Hebrew slave spoke to us whenever my aunt and uncle were not around.

Pushing Lukio from my lap, I stood and brushed sand off both of us, then turned a bright smile on my aunt. "How can we help?"

"There are three baskets of goods, and that old woman only

has two hands," said Jacame, as if such a thing were an affront to her. "You children can each take one."

My mother's sister was not unkind to us, but there was little warmth in the woman. The deep lines between her eyes attested to a lifetime of furrowed brows and she had none of the graceful beauty my mother had been famous for. Still, she had been more than generous to take us into her home five years ago when my father dumped us, along with Azuvah, at her threshold before he boarded a ship for the last time, heading back to the distant northern shores his ancestors hailed from.

Not wanting to chance being separated from Lukio for anything, I dutifully gripped his hand in mine and followed my aunt back up to the market near the port, vowing to never again take my eyes off my brother. He was my responsibility and had been since our mother died giving him life. I loved no one in this world more than Lukio.

Azuvah, the slave who had been with my family for as long as I could remember, stood waiting for us, three large baskets at her feet. Although her expression remained neutral, her deep brown eyes flitted to my brother and me, relief in their murky depths that made me wonder whether she'd seen Lukio go under the water. The old Hebrew woman saved her smiles and stories and songs only for Lukio and me in private; to Jacame she displayed only blank-faced submission, as was expected of her. Like me, I suspected she would do anything to please my aunt, not wanting to jeopardize her position in the household.

Once the three market baskets had been distributed—mine full of fish, Azuvah's a variety of shellfish, and Lukio's a large bundle of the finest papyrus and an assortment of imported spices—Jacame led us to the river, heedless of the weight we carried for her.

Lukio had been thrilled when our aunt insisted we accompany her to the port north of the city, not only because it gave him a chance to enjoy the sea, but because it was necessary to ride on one of the shallow-bottomed boats that ferried goods up and down the river. Once he was safely tucked into the hull between Azuvah and me, his eyes sparkled with excitement for the return trip as he watched the men push the vessel away from the shore and begin to row against the current. He was enthralled by every stroke and every guttural command the leader of the team spat at the rowers. But as for me, no matter how lovely the boat's bird-headed prows might be or how swiftly it cut through the water, I could not help but remember that a ship had been the very means by which our father abandoned us.

The sun had not even reached its high point by the time the enormous walls of Ashdod rose up before us, the most prestigious of the Five Cities sprawling like an overindulged queen at the conflux of the river and the most important trade road between Egypt and Damascus. Colorful banners danced on the ramparts in the distance, welcoming us home.

The moment the boat touched land, Jacame hissed at us to disembark with all haste. Messengers had spread word that the army would arrive back in Ashdod today, two months after heading off to war against the Hebrews. With her three sons among its ranks, she was determined to provide them with a lavish homecoming feast this evening, which is why she'd insisted on meticulously tending to every detail. I knew little about this latest struggle against Azuvah's people but had heard my uncle Harrom describe them as a plague over the hills and valleys to the east. This was only one of many battles we'd fought with the Hebrews since our people had arrived on the shores of this fertile land, but it was the first major one since their champion had brought a temple down on the heads of a large number of our commanders and leaders a few years ago.

Stumbling as she stepped out of the boat, two of the fish Azuvah carried tumbled out of her basket and plunked into the muddy water with a small splash.

"Look what you've done, you clumsy old woman!" snapped Jacame. "I selected each one of those fish myself! Now we will have two less to serve this evening. The feast will be ruined! I should make you walk back to the fish market and purchase more."

Her harsh rebuke was sliced in two by a chorus of horn blasts coming from the direction of the trade road, and I hoped it was enough to make her forget her threat of forcing Azuvah to walk back to the port, a journey that would take many hours.

My aunt's face went pale as a hand flew to her heart. "Have they returned already?"

Another joyful blast of the horns answered her question; the army had indeed returned. All around us people began moving toward the sounds of rhythmic drumbeats and shouts that announced a triumphant arrival.

The third blast of the rams' horn rang with such a distinctive warble of victory that it seemed to vibrate my bones. We must have won a great battle against the Hebrews.

Jacame demanded we hurry, anxious to catch sight of her sons among the long parade of soldiers that would soon be entering the city gates, their long spears held aloft and round shields tucked against broad chests in an impressive show of Philistine military might. She pushed through the crowd, caring nothing for the fact that Azuvah, Lukio, and I still hefted overflowing baskets.

We allowed the current of bodies to carry us along, keeping pace with the soldiers as they headed toward the center of town, where Dagon stood watch over Ashdod within his imposing and ornate temple, bestowing prosperity and fertility on the people who'd adopted the once foreign god as their own. Today, our victorious soldiers would deliver the spoils of the battle to his feet, and the leaders would offer libations and sacrifices in thanks for his favor.

"Stay close. I don't want you to get lost in the crowd," I said to my wide-eyed brother as the curious crowd around us began to thicken and came to a halt before the temple.

Lukio pressed in close to me, and I encouraged him to place his basket at his feet like I had and keep a tight hold on my hand. I was unable to see much of anything with the shifting, roiling crowd in my way, but he was enclosed by a wall of bodies and likely frightened by the chaos.

Through the gaps between shoulders, I caught a glimpse of the commanders of the procession, their bronze-scaled armor flashing in the sunlight and their feathered headdresses regal and bright against the blue sky. At the very front of the parade was the *seren* himself. The young king of Ashdod perched atop an enormous stallion, his own polished armor bearing the marks of the recent battle, and both his thick-muscled arms were wrapped in linen, evidence of his bravery on the battlefield. One of the tallest and most handsome men I'd ever seen, the seren was known to be ruthless in his dealings with enemies and fearless on the battlefield. Even among the other four kings of Philistia, he stood apart. Regal and well-deserving of his scepter, there was no better man to rule the region. A warm swell of pride in my people and my king rushed through my whole body.

"What is that?" I asked Jacame when I caught the barest glimpse of something sparkling in the bed of an ox-drawn wagon. "I can't see."

"It's some sort of box," said my aunt. "Made of gold and with winged creatures atop the lid. It must be a trophy of the battle, depictions of the gods of the Hebrews, I would guess."

God, my mind silently corrected. Azuvah was very firm that her people only worshiped one god. An all-powerful one. I'd heard stories of Yahweh from her lips since I was tiny, always whispered in secret or sung about in her Hebrew lullabies. It was implicitly understood that the stories of Yahweh and his deeds were to be kept between Azuvah, Lukio, and me, and since I did not want them to end, I had never breathed a word about them to anyone else.

The urge to see the box for myself pulsed through my limbs. Something about Jacame's description seemed familiar, and I glanced at Azuvah for confirmation that this golden box was indeed a Hebrew treasure.

Azuvah was no young woman—her hair had been gray for as long as I remembered—but in the past four years, it seemed her wrinkles had multiplied and her back stooped further every month. I wondered sometimes if her aging had been compounded

14

by her additional labor as a kitchen slave, instead of tending only to Lukio and me as she'd done in my father's house. But now every remnant of color fled her skin as a look of absolute horror settled into the lines of her face.

"Mercy," she whispered in her own tongue, her eyes following the wagon with a strange look of longing as it passed almost directly in front of us. "Have mercy on us."

Regardless that the day was warm, with a gentle breeze sweeping around me and brushing across my shoulders, a cold finger of dread slipped up my spine. How could a box frighten her so?

"Make way!" shouted one of the soldiers. "Make way for the shame of our enemies! Make a path to Dagon!"

The crowd scuttled back a few steps as the wagon rattled along, and the shift in movement afforded me a few moments to see the golden box with my own eyes. There were indeed some sort of winged creatures, their feathers curled as if in protection over whatever might lay inside. I wished I could ask Azuvah if she knew about the contents, but I dared not speak of it in front of Jacame.

The crowd jostled again as a loud buzz of voices rose up, mocking, jeering, whistling derisively at the box, like it was the very embodiment of our foes. The closer the soldiers came to the temple porch, the louder the people around us grew. A few pieces of soft fruit were thrown at the box, the pulpy missiles striking its sides with a wet crash. Each time it was hit, the delighted crowd roared, their fervor going nearly wild as the soldiers maneuvered the wagon until the bed was at the steps of the temple of Dagon.

I, however, could not take my eyes off the intriguing object. Even as the soldiers slid it off the end of the wagon, it shimmered in the sunlight, looking like its surfaces were alive and glowing. I had the odd urge to push through the assembly, race to its side, and place myself between it and the rabid crowd.

Four soldiers lifted the chest with poles that were slipped through loops on the sides and hefted it atop their shoulders. Then they took the four steps up to the temple porch and none too gently dropped the golden box just at the threshold, an offering to the enormous depiction of Dagon within. The chest sat on the porch, looking small and sad between the towering scarlet and blue columns on either side.

The seren ascended the stairs, his two high commanders at his heels, to confer with some of the priests who'd been watching over the procession in delighted anticipation. My uncle Harrom, the High Priest of Ashdod, was included in the discussion, a smug grin on his clean-shaven face, but I could not peel my eyes away from the shining box.

"I want to go home, Risi," yelled Lukio over the melee. No matter that he was tall for his age, my poor brother could see little more than backs and legs and arms all around him.

"Soon," I said, drawing him closer. Even if Jacame desired to leave—and the elated expression on her face told me she had no intention of doing so—the shifting, crowing crowd would never allow us to pass through.

At my other side, Azuvah stood perfectly still, her eyes fixed on the box and her lips moving silently, while her fingers worried at the knotted threads she wore around her wrist.

My uncle finally stepped forward, then lifted his hands, palms outstretched. A breeze off the ocean fluttered the tall crimson feathers on his ceremonial headdress as he waited for the crowd to settle. When the taunts and hisses finally melted into uneasy quiet, the priest slid a slow and steady kohl-lined gaze over the crowd.

"People of Ashdod," said Harrom, a benevolent smile spreading across his face as he gestured toward the seren, who looked over the crowd with regal satisfaction. "Our exalted king and his faithful men have returned with news to gladden our hearts. From the time the gods brought our ancestors across the Great Sea and, in their divine wisdom, led them to these shores, we've been fighting for our place in this fertile land. But as you have guessed, our valiant warriors have finally brought the Hebrews to their knees. The victory was decisive and our enemies' losses extensive. This land is ours!"

The crowd erupted again, the roar of approval for such news nearly deafening. With satisfaction on his face, Harrom allowed the chaos for a while longer before again gesturing for quiet. Once the people settled down again, he lifted his palm toward the golden box, which sat forlorn and askew before the threshold of the temple that threatened to consume it whole.

"Behold, people of Ashdod, Dagon has bested the God of the Hebrews," he bellowed, victory lifting his voice to impossible volume. "Yahweh. Is. Vanquished."

Two

On secretive feet I padded through the adjoining rooms and slipped into an alcove just outside the door to the main hall, lured by the sounds of celebration. A large group of Harrom and Jacame's family and friends were gathered around the blazing fire on the circular hearth at the center of the grand room, glorying in the downfall of our enemies. My aunt had spent the rest of the day after our return from the temple snapping at Lukio and me for being under her feet and scolding the kitchen slaves for not working fast enough or to her exacting standards, but the moment her guests stepped across her threshold, she'd been the queen of graceful hospitality.

"The battle could not have been more simple," said Senamo, the eldest of my cousins, raising a boar-headed rhyton to his lips for a long draft of wine. "There was a small scuffle when the Hebrews showed up with their magical box. We'd all heard rumors about it having great power."

Their youngest, Mataro, barked a harsh laugh. "That thing is no more powerful than my left sandal. Those ridiculous Hebrews came out onto the battlefield with it in the lead, blasting horns and shouting all sorts of pompous nonsense. But before the sun reached its zenith, their precious weapon was in our hands. The ones we didn't slaughter ran off into the hills like squalling coneys with their tails on fire."

A round of derisive guffaws followed.

"You did well to bring the Hebrews' sacred chest back to Philistia," said Harrom.

"What will you do with it, Father?" asked Senamo. "Destroy it? The gold could certainly be melted and used again."

The distinctive clunk of pottery hitting pottery followed Senamo's question.

"Azuvah," snapped Jacame. "Watch yourself. You nearly spilled the wine."

Disturbed by the excessively sharp tone of my aunt's voice, I took a chance at peeking into the room through the crack near the door hinge. Azuvah stood next to a large wine krater, head down and her face sufficiently blank, but her knuckles were white where she gripped the handle of the juglet she'd just dipped into the wide-mouthed vessel. A few drops of crimson liquid dripped onto the floor near her feet.

"Oh now," said Senamo, the compassion in his tone as false as the Egyptian wig he always wore to appear more powerful—and perhaps to cover the bald spot on his head. "The Hebrew crone is likely just embarrassed by her kinsmen. Aren't you, old woman? Not much to boast of when your people are little more than a herd of barely civilized she-goats."

Azuvah did not respond; she was no fool. She simply kept her head down as the entire room exploded into cackling laughter. Instinct wound tight in my belly. Azuvah may not be a Philistine, but she'd been the only person in the world who cared for Lukio and me since my mother died. I shifted, muscles tensed to put myself between her and their mocking.

Without moving her head, Azuvah's eyes suddenly glanced up, pinned on the place where I peered at her through the narrow gap. How she knew I was there, I could not explain, but so slowly that she barely seemed to move, she shook her head once, a clear command for me to stay where I was. I fisted my hands but obeyed.

"At least we've had satisfaction for what your pathetic champion did to the temple at Gaza," said Mataro, the youngest of my cousins. "Along with the rest of the honorable Philistine lives he wasted before being bested by one of our women."

I knew little about the man called Samson, who'd at one time been feared among our people for his vast strength but whose life ended beneath the rubble of the temple after being captured, shorn, and blinded. Although I had heard the whispers that he'd somehow pulled down the enormous twin columns that held up the roof in one final burst of strength after being outwitted by one of our women. Regardless of how many Philistines died in that temple, and she among them, Delilah was still held as a heroine in our cities.

"Perhaps next time we'll send *you* to thrash the Hebrews, Mother," said Mataro. "They've proven to be nothing but a whimpering crowd of little girls anyhow."

Grinning, Jacame playfully slapped at her favorite and by far the most indulged of her four sons, even though he was fully grown at eighteen.

Harrom lifted his cup of wine. "Our ancestors are no doubt looking on with pride in all of you now that you've fulfilled their wishes to take this land as our own. And to think, our own sons were involved in finishing the work our forefathers began when they set foot on these shores so many years ago. We are truly blessed by the gods."

The group of them drank to the memory of our valiant ancestors and to Dagon, who'd led those brave men and women across the Great Sea from Caphtor to the shores of this fertile land.

Once talk turned to an unexpected shipment of goods from Sidon that had arrived in port two days before, I slipped away and skittered back down the hallway into my room, overflowing with questions about the golden box that had drained the color from Azuvah's beloved face and determined to stay awake until she returned.

Lukio was restless, shifting back and forth on the bed as I sang the same songs Azuvah did each night. However, my version of the Hebrew lullabies was not adequate to soothe his unease tonight, and neither were my reassurances that she would arrive soon.

Not only had he been frightened by the crush near the temple earlier, but after Harrom had declared triumph over the God of our enemies, the crowd grew so wild the four of us barely escaped without being trampled. Now, Azuvah's absence in our room after so many hours had us both unsettled.

I could not remember the last time she'd been forced to serve Jacame and Harrom so late into the night. And after what I'd seen and heard earlier, I could only imagine what further indignities she was suffering, as voices down in the hearth room had been growing increasingly louder and more slurred. I was grateful that Lukio had not heard Mataro and Senamo mocking her in front of everyone, since he was prone to flashes of temper and loved Azuvah too well to refrain from coming to her defense.

The relief that poured into my limbs when the door finally opened and Azuvah slipped inside was so acute I let out a grateful sigh. From his place curled up next to me, Lukio sat up, blinking at the light from the oil lamp she held in her hand.

The flame flickered as she flinched from surprise. "You are both still awake?"

"Lukio refused to sleep until you returned," I said, although I had been just as determined to keep my eyes open until she lay beside us, with Lukio in between, just as she had for as long as I could remember.

Nightmares had plagued me after the death of my mother seven years ago, and no matter how many times Azuvah carried me back to my bed in the middle of the night from the servants' quarters, she'd always found me back on the pallet next to her and Lukio in the morning. Eventually, she'd given in and the two of them had remained with me. Our father hadn't cared where she slept as long as she kept the two of us quiet and out of his way. And thankfully Jacame had not argued when I insisted on continuing the arrangement when she took us in.

After she extinguished the lamp, Azuvah slid between the linens, a low groan coming from her lips as she allowed herself to relax, likely for the first time since her eyes opened this morning. In my father's house, she'd spent most of her time tending to the two of us children and overseeing the rest of the slaves my father could not bother himself to manage, but in Jacame's house, she worked from before first light until sundown, tending to a wide range of duties.

We barely saw her until bedtime most days, but it was in those quiet moonlit times she shared stories of her people with us, whispering in her mother tongue until our rebellious eyes finally fluttered closed. Both Lukio and I understood the language of the Hebrews well since Azuvah had always told her stories using the words in which she'd learned them and had openly spoken it to us within my father's home. But after Jacame had overheard Lukio asking Azuvah a question in Hebrew and viciously chastised our servant for speaking anything other than the Philistine language, neither one of us had dared to use those words outside of our tiny room in the far back corner of the house.

However, I spoke it now as I finally asked the question I'd been holding in for the better part of the day. "What was in that gold box the soldiers brought to Ashdod?"

She waited so long to speak that I wondered whether she'd already drifted off in her exhaustion, but then she turned to peer at me, moonlight washing away the lines and grooves that testified to her many years.

"I was just a girl when I was snatched," she said, as if she'd not even heard my question. "Only eleven years old. A year younger than you now, Arisa." Lukio settled his head on the pillow between us, knowing one of Azuvah's stories was forthcoming. Already the tension in his small body had lessened.

"I'd been herding goats with my older siblings," she continued, her gnarled fingers brushing through Lukio's curls in a smoothing motion, "and wandered just a little too far from their view. A man came up from behind, slipped his hand over my mouth, and just like that—I was taken. Brought here to Ashdod and sold into your grandfather's house. I had no idea what slavery was among your people . . . or the indignities. . . ." Her voice trailed off. I held my breath, bursting with curiosity. Over the years she'd told us many stories, but never her own.

"But when your mother was born a few years later," she continued, "just after my own child, I became her wet nurse. And she was so beautiful. So sweet." She smiled and brushed her callused palm over my cheek. "She was a bright light in the midst of great darkness, just like you and Lukio. And after that, slavery was not quite so painful as it had been before."

I'd not known that she had nursed my own mother. No wonder she'd held such an honored place among the other slaves before my brother was born.

"But all throughout those years, I remembered," she said. "I remembered the stories of my people. I remembered the histories written by Mosheh in the wilderness and the saga of our rescue from Egypt. I told them to myself whenever I was alone, singing the songs of my people under my breath so I would not forget."

Azuvah had told Lukio and me many tales of Mosheh, the revered leader of the Hebrews, and how he thwarted Pharaoh with his magical staff and how the entire land of Egypt was battered by plague after plague until Pharaoh finally relented and let them go.

"And the box?" I whispered.

"I have never seen it before with my own eyes. It has been in our holy sanctuary at Shiloh for over three hundred years. But I knew the moment I saw it that it is the Ark of the Covenant, the vessel that contains the Ten Words written on stone, along with the staff of our first High Priest, Aharon, and a portion of the manna that sustained our people for forty years in the wilderness."

"And the winged creatures on top?"

"Those are cherubim, the guardians to the throne of Yahweh."

A whisper arose in my mind. She must have told me stories

about this Ark long ago because I suddenly remembered something. "Your priests carried it, didn't they?"

"They did. There are men designated to serve Yahweh who are called Levites. They've been given specific instructions on how to carry and protect the Ark with the reverence and fear due its powerful nature."

I thought of the way the golden box had been so unceremoniously dumped onto the ground this morning and the forlorn way it sat on the threshold of the temple of Dagon. "How powerful could it be if our soldiers took it in battle?"

"I don't have an answer for you. I cannot understand how it was taken from my people. Not when in ancient times it preceded so many successful battles under the command of Yehoshua."

"Is that your king?" asked Lukio, perking up at the mention of war.

"No," replied Azuvah, "the tribes of Israel have no king. Yehoshua was the commander of our armies when our people came to this land after forty years of wandering in the wilderness."

"No king?" Lukio's small face scrunched in confusion. "No wonder they lost the battle. Our seren is the tallest and strongest of all of the kings."

She smiled indulgently at his prideful statement, brushing a knuckle down his nose with affection. "He *is* a powerful man among the Philistines. That is no question. But we have no need of a king because Yahweh is our God, and it is he who guides and protects us, and he is far more powerful than all the earthly kingdoms put together. There have been times since Yehoshua's death when we lost our way, years in which we turned to other gods and when foreigners overtook us, but Yahweh has always raised up *shoftim* to rescue us from our own folly."

"What are shoftim?" asked Lukio, on a yawn. I wondered if he would even hear the answer, fighting as he was against the weight of his eyelids.

"Men and women appointed by Yahweh himself to call our armies to war, to fight against oppressors, and to urge the people to turn back to worship of the Most High God. They are famous among us—Othniel, Ehud, Devorah, Gideon, and many more. They have served as military commanders and wise judges over some of the tribes, but they were not kings and never purported to be."

"Who leads your people now?" I asked.

"I don't know," said Azuvah. "When I was a girl, things were relatively peaceful between the Hebrews and the Philistines. Trade was frequent between us, although there were skirmishes on the outskirts of our territories every so often and, of course, sometimes towns were overrun or people snatched away."

Like she had been, I thought.

"If anything we were far too entangled. Too comfortable with the gods of those among us," she murmured. But before I could ask about the strange statement, she continued.

"I have been trapped here in Ashdod for so many years without contact with other Hebrews that I could not tell you what life is like for my people now. But the Ark being here . . ." She sighed, and the sound was full of grief. "With the Philistines in possession of our most sacred object after such a terrible loss on the battlefield, something awful has happened to the sons of Yaakov. Something that I fear may threaten our very existence as a nation."

"Perhaps the box simply no longer holds any magic," I said. "If that is even the same one the Hebrews carried in the wilderness, then it is very old. Perhaps it wore off."

"There is no magic in the box itself, Arisa. The power is that of the hand of Yahweh. It is merely a vessel, but one that signifies the sacred covenant between Israel and our God and above which has hovered the very *shekinah* of the Eternal One." She shook her head, her tone foreboding. "These Philistines do not know what they have done. They have stolen something that they cannot comprehend or control. But no matter what, Yahweh's glory will prevail. I have no fear for the Ark itself, only for those who do not handle it with respect."

A shiver slithered down my back, so I settled closer to Lukio's warmth. It seemed he'd lost the struggle against sleep at some point, his breathing now slow and rhythmic against my chest.

"Azuvah?" I chanced one more question now that Lukio was unconscious. "You had a child?"

Her breathing hitched audibly. "I did. But he was taken from me."

"Where did he go?"

Her responding whisper was mournful. "I am but a slave, sweet child. I will never know. But you know your people and their hatred of mine. He was probably left on the rocks to die, swept into the sea. I was only able to hold him once."

She lifted her hand, stroking the dingy and frayed knotted threads she wore around her wrist at all times, something she once told me was a reminder of her God and his laws. "I had just enough time to wrap one of the *tzitzit* I'd cut from my garment around his tiny wrist before they took him away. A paltry consecration to Yahweh, but it was all I had to give him."

This woman had nursed my own mother, wiped my every childhood tear, and kept my brother and me alive in a house with a father who had barely fed himself after his wife had died. Not for the first time I wished the relationship between my people and hers were different. Wished the magic box of the Hebrews could heal the hurt I heard in her voice.

"Rest now, *lior*." She reached across Lukio to cup my cheek in her warm palm, and I leaned into the familiarity. She'd used that endearment—*my light*, in her tongue—for both Lukio and me as far back as I could remember, and it never failed to remind me how precious we were to her.

Once Azuvah began breathing deeply, succumbing to a long day of attending to Jacame's every unreasonable demand, I fell into a sleep marred by images of golden boxes; of the lone wail of an infant being consumed by the sea; of a terrifying man on a mountain with a glowing face; of blood and locusts and suffocating night.

But however violent my dreams had been, nothing prepared me for being awakened at daybreak by the world being shaken to pieces.

Three

The washpot near the door shattered on the floor with a violent crack as the ground below us heaved and convulsed. A lamp also met its demise in a mess of broken clay and olive oil while our bed juddered and shook, the ropes beneath us groaning as Lukio's screams rose above the pounding roar of the earth. He clung to me as Azuvah called out frantic assurances that the quaking would soon cease.

Shrill cries came from somewhere in the villa, joining the repeated sounds of pottery slamming to the ground. Cracks webbed across the plastered walls, and a corner of the ceiling caved in across the room, letting in the gray light of dawn. Azuvah threw herself over Lukio and me with grim-faced determination to protect us from whatever might fall from above. But if the floor beneath us crumbled, pulling us down to the bottom level, there would be nothing Azuvah could do to keep us from being swallowed up in the destruction.

And then it was over. The earth stilled. The shaking stopped, and all that could be heard was my shallow breathing and Lukio's muffled sobs against my chest.

"Are you both unharmed?" asked Azuvah.

"I . . . I think so," I said, smoothing my brother's sweat-soaked hair away from his face. "Lukio?"

He dragged in a shuddering breath and nodded, then his mismatched eyes went wide as he took in the damage around us. "What happened?"

"An earthquake," said Azuvah as she crawled out of the bed with a groan. "It has been many years since one so large has shaken this city." Her gaze went to the high window on the opposite wall, where the glare of sunrise was now visible. Her lips pressed into a thoughtful line, then she nodded, as if making a determination in her head.

"Come," she said. "Jacame will need me, and she'll likely want to ensure that you two are safe. But take care where your feet go. There will be many splinters and shards on the floor until we can sweep everything up."

Mumbling promises that we would be vigilant, Lukio and I scooted out of the bed, waited while Azuvah swept aside the disaster in front of the door with one of my extra sandals, and then followed her into the next room, hopping over the mess as we crossed the threshold. Each room we passed through was just as damaged as ours had been, but downstairs, where Jacame's many treasures decorated her luxurious home, the destruction was even worse.

Nearly every shelf had been swept of its contents. Idols and vases and jars littered the floor in every room. The air was full of dust and the tinge of smoke tickled my nostrils. Shouts and calls from both inside the house and outside joined the haze.

When we finally entered the main hall, where just last night Jacame had entertained her returning sons in lavish fashion, I gasped. The entire roof had given way, leaving only a canopy of blue sky overhead and four solid cedar pillars in the center, holding up nothing. The elaborately tiled circular hearth, around which every family meal was enjoyed, was buried beneath a pile of rubble.

My aunt, her face covered in dust and despair, darted around the wreckage. "Azuvah," she commanded, "go tend the kitchen slaves. Two of them are injured."

The Hebrew woman complied, although the look she cast over

her shoulder as she slipped away told me that it pained her to leave us after such a horrific event.

"Are you wounded?" my aunt demanded, her gaze barely brushing over the two of us before turning back to the devastation.

"No, just frightened." I slipped my arm about Lukio's shoulders, and he leaned against me. Although he was trying to be brave, most likely for my sake, his face was a mess of dirty tear streaks.

"Good," Jacame murmured distractedly as she wrung her hands and surveyed what remained of the room. "So much destroyed. Oh no! Harrom had these brought all the way from Tyre. . . ." She bent to pick up the crushed arm of one of the costly cedar chairs from the ground near her feet. "Even the sanctuary is a mess. . . ."

Suddenly, Jacame's eyes flew wide as she gasped, a hand loosely pressed to her mouth. "Harrom! What of Harrom? He left for the temple before dawn. And Senamo and his wife! They passed the night with Portea's family across town. What if they have been hurt? Or the children?"

I'd never seen my aunt so undone. For as cold as she was toward Lukio and me, and for as ruthless as she was with her servants, she worshiped her family. I felt a pang of compassion at the tears welling in her eyes.

"Would you like us to go see how they fared?" I asked.

"Excellent idea," she said, then grabbed my shoulder far too tightly. "No, go to the temple instead and ask after Harrom. I will go to Senamo and Portea and the children. I need to see them with my own eyes."

Mataro emerged from the next room. "Mother—"

"Oh! Mataro!" Jacame flew to him, arms outstretched. "Where are Hektor and Arguro?"

"They are fine," he said, scowling as he slithered out of her urgent hold. "They are digging out one of the manservants from beneath some rubble."

"Are you certain they aren't injured?" she said, ignoring the plight of the unfortunate manservant.

"No," he said. "Hektor and his wife were in a room that sustained minimal damage, and although one wall of our chambers crumbled, Arguro and I were able to flee before that portion of the roof collapsed."

He looked past his mother at me, his dark brown gaze taking in my disheveled state, then traveled to the tear tracks on Lukio's dusty cheeks. He sneered at my brother. "What are you sniveling over? It was only a bit of shaking." He made a show of scrubbing at his eyes and mock crying.

Lukio's body went stiff against mine. Regardless that Mataro was, in my opinion, as rotten as a fig left far too long on the branch, Lukio seemed drawn to him and worked hard to attract his attention. I tried to draw my brother closer, hoping it would reassure him that his tears were nothing to be ashamed of, but he used his elbow to push against my side, putting a small bit of distance between us that made my heart squeeze painfully.

"Go on now," said Jacame to me, ignoring her son's rude behavior. "Get to the temple and ask after Harrom. Don't stand about gawking."

I nodded, tugging Lukio along behind me, but he slipped his hand from mine with a furtive look at Mataro. Our cousin had already turned back to his mother, listing off a number of his belongings that the servants must search for with all haste. Leaving Jacame to fret over her favorite son, Lukio and I crossed the threshold and headed into the street.

The sight of our city was a shock. The damage to Harrom and Jacame's home was much less than most. Some were nearly leveled, and smoke rose from more than a few caved-in roofs.

Many of the residents of Ashdod stood in the streets, dazed and covered in dust, surveying the damage, but a few mournful wails had gone up as well, making it clear that more than just property had been lost this morning.

When we came within sight of the temple, it was plain to see that damage had been done, but not nearly as much as I'd expected. One mudbrick wall of the courtyard fence had crumbled, and the two enormous incense burners near the entrance had toppled, their shattered remains scattered across the ground.

It would be easy enough to report to my aunt that Harrom had escaped injury, since he and the other priests stood on the porch of the temple, gathered near the place where the Hebrews' box had been dropped in front of the entrance. I could barely make out the glint of its golden sides through the many bodies surrounding it.

"What are they doing?" Lukio asked, rolling to the balls of his feet.

"Prepare!" cried my uncle, and we watched in fascination as the group of them bent together in one unit around something that lay on the ground near the threshold. "Lift!" commanded Harrom, and in one accord they obeyed.

"It looks like Dagon fell during the earthquake," I said, incredulous. "They are putting him back in place."

Using a complicated system of ropes strung up into the rafters, along with their collective might, the priests heaved together, dragging Dagon back onto his wide pedestal, where he settled with a grinding thud. The priests hovered about, a few of them pushing in tandem against the base of the idol from each angle to ensure that he would not topple again, now that he had returned to his place of honor. Then, brushing their dirty hands on their tunics, they began to head off in different directions, likely returning to gauge the damage on their own homes after having dealt with the most important task.

Their dispersal meant that I was able to see the golden box more clearly than I had the other day. My eyes were drawn to the winged creatures atop its lid, the ones Azuvah said were the guardians of the throne of her God. Even beneath the shadow of the temple, their outstretched feathers glinted, giving the illusion of mid-flight. In fact, the casket itself seemed to shimmer with life, making it nearly impossible to peel my eyes away. Just as I had yesterday, I felt the strangest urge to run toward it and lay myself on the ground at its base, but at the same time, something deep inside told me to flee in terror from whatever awful power it represented.

Instead of submitting to either urge, I ushered Lukio back toward my aunt and uncle's home, knowing Jacame would be angry if we tarried, but I could not help but peer back over my shoulder as we walked away, struck by the strangest realization.

Although the entire city of Ashdod seemed to have been shaken, the Hebrews' Ark had not moved.

Although the next morning arrived without shaking, the house was still in disarray. As Lukio and I made our way through what was once one of the most lavish homes in Ashdod, we found every servants' hand occupied with picking up the pieces of our aunt and uncle's wealth—a task that, from the looks of the destruction, would take days or perhaps even weeks to complete. Although it had been determined by Harrom's steward that the building itself was not in danger of caving in, there were at least three rooms that were unusable, including the main hall.

Since Mataro had mocked him yesterday after the earthquake, my brother had spoken no more than a few words to me. He'd even refused to let me help tie his sandals this morning, setting about the job with an iron set to his small jaw and none of the usual light in his eyes. The change unsettled me and made me furious with my cousin for his callousness, so today I was determined to do all I could to distract Lukio and give him a reason to smile again. It was the only way I could win against Mataro's spitefulness.

With as occupied as Jacame was with the destruction of her home, she'd likely not even notice that we'd gone down to the market to explore. While Lukio loved to seek out exotic treasures brought into the port by sailors from far-flung places, I could not resist looking for my father among the men who landed on our shores, even after so many years. I tended to avoid the market whenever possible, but for my brother, I would ignore the pangs of longing the sailors' gruff voices and sea-weathered faces inspired.

However, my plans to escape the house were waylaid when my uncle burst through the front door like a thunderstorm. His priestly robes were covered in dirt and ashes, torn from his neck to his navel. His shaven head was also stained with soot, the kohl around his eyes a smudged mess, and there were four gashes on his arms, the blood already drying in streaks along his skin.

Startled by the sight of Harrom in such disarray, Lukio smashed his body into mine and gripped my waist, seemingly forgetting his earlier reticence. My uncle, however, did not even acknowledge us as he brushed past. In fact, his bloodshot eyes seemed glazed, as if he did not even see the two of us standing there at all.

He'd not gone far into the next chamber when he was met by Jacame, who'd been bustling about all morning, screeching at the servants to work faster. My aunt gasped at her husband's shocking appearance, reaching out to pull him to a stop. "Harrom! What is it?"

"Let me by," he demanded, yanking his arm away. "I must get cleaned up and then go back to the temple. There is work to be done."

"What do you mean? What has happened?"

I expected Harrom to push past her as he'd done Lukio and me, but instead, he stopped, his head dropping forward and a sigh heaving from somewhere deep inside his chest. Neither one of them noticed that my brother and I were watching their exchange, so I held Lukio tight against me and hoped he would not make a sound.

"He fell," Harrom grated out.

"Who?"

"Dagon."

"But the earth did not move again. All has been still."

He shook his head. "I cannot explain it. When I arrived this morning, he was on the ground."

"That makes no sense," Jacame countered. "You said your men lifted him back into place and made certain he was secure."

"He was secure," said Harrom. "I ordered them to check once again before the sun went down yesterday. He was immovable, even with five men pushing on every side."

"How can he have fallen, then?"

He placed his filthy hands atop his head. "I don't know," he rasped. "But he is face down on the floor."

The desperation in Harrom's voice caused a spike of confusion to pass through me. For as long as I could remember, the High Priest of Ashdod had never betrayed even a shadow of fear or doubt, his every word and move calculated and certain, but right now my uncle looked terrified and on the edge of panic.

"Well, it is nothing to be so upset over. Perhaps the earth moved again and we slept through it. Simply have your men put him back up again."

"But that is just the thing," he said, rubbing his soot-stained face with both palms, further smearing the mess across his skin. "Not only did Dagon fall, but both of his hands and his head were severed from his body. They are lying on the threshold of the temple, only three paces from that Hebrew box."

Taking a step backward, Jacame shook her head in disbelief. "Surely not. What could it mean?"

"The breaks are clean, wife. Like an impossibly sharp sword sliced through the rock with perfect precision."

"What will you tell the people?" she asked, her voice warbling. "They will want to know how this could happen."

"I don't know. For now, I have guards blocking the entrance to the temple. No one can know what has happened until I confer with the other priests and the king. We might have a revolt on our hands if word of this got out without a plausible explanation."

"Are we under a curse?" she asked. "Is Dagon displeased with us?"

He shrugged. "We have been faithful in our daily offerings. And we delivered the Hebrews' most sacred treasure to his feet."

"And now he is laying at the foot of it instead," mused Jacame, her tone thoughtful as she stared at the wall across the room, tapping her chin with a long finger.

"I must go," Harrom said, his voice strangled. "We must decide what to do before anyone hears of this."

"Tell the people that the idol was damaged during the earthquake and that you've commissioned an even grander image to replace him," said my aunt, all grief suddenly wiped away by decisiveness. "Tell them that you want to honor his might and power with a fitting depiction. They will not question your wisdom in that."

"Yes," said her husband. "Yes. . . . That may work to allay any fears, at least among the people. But the other priests will not be so easily placated. Most of them are too terrified to even approach the porch, saying that the Hebrew god has felled Dagon."

"You are the High Priest, Harrom, the man chosen to lead our people with the wisdom of the gods," she said with a strident gesture toward his ruined robes. "Convince them it is nothing more than faulty stone or shoddy craftsmanship."

He took a noisy breath. "Perhaps you are right."

"I am. Now go, clean off the evidence of mourning and return to the temple," she said, unabashedly commanding her husband like he were one of her slaves. "Show them there is nothing to fear. In the meantime, hang a curtain in the entrance, declare it out of reach until the new, larger image is unveiled. Build expectation with the people by boasting of the grandeur of Dagon and they will forget this small thing."

"Yes," my uncle said, then walked away, muttering to himself. "Yes, I shall do just that. Nothing to fear. Simply damage from the earthquake. Flaws in the stone."

But perhaps there was something to fear after all. Azuvah certainly thought so. I remembered the way my skin had prickled as she'd whispered *"Mercy. Have mercy on us"* when the soldiers returned with their war trophy. She'd said the box itself did not contain magic, but what other explanation was there for what happened this morning? And would this be the last such occurrence?

The image of Dagon filled my mind: his once-powerful hands useless on the ground and the obsidian eyes now like black holes in the severed head that lay at the threshold before the golden box. Somehow I suspected that it would not matter how grand a replacement Harrom lifted in its place. For if Dagon was now powerless and sightless, perhaps the God of the Hebrews had not been bested after all.

Four

I dodged a mule-drawn wagon as I passed through the market-place, desperate to find Lukio before the sun melted into the sea. He'd never been this late coming home from roaming the streets with his friends, and the gnawing worry in my gut had driven me to leave behind the floor I'd been scrubbing to look for him. Thankfully, Azuvah had promised to finish the task I'd abandoned.

Instead of the insistent calls of traders hawking pottery decorated with red and black swirls or fabrics from places I would never see with my eyes, the market was nearly as desolate as the dusty wheat and barley fields all around the city. Although a few tenacious merchants still tended their stalls, their goods were offered for nearly twice their worth and their stock was of questionable quality. Outside traders refused to come inside the gates of Ashdod anymore.

A plague-ridden city and its impoverished inhabitants did not make for good business, after all.

Two rats scuttled across the road in front of me as I jogged toward the place Lukio and a few of the other boys gathered to play games almost every day. There was a time when I might have jumped and squealed at the sight of rodents so near my sandals, but they'd become as common as stones in the street over these past few months. After consuming the majority of our crops and a fair amount of the grain in once-overflowing community silos, they'd taken to scavenging in our homes. At night they skittered over the plastered floor beneath our bed, making the skin on my arms crawl until I forced myself to sleep, praying to any god who might listen that the horrible creatures would not find their way beneath the blankets Azuvah tucked so diligently around us. The few remaining dogs that braved the streets had given up the fight against the invasion, as they were too busy fleeing the cooking pot to bother chasing their own prey.

Even months after the Ark of the Hebrews had been whisked away following an outcry by the people of Ashdod, its effects lingered over us like a foul odor, as permeating as the smell of death. A scent I knew only too well now.

Within weeks of the fall of Dagon, Harrom had perished, his body overtaken by black boils that not only distorted his face beyond recognition but had choked the breath from his lungs. After days of hiding in her chamber while the growths enveloped her body, Jacame succumbed as well. Three of their sons followed them to the grave, along with two of the wives and at least six of Jacame's grandchildren. There'd been so many deaths over the last few months that bodies were now either dumped in mass graves or taken out to sea to be tossed overboard before fishermen dropped their nets. Any respect for the dead had been drowned in the overwhelming number of corpses.

I scratched just above my elbow, where the last of my own boils had healed months ago, but still felt tender to the touch. Not long after Harrom had died, both Lukio and I developed painful sores on the inside of our thighs, the first sign that we too had been stricken with whatever plague had descended upon Ashdod. But Azuvah had stolen a portion of olive oil in the chaos, anointed both Lukio and me with it in secret, and prayed over both of us in the name of her God as she tended our fevered bodies, washing us with water tinged with strong-smelling herbs and feeding us hearty vegetable broth. Although I'd not expected anything more than to watch my brother die in the same horrific way my uncle had, somehow both of us had recovered within a few days, and any sores we'd developed withered away.

Through it all, Azuvah's skin had remained untouched—a fact that Mataro, the only survivor among our cousins and inheritor of all, did not miss. Nor did he forget where the blame for these plagues lay: with her people and their sacred Ark. Jacame had treated Azuvah no better or worse than any of her other slaves, but Mataro seemed to take pleasure in humiliating her, entertaining his loathsome friends with a litany of foul epithets for her as she served them. And last night she'd crawled into bed far past the rise of the moon with a deep bruise along the edge of her jaw. Seeing the woman who'd always protected me and my brother beaten like a dog had filled me with equal parts disgust and fury, making me wish Mataro had joined his parents and his brothers in the grave. And yet, for Lukio's sake, I could say nothing, do nothing. Mataro had made it very clear that the two of us stayed in the household he now lorded over only at his pleasure.

Lately, I'd been too busy acting the part of a servant to keep a close eye on my brother at all times, as I had done in the past, so Lukio had been increasingly unruly and prone to wander around the city with his equally unruly friends. I hurried along the desolate streets, determined to find Lukio and return to the house before Mataro discovered I was gone. The longer I was away, the greater the chance he'd discover I'd left my duties behind.

The sounds of cheering met my ears as I neared the wide alleyway where I knew Lukio and the other boys passed their time tossing sheep knuckles, a favorite game that mimicked those of the men who wagered far more than shells or bragging rights on the roll of a die. However, when I came around the corner, it was not only young boys gathered in the alleyway but a group of grown men whose shouts and jeers echoed off the two-story buildings on either side.

Confused, I hovered near the corner, trying to discern why they would be circled around a youthful dice-throwing game, carrying on as if the outcome were of some importance.

A final roar of approval went up as I scanned the crowd for Lukio's golden-brown curls, but there were too many bodies crammed into the alley. I had little doubt my brother was there in the midst of the melee since he liked nothing more than a raucous game of dice. I did not like the older boys he'd been passing time with, but they seemed to accept him easily, the unusual height he'd inherited from our father fooling them into seeing him as their equal.

The crowd began to dissipate, the men moving off in pairs or threes, some exchanging silver as they walked away. The clench of my stomach tightened, and my heart thudded sickly. I'd never seen grown men wager on a boys' game of dice . . . but a fight was a different matter.

And then, to my great relief, I saw Lukio coming toward me with an enormous smile on his dirty face. He slipped free of the crowd and broke into a run, his hand outstretched and my name on his lips.

"Risi! Risi! Look what I won!" he called out at the same time I realized it was not only dirt on my brother's sweet face but blood. A dark smear of crimson trailed from his nose to his chin and already a bruise was forming just below his left eye. By the time he reached me, panic had me tightly in its grip.

"Lukio, what did you do? Why are you bleeding?" I demanded, caring nothing for his spoils.

His mismatched eyes fluttered in confusion. "I'm all right Risi. I won."

"You won? What sort of dice game causes a bloody nose and a black eye?" I swiped at his face, my palm coming away red.

"No, we weren't playing dice. Well, we were. But Tombaal tried to cheat, and he stole my best die. But I got it back," he said, digging into the little pouch at his neck where he carried his treasures. He held out a sheep knuckle that had been smoothed on all four sides and had tiny holes drilled into each side. "Look! I couldn't let him take that one. It's my favorite."

"Lukio, I don't care about your dice. Why are you bleeding?"

"I told you, Tombaal tried to steal it. So I knocked him down and took it back," he said with a shrug, tucking his reclaimed die back into his pouch. "And Mataro saw me."

I sucked in a breath, my eyes darting around until they landed on none other than my only remaining cousin. He stood a few paces down the alleyway, talking with a few other men, with a large grin spread across his face. Nausea rippled up my throat.

"He saw you?" I choked out.

"Yes, and then he said I would be rewarded if I fought Tombaal for real. And I did. See!" He stretched out his palm to display two lumps of silver the size of my smallest fingernail.

"You fought another boy?"

"It was easy, Risi." His voice pitched high with excitement. "After I won over Tombaal, I wrestled Nasso. That's why I got two pieces instead of one."

It had been months since I'd seen Lukio so excited about any-thing. The excruciating deaths of our aunt and uncle had been horrifying, and he was not unaware of the large numbers of other casualties, some of his friends among them. I was torn between gladness that he was not curled up on our bed weeping and horror that Mataro had somehow cajoled my gentle little brother into this world. Wrestling and fistfights were among the most popular activities in Ashdod, the wagers far more than the tiny pieces in my brother's palm. It was common for boys to take part, but it turned my stomach to think of Lukio pummeling other children for gain.

"You earned it, cousin," said Mataro, who'd appeared beside us as I reeled from the revelation that it had been Lukio in the center of that crowd of bloodthirsty men. Mataro clapped a palm on Lukio's shoulder. "Those boys were at least two years older than you."

"Tombaal is ten," chirped Lukio, beaming.

"Even better," said Mataro, who then leaned down to look him in the eye. "He didn't have a chance. They'll be much more silver in your future, little man."

"He can't fight," I said, pulling Lukio toward me and wrapping an arm around his shoulders. "He's too young."

Mataro narrowed his eyes at me, the glare causing the flesh on the back of my neck and arms to prickle. "Why are you here?" he said. "You were told to scrub the sanctuary floor."

A spike of pure fear shot through my blood. "I . . . I will finish. I was worried about Lukio. The sun will set soon."

"You were not given permission to leave."

"But Azuvah said she would finish—"

"You are under my authority." He leaned down a handspan from my face. "The house is mine and mine alone. You do what I say or you will regret it. Understand?"

Trembling head to foot from the menace in his voice, I nodded.

"Good," he said with a sneer. "And I will make sure that crazy Hebrew sow understands it as well."

The memory of Azuvah's bruised jaw arose in my mind. He would mete out my punishment on her skin, I had no doubt.

"It was my fault alone," I pled. "I won't disobey you again, Mataro. I promise. I lied to Azuvah and told her you said I could go."

His lips pinched together as he stared at me, seeming to gauge whether I was telling the truth now. "All right," he said. "But this is the last time I grant mercy. Next time the Hebrew pays your debt. Is that perfectly clear, *cousin*?"

I nodded, my eyes burning.

"Go on home," he said. "And tomorrow you'll scrub the walls of the sanctuary as well."

"Of course. Thank you, Mataro," I whispered, then slipped my hand into Lukio's before turning toward home.

Behind me Lukio jerked to a stop, causing me to nearly stumble. When I turned back I realized that Mataro had my brother's arm in his grasp.

"Oh no," said my cousin, drawing Lukio back toward himself. "He stays with me. We'll be along shortly."

My gaze flew back and forth between Mataro's arrogant smile

and Lukio's wide eyes. The thought of walking away from my brother caused every bone in my body to turn to water, but if there was anything I knew about Mataro, it was that he was ruthless. The threat on his face was evident as his large fingers dug into the skin of Lukio's arm.

It was not only Azuvah he would go after if I disobeyed.

I had no choice. Choking back a sob, I released Lukio's hand, and then, on shaky legs, I turned and walked away, feeling every step of separation between my heart and his.

Five

Water dripped down into the arms of my tunic, tickling my sides as I pressed harder on the sodden rag. My shoulders ached from scrubbing up and down for hours, and my knees throbbed from kneeling to reach the corners, but I was certain that not even Mataro would find fault with my meticulous handiwork.

Years of incense and smoke had dulled the bright murals in this small sanctuary, but my diligence had brought them back to life. They gleamed in the sunlight that shone through the window, greens and blues and reds depicting the glorious arrival of our ancestors on this shore, as well as the distant island from which they originated. Thanks to me, the story on these walls was no longer hidden.

These depictions were full of triumphant boasting for the heroes whose blood ran in the rivers of my own body, yet somehow Azuvah's stories of the Hebrews were more real to me. Mosheh, Avraham, Yosef, Yehoshua, and Rahab felt more like my people than those I had been born to. The thought made me glance over at the altar in the corner, as if the collection of silent statues arranged there on the low stone pedestal might have overheard my treachery.

The earthquake seven months before had destroyed many of the gods within this household sanctuary, their parts carelessly strewn across the floor like dice tossed by Lukio and his friends.

But Jacame had replaced them with ones that were far more costly than those that had been damaged, and two new oil and incense burners hung from the rafters, the large ceramic rings decorated with ornate depictions of seabirds and swans.

Taking a moment to rest my weary arms, I sat back on my haunches and looked over the *baalim* my aunt had selected with so much care. Foremost among them was the Great Mother goddess, the ancient deity worshiped by our people back in our homeland, her exaggerated bosom and benevolent smile a promise of great fertility. The rest were a collection of Egyptian deities: Isis, Osiris, and Thoth, and a few Canaanite ones as well, such as El, Ba'al, and Ashtoreth. But regardless that most of them glittered with jeweled and gold-plated glory, and regardless of the countless sacrifices offered on their behalf, none of those gods had saved Jacame or Harrom from excruciating deaths.

Azuvah claimed that the fervent prayers she offered to her God on Lukio's and my account had healed us, and truly they had seemed to protect us from the worst of the tumors. However, the Ark of the Hebrews had disappeared from the temple porch within days of the fall of Dagon, likely melted down as Senamo had suggested in an act of retribution for the plagues that befell us in Ashdod. How powerful could a god be if its most sacred treasure could be so easily destroyed?

If even Azuvah's Yahweh could not be trusted, then there was no god I could plead with for help. No one to beg protection from our cousin's capricious whims and whatever plans he had for my brother.

Lukio had returned well after sunset last night, full of excitement over his victories and talk of more in the future. He'd balked when I said I did not want him to fight again, but after I'd tearfully explained how frightened I'd been, he'd apologized and meekly crawled into bed. Even so, I could tell that he'd been torn between pleasing me and pleasing the cousin who had filled his head with grandiose tales of fame and fortune.

What Lukio did not comprehend was the savagery of such

matches, of men beaten until they were unrecognizable, of broken limbs and shattered teeth, and the fickle affections of the crowds once their favorite fighters were no longer lining their purses with silver. I'd heard such talk from my uncle and cousins for years, not to mention witnessing the aftermath of my own father's bouts, and I refused to let Lukio be abused for sport. This was a boy whose thumb had only stopped finding its way into his mouth at night a little over a year ago. I could not allow the last of his innocence to be pummeled from his young body on the fighting grounds. But how could I protect him from Mataro's schemes? The filthy rag in my hands and the ache in my neck and shoulders was a reminder that although I'd been born into wealth and privilege, I was little more than a servant in this house now, a young girl dependent on my tyrannical cousin for every bite of food and every scrap of clothing. I was nothing. Alone.

Azuvah padded into the room, pulling my attention from the powerless gods in front of me.

"I'm nearly done," I said, my smile as weak as my legs as I stood.

Instead of inspecting my work, Azuvah moved in front of me and lifted her hands to cradle my face, her dark eyes seeming to peer directly into my soul and past any pretense I could conjure. "What is wrong, Arisa?"

I could do nothing to prevent the tears that slipped down my cheeks. "Mataro means to have Lukio fight against other boys. Older ones, most likely. You know what those vicious matches are like. I cannot stand to see him beaten, Azuvah—or worse. Especially when it is only for Mataro's gain."

She pulled me close, stroking my hair as I wept against her shoulder.

"What can I do? I can't stop Mataro from doing whatever he pleases. No one can."

"Give me some time," she said. "I will think of something."

I pulled back to stare at her. "What could you possibly do?"

"You and Lukio are the brightest lights in my sky. There is nothing I would not do to protect the two of you." She pulled me back in for another embrace, her strong arms and familiar smell smoothing the sharpest edges from my fears for my brother. "You will never be alone, lior."

The door slammed open, jerking both Lukio and me from a deep sleep.

"Get up," said Azuvah, her eyes wild. "Now."

The fear in her tone caused me to leap from the bed, Lukio scooting out behind me. "What is it?"

"It is time to go," she said, closing the door behind her and jamming a wooden dowel in the latch, locking us inside. A full wineskin was slung over her shoulder, and she carried a linen-wrapped parcel.

"What is happening?" I asked as Azuvah knelt to drag a large leather satchel from beneath the bed, one that looked to have already been packed. The promise that she'd made to me last week in the sanctuary came immediately to mind.

"Mataro's lecherous friends are here," she said, opening the pack and digging through it with purpose before pressing the wineskin and the linen bundle inside. "They are drinking themselves into oblivion and boasting about their plans." Her voice held a menacing edge I'd never heard before from the gentle old woman.

"For a fight?" I asked, my hands shaking as I gripped Lukio's shoulders and tugged him close to my side. Thankfully he was too sleepy to struggle against my embrace. He leaned heavily against me, his eyes fluttering closed.

"I wish it were only a fight," Azuvah said as she sailed across the room to snatch up both my and Lukio's sandals. "Mataro has sold you, Arisa. To one of the priests of Dagon."

Everything went still around me as the world tilted sideways. "Me?"

She returned to push our sandals into the satchel. "The man plans to take you with him as soon as this debauchery is finished."

"I'm to be a slave in the temple?" The words were too terrifying to speak louder than a whisper.

Azuvah tied the pack closed and dropped it on the bed. "Worse than a slave, my sweet girl. Far worse." Although I did not understand exactly why her tone made the skin on my neck and arms prickle, I did not doubt Azuvah. "That is why we must leave. Now."

"I don't want to go anywhere, Risi," said Lukio on a yawn. "Mataro said I am the best fighter and soon everyone in the Five Cities will know my name, even the kings."

Before I could respond, Azuvah knelt before my brother, an earnest expression on her wizened face as she gazed up at him with affection. "Mataro is right about one thing, Lukio. You are the strongest boy I know. One who will grow into a man of integrity and honor if you choose the right path." She grasped his hands and turned them palm up. "These hands were made to defend those who cannot defend themselves. And tonight, that means protecting your sister by fleeing Ashdod."

His brows pinched together as he glanced up at me. "Risi is in danger?"

She nodded. "There is no other choice but to go, lior. Your sister's life is at stake."

He blinked at her, taking in her plea wordlessly. Then his gaze darted to the door before coming back to rest on me.

"Please, Lukio," I whispered, through the burning knot in my throat. "Please."

It seemed a hundred years passed before he finally nodded and I was able to release the breath I'd been holding back.

"Good," said Azuvah, who then stood and placed a kiss on his forehead and then one on mine. "We don't have much time. We must be far away before anyone notices I am missing."

"How will we get out of the villa? We'll be seen," I said. We'd be forced to walk directly through the rebuilt hearth room on our way to the front door.

"We are going out that way," Azuvah replied, gesturing to the window that looked over the alleyway behind the villa.

"But it's so far to the ground!" I said. "How will we get down?"

With a smug little grin, Azuvah pulled a pile of braided linens from beneath the bed as well. "With this," she said, stretching the cloth between her outstretched arms so I could see the knots she'd tied along its length. "I found a bin of forgotten linen sheets and prepared this over the past few nights. It is as strong as any rope."

She took the long braid and tied the end to the sturdy frame of the bed we shared, then together the three of us moved it directly beneath the window.

"Lukio first," she said. "Then you."

My brother scrambled onto the bed without argument, far from fearful over the prospect of climbing down from the second story since he spent much of his time scaling trees with his wild friends.

"Hurry," she said, waving her hands at me. "He will come to fetch you soon and you must be away from this place."

After taking a shuddery breath, I helped Lukio climb onto the sill, encouraging him to be as quiet as possible as he slithered down the linen rope. Once he was safely on the ground, I took the leather satchel from Azuvah and slipped the strap over my chest. Then I gripped the stone ledge with both hands and, with Azuvah's help, managed to maneuver myself until my legs were outside, bare feet propped against the wall and the rope gripped tightly in my fists.

A loud sound at the door halted my progress.

"Let me in," shouted Mataro, pounding on the wood. The dowel Azuvah had jammed into the latch wiggled as he shook the handle.

"Go!" whispered Azuvah, her eyes wide. "Now!"

"Not without you," I said, my hands already aching from holding my weight.

"Open this door, you stupid cow," screamed Mataro, jerking the door so hard that it juddered on its leather hinges. "I know you are in there."

"Arisa," said Azuvah, her tone solidifying into a firm demand. "You must get Lukio to safety. There is no one else who can do so."

I shook my head vehemently, the memory of the deep purple

bruise on Azuvah's face rising in my mind. Mataro would not stop at a strike when he discovered us missing. From the bellowing threats he was spewing from behind the door, he would not stop at all. Agony flooded through me. I had no choice but to obey her, or all of us would suffer his wrath.

"But where do I go?" I choked out.

Her gaze fluttered about the room, as if the answer were written somewhere on the walls. "The Ark," she said on a gasp, her eyes flaring. "It is just as in my dreams. You must follow the Ark."

"Where?" I gasped, her strange statement addling my mind further.

"It was taken to Ekron, after being sent away from Gath," she said. "Go north on the trade road and then follow the river eastward."

"But I—"

"Follow the Ark, Arisa. Do not turn to the right or to the left, and do not stop until it dwells among the cedars and you are sheltered in perfect peace."

Pain ripped through my chest at the thought of leaving her, but the bone-deep trust I had in her made my decision for me. I nodded and through a haze of tears, I saw her smile one last time, all the love in the world shining in her deep brown eyes.

"I promised you would not be alone, and I vow that it is true," she said. "Yahweh will be with you. Now go!" She whirled around, slipped off the bed, and then with a strength I did not know she possessed, slid a heavy wooden chest in front of the door. Although it was a futile gesture and Mataro would no doubt burst through, she was giving us a few extra moments to get away.

Hand over hand I used the knots Azuvah had tied to let myself down the length of the rope, repeatedly scraping my knees on the plastered mudbrick as I attempted to keep myself from sliding to my death. When I was only a few cubits from the ground, I heard a loud crack as Mataro broke through the wooden dowel and the groan of the chest being shoved aside as he fought his way through the barricade Azuvah had made. Knowing I was out of time, I let myself drop, hissing at the spike of pain in my feet when I hit the ground.

Even though everything inside me screamed to run back in the house and plead with Mataro to leave Azuvah alone, I ignored my instincts and grabbed my brother's hand.

"Run!" I commanded in a rasping whisper, fixing my eyes on the dark street ahead of us and wishing I could not hear the horrors that emanated from the window above us. Curses. Moans. The sound of fists meeting flesh and the vow from my cousin to choke the life from the woman who'd sung me to sleep every night of my life.

I had no idea what lay before us on this dark road, but I would not waste Azuvah's sacrifice.

Six

Turning away from the river we'd followed for the past few hours, Lukio and I made our way up the wide road toward Ekron. Lording over a region that teemed with olive groves and fertile farms, this famous stronghold was on the frontier of Philistine territory, and I could only hope that within its thick walls we would find the box Azuvah had charged us to follow.

"Where are we going?" asked Lukio for the hundredth time since we put Mataro's house at our backs and flew into the night.

"I told you. We have to find the Ark of the Hebrews. Azuvah said that it was brought here."

"And then we will go home?"

I studied his beloved face as he blinked up at me, my gaze going to the remnants of the bruise beneath his green eye and the gap where one of his lower teeth had been knocked out. Already a new one was pushing into its place. The memory of the blood trickling from his nose the other day wiped any lingering uncertainty from my mind.

I stood tall to assert my authority. "We can never return to Ashdod."

His eyes went wide. "Never?"

I shook my head. "It is too dangerous."

"But how will Azuvah find us here?" he asked with a deep furrow between his brows.

My heart wept at the innocent question, but at the same time, I was grateful that he seemed not to have noticed, or understood, the sounds of Mataro destroying the woman who'd laid down her life for us. Lukio loved her just as much as I did.

"She wanted to come but had to stay back in Ashdod." The lie slipped from my tongue easily, determined as I was to keep him from knowing the extent of my fear.

He frowned, gazing back toward the expansive stretch of coastland from which we'd come.

"I have an idea," I said, thinking to distract him from our new and terrifying reality. "We must find that golden box, Lukio. The first one of us to catch sight of it will earn a double portion of bread."

Lukio's green and brown eyes sparkled as he rubbed his belly. "Truly?"

We'd already eaten half of the bread Azuvah had packed, but at least the skin of watery wine was almost full since we'd knelt on the bank of the river this morning and drank until our bellies sloshed. No matter what we discovered today, I would ensure he had the double portion anyhow, but Lukio was always up for a challenge.

"First, we need to get inside the gates." My eyes followed a small caravan of traders, their camels slowing into a loose-limbed cadence as they climbed toward the grand entrance to Ekron. "There," I said, gesturing to the last animal, which bore two small children among its burdens. "Let's follow closely. Perhaps the guards will assume we are part of that group."

He nodded and slipped his palm back into mine. He'd grown so much in the last few months that he stood just past my shoulder now. One day soon I knew he would surpass me in height—greatly, if my father's size was any indication—but I would never forget the first time Azuvah placed him in my arms, saying that he would always look to me for care and protection. A statement that proved to be absolutely true in the years since then and even more so now.

"Eyes on the ground," I hissed as we approached the gates.

He scowled, annoyed that I'd prevented him from gaping at the guards who stood watch, their iron swords gleaming in the sunlight.

As much as I regretted snapping at Lukio, we could not chance anyone taking notice of us. Like Azuvah had predicted, it took all night to find our way here, stopping only for a few hours' rest within a stand of bushy junipers alongside the river. We'd made it this far without detection, and I was determined to remain unnoticed. I kept my head down and hurried to catch up with the traders, pleading with the gods to cloak us with invisibility as we passed beneath the wary gazes of the guards.

When my plan worked and none of the men took notice of two dusty children trailing behind the line of camels, I took a few deep breaths, willing the tight knots in my stomach to unwind. I patted the strap of the leather satchel, reassuring myself that our only worldly possessions were still slung across my torso.

Tightening my grip on Lukio, I peeled away from the crowd, feeling the urgent need to put distance between us and the gates.

"You're squeezing my fingers," said Lukio, making an attempt to shake off my hold, his feet dragging in the dirt.

"There are too many people in this city," I said, firming my grip as I gestured to the river of bodies swarming toward the marketplace. "We cannot get separated as we search for the Ark."

"Why do we have to find it?" he asked, trudging along beside me. "Tombaal said it was full of evil spirits."

I had no answer, other than Azuvah's strange mumblings about dreams and assurances that we would find peace among cedars— none of which I was certain I believed—so I tugged on his hand and headed toward the center of the city, assuming that the best place to find a sacred object would be a temple.

We passed through the bustling marketplace where Philistines, Canaanites, Amorites, and other foreigners vied for goods or customers, just as they'd done in Ashdod before the plagues had struck. It seemed that Ekron had had no such misfortune, for every stall overflowed with bounty and the sounds of commerce rang from every corner.

After winding our way through narrow streets toward the center of town, where an assortment of grand homes and minor temples lined the streets in well-maintained grandeur, we came upon the largest and most ornate of all. An engraving near the entrance to the courtyard offered the sanctuary to Baalzebub, Lord of Ekron, who was revered for his powers of healing. But there was no golden box sitting on the porch before his likeness and no bevy of priests trying to decide what to do with the Hebrews' sacred chest. In fact, it seemed that none of the terror that had fallen over Ashdod was on the faces of the people here. They moved about the streets without a care, unmarred by boils, and the obvious bounty in the market making it plain that they'd suffered no horde of rodents devouring their crops. Had Azuvah been wrong about where the Ark had been taken? Or had it indeed been destroyed?

Despondency settled atop my shoulders and tears stung my eyes. My brother and I were alone in a strange city, Azuvah was dead, and I had nothing more than three remaining rounds of bread and a skin of wine to sustain us. My stomach roiled and pitched as I wondered whether we would be forced to return to Ashdod after all.

Swiping at my eyes before Lukio noticed my hopelessness, I cleared my throat. "Looks as though it's not here. But let's go back to the market and keep our eyes open for any talk of it, all right?"

"But who will get the extra loaf of bread?"

I ruffled his curls, laughing as he ducked away from my affectionate gesture. "The first to overhear any clue as to where it is."

"Like a spy?" he responded, grinning.

"Exactly."

For the next couple of hours, we wandered through the marketplace, strolling past stalls stacked high with fabrics of every variety, pots of pungent spices, tables lined with idols both large and small, and fresh produce that practically begged to be snatched. But although my stomach pleaded with me to succumb to temptation, we could not chance someone noticing our presence. I glared at Lukio every time I caught him staring longingly at baskets of ripened olives or fragrant fruits.

But although we hovered around countless booths and shop windows, listening for any mention of the Hebrews' treasure, I heard nothing but the usual arguments over weights and measures, and the everyday gossip between friends and neighbors. Discouragement weighed heavy on me as the heat of midday leached the strength from my bones.

However, during our largely fruitless search, I had discovered something shocking: a large number of Hebrews were among the customers here in Ekron, a few wearing tassels on the corners of their garments that were identical to the knotted white-and-blue threads Azuvah had always worn around her wrist. Those who did not wear the fringes looked no different than the other customers, their dress and mannerisms so similar to the other tribes in this region that it was difficult to distinguish them. But after living with Azuvah for my entire life, I knew the distinctive lilt of her language as much as I knew my own, and I'd heard more than a few Hebraic tones bartering goods and haggling prices. Why, when we'd devastated the Hebrews' army and stolen their greatest treasure, would these people continue to intermingle with their enemies?

"I'm hungry. When can I have the bread?" Lukio whined, his belligerent pout belying his actual age and contradicting his size. There were purple shadows beneath his mismatched eyes, and his lips were cracked after hours in the sun.

"All right, let's find some shade and eat," I said, my spirits flagging further as I contemplated what we would possibly do once our meager provisions were gone. Would I end up having to steal to prevent my brother from starving? Or worse? I swallowed hard against the glut of hot tears that was making its way up my throat. It was my responsibility to protect Lukio and already I was failing.

". . . glad they didn't let that thing through the gates," said a woman as we passed by a handcart laden with a strange assortment of goods: a tilting pile of what looked to be well-used pottery, a mound of fabric scraps, and produce that looked to have passed its prime two days before. The couple whose conversation had snagged my attention away from Lukio's empty belly looked to be peddlers—their clothes threadbare, their bodies filthy and gaunt. Although the market was bursting with customers, none seemed interested in their paltry offerings.

"I am as well," said the woman. "I heard even more people died in Gath than Ashdod."

Thrilled that I'd finally heard talk of the Ark, I swung back around, dragging Lukio behind me without explanation as I slipped behind a pottery stand where the couple could not see us.

"Indeed," said the man, his fingers sliding over his greasy pate. "But the seren is no fool."

Pulling Lukio behind me, I stepped out from behind the pottery stall, too desperate to remain hidden.

"Where is it now?" I said to the man.

"Where is what?" The peddler scowled as he placed his hand atop a stack of ceramic bowls that shivered when Lukio knocked into the handcart in a bid to peer inside.

"The Hebrew box," I pressed. "Where did they take it when it was turned away at the gates?"

The man furrowed his brows. "How am I to know? It's gone. That is all that matters."

"I need to know. Please."

"Why, dear?" asked the woman, the words lisping through her rotted front teeth.

How could I explain that I was looking for a supposedly cursed object that an old Hebrew woman told me to follow because of a dream? My mind stuttered as I tried to think of an explanation, hoping it would be convincing.

"Because it killed my aunt and uncle, and I want to make sure that my brother and I are far away from it," I said, allowing nerves to wobble my voice. "Please tell me where it is so we can stay far, far away."

Although the peddler continued scowling at us, the woman stepped closer. "There is no need to worry. I heard that all five kings are meeting somewhere to the east of here, making a plan for what is to be done with the Hebrews' magic box. It won't be brought back here. You have no cause to fear." She placed her bony hand on my shoulder, her gaze skimming over Lukio's dirty face before coming back to me. "Are the two of you alone?"

Although her body smelled of stale sweat and other foul things, the instinct to unburden myself was strong. But something in her red-rimmed eyes gave me pause, causing me to snap my lips closed before I could divulge our secrets to these strangers. And I did not like the way her man was looking at us now, chin tilted and eyes narrowed, like he was weighing us on a bartering scale.

"My cousin is here somewhere," I said, letting my gaze break away as if I was searching him out. "We should go find him. I'm sure he is wondering where we are."

"Who is your cousin? Perhaps I can help you find him," said the woman, her fingers tightening on my shoulder.

"No need. We will be fine," I said, hoping she would not press further.

"Your accent is not local. Where are you from?" A note of suspicion dropped into her voice, and a strange look passed between her and the peddler, one that made the hair on my neck stand on end.

"We need to go," I said, snagging the back of Lukio's tunic and shrugging away from the woman's hold as I spun around and yanked him along with me. A silent warning blared in my head, and I cursed myself for even approaching the peddlers. I would not be so foolish next time.

"Wait! I'll help you find your cousin," the woman called out, lurching toward us and swiping for Lukio. But her hand swished through the air as we bolted away, and I thanked every god in the sky that my brother did not balk at my hasty retreat.

"Run!" I shouted, gripping his hand tightly and leading him into the crush of bodies.

More than a few shouts and snarls accompanied our flight as I pushed through the market with my brother trailing behind me and my heart thundering in my chest.

By the time I slackened my pace, we were well free of the market but also far from the gates. In my panic, I'd headed in the opposite direction, and we were now on the far side of Ekron, where the air was tinged with acrid smoke from kilns and forges. These streets were filled with tradesmen carrying pots or baskets on their shoulders, or hefting bushels of sticks to fuel fires. The persistent clang of metal on metal echoed from smoky blacksmith booths.

"Look, Risi!" said Lukio, skidding to a stop. "They're throwing dice."

I followed my brother's exuberant gesture to a group of boys gathered in the shadow of a trio of acacia trees down the street. They cheered and whooped at the latest toss, and Lukio began to walk toward them, his hand wrapped around the leather pouch at his neck.

I grabbed his arm. "No. We need to leave this city." Although it seemed we'd successfully dodged the peddlers, I had no desire to remain in Ekron. Especially if the Ark was nowhere within its walls.

"But I can win, Risi," he said. "And then I will buy you some food."

The dull gleam of silver pieces winked at me from the dirt in the center of the game. Unlike in Ashdod, these boys seemed to be wagering for more than just shells or trinkets.

"We will find food elsewhere," I said, touched by his offer to procure food, as if he was the one responsible for our sustenance. "It's time to go."

"But I am good. Only Tombaal was better than me," Lukio said, his jaw setting and a stubborn crinkle forming between his brows. "And Mataro taught me some new tricks too."

The name of our cousin halted any softening I might have had toward the idea. I had no doubt that what taught Lukio were dishonest. He would himself beaten up by those older boys.

"No," I said, my resolve hardening. "V

"But, Risi—"

"We will find another way," I said, pul headed in the other direction. "For now we need to get out of this city and find someplace to pass the night."

Although he struggled against my hold for a few moments, grumbling that I was being unfair, he followed me through the maze of back streets, since I was determined to avoid another run-in with the peddlers.

However, to my dismay, some sort of commotion blocked our exit from the city. A large group of men and women had congregated just inside the entrance, all with expectant eyes turned toward the gates. As a glut of people entered Ekron, moving in our direction with loud voices and shouts, Lukio and I skittered off the side, then climbed atop an empty stone bench and pressed our backs to the wall.

"Is it a parade?" asked Lukio.

Could it be the Ark being brought into Ekron? My heart fluttered at the idea, but then I remembered how the woman had said it had been turned away a few days ago when the people rebelled.

When the true reason for the furor was made clear, I was just as slack-jawed as Lukio at the incredible sight.

He stood nearly three heads taller than anyone else in the group of soldiers that accompanied him, his body built like a ship at full mast. With the feathered headdress of a Philistine soldier and a gleaming iron battle-ax slung between his wide shoulders, the giant of a man drew every eye as he passed through the gates, each stride equal to three of my own.

I'd heard of a few of these enormous men in our midst, mercenary warriors whose imposing size and vicious natures made our enemies' knees tremble, but I'd never seen one with my own eyes.

"Who is that?" Lukio asked, without removing his gaze from

ormous man, whose smug grin and swaggering gait seemed inflame the burgeoning crowd. They screamed and whistled, jostling to be closer.

"One of the last of the Anakim," I replied, having heard the word from Azuvah when she spoke of the giants who inhabited the land of Canaan before the Hebrews cut most of them down. "There are said to be fearless in battle."

"I want to be that big someday," he said. "And fearless too."

Amused by the awe in his voice, I slipped an arm around his shoulder and squeezed him to my side before placing a kiss on his sweaty curls. "I have no doubt you will be."

Taking advantage of the distraction that the giant man caused with his ostentatious arrival, Lukio and I jumped from our perch and slipped through the crowd and out of the gates, directly beneath the noses of the preoccupied guards.

The old woman had said that the kings were meeting east of the city, so instead of returning back toward the stand of junipers where we'd slept the morning away, I led Lukio onto the eastern road toward the rolling hills on the horizon, determined to obey Azuvah's commands to the very last.

Lukio found a stick on the side of the road and entertained himself by tossing rocks into the air and attempting to hit them as we walked. I was surprised at how many he was able to send flying off into the weeds, but then again my brother had always been able to accomplish uncommon physical feats as far back as I could remember. It was no surprise that Mataro had recognized his potential, even at his young age. Perhaps one day Lukio would indeed rival the giant in brawn.

Our father had been the same way—a champion in wrestling matches, a towering and thick-muscled warrior, and a seafaring trader who hefted enormous jugs full of olive oil into the hull of his ship like they were nothing more than feather pillows. Lukio was similar to him in so many ways, like the gods had remade my father into a perfect replica. I'd survived when my father had taken his grief with him and left us behind, but I was determined that nothing would separate Lukio and me, no matter what cost I had to pay.

The sun was near to setting by the time we approached a small hamlet, the tiny group of four houses set away from the road and near the river. Seeing nowhere else to pass the night and knowing that darkness would soon be upon us, I decided to take shelter in the nearby olive grove, hoping that none of the inhabitants of the homes would stumble upon us.

Before I guided Lukio into the orchard, I stood on the road, wondering where the kings of Philistia would have possibly taken the Ark. There was nothing to the west of us except a herd of cattle grazing the fertile pasturelands, and nothing to the east but a dark ridge of mountains in the far distance.

Where is it, Azuvah? Was your dream a lie? I shivered at the implications that Lukio and I had come so far in pursuit of nothing more than a mirage.

Turning my back on whatever ghosts we were chasing and desperately wishing Azuvah were here to calm my fears so I could do the same for Lukio, I led my brother off the road and found a place at the foot of an ancient tree, where the thick roots created a natural cradle large enough for both of us.

After we fashioned a nest from fallen leaves and weeds and settled into its lumpy embrace, I reached into the leather satchel to retrieve the three remaining portions of bread. I handed Lukio two of them, telling him that although I'd been the one to win the contest between us, I was not hungry enough for both pieces. He frowned at me, likely seeing through my lie, but his stomach must have overcome his hesitation because he devoured the bread without further comment.

I divided the watery wine between the two of us, again ensuring that the greater portion went to Lukio, but tipping the last of the bitter liquid into my mouth made my stomach hollow out. When would we be able to find more food? And how would I make sure the two of us survived out here in the open? I'd lived my entire life in Ashdod, with every meal provided to me and no wild animals to fend off. We had nothing more than a small knife Azuvah had put in the satchel and the one woolen blanket between us.

Meaning to cover Lukio, who'd already curled up in the bed of leaves like a contented pup, I pulled the blanket from the pack. Something fluttered to the ground. Something blue and white and all too familiar. Azuvah had severed the knotted strings from her wrist and sent the makeshift bracelet with us.

Intuition slithered through me. Somehow Azuvah must have known she would not be with us on this journey. That we would be alone and would have need of a reminder of her devotion to us. With my eyes burning, I tied the ends together in a sturdy knot and slid it over my own wrist, knowing that I would never again remove the worn but precious gift.

Lukio was already asleep, his mouth slack in his exhaustion. For a long while, I watched my brother breathe steadily, glad that he was oblivious to the dangers that lay beyond this small clearing. I could not fail him. I would not.

Laying my weary body down beside his and nestling close to share warmth, I prayed that we would be invisible to both man and beast alike. Pushing aside the barrage of fears and doubts, I squeezed my eyes tight, hoping that tomorrow some idea of how to survive in this new and frightening world would make itself known.

Seven

The insistent bawling of a calf woke me. I sat up, peering beneath the lowest branches toward the empty road about twenty paces away. The calf bellowed again, the thready call slicing through the hush of dawn and was soon joined by another of a similar pitch.

Lukio stirred to life as well, scrubbing the sleep from his eyes. "What is that?"

"Nothing," I said. "Sounds like a farmer weaning a couple of calves." I'd heard talk of such things from my uncle as he discussed management of the herd sanctified for temple sacrifices with his steward, but the brays from the calves were so high-pitched and reedy it almost seemed as though they were newly born instead of ready to wean from mother's milk.

My brother's empty stomach made its own call of displeasure and when he rubbed his belly, as if somehow his palm could wipe away the hunger, I decided that I'd been too hasty in rebuffing his offer yesterday.

First, we would search out water. There must be some source nearby that the farmers used to water their crops and stock, and then we would return to Ekron and I would let him throw dice. If there was even a small chance he could win and earn something to fill our stomachs, we had to take it. When our hunger was assuaged, I would think about where to go next.

I explained my plan to Lukio as we scrambled from our hiding place, shaking the debris from our tunics. The sun had only just parted ways with the horizon, the dawn rising over the low hills that divided the coastal plains upon which our people had settled from the peaks and valleys wherein the Hebrews resided.

"Look, Risi!" said Lukio, gesturing through the trees toward the road. A lone wagon plodded by at the same time the two calves in the distance cried out again.

The wagon jerked to the right as one of the red-coated cows stumbled as she called back over her shoulder, her heavy udders swaying. The other cow, who also looked to be nursing, did not return the plaintive plea of her calf, which must be penned up within one of the houses in the hamlet, but instead continued on, head down, looking determined as any ox trained to the yoke as she forced her companion to keep moving forward.

What was even more bewildering was that no one seemed to be driving the cows. The two-wheeled cart held something covered with a swath of white linen as it bumbled along the road, driver-less and unaccompanied.

But before I could make sense of the strange situation, the crunch of wheels off to the southwest startled me. I jerked Lukio down into the tall weeds, the sight before me even more confusing than two milk cows pulling a wagon. A caravan of chariots was following fifty paces behind, their polished iron wheels flashing a circular rhythm and the riders inside them dressed in full military regalia.

My eyes were likely just as wide as Lukio's as the eight regal vehicles and a large company of foot soldiers passed us in the same achingly slow cadence as the cow-drawn wagon. The noise of wheels and sandals on the rutted and stony path drowned out both the thudding of my heartbeat in my temples and my brother's exclamations about the heavily armed men who rode by with their eyes on the unmanned wagon ahead of them.

Two of the chariots carried priests, their embroidered tunics similar to the ones my uncle Harrom had worn during temple

services. The other five seemed to be carrying men of great importance, who wore headdresses more ornate than the other soldiers
and decorated with tall feathers dyed a deep purple. One of the
faces was well-known to me. I'd caught glimpses of him many
times during celebrations, seen him ride through the city on a
black stallion dressed in royal garb, and watched him gloat over
the Hebrews' defeat on the porch of Dagon's temple—the king
of Ashdod.

I was reminded of the words of the woman in the marketplace
"... *all five kings are meeting somewhere to the east of here, making a plan for what is to be done with the Hebrews' magic box.*"

In the distance, the wagon plodded forward at an excruciat-
ingly slow pace, wandering from one side of the well-worn path
to the other like a pebble rolling haphazardly down one of the
storm drain channels in the streets in Ashdod. One corner of the
linen had slipped away from the cargo, and the barest glint of
gold shimmered in the morning light. Any worry about where we
would find food and water dissipated as I realized exactly what
the wagon was carrying.

As soon as the final chariot and its escort ambled by, I turned
to Lukio, both of us still crouching in the shoulder-high weeds.

"We have to follow that wagon," I said. "The Hebrew box was
inside."

His brows furrowed deeply. "But you said we would go back to
the city so I could throw dice. I want to win you some food, Risi."

"I know I said that. But this is more important."

His gaze floated off toward Ekron in the distance.

"Listen," I said, gripping his shoulders so he would look at me.
"I know it is hard to understand, but this is what Azuvah told us
to do, Lukio. She always watched out for us, didn't she?"

He nodded his chin.

"And she never told us a lie or mistreated us, correct?"

Although he scowled, he did not argue the point.

"She told me to follow that box, no matter what. She even had
dreams about it."

He grimaced in confused disbelief.

"I don't understand it either, but I know this is the right way." I placed my hands on his face, staring into his uniquely colored eyes. "Please. Trust me."

After a few moments, he nodded again, and I sighed in relief.

"Won't those soldiers see us?" he asked.

"We won't let them," I said. "We will keep off the road, walk behind the trees and in the brush."

"Like spies again?" he asked, a note of intrigue tugging his voice upward.

"Exactly like spies." I grinned at him, making my eyes go wide. "Spies who will outsmart the kings of Philistia and all their men."

Lukio's mischievous laugh was all the sustenance I would need for at least the next few hours. So we placed everything we'd ever known at our backs and followed the Ark.

The slow progress of the caravan made it easy for us to keep pace, and much to my delight, we passed by two separate creeks along the way, giving us the opportunity to not only drink deeply of clean, sweet water but also to refill our wineskin. To add to our good fortune, our path took us directly through a number of orchards, so our leather satchel was now full of apples, pomegranates, olives, and walnuts, and our bellies were satisfied.

We stayed far enough behind the parade of chariots that none of the men noticed us, or if they did, they saw no danger from the two children shadowing the procession. But Lukio took great pleasure in keeping watch, hissing at me to duck down every so often whenever he saw one of the men turn back to survey the road behind them.

The cows continued to meander back and forth like drunkards, but had not stopped moving forward. Somehow they remained on the well-beaten trade road, even without a driver to keep them on task.

The foothills rose up around us, each summit higher and more imposing, as the sun reached its high point. This was the area Azuvah had called the *shephelah*. My legs ached from the upward climb, and I wondered whether the wagon would ever reach a destination, or if the cows would continue walking through the afternoon and into the night. By now we must be deep into Hebrew territory, and I could not understand why the kings of Philistia were still following behind the wagon when our enemies may already be aware of the strange caravan heading their way.

Without warning, the chariots stopped moving forward just below the top of a ridge. The five kings stepped out, and, accompanied by a number of their men and the two priests, they hiked up a hillside that overlooked a wide and fertile valley. After removing their distinctive headdresses, they squatted down behind a few boulders and watched the wagon as it continued on.

Spotting another outcropping of boulders up above them, I led Lukio in that direction with a warning to stay quiet as we crept through the thick trees and up the hillside. We settled in a gap between two enormous granite rocks, out of sight of the Philistines below but near enough that their voices echoed back to us.

"Will they accept the gifts?" asked one of the kings.

"The gods have foretold that they will. Both the bones and the entrails have made that very clear," said one of the priests, a man I remembered from my uncle's lavish feasts. "Besides, that is no small offering inside that wagon."

"Any amount of gold is worth ending these plagues," said another king. "Otherwise our cities will be laid waste."

The king of Ashdod muttered something under his breath, shaking his head in obvious disagreement. With his jaw locked and a scowl on his face, he began to push to his feet, but the king next to him, one with a thick head of silver hair, grabbed his arm and pulled him back down.

"I have no interest in watching this foolishness," said the seren of Ashdod.

"We wait, Nicaro," said the older king, his tone brooking no argument. "Your father would have agreed."

"I am not my father," said Nicaro.

"No," said the older man, his eyes narrowed. "No, you are not."

Although the seren of Ashdod went stiff at the blatant slight, he remained silent and did not retreat.

Far below us, the cow-drawn wagon had meandered off the road and into a golden-brown field of ripe wheat. After so many hours of bumping along on the pitted and scarred path, half the linen covering had slid away, and the sparkling wings of one of the otherworldly creatures were plainly visible, glittering with strange magnificence in the bright sunlight. I watched in fascination as the vehicle that had carried the gold box from Ashdod to Gath to Ekron to this valley plowed through the gently waving stalks.

Then, in the distance, I saw a group of men—farmers bent over in the field, harvesting the wheat with sickles. One of them noticed the wagon approaching and let out a shout to alert his companions. The cows finally came to a halt near a flat boulder that sat near the center of the field, as if that had been their destination all along.

"Should we go now?" asked one of the kings. "It's in their hands now."

"No," said the silver-haired king. "Not until we know they aren't planning to turn it around and send it back. I want to assure my people that it has no chance of returning."

Soon the entire group of farmers had congregated near the wagon, some looking up to search the hills around, their sickles still in hand, as if guarding against attack. But then one of them reached over the lip of the cart and slipped off the rest of the linen, revealing what lay beneath.

As if in one accord, the group of them darted away, gathering about fifty paces from the wagon, their animated gestures making it clear they were discussing what to do with the treasure that had been returned to them. After a while, a few of them ran off, headed toward the town in the distance.

The Philistine kings then slipped away from their perch overlooking the valley, quietly making their way down the hillside to their chariots, slinking away like dogs with their tails tucked firmly between their legs. The seren of Ashdod trailed behind the rest, a troubled expression on his young, handsome face as he took one last look over his shoulder toward the valley.

"Shouldn't we follow?" Lukio said as he watched the kings and priests mount their chariots and turn them back toward Ekron.

My chest ached as I watched the last of our countrymen drive away, leaving the two of us alone in enemy territory. Perhaps we should turn back as well. It had only been a few hours' walk between Ekron and this valley, after all. But I'd obeyed Azuvah this far, and I would not stop now.

Besides, the draw that golden box had on me since the very first moment I saw it had not relented. Even across the valley I could sense it calling to me. I imagined the winged creatures atop its cover were whispering my name, imploring me to press on in spite of the danger.

One last shred of courage curled around my spine, lending me strength.

"Azuvah said to remain with the Ark," I said, hoping that Lukio could not see my hands shaking in my lap, nor sense the double-mindedness beneath my show of certainty. "And that is what we will do. No matter what happens, we stay."

Eight

After eating most of the remaining fruit in our satchel, we decided that it would do us no good to remain perched up so high. None of the farmers that remained near the wagon had noticed us, so I led Lukio down the hillside, staying within the cover of the trees and picking my way carefully down the steep incline. But just as we neared the valley floor, I skidded on a patch of loose stones, my foot twisting as I pitched backward and landed hard on my elbow.

"Risi!" gasped Lukio, darting to my side.

"I'm all right," I lied, squeezing my eyes hard against the hot prickle of tears as I gripped my ankle and swallowed down the sob that threatened to burst from my lips. Worry furrowed deep between my brother's brows, and his gaze flew back toward the bend in the road where we'd last seen the kings of Philistia.

"Give me your hand," I said. "I need help standing, but I can walk."

With his lips pressed tightly together, my brother pulled me to my feet, then slipped his arm around my waist, doing his best to prop me up as I gingerly hopped forward.

With a grim expression that belied his years, Lukio helped me hobble toward a stand of trees at the edge of the valley, where we found a well-protected narrow gap between the largest of the sprawling oaks and the crumbling stone wall of what looked to be an abandoned sheepfold.

Dropping our satchel on the ground, I sat and propped my back against the tree trunk, sighing in relief and grateful for the shade. Both of us were panting, soaked in sweat, and covered in dust from head to toe. Moisture pricked at my eyes as my twisted ankle and bloodied elbow throbbed in tandem. I squelched the urge to let the tears fall, determined to be calm for my brother and not stoke his fears any higher than they already were.

"Where do we go now?" asked Lukio, slipping his hand into the satchel for an apple.

"I don't know," I answered honestly, examining the abrasions on my elbow and restraining a hiss as I brushed away the tiny blood-encrusted pebbles that had lodged themselves into my skin. "Azuvah told me to follow the Ark, so I suppose we wait."

Lukio frowned. "We should go back to Ekron."

The same thought had cycled through my mind again and again. I did not know how to explain why I felt certain we should stay when I could not reconcile it even to myself. I just knew we must not retreat. At least not yet.

Voices echoed across the valley, so Lukio and I peered over the crumbling stone wall to where the wagon sat only a hundred paces from our hiding place.

A large group of people had joined the farmers, mostly men dressed in white garments, but there were women and children among the numbers as well. A few of the men removed the Ark from the wagon, using the poles attached to its sides, and placed it atop the boulder that stood at the center of the field, as if the flat-topped rock had been laid there for the purpose of serving as a sacred *bamah*.

Once the golden object rested securely, another group of men unhitched the cattle from the wagon. Then, to my great shock, one of them unsheathed a knife and with swift efficiency slit the throats of both cows, watching dispassionately as they dropped heavily into the dirt one after the other. Then he, along with a few others, began the grisly task of butchering the unfortunate beasts. I'd seen many bloody carcasses in the marketplace—goats, sheep, dogs, pigs—and the sight never bothered me before, but somehow watching the men at work gutting, skinning, and slicing up cows whose calves were likely still bawling for their milk made my stomach curdle. At the same time, another group of men began to break apart the wagon, and the rest of the people scattered around the valley, gathering rocks.

"What are they doing, Risi?" asked Lukio, his mouth full of fruit.

"I don't know," I replied, reaching out to brush juice from his chin. "Building something, it would seem."

We watched the group arrange the rocks into a pile that swiftly grew larger with so many hands working together. Stone by stone, an altar formed near the boulder upon which the golden box was perched.

As the sun slid behind the hill at our backs, the men constructed a fire atop the makeshift altar and laid the carcasses on the flames. The enticing smell of roasting meat wafted on the breeze, making my stomach protest. More people from the city had gathered but stood some distance away from the boulder, seeming fearful of coming any closer. But the sounds of celebration reached my ears—laughter and song and the screech of a few children playing a game of chase on the far edge of the valley. A few pipes and drums echoed across the field, and a circle of women took up a joyful dance as the first star of twilight winked into sight and the full moon peered over the horizon.

The group of white-clad men was now circled around the boulder, facing the golden box. Four of them carefully lifted the lid with its winged creatures, most likely to ensure that my people had not removed its contents. Azuvah had told me what was inside—magical food and a staff that bloomed with almond blossoms and stone tablets upon which Mosheh had chiseled important laws—none of which the kings of Philistia would have any interest in, even if they had opened the box.

"I'm hungry, Risi," said Lukio. "That meat smells so good."

"That it does," I said, my own belly snarling in agreement.

A rumble in the sky jerked my attention away from my brother, who'd found a few leftover olives at the bottom of the satchel and was making short work of devouring them. A cloud had formed over the golden box, an otherworldly swirl of color and light that looked like no storm I'd ever seen. Another roll of thunder echoed across the valley, one that grew louder and louder instead of fading away. All the hair on the back of my neck, my scalp, and my arms rose as a crawling sensation moved over my skin like water. I was simultaneously struck by an urgent need to flee and the feeling that a heavy weight was pressing down on me from above.

Lukio buried his face in my shoulder, trembling. "Is the earth shaking again?"

Before I could answer, a brilliant light flashed above the Ark, one that seemed to come directly from the void between the wings of the creatures on its lid. The light suddenly shattered, snaking into a hundred threads of blue-white light, and between one blink and the next, every man who was standing around the box had been struck down, their bodies smoking where they lay.

Clapping a hand over my mouth to contain the shriek of horror that ripped up my throat, I dropped my head, squeezing my eyes shut as I yanked Lukio down to the ground behind the stone wall.

"What is it?" he squeaked.

"Shhh." I petted his head, whisking my fingers through his thick curls, again and again, hoping to keep him calm but unable to brush the terrible sight I'd just witnessed from my own mind. My stomach churned with nausea as I rocked us both back and forth. "We are all right," I said, needing the reassurance just as much as he did. "We are safe."

But the keening cries that went up in that moment and the terror-stricken shouts that followed told a different tale. Although the fire seemed to have consumed the men around the makeshift altar and the Ark, many townspeople had been spared. The sounds of their panicked voices and the shrieking of the children moved farther and farther away as we huddled against the stone wall. The survivors were fleeing the carnage, but Lukio and I were trapped here by my injury and were now exposed to whatever had just slaughtered so many men a hundred paces away.

I had made the wrong choice. I'd followed an old woman and her wild dreams, leading Lukio directly into unspeakable peril. Perhaps, as Mataro had accused many times, Azuvah *had* been touched by madness. I should have stayed in Ekron, hired myself out as a servant, begged for scraps, let Lukio toss dice—whatever it took to stay alive.

With my arms wrapped tightly around my brother, I continued rocking us back and forth, whispering into his ear, "We are safe. It is over." Meaningless words that I did not believe as darkness descended over us like a shroud.

When my brother finally succumbed to exhaustion, his body going slack in my arms, I laid him on the ground and pulled out the wool blanket to tuck around him. For as frightened as I'd been last night when we slept in the cradle of the olive tree, my terror now was tenfold. Something far more dangerous than wild animals waited out there in the dark tonight.

Giving in to my morbid curiosity, I sat up on my knees and peered over the stone wall. The moon was high now, casting its brilliant gaze over the wheat fields and illuminating the golden box, but thankfully the charred bodies were hidden in the shadows. Contrary to Azuvah's assurances, there were no tall and lovely cedars in this valley where Lukio and I would find rest and peace. There were only horrors and death beneath the open sky.

The Ark shimmered in the moonlight, reminding me of how captivated I'd been by its sunlit sparkle, even as the soldiers hefted it toward the temple porch and the crowd mocked and jeered. But as harmless as it appeared now, alone atop the rock and no longer alive with fire, I determined to keep my eyes on the dangerous object all night long, just in case something else happened and we needed to flee right away. And no matter that it still seemed to whisper my name, tomorrow I would push aside the screaming pain in my ankle and put as much distance as possible between the two of us and that box.

Nine

The lingering smell of charred flesh made me grateful that my uncle had forbidden me from coming within a hundred paces of the Ark. One by one, the bodies of the men who'd foolishly remained in the center of an open field during a lightning storm were wrapped in linens and loaded onto ox-drawn carts, bound for their graves outside the town of Beth Shemesh nearby.

Shifting my seat, I juggled a smooth stone between my palms as I waited for the grisly task to be complete. After being told to stay as far away as possible from the carnage—and the golden box that the Levites insisted was dangerous—I'd settled in the shade of an oak, atop the last crumbling wall of an abandoned sheepfold, one that seemed to have been mostly dismantled, the materials hauled away for other purposes.

I did not understand why my uncle had even insisted I come today, since I was relegated to the far reaches of the valley while he and the other Levites tended to the dead. But as his apprentice, obligated to learn the sacred duties our tribesmen had performed at the Mishkan for many generations, I had no choice but to obey.

The fact that the Mishkan no longer stood, and Shiloh, the city that had housed it for hundreds of years, had been mostly razed by the Philistines seven months ago, changed nothing. We were Levites. We served the people and our God without question—whether we believed it mattered, or not.

My uncle and the others had been summoned to Kiryat-Yearim for meetings nearly two weeks ago to strategize with the other Levites how to address rumors and frustrations among the people. Many were not only frightened that the Philistines would invade again soon, but also wondered whether Yahweh had abandoned us completely. Over the past few months, I'd begun to question whether he'd ever cared in the first place.

My gaze was drawn to the chest atop the flat boulder at the center of the valley. A fresh new swath of linen had been draped over the relic by the four eldest Levites with painstaking reverence. It was not the first time I'd seen the Ark with my own eyes. I'd been in Shiloh the day the High Priest's sons had ordered it removed from the Mishkan and carried to the battlefield at Afek—where my father, along with my two older brothers and nearly a hundred other Levites, had been slaughtered protecting the useless thing.

Like every other Hebrew child, I'd been raised on the stories of the larger-than-life Mosheh defeating Pharaoh, splitting the sea, and constructing the golden casket said to be in-dwelt by the very presence of the Almighty. But I'd stopped believing such fantastical tales the day the Philistines cut down three of the best men I'd ever known while easily snatching the Ark and hauling it away without suffering even a scratch. If the ancient object was so powerful and holy, how had such vicious and foul-hearted men even approached it?

It seemed almost laughable that as soon as messengers had arrived in Kiryat-Yearim in the middle of the night with a wild story about an unmanned wagon wheeling itself into their midst, my uncle and the other Levites began cleansing their bodies and preparing themselves ritually to approach it. The Ark was nothing more than a gold-covered box of acacia wood, built up by myth and legend into something of a great mystery. An object for which my father and brothers had died needlessly.

I let the rock slip from my fingers and closed my eyes, allowing the new song that had been stirring in my belly for weeks to pour from my mouth and diving into the pool of delight I always found when I blocked the world around me to create music.

For as uninspired as I was by thoughts of my future Levitical duties, the fact that the men of my lineage were descended from some of the first musicians to worship in the Mishkan in the wilderness was a point of great pride. I could endure any tedious task for the privilege of learning the sacred songs and instrument-making techniques they'd passed from generation to generation.

Pausing to consider where the melody of my new song might go next, I took a breath, but just as the next flurry of notes came to mind, a whisper at my back startled me into awareness of my surroundings. Spinning around with my heart pounding against my ribs, I leaped from my perch on the low wall and drew my small flint knife from my belt.

All was silent again as I searched the deep shadows beneath the spreading oak tree, confused as my gaze found nothing but dirt and weeds. I'd heard a voice; I was certain of it. The hair on the back of my neck rose as I glanced back toward the Levites, remembering another of those impossible tales I'd been told about a young boy named Samuel, who'd heard the voice of Yahweh call his name. I nearly laughed at myself for the wild comparison. The maker of the universe did not speak to little boys, and he certainly did not speak to me.

Something scuffed against the backside of the stone wall. Praying it was some small animal scrabbling about for food and not a stray Philistine lying in wait, I crouched down, then slowly crept along the base of the wall with my pulse throbbing in my ears.

Taking a deep breath and gripping my knife tight, I peered around the end of the wall with my stomach looped into a hundred knots. There, huddled against the stone fence, were two bedraggled children, clutching each other with terror-stricken expressions on their pale, dirty faces as they looked back at me.

Letting out a shuddering breath mixed with a self-deprecating laugh, I put my knife back in its sheath. "It's all right. I won't hurt you."

The oldest—a girl of perhaps twelve or thirteen with the most enormous green eyes I'd ever seen—pulled the younger child closer to her side. Perhaps they were survivors from the terrible happenings during the storm last night. If so, then they must have been horrified by the sight of seventy men being struck by fire from the sky.

Compassion bloomed in my chest. I took a few cautious steps forward, palms upraised. "I mean you no harm."

The girl shrank back at my proximity, but the boy's jaw hardened and he shifted his body slightly, as if preparing to protect his companion from me. I suppressed a smile at his mettle. He could not be more than nine or ten, a full eight years younger than me, but it was clear that he was willing to engage me to protect the girl—his sister, most likely, by the striking resemblance between the two.

"Are you from Beth Shemesh?" I asked, gesturing over my shoulder.

After a long pause, the girl shook her head. The fertile valleys within the shephelah contained any number of small farming hamlets that they might have wandered away from.

"Another village?"

The girl gripped the boy's tunic in a tight fist, either to hold him back or to reassure herself, her gaze flitting around the hills. Then, to my amazement, she lifted a trembling finger and pointed toward the western horizon, speaking in a small but sweet voice laden with an unfamiliar accent. "Ashdod. Near the sea."

I could not have been more shocked than if the lightning had returned at that moment to strike me down as well. These children were Philistines?

"But . . . but you speak my language," I spluttered out, my

mind flailing about for an explanation as to why they would be in Yehudite territory. I knew Ashdod to be one of the largest of the enemy strongholds, a major port city, and at least two days' walk from here.

"Azuvah—" she stopped herself, blinking a few times before she continued. "A slave spoke your words to my brother and me."

"You are far from home. How have you come to be here?" I swept my eyes around the valley, instinctively searching out enemies among the many shadows on the thick-wooded hillsides.

Her long lashes fluttered before her deep green eyes met mine with shy determination. "We followed the box. The kings left, but we stayed."

Stricken by the odd statement, I opened my mouth to ask more but someone called my name, drawing my attention away. My uncle Abiram waved to me from twenty paces off, gesturing for me to return.

"That is my uncle," I said to the two children still huddled like field mice against the wall. "He will want to meet you."

The girl let out a small gasp, fearful of yet another stranger discovering their hiding place.

"You have no cause for alarm," I said, gentling my tone even further. "Neither one of us will harm you. I vow it in the name of Yahweh, the Holy One."

By the time Abiram neared the tumbled-down sheepfold, a heavy dose of concern lay within his confused gaze. He frowned as his steps slowed. "What is it? Another body?"

"No," I replied, waving him over. "Come see for yourself."

Cautiously he came around the end of the stone wall, then stopped short when he saw the children. "Whose young ones are these?"

"That is just the thing. They claim to be Philistines. From Ashdod."

My uncle's jaw slackened as he examined them more closely. "How did they come to be in Beth Shemesh?"

"They say they followed the Ark. And remained when the kings left."

"The kings . . . ?"

I shrugged, having no more understanding than he of what the girl meant by that statement.

Abiram pulled me a few steps away and lowered his voice. "What else have they told you? Did they see what happened here?"

"I don't know. I only just discovered them hiding behind the wall."

Turning back to gaze across the valley, he hummed and stroked his graying beard, a habit he turned to whenever mulling over a tangled issue. "The Ark is secure, and the bodies have been removed. We are returning to Kiryat-Yearim for the time being to discuss the next steps. But if they were witnesses to this "—his palm fluttered in the air behind him—"then I am certain Abinidab will want to speak with them, no matter what their heritage is. Perhaps they can give us more clarity about where the Ark came from and why." He lowered his chin, pinning me with a pointed stare. "See if you can find out more while I fetch the others."

"They are frightened. I'm not certain they will tell me much. The girl seems quite reticent, and I don't know that the boy can even speak our language."

"You have a knack for these things, Ronen. You'll think of something."

Before I could argue with his assertion, Abiram walked away, determination in his stride as he went to retrieve the other Levites. Turning back to the children, I sighed, rubbing my forehead. They looked back at me with curious expressions, and I wondered how much of the conversation they'd overheard or understood. Thinking to make myself appear less threatening, I took a seat on the ground a few paces away.

"I come from a village far from here as well," I said, hoping to ease them into revealing more. "Up near Shiloh. Have you heard of it?"

The girl nodded, gesturing with her chin toward the northeast. "Your gold box is from there."

I lifted my brows in surprise. "That is right. It resided within the Mishkan for hundreds of years."

"Mishkan?" she echoed.

"Our holy sanctuary for as long as our people have lived in this land. It began as an enormous tent constructed in the wilderness—"

"By Mosheh," she interrupted.

"Yes," I said, stunned that she knew anything of our history. "Mosheh instructed the people to build the tent after our people were freed from slavery in Egypt. I am from the line of Levi, the men tasked with caring for that sanctuary and all its implements."

Her brow furrowed. "But you are here."

I tilted my chin, studying her face for a moment. Distracted at first by the shock of her presence, I'd missed the foreignness of her features—the paleness of her skin, the shimmering golden tones in her light brown hair, wide-set eyes the color of a sunlit forest—but the closer I looked, the more I could see that these children did somewhat resemble the few Philistines I'd seen in the last few years, either traveling on roads through our territory or passing through the marketplace in Shiloh before the war. No matter that our two peoples were constantly at odds—and theirs had vowed long ago to wipe us from this land—trade and intermingling between us and our enemies was commonplace. Far too much so.

"Your people destroyed it," I said, working hard to contain my bitterness as I thought of the way the Philistines had marched into Shiloh and razed the holy places only a few days after cutting down thousands of our men. "There is little left of the city, and the stone walls that once protected the Mishkan were torn down."

Her dark eyelashes fluttered. "This would make Azuvah very sad." Her tone indicated that the revelation disappointed her as well, which made no sense coming from the child of our sworn enemies.

"Who is this woman you speak of? The one who taught you our language?"

"She cared for my brother and me." She placed a possessive hand on his shoulder. "Our mother died when Lukio was born, and our father is . . . he is gone. But Azuvah protected us. Taught us many things. Even your words and stories."

"And where is she now?"

She pressed her lips together, those green eyes shimmering as she shook her head and darted a glance at Lukio. She must not want him to know that the slave was dead, so I said nothing.

"And the rest of your family? Do you not need to return to them?"

"They are gone too. The plagues from your golden box took them."

We'd heard rumors that some sort of tragedy had befallen Ashdod. A few Hebrew tradesmen returned from the coast with stories about an epidemic and widespread famine, but this was the first I'd heard of the Ark being accused of causing them.

"My uncle thinks our leader would like to speak with you. Are you willing?"

Her face seemed to pale further, and her eyes grew impossibly large.

I placed a palm on my chest. "I promise, no one will lay a hand on you. We are men set aside for service to our God. Men of peace, not soldiers. Abinidab will only want to hear your story."

The girl shifted, her gaze downcast as she fidgeted with a clump of grass near her knee, but Lukio's eyes were pinned on the center of my chest, where a keepsake hung from a leather strap. I noticed that his eyes were mismatched, one walnut brown and the other similar to his sister's eye color.

"Do you like this?" I asked, seizing on the distraction as his sister contemplated my request.

He did not answer, but curiosity seemed to override his wariness as he peered at the necklace. I lifted the pendant to give him a clearer view. "This is very special."

"What is it?" The question was spoken with a boyish huskiness, foretelling a voice that would eventually deepen to a low rasp in the years to come.

"A lion's claw. My great-great-grandfather Remiel killed the beast when it attacked his camp during a hunt. It stalked them for three days, keeping mostly out of sight. But just when they thought it had disappeared, the beast pounced on one of the men that strayed from the fire late at night. Remiel heard the shriek and took up his dagger, racing toward the commotion."

Fascinated, Lukio was now leaning forward, his brows high in a silent invitation to continue my tale.

"Although the lion was fearsome, my forefather prevailed, emerging from the fight with only a few scratches. The other man survived too, though without the use of his arm. This claw"— I wrapped my fingers around the treasure—"was saved as a reminder of that day. It is said that anyone who wears it is blessed with divine protection, along with those around him."

Though I believed the idea of a protective charm to be nothing more than another of the myths I'd been told in my lifetime, I could not restrain the irrational guilt that, had my father not given it to me the day he left to guard the Ark, he and my brothers might still be alive.

Movement from the corner of my eye announced the return of my uncle, along with Abinidab and his eldest son, Elazar. "They are here," I said to the girl. "Will you come out and speak with them?"

She clutched at her brother, her breaths coming faster, but Lukio murmured something to her in their language, his tone indicating that my storytelling had smoothed the sharper edges from his wariness.

"Abinidab is a kind man, I assure you. Besides . . ." I patted the lion claw with a wink at Lukio. "You will be safe with me."

They exchanged a few foreign words before they stood in tandem, both of them taller than I'd expected, making me wonder if perhaps I'd guessed their ages incorrectly. When they followed me around the stone wall toward the four white-clad Levites, the girl favored her left leg, her face pinched with each step. Lukio kept close to her side, sliding worried looks at his sister every so often, his protectiveness in full bloom, no matter his age.

Abinidab smiled broadly, his eyes crinkling as he regarded our approach with gentle curiosity. I'd enjoyed only a few brief moments in the older man's presence since we'd come to Kiryat-Yearim, but I'd never met a more kind and good-natured soul. He was the most widely respected Levite elder in the territory of Yehudah, both for his long service at the Mishkan under the leadership of Eli and his commitment to preserving our way of life after the High Priest's death and the destruction of our holy sanctuary.

"Young Ronen," he said as we met in the middle, "who have you found?"

The children stood together, hands entwined. Whatever headway I'd made in gaining Lukio's trust looked to have melted away. His jaw was set, eyes wary, and his stance full of tension.

"Lukio and . . ." Realizing I'd not asked her name, I turned to the girl with lifted brows.

"Arisa." The name was offered barely above a whisper.

Abinidab gave them both a warm smile. "I have been told that you are from Ashdod. Is this true?"

Arisa's eyes bounced to me for a moment before she nodded. "Yes, my lord," she said, her gaze downcast again.

"And how did you come to be in this valley?" he asked, tilting his ear to hear her soft answer.

She swallowed hard, a pinch forming between her brows. "We followed the Ark, my lord, and the kings of the Five Cities as they trailed after it in their chariots." She pointed to a ridge on one of the hills at our backs. "The kings watched from up there until the men removed the box from the cart. And then they left."

"Why did you stay, child?"

For the first time, Arisa lifted her eyes to meet Abinidab's stare. "Because I was told to stay with the Ark until it dwells among the cedars in peace."

Abinidab's lips parted on an audible exhale. "Among the cedars?" he echoed.

Arisa nodded, her gaze once again on her dusty toes.

The old Levite was quiet for a long while, studying the two children and then looking back to where the Ark awaited transport to Kiryat-Yearim. "I would very much like to hear more about what happened in Ashdod over these past months, Arisa. Will you join us this evening at our camp and tell me?"

Lukio scowled at the suggestion, again muttering something in his own tongue that sounded distinctly belligerent.

"We will make sure the two of you are safe and fed," promised Abinidab. "And whenever you desire to return to your own territory afterward, I will appoint an escort to transport you back to Ashdod. You are not our captives, my young friends, but honored guests." He pressed a hand to the center of his chest. "This is an invitation, not a demand. You are free to go now if that is what you wish."

Arisa contemplated, her green eyes roving the valley, glancing off me and then her frowning younger brother, and finally landing on the linen-covered chest on the horizon. Her slender shoulders straightened, determination in the lift of her small chin even as her voice quavered like a wounded bird's. "Where the Ark goes, we will follow."

Ten

The camp was made in the valley, with a few of the Levites appointed to guard the Ark on the boulder a thousand cubits away. Although the people of Beth Shemesh were in deep mourning for the losses they'd suffered, they were so grateful for the retrieval of the bodies and our willingness to remove the Ark from their midst that a group of women appeared just before the sun set with basketfuls of food and drink.

The offering was taken with solemn humility, Abinidab expressing his sincere regret for the lives that had been lost, while refraining from speaking any words of censure. My uncle had told me that the lid of the sacred chest was askew when we arrived, making it clear that the men from Beth Shemesh had taken it upon themselves to look inside—a grievous mishandling, and one that, as Levites, they should have known not to do. I was doubtful that their transgression had brought about their collective demise, whether they touched the box or not.

Although I was fiercely curious to hear the rest of Arisa and Lukio's story, I'd been tasked by my uncle to retrieve firewood and help prepare the camp. I bristled at the dismissal and the attitude that I was too young to take part in the discussion surrounding the children when I'd been the one to come across them in the first place. However, I was not yet of age to be counted among the active

Levites, and since I would be in training for the next seven years, both in Torah instruction and my duties, I was therefore bound to obey my uncle's every command. And as much as it grated to do so, I would gulp down my pride, haul water and wood, clean tools, and perform any other menial task for the sake of my father and brothers, who'd desired nothing more than for me to join them in the work they treasured.

Seated about fifteen paces away from the fire, Arisa and her brother had devoured every bite of food set before them, and now she was quietly answering questions from the old Levite and his son, Elazar, no doubt expanding on the scant details she'd offered back at the sheepfold. She seemed no more settled speaking with them than with me, her gaze anywhere but upon the men, but her lips were moving and the stiff set of her shoulders had relaxed just enough that I knew Abinidab had persuaded her that there was little cause to fear us.

Both children began yawning, the long day of cowering behind the stone wall and whatever horrors they'd endured the night before catching up with their small bodies. Elazar prepared them a place to lie down, far enough from the fire that they might sleep undisturbed, but close enough that we could watch over them.

Elazar had five children of his own, some near Arisa and Lukio's ages. I wondered if he might be thinking of his own young ones in such a situation, alone in enemy territory and surrounded by strange men. Once he'd settled Arisa and Lukio, he returned to fold himself down beside his elderly father, his eyes locked on the flames nearby as the two of them murmured together. After a time, they rose and joined our circle on the other side of the fire, settling down among us with serious expressions.

"They do indeed come from Ashdod," said Abinidab without preamble. "And they were there the day their soldiers returned after the battle of Afek."

Briefly, he told us the story Arisa had related to them: of the Ark being brought in on a cart, dumped in front of their heathen temple, and then the unbelievable account of the image of Dagon falling before the golden chest. When the story of the morning after the earthquake was told, and Abinidab revealed that not only had the statue fallen without cause but that the hands and the head of the idol were cleanly severed, more than a few awed gasps and exclamations of praise went up.

I had no doubt Arisa believed these stories, and perhaps the idol had indeed fallen, but it was plain to me that the earthquake had caused it to topple both times, not some divine action. Trembles underground were not that uncommon in this land, after all, and some places were more prone than others to violent rumblings. Unseen cracks must have formed within the stone and the base made unsteady from the shaking the day before.

But whatever had happened to make the Philistines return our sacred object, I was glad they'd found cause to fear. With the Ark back in our hands, the holy sanctuary could now be reassembled and restored with even greater glory and richer materials, and by more skilled artisans than a horde of former slaves out in the wilderness.

Perhaps the Mishkan at Shiloh had once been a sight to behold, but the last time I'd seen it standing, the curtains were near to disintegrating and the mudbrick walls built around the once moveable Tent of Meeting were crumbling like week-old bread. Under the leadership of Eli and his sons, little had been done to return it to its once laudable state—a point of contention that my uncle and many of his friends frequently brought up in their discussions over the future of Shiloh. What remained of the original structure, the altar, and the other consecrated objects had been spirited away to some unknown location by the priests before the Philistines desecrated the holy hill upon which it once stood.

Without the Ark, it was inevitable that the Mishkan would have remained hidden away for generations, or perhaps for good. For what use was a sanctuary without its most revered relic? But now, for the first time in months, the people of Yahweh could finally hope for its restoration. Because in my estimation, the true power in the golden box lie not with flashes of fire, but in its ability to resurrect the spirits of the people who would again offer the tribute necessary both to sustain the Levite tribe and to reestablish the holy places.

"Arisa said that soon after Dagon fell, an epidemic hit the city. Black boils covered the people, killing many. Rodents swarmed the fields, stripping the crops, and then when the fields were bare, they moved into the city and devoured the granaries. Those not struck by the sickness were in danger of starvation, and many, especially children and the elderly succumbed quickly."

"Fitting justice for stealing our holy implements," snarled Bezor, one of my uncle's closest friends. "It's unfortunate they all did not perish."

A few nods of agreement bobbed around the circle.

"None of us dispute that the Philistines are the enemy, Bezor, nor that they have oppressed, slaughtered, and enslaved many of us," responded Abinidab. "But let us find a touch of mercy within our hearts, shall we?" He waved a hand toward the sleeping children, reminding us all that they were survivors of such happenings.

A scowl was Bezor's only response.

"How did the Ark end up here?" asked another man, whose name I did not know.

"From what Arisa says, Ashdod sent it away, their priests making clear that it was the appearance of the Ark that had caused the plagues. It was sent to Gath, where the same thing happened. And when Gath was struck with the same terrors, it was sent to Ekron. But Ekron rejected it outright, the people having heard the rumors of the tragedies in the other cities and revolting before it even reached the gates."

"What did the girl say about the kings?" asked Abiram.

"The children awoke outside of Ekron to the sound of calves crying out. They emerged to find the cart, hitched to untrained milk cows who'd been separated from their young, plodding along the road without a driver. And all five Philistine kings were following a long stretch behind, their chariots escorted by soldiers. The children had been told by their nursemaid, a Hebrew slave named Azuvah, that they should follow the Ark, and so they did, all the way here."

"What if this is nothing more than a ruse?" said Bezor. "Sending in our sacred object and a couple of children to distract us? There could be an army lying in wait just beyond the hills."

"Then why did they not attack Beth Shemesh after the Levites were struck down? Or even when they were celebrating with all their women and children out in the field earlier in the day?" asked Elazar. "It would have been the perfect opportunity for an ambush. And we know they are not above such atrocities."

"Agreed," said Abinidab. "It seems that the kings of Philistia were much more concerned with getting rid of the Ark than using it as part of some plot."

"And the gold?" asked one of the others.

"She knows nothing of what was inside the cart," said Abinidab. "But Elazar and I believe the five golden rats inside are an offering. One for each of the Philistine capital cities."

"It's no small amount of gold," said Bezor, a satisfied grin curling his lips. "They must be quite desperate to assuage Yahweh's wrath."

Abinidab nodded, his wizened eyes full of contemplation. "Indeed."

"And so," asked another man, "what comes next? Shiloh is in ruins."

Abinidab stroked his beard, looking into the flames as if the answer flickered in the orange glow. "I do not believe it is a coincidence that we were in the midst of gathering to discuss that very thing when the Ark found its way back to us. Yahweh directed its path, leading the cows here to Beth Shemesh, a Levitical community."

"Much good that did," said Bezor. "Apparently the Levites in this city have forgotten the stories of the Ark's power."

"I would venture to guess that we all have been remiss in our treatment of holy things," said Abinidab. "There was little outcry when Eli's sons removed the Ark from Shiloh in the first place."

An uneasy silence followed, and I wondered how many of the men in this circle had held their tongues when the High Priest's contemptible sons ordered the Ark to be carried into battle. My tortured imagination spun with conjured images of my father's and brothers' final moments. Had they believed until their last breaths that the Ark would save them? Or had they watched from their bloody deathbeds on the field as the chest of gold they'd put such faith in was carted off by the enemy? My only consolation was that the sons of Eli had been killed that day as well and their father had broken his worthless neck falling from his judgment seat near the city gates when he heard of their deaths.

"The Ark should return to Shiloh without delay," said Bezor. "There is no question."

"And where would it be housed?" asked Elazar. "The city is a ruin and what remains of the Mishkan in pieces, stored away in Nob, where it is safe from further desecration. Who knows how long it will take to restore the sanctuary? And where it should be done?"

"That can be determined when we arrive," said Abiram. "The priests will have a solution."

"And how do we know that it would even be safe there? The Philistines already swept in and took it once," said another man.

"From what Arisa says, I believe they've quite learned their lesson," said Abinidab, his gaze again sliding toward the two children in the shadows. "But it does need to be protected from the elements until a suitable sanctuary can be reconstructed."

"Returning the Ark and rebuilding the Mishkan will send the message to the Philistines that we do not fear them," said my uncle, pounding a fist into his palm. "Also, it will make clear to our own people that we are not twigs to be crushed beneath our foes' chariot wheels. With Eli and his sons gone, it is time to rebuild— and past time to restore the office of High Priest to the sons of Eleazar ben Aharon, as it should be."

A flurry of overlapping arguments erupted at this idea. The seat of the High Priest had been filled by men who descended from Eleazar, the son of Aharon and nephew of Mosheh, since our people had come into the Land of Promise. Eli, however, had been a descendant of Itamar, another son of Aharon. And even before he'd been installed as the High Priest decades ago, a deep divide formed between those who felt the blessing had been permanently passed to the line of Itamar and those who insisted that the honor belonged to Eleazar's descendants alone. My uncle was firmly of the opinion that Eli and his sons were an abomination, corrupt to the bone, and should be replaced with a man of the correct—and divinely appointed—lineage.

Abinidab attempted to rein in the conversation. "We must not harbor such antipathy toward each other as we await Yahweh's direction—"

Undeterred by the older man's admonition, my uncle spoke over him. "You've been down here in Kiryat-Yearim these last two decades, Abinidab, you did not see just how despicable those two were and how impotent Eli was in reining them in. Bribery. Extortion. Thievery. Taking female worshipers to their beds. There was no honor among those men, nor those who consorted with them. My brother and sons were slaughtered because of their arrogance and contempt for the Torah." His flinty eyes glinted in the firelight. "The High Priesthood should return to the line designated by Yahweh at the Holy Mountain."

It was a bold statement, and one that was loudly refuted by a number of the other Levites, a few who sprang to their feet to make their points known. One thing was very clear: The divide between the two opinions was deep and each side was passionate in their beliefs.

"If anything is plain," said Bezor, raising his voice over the melee, "it is that we must no longer suffer corrupt leadership. Samson, and the disaster that was his time as judge over this region, made that all too apparent."

"Samson was a hero," shouted one of the younger men from across the fire.

"He was a drunkard with no respect for the Nazirite vow he was supposed to have taken," snarled Bezor. "And more interested in Philistine whores than in bringing Israel together against our enemies."

"He killed thousands of Philistines!" said the young man. "With his own hands! And took many more with him as he sacrificed his own life. He wasn't content to sit around with his companions, clucking over the state of the tribes like a bunch of toothless old women."

"How dare you disrespect—"

Elazar spoke over Bezor. "While Samson was not the wisest of men and not the most discerning of leaders Yahweh has raised up over these past centuries, at least his intervention awoke many of us from our complacent attitudes toward the Philistines. We must separate from them, body and soul, or they will swallow us up. Perhaps the next *shofet* raised by Yahweh will build upon Samson's victories—and his failures—and call the people back to pure worship."

"We need no more shoftim," said Bezor. "The tribes need to come together and install a king, one who will ensure the Philistines have no thought of returning. We are made fools by our constant discord. A king would have kept Eli and his sons in line. Held them to account."

"The priesthood should not be subject to a human king," said Elazar, with a sharp edge of frustration I'd not yet heard from the stoic man. "It is under the authority of Yahweh alone."

"And what has Yahweh done to direct the priests? Has he lifted a finger to write on more stones?" challenged my uncle with a scoff. "We are at the mercy of the foreigners around us, ones who grow more powerful every day. And without a king, we look even weaker than we are. We fight more among each other than we do the true enemy."

"These matters will not be settled tonight, my friends," said Abinidab, his tone deliberately soothing as he looked over the group. "We've been discussing them for days now and have come to little conclusion. And with the Ark returned to us, the stakes are even greater. For now, we will return to my home in Kiryat-Yearim. I've already sent a message to Samuel. We will wait for his direction before we decide anything further."

Chaos erupted around the fire again.

"Samuel has no authority here!"

"A pretender . . . !"

". . . as corrupt as Eli's sons were!"

"His prophecy was proven by Eli's death!"

My uncle's face was flushed in the light of the fire, his voice louder than all the rest. "The Ark belongs in the holy Mishkan, *not* your house."

Abinidab lifted both palms, his expression expectant. Although nearly half the men seemed to side with my uncle, they hushed, giving respectful deference to a man whose years were far beyond their own. "I know that some of you are unsure of Samuel's divine appointment. But I was there when, as a boy, he delivered the words of Yahweh to Eli, instructing him to take his sons in hand or suffer the consequences."

No one interrupted, since none of them would have been old enough to witness such an event, nearly thirty years ago. Abinidab let his gaze travel over the men, challenging them to defy his testimony. "Young as he was, he spoke with a clarity of mind and an authority that shocked us all. And since that time, I have carefully watched him. He possesses a wisdom that belies all reason. A steadfast heart that is firmly set upon Yahweh. And he is a lifelong Nazirite with unparalleled dedication. So yes, we will wait for Samuel, and we will trust his judgment."

My uncle muttered beneath his breath. If there was anything I'd come to understand during these past couple of weeks we'd been at Kiryat-Yearim, it was that, like the division over the High Priesthood, there was a stark delineation between those who looked to Samuel as a prophet and those who did not. Abiram was firmly within the camp of those who did not.

"All of you will have a chance to voice your opinion when Samuel arrives, along with elders of the *kohanim*. And the children have agreed to stay with us for a few more days, so everyone can hear their story. But for now, we will sleep. I'd like to arrive in Esthaol before the sun is too high so we can reach Kiryat-Yearim before nightfall tomorrow." The definitive authority in the old man's voice seemed to close the mouths of those around the circle who disagreed. But from the way my uncle shifted in his seat, his jaw working back and forth, I knew he had much more to say on the subject. He and Bezor would not be satisfied until we were on our way back north with the Ark, headed for Shiloh.

Silently, I found a spot nearby to lay down my mantle, although I could not calm the storm of questions that tonight's argument had provoked in my mind. Although my father and brothers had been resolute that Yahweh had given Eli authority for a purpose, I could not dispute Abiram's reasoning. I knew that many Hebrews had been clamoring for a king for a long while now, but the priests had blocked every attempt to raise up a man to govern the tribes as a whole. Perhaps now, with the priesthood fluttering about in the wind, someone would step forward to accept the call. Someone who would bring us back together, rebuild the Mishkan, restore our prosperity, and push the Philistines from our lands once and for all. The thought made my heart swell with hope for the first time since the travesty at Afek. Perhaps within the next few years, I would be singing one of my own compositions in the holy sanctuary, using the lyre I'd inherited from my father to worship alongside my fellow Levites.

Inspired by the idea, a new line of notes fluttered through my mind, and I hummed the tune as I settled onto the ground, but just as I moved to lay my head on my folded mantle, movement beneath the oak tree caught my eye.

Arisa, whom I'd thought long asleep, was sitting up. The gleam in her large eyes made it clear that she'd been disturbed by the raised voices and vehement outbursts around the fire. She shivered, her slender figure illuminated by moonlight, and for the briefest of moments met my gaze. Then she lifted her chin to the sky, perhaps beseeching the stars for comfort, but likely just avoiding my stare. I wondered what sort of stories she might have to tell her people when she returned to Ashdod. Through her, would word of the cracks and splinters among us reach the lords of Philistia? Or would the two children fade into the masses, their strange encounter with us Hebrews long forgotten in their relief at being back among their own?

I shrugged off the thoughts and laid my head down, determined to fill my mind with the song I'd been weaving together instead of things that were far beyond my control. I'd leave the power struggles to my uncle and his friends and bide my time in training until I could become the Levitical musician I was born to be.

Eleven

Arisa

The path up the back of the mountain was steep, but Abinidab said it was the only way the Ark could be transported. The other way was too narrow and winding for the six white-clad men who'd been taking turns carrying the burden since dawn. Lukio and I followed a safe distance from the golden chest at the head of our strange procession, both of us in awe of the enormous trees on either side of the path that stretched toward the sky in clusters of green-headed splendor. A storm was threatening, the stir of dark clouds gathering above us as we pressed toward the summit. It seemed like we were climbing into those same clouds as we ascended, and I wondered if the gods were nearer here, where the mingled scents of bark and decaying vegetation spoke of the cycles of life and rebirth.

Ronen walked a few paces behind us with his eyes on the ground, humming something to himself. He'd said little to me this morning before we began this second leg of our journey but had asked Lukio about the pouch at his neck. At first, my brother had been suspicious, clasping the leather purse in his palm with a determined set to his chin, but Ronen had not been deterred, inviting Lukio to take a closer look at the lion claw necklace he was so fascinated by, and soon the pouch was emptied and all of my brother's treasures displayed with pride.

During one of our rests over the past few hours, Lukio had even taught Ronen the game of dice that he and his friends spent so much time playing. Why tossing sheep knuckles in the dirt and then counting holes on each side once they shuddered to a stop was so fascinating to boys, I could not begin to guess, but if it caused Lukio to relax a small measure and cease scowling like a cat in a washtub, then I was glad for the distraction.

The pain in my ankle had been greatly diminished by this morning, thanks to a strong-smelling herb poultice administered by one of the women of Beth Shemesh, and I'd been able to walk most of the day. But after so many hours on this upward road plagued by uneven ruts and hard-packed dirt, my ankle had begun to swell and throb once again.

My next step landed on the wrong edge of a loose stone, and it jostled beneath my sandal, knocking me off-center and nearly pitching me to the ground. I sucked in a breath as new pain spread across the top of my foot, making the soreness in my ankle a distant memory.

A hand gripped my arm as I wobbled, saving me from falling forward in a graceless heap.

"There now," said Ronen, holding me upright. "Are you all right?"

My throat closed shut as his brown eyes, the color of rich earth, surveyed me carefully. He looked to be close in age to Mataro, but the thick black hair curling around his ears made him seem far more youthful than my awful cousin. And the concerned furrow between his dark brows made it clear there was little similarity between the two.

"Is your ankle hurting again?" he asked when I failed to answer.

Blinking in embarrassment, I nodded.

"Can you walk?"

"Yes," I replied, the word so small it likely was borne away on the breeze.

I did not know why Ronen made me feel so timid. I'd never been the type of girl who fluttered and preened over older boys deemed handsome by others. All I knew was that whenever he looked my way, my chest squeezed tightly, my palms sweated, my voice pinched tight, and I had to look away from his potent gaze.

I lifted a tight smile and took another step, but the pain was so sharp that colors swirled in my vision, and I could not restrain the strangled cry that burst from my lips. Hot tears of humiliation gathered in my eyes.

"You're truly injured, aren't you?" he said, looking ahead to where the rest of the men trudged upward, ignorant of my struggle.

I replied with a small shrug, wishing he'd just go on and let me limp behind and pray to whatever god lived on this mountain that Abinidab's house was not much farther up this untamed road.

Ronen moved in front of me and crouched down in the dirt, patting his back. "Climb on."

I skittered backward, gasping as another shock of pain gripped my foot.

"I may not look like a camel," he said, with a grin over his shoulder. "But I do a passable impression of one. I promise not to spit." He winked at me, the gesture causing another of those unfamiliar flutters in my stomach.

When I did not respond to his jest, his lips curled into a gentle, reassuring smile, and his tone softened. "I understand that you don't know me, Arisa, and this is all very confusing and frightening for the two of you. But I would never hurt you or your brother. I only want to help. It's not too much farther, but the sun is going down, so we need to be on our way. And I promise that once we reach Abinidab's home, you will be fed and cared for with utmost hospitality."

Lukio nudged me at the mention of food. "Hurry," he said, in our own tongue. "I'm hungry."

Resigned, I sighed and with heat flooding my face, I inched

closer as Ronen turned around, giving me his back again. My stomach twisted about like a fishing net caught on the rocks, but I placed my hands on his shoulders and allowed him to hoist me up, his arms wrapped beneath my knees to keep me steady. His muscles strained beneath his tunic, and he bounced once, jostling me into a position that forced me to wrap my arms around his neck. Then, tipping his head in a silent command for Lukio to keep pace, he began to walk.

Mortified by my helplessness, especially in front of a man who made my insides flip and squeeze, I held on tight and kept my eyes pinned on the road in front of us, straining for any glimpse of the old man's home.

But then Ronen began to sing.

When he'd woken the two of us with his presence yesterday by the wall, I'd been tempted to snatch up Lukio and flee the valley, regardless of the pain in my ankle. But I'd been so drawn to the lovely sound of a deep voice singing in Azuvah's language and desired to listen for just a while longer. He'd fumbled with the sounds, altering the order every so often, just like how I'd seen one of the stoneworkers shifting rocks back and forth as he devised a swirling pattern on the new hearth Jacame had commissioned after the earthquake. However, when Lukio had whispered my name during one of the pauses in the melody and we'd been discovered, I'd cursed myself for being so foolish as to be lured into danger by a song.

Now the same melody he'd been experimenting with on the sheepfold wall spilled from his lips, and though there were gaps in my understanding of some words, I grasped the meaning fairly easily. It was the story of a boy tending sheep on a hillside at sunset, watching the clouds slide along the canopy of fading blue overhead and wondering what lay beyond the stars that winked into sight one by one.

Ronen's deep voice vibrated in his chest, and I felt the echo of it in my own as I held my breath, enthralled by the sounds that emanated from his mouth as he effortlessly carried me toward the summit.

Lukio seemed unimpressed by the singing, caught up as he was in plucking stones from the ground to aim at tree trunks or toss into the babbling stream that ran alongside the path. But as Ronen's song came to an end, I kept silent, hoping he might sing another.

"We've arrived," he said, to my great disappointment. For as much as I'd been ready for this eternal climb to be over, the music that came from somewhere deep inside Ronen captivated me.

Two homes appeared between the trees. Flat-roofed and fashioned from stone, they perched on the hillside like a pair of gray quail. The other men had already arrived and were gathered in front of the largest home, which I assumed to be that of Abinidab, who seemed to be the leader of this group of white-clad priests. The golden box was nowhere in sight.

As Ronen approached with me still clinging to his back like one of the monkeys from Egypt I'd once seen for sale in the market, Elazar came forward to meet us, a woman at his side, both of them with matching expressions of alarm.

"What happened to her?" said the woman, her pace quickening as she came nearer. Her pale green headscarf fluttered in the breeze, and a few black curls slipped from beneath the cloth, framing her round face.

"She hurt herself before I found them yesterday, and it looks as though the long walk aggravated the injury." Ronen bent his knees, silently giving me permission to climb down.

Gingerly I slid to the ground but winced as soon as my left foot touched the dirt and sucked in a hissing breath.

The small woman practically shoved Ronen out of the way to get to me and slipped her arm around my waist. "You poor girl, how long did you walk on that foot?" She scowled at Elazar, wordlessly chastising the tall, thick-bearded man—her husband, if their familiarity was any indication.

"She hid it well, Yoela," he said, large palms uplifted. "If I'd known she was hurting, I'd have had us all take turns carrying her."

Last night, as I'd told this big man and his elderly father my tale, he'd been so kind, never pushing as my voice halted and stumbled over words I'd used only infrequently with Azuvah in secret. And he'd gone out of his way to fashion a soft pallet for Lukio and me at the foot of an oak tree, giving up his own mantle to add to the blanket we'd carried from Ashdod. I'd been stunned by the gentle treatment, especially from a man as large and rough-featured as Elazar, but also struck by a pang of latent grief for the father who'd once carried me around on his shoulders but who had not looked back after leaving us at Jacame and Harrom's threshold.

Ronen voiced his agreement with Elazar's words. "It's true. I walked behind her all day, and it was not until this last stretch that I even saw her falter."

"Thank you for carrying her, young man," said Elazar's wife with a kind smile, her tone gently dismissive. "I'll make sure she is tended to properly."

With a respectful nod of his head, Ronen walked away, joining his uncle in the cluster of men who were congregated near the house, discussing something in low, but animated tones. These men seemed to do little more than argue, as I'd witnessed last night. It had taken a long while to relax into sleep after their loud and vehement disagreement, and it seemed that whatever matters they'd been discussing were far from settled.

Lukio had found his way to my other side as Yoela fussed over me, his cheek pressed against my shoulder and his wary gaze darting between Elazar and his wife.

"Come," she said. "We have just called everyone to gather for a meal. We have much to celebrate and we are delighted you are with us!" Yoela craned her neck to smile at my brother. "And you, my friend, look as hungry as a wandering jackal." The twinkle in her honey-brown eyes made her seem far more youthful than her husband, whose temples were brushed with silver.

Although he did not respond to her gentle tease, Lukio's stomach answered for him, and Yoela laughed, the sound nearly as enchanting as Ronen's music. A rush of something new flooded through my limbs, something that reminded me of the countless nights Azuvah lulled us to sleep with her stories and songs, and the faint memories of being tucked securely against my mother's warm body.

Any lingering thoughts that Azuvah had led us astray by insisting that we follow the Ark withered away as Yoela guided us to her home, exclaiming over our bravery for making such a treacherous journey alone and telling us how excited her children would be to meet us. And even as two older boys and three girls, all with Yoela's black curls, emerged from the house to watch our approach with open curiosity, somehow I knew that we'd taken the right path, even if it led us to the top of a mountain deep in enemy territory.

Part Two

And he struck some of the men of Beth-shemesh, because they looked upon the ark of the LORD. He struck seventy men of them, and the people mourned because the LORD had struck the people with a great blow. Then the men of Beth-shemesh said, "Who is able to stand before the LORD, this holy God? And to whom shall he go up away from us?" So they sent messengers to the inhabitants of Kiriath-jearim, saying, "The Philistines have returned the ark of the LORD. Come down and take it up to you."

And the men of Kiriath-jearim came and took up the ark of the LORD and brought it to the house of Abinadab on the hill. And they consecrated his son Eleazar to have charge of the ark of the LORD. From the day that the ark was lodged at Kiriath-jearim, a long time passed, some twenty years, and all the house of Israel lamented after the LORD.

1 Samuel 6:19–7:2

Twelve

Eliora (Arisa)

1062 BC
KIRYAT-YEARIM, ISRAEL

Clutching the soft stack of cushions I'd collected to my chest, I
paused to take in the awe-inspiring view from the rooftop, one that
even after eight years never ceased to steal my breath. From this
vantage point, I could see the entirety of the valley below and the
thick-forested hills all around it, dressed in every shade of green.
I inhaled deeply of the crisp smell of the woods and the delicate
hint of smoke from the cookfires in the courtyard, enjoying the
chorus from a trio of songbirds in nearby pine branches. The
sweet familiarity of it all wrapped me in bone-deep contentment.

When my brother and I had arrived on this mountain, desperate and confused, I would have never imagined how much I would
come to love every leaf and flower and rock on its slopes. Nor that
Elazar and Yoela would not only invite two enemy children into
their house, but also welcome us into their family, treat us as their
own, and give us new names when we joined ourselves in covenant
with the Hebrews. Even if Lukio still struggled with being called

Natan, I was ever grateful to leave Arisa behind in Philistia and to be known as Eliora to everyone in Kiryat-Yearim.

Although there were times I missed the tang of sea salt in the air and the distant crash of waves on the shore, this place among the clouds was home—far more than Ashdod had ever been. I would not trade my adopted mother and father—nor any one of my nine adopted siblings—for any amount of time back on the coastal plain where I'd been born. That place and all the terrible memories it harbored was firmly in my past, where it belonged.

Miri appeared at the top of the stairs, her sweetly rounded cheeks flushed and the coils of black hair she'd inherited from Yoela refusing to be tamed by her loose braids. "Eliora! I've been searching all over for you!"

My younger sister bounded across the roof to meet me near the parapet. "Safira wants me to remind you that the braziers will need to be filled before dark, and that additional fuel should be fetched. I told her that Natan stacked the woodpile almost to the roof of the shelter, so we have plenty at hand, but she doesn't believe me."

I could practically see the pinch of worry between Safira's dark brows as she'd directed Miri to relay the message. But although her anxieties were rarely based in truth, I had no desire to see our sister fret over any detail during tonight's wedding festivities. Especially when she was the bride.

I sighed, letting my eyes wander over the eastern hills again. This would likely be the last quiet moment I would have for the next few days. Many of the townspeople would already have begun the hours-long, winding trek up the hillside to join our family in celebrating Safira's marriage to one of the young Levites who lived here on the mountain above Kiryat-Yearim, and I refused to fall short in my duties. Our mother had instilled her devotion to hospitality in her children, so everyone—from Gershom, our eldest brother, down to little two-year-old Dafna—had duties to perform to ensure that Safira's marriage celebration would be one to remember for years to come.

"Help me with the rest of these, won't you, Miri?" I gestured toward the last of the colorful cushions left atop the roof from a Shabbat gathering two nights ago. "Thankfully the rain held off this week or they'd all be soaked through."

"I'd be happy to," she chirped, thirteen years of exuberance wrapped up in her youthful smile as she moved to comply. "But Ima says I must fetch more bowls from the storage room next. And Rina needs help turning the meat spits since Shai and Amina have taken off somewhere."

Rina, the eldest of my sisters, was the most skilled with cooking, next to our mother. Since her marriage last year to another of the Levites who lived here on the mountain, Rina had taken over much of the cooking for the unmarried guardsmen. She was more than capable of overseeing the wedding feast, but I could almost feel her vibrating with tension as she ground something in a mortar across the courtyard. A flash of guilt swept through me at seeing her so on edge and not being able to help her, but I had plenty of my own tasks to attend and could not disappoint anyone by letting a single one fall by the wayside.

Besides, soon the other women of our clan would join Rina and Miri, bringing their own offerings of bread and stews and other savory dishes to add to the feast, and plunging into a swirl of chattering ladies made my skin feel too tight and my stomach writhe like a pot full of caterpillars. Even if none of them had ever said anything unkind in my presence in all these years, I still could not help wondering what they might be saying about the "foreign girl" when I was not around.

I frowned as I peered over the parapet into the courtyard, searching for the twins. "Shai and Amina cannot stay still for an hour, can they?"

Miri shrugged. "They are five. To them, sitting near a fire for hours to ensure a lamb is roasted evenly is akin to torture, even if they're taking turns."

Our twin brother and sister were the very definition of life, with boisterous voices that constantly overlapped the other, legs that seemed to be always in motion, and hands that were compelled to touch anything that came into view. They never balked at helping, and in fact begged to be included, but rarely did they finish the tasks assigned to them. I almost dreaded times when they offered to help me in the gardens, as I usually spent most of my efforts directing them and protecting plants from their curious fingers and wayward toes. But their adoring smiles and plentiful hugs made up for any frustrations caused by their enthusiasm.

With our arms full of cushions, Miri and I descended the stone steps into the courtyard, which was the bustling center of preparations for tonight's feast. After we spread the cushions on the ground in the approximation of a circle to encourage conversation, Miri bounced off to help Rina.

My two oldest brothers, Gershom and Iyov, were hefting a long, low table between them, following my mother's direction about its placement at the center of the courtyard.

"Oh, Eliora, there you are," said my mother, with a lighthearted clap. "Do you think this is the best place for the bride and groom's table?"

I surveyed the wide area, gazing over the scattered groupings of rugs and cushions and pillows, upon which our many guests would soon be seated. "I do. They'll be visible to everyone that way."

"And you have enough flowers?" she asked, with a tiny wrinkle between her black brows. "Or shall I send a couple of ladies to make more cuttings?"

"I have plenty, Ima. Miri helped me gather so many blooms yesterday that this courtyard will look more like my gardens than the real ones do."

Miri and I had spent the entirety of the last evening fashioning sturdy vines and blossoms into long garlands that I meant to string up between columns. I'd been waiting until nearly the final hour to remove them from the pots of water they'd been sitting in, soaking up as much moisture as they could.

My mother looped her arm around my waist, her head coming only just to the top of my shoulder. "Thank you for all you have done to prepare for this wedding feast." She sighed, leaning into me a bit. "I just wish I wasn't so tired these past few days. I haven't even been able to help Rina much with the food."

I pulled her tight to my side, having a vague notion of just why she'd been in need of extra rest lately. "It is my pleasure, Ima. And Rina, Miri, and the other ladies are capable of handling the food for now. We all just want Safira to be pleased."

"She will, daughter. Of that, I have no doubt."

I could only hope so. I could not wait to see Safira's face when she caught sight of this courtyard, bedecked in flickering oil lamps, flowers of every variety, and clusters of joyful guests with well-wishes on their lips. I had forgone most of the night's sleep to make sure that everything would be perfect and spent every other waking minute worrying that I'd missed some important detail that might upset my mother or the bride. I would sleep when this celebration was over and everyone was happy.

My mother slipped away, darting over to where Gershom and Iyov were standing by the long table. "Oh! No, turn it the other way," she admonished, her small hands fluttering about like sparrows. "That way they'll be able to view the dancing easily."

Yielding to her demand, my older brothers situated the table facing north to south, so not only would Safira and her new husband enjoy the music and dances, but they'd have sight of the sunset as it painted the sky above the sea on the far horizon.

My grandfather, Abinidab, had told me many years ago that when he and his family had migrated to Kiryat-Yearim to settle atop this mountain, he'd chosen this very spot to build his home because he could watch the sun rise and set without moving from his roof, and therefore could praise Yahweh from dawn to dusk without ceasing. And now, in addition to the home he and my father and uncles had built when my father was just a boy, there were three more large houses here, all adjoining, sharing common space and housing extended family, as well as a number of the Levites who guarded the Ark of the Covenant in its secret location nearby. I missed my grandfather so much, his magnanimous and wise presence having left a giant hole in our home when he went to the arms of his ancestors a year ago, passing the entire mantle of responsibility for the Ark and our clan onto my father's shoulders.

Once the table was situated to our mother's satisfaction, Gershom wiped his hands on his tunic, amusement in his dark eyes as he took in Yoela's harried expression. "What else can Iyov and I do to help you, Ima?"

"We'll need at least five more jugs of wine brought up from the cellar for tonight," she replied. "But only five. I don't want to run out too soon."

Nodding, Gershom gestured for Iyov to follow along, then gave me a wink as the two set off to do our mother's bidding. My two eldest brothers were a few years older than me, and deep into their intensive training for Levitical service, so I'd seen little of them lately. Both were also betrothed but would wait until they were of age at twenty-five and prepared to accept their duties as Levites before completing their marriage covenants. In Gershom's case, it was only a few more months until he and Adi would be united, but Iyov would have two more years before he'd be allowed to claim his sweet young bride, Hodiya.

Their future wives were daughters of one of the Levite guards who lived down in Kiryat-Yearim, so when Gershom and Iyov were not learning Torah and discussing Levitical laws, they were visiting the sisters with whom they were eager to wed. I adored both of my brothers and would always be grateful for how easily they, along with the rest of Elazar and Yoela's brood, had accepted our adoption into the family.

Even if Natan felt differently.

"Where is Natan?" I asked my mother, realizing that I'd not seen my brother since early this morning as I was departing for the terrace gardens with Miri.

She hummed thoughtfully. "I believe your father sent him down to the village with a message for one of the guards, and Yonah went with him. They ought to be back by now."

Yonah had been Natan's shadow for the past few months, at least whenever he deigned to allow the boy to tag along. At eight,

Yonah thought Natan could do no wrong, even though I'd had to quietly chastise Natan a number of times for being short-tempered with our younger brother when he struggled to keep up, due to the twisted leg that hindered him. I hoped that today, of all days, Natan was being kind. Nothing put me more on edge than the creeping fear that Elazar and Yoela would once and for all tire of his sullen attitude.

After settling the last of the cushions around the bride and groom's table, where they would be joined by our parents and those of Safira's new husband, I slipped out of the courtyard gate and headed for the woodpile on the eastern side of our home, located beneath a sturdy shelter. As Miri had said, Natan had indeed stacked the wood so high that I was forced to stand on the balls of my feet in order to reach the top.

As I was reaching for one of the smaller logs and hoping not to topple the rest, Yonah stormed past, with his small face flushed and brows pinched, ignoring me when I called his name as he limped his way into the house. The door flew closed behind him with a thud, but the latch refused to catch, and it bumped back open a crack.

Natan appeared at my side, easily plucking the wood that I'd been stretching to reach and then holding it out to me with a condescending smirk. No matter that I was as tall as both Gershom and Iyov, Natan was a wide handspan above us all, and likely still growing—a fact he never ceased boasting over.

"What did you do to Yonah?" I asked, grabbing the log from his hand. His golden-brown curls fluttered in the breeze as he shrugged shoulders that seemed far too broad for a boy of fifteen years. Something about the way he carried himself now reminded me so much of our birth father that at times, I had to blink my eyes to clear away the memories.

"I told him he needed to go home. He can't follow me around all day."

"He only wants to be with you," I admonished. "He practically worships you, wishing he could do half of what you can do."

He winced, a flash of guilt moving over his features as his eyes darted to the door Yonah had slammed behind him. But just as quickly, his face went blank. "He will be fine. He must learn to have thicker skin, anyhow. Besides, Adnan and Padi will be here soon to fetch me."

"You can't go off with your friends," I said, one fist on my hip. "We need your help today."

His lips pursed, his green and brown eyes narrowing. "I already hiked up and down this mountain twice with messages and hauled three huge pots of grain up from the storeroom—by myself. I've done enough."

"What possible reason do you have for leaving right now? It won't be long until guests begin arriving. And I could certainly use some help lighting the braziers."

"Adnan says there is a fallen oak not too far off. We're going to begin cutting it up before it rains again." Although he sounded insistent on leaving with his friends, he began pulling kindling from the woodpile and stacking limbs in the cradle of my waiting arms. "It's quality wood. I don't want it to go to waste."

The two young men with whom Natan had been spending time lately were not Hebrew at all, but of a Gibeonite tribe that settled in this area long before Mosheh led the tribes of Israel out of Egypt.

Many of the Gibeonites were so intermingled and intermarried with the Hebrews that they'd all but forgotten their heritage. But some, like the family of Adnan and Padi, proudly boasted of their ancient Amorite ancestry and the way their forebears used an elaborate ruse to convince Yehoshua they were travelers from a far land, instead of from within the territories allotted to the tribes of Benjamin and Yehudah. They'd also not forgotten that the city of Kiryat-Yearim itself had once been theirs.

I'd wondered if Natan felt a sense of kinship with the Gibeonite boys because of their foreignness, and therefore chose them above Hebrew boys to associate with. But that did not stop me from being uneasy with their friendship. For the most part, Gibeonites adhered to our civil laws, a stipulation of their agreement with Yehoshua, but that certainly did not mean they worshiped Yahweh.

"I am sure the tree will be fine for a few days," I said, shifting the burden in my arms, "and you need to be with your family."

From the corner of my eye, I noticed that Adnan and Padi had appeared at the head of the trail, both with axes on their shoulders. The two of them were nearly equal to Natan in height, although both were a few years older than him. But something about the way they stared at me as they approached made the hair on the back of my neck prickle.

After adding one more piece of wood to my armload, my brother turned, his long-legged stride carrying him a few paces away before I could react.

"Natan!" I called out, but he did not answer.

"Natan!" I repeated, louder this time, but still he refused to respond as he walked away. I gritted my teeth, knowing he would not relent, and annoyed that he would win this battle.

"Lukio!"

Finally, he halted, turning his neck to look at me with a smile tainted by mockery.

"Be back before nightfall," I said, my stomach curling in on itself at the sneer on my beloved brother's face as he turned away.

"Please!" I rasped in desperation. "For me. And for Safira."

Without looking back, he lifted a hand, as if silently assenting to my plea. The tightness in my throat eased a bit. Out of all of our adopted siblings, Safira was the most tenderhearted, and I knew he would not hurt her willfully.

But even as I headed back toward the courtyard with my load of kindling and back toward the many duties that awaited me before the wedding feast, I was plagued by the unrelenting feeling that the tides were pulling my brother farther and farther out to sea.

Thirteen

The entire town of Kiryat-Yearim seemed to be gathered within this courtyard, its overflow filling the flat-topped roofs all around with chattering wedding guests. Since the death of his father, Elazar had headed this set-apart community nestled near the thick-forested summit, and it seemed that the once-small settlement had grown into a formidable compound under his leadership.

Upon our arrival earlier, my cousin Machlon and I had been told that tonight was the culmination of a days-long wedding feast, the invitation open to all who lived in the homes scattered about the slopes below, and therefore we'd seized upon the opportunity to look around without cause for suspicion.

Across the courtyard, Machlon was deep in conversation with a few of the Levites we'd be living among over the next few weeks, his hearty chuckle ringing out in response to some jest. As usual, his honeyed charm drew in the flies, a skill he was putting to good use tonight.

I accepted a refill from one of the women who strolled about the courtyard, wine jug in hand, giving her a distracted nod of thanks as I skimmed my gaze over the line of the roofs, the placement of each window, and the path of each stairway that led to the rooftops.

The notes of a familiar tune fluttered to life from a double-pipe, drawing my attention from my surveillance toward the lively dance that was forming to one side of the gathering. Soon a ring of men encircled another made up of women, moving in opposite directions as the melody chased back and forth between the pipe and a long-necked lute.

The dancers laughed and teased one another as they wove in and out, the men's deep voices chanting questions to the ladies, who responded in sly tones. The bride and groom eventually were looped into the center of the circle, the rest of the dancers whirling around them with claps and shouts of blessings for a long life together. I'd seen this dance performed many times, each with slight variations, but had never participated myself, being still unmarried. I had no desire to be within such a circle any time soon. I had far more important plans that took precedence.

Perhaps when this was all over, I'd settle and have children, ease into my life serving at the Mishkan whenever my turn came along. But not until my task was complete.

As the dance ended, someone announced that the daughters of Elazar would be performing next, and the dancing ground was cleared for the bride and her five sisters, including the two youngest, who appeared to be about three and five years of age. Elazar and his wife must have been blessed with more children after I'd left Kiryat-Yearim. His quiver was certainly full now, although I'd thought he'd had only three daughters back then, so I must have been mistaken. This dance was slower, led by the gentle pluck of harps and incorporating a variety of colorful scarves that floated through the air in well-coordinated grace. But my eyes were drawn to the tallest of the four young women. Her hair was hidden beneath a tightly wound headscarf the color of mud, but it seemed to be a much lighter shade than that of her sisters. And her skin was paler, more like unfinished sycamore than varnished olive.

Though she moved smoothly through the dance, her long limbs creating graceful arcs as she dipped and swayed to the music, she kept her eyes cast down, seeming embarrassed that so many were watching. I suspected that were I closer I would even see a tinge of rosy blush on her cheeks. But in spite of her discomfort at being the center of attention, or perhaps because of it, I could not look away from her as she swirled her scarves, one green and one blue, in a flashing circle of color around her body.

When the dance concluded, many in the crowd rushed forward to praise the performance, but the tall woman seemed to be excluded from much of this. With a tight smile, she nodded acceptance of a few exclamations, but then crouched down to embrace her youngest sisters and kiss their foreheads, pride for their contribution to the dance evident in her glowing smile. However, as soon as the little girls darted away, she slithered through the crowd, head down, and moved toward the far edge of the courtyard, where she grabbed one of the lit oil lamps from a nearby table and then mounted the stairs, her long legs taking the stone steps two at a time.

Without examining too closely my reasons for choosing her instead of one of the other sisters, I began to follow at a discreet distance. My goal tonight was to ask the right questions of those closest to Elazar, and I would not let this opportunity slip away. Having grown up in this compound, she would know every tree and rock on the mountain and therefore was a valuable asset.

Standing in the corner where the parapets met, the woman peered over the edge toward the path that led to the town below, her lamp flickering near her elbow. Intrigued, I leaned against the low wall a few paces away and waited, wondering what she could possibly be searching for out there in the darkness when the entire city was within the walls of her family's well-lit compound.

She ran a palm up and down her arm, an action that I took more for unease than a chill, since even up here on the mountain the air was pleasant. She rolled to the balls of her feet, her long neck stretching as she peered into the deepening shadows. Then, slumping, she bowed her head and remained still for a long while.

"What are you looking for so intently out there?" I asked, glad she'd handed me a reason to initiate conversation. She flinched and spun around, eyes wide and a hand over her heart.

I lifted my palms. "I apologize for startling you. But you seemed upset."

Her brows came together as she searched my face, which was likely as shrouded in shadows as her own, now that the sun had nearly melted into the horizon. "My brother is missing, I'm afraid."

"Your brother missed the wedding feast?"

She sighed, a sardonic smile tilting her full lips. "It's not the first important gathering he has avoided. And I doubt it will be the last."

"He's run off like this before?"

She sighed wearily. "He has. Although never for so long." She scrubbed at her arm again, a deep pinch between her brows. "It's been nearly three days."

"How old is he?"

"Fifteen years."

"Ah. Plenty old enough to know better than to worry his family."

"One would think," she said, and the sound of grief was heavy in her tone. "But it is not so simple as that."

Strange that only this young woman was so distressed about the missing boy, while the rest of his family members were occupied with entertaining their guests below. Something about the way she clung to the edges of the celebration, engaging but not fully participating, unsettled me, like the last in an upward line of notes left unplayed.

"What is your name?" I asked.

She tilted her chin, studying me for a moment. "Eliora."

"A lovely name," I said with a smile that usually set lashes to fluttering back in my hometown. I took two slow steps toward her, hoping she would not bolt. "I am Ronen, one of the Levitical musicians who've been sent here to assist with the upcoming celebrations."

"I know," she said. "My father told me you were coming with the others."

A strange response, as if she expected me. As if she knew me.

Intrigued, I ventured closer, leaning my hip against the wall beside her and relaxing my posture. "I don't remember meeting you when I was in Kiryat-Yearim last time. And I thought I'd met all of Elazar's children."

Her lips quirked. "Don't you?"

"I would remember *you*," I said, allowing another slow smile as my eyes traveled over her face with its high, wide-set cheekbones, narrow chin, and full lips. There was something so unique about her, more than just the color of her hair or the paleness of her skin. Whatever had snagged my attention as she danced had not relented.

She huffed a soft laugh and shook her head, as if she suspected the game I'd barely begun to play. "Perhaps your memory is not as well-honed as you think it to be." She lifted her brows, and somehow I felt she'd turned the game board around on me and now awaited my next move.

As tall as she was, she was almost able to look me in the eye, so I leaned forward to search hers in the meager light from the oil lamp sitting between us on the wall. Her eyes were large, almost impossibly so, and a deep green color that I'd only seen one time before.

The truth struck me so suddenly that I gasped out a name I'd not uttered in all these years. "Arisa?"

She dipped her chin in acknowledgment, those green eyes now alight with laughter.

My jaw gaped as I conjured up my memory of the Philistine waif I'd discovered behind the sheepfold. I would have guessed that she and her brother had been escorted back to Ashdod long ago, as Abinidab had promised them.

"But . . ." I sputtered, remembering the way she'd danced with the sisters of the bride. "But you aren't Elazar's daughter."

A flash of hurt crossed her face before her chin lifted and her gaze hardened. "Natan and I were adopted by Elazar and Yoela and have the same rights as any of their blood-borne children."

Again I lifted my hands in apology. "I meant no offense. I am merely surprised. I did not expect you to still be here."

The nearby flame reflected against those luminous eyes as she spoke. "They saved us," she said softly, her body relaxing into the wall again. "Took us in and from the very first treated us with unwavering kindness. Never once did I feel like an enemy. After a few weeks, they asked if we wanted to stay. Not only did we have nothing to return to, but by that time I was desperate to remain with such generous people. When Elazar came to me with the proposal that we become part of the family a few months later, I accepted without a thought." Her gaze floated back toward the dark tree line. "Natan still struggles with that decision. But it was the right one."

"So Natan"—I gestured off toward the path she'd been keeping vigil over—"is Lukio?"

She nodded. "We both were given new names—Hebrew names—when we became part of the family and joined in the covenant with Yahweh. A reminder of our new identity." A distant look came into her eyes. "The old Hebrew woman who cared for us, Azuvah, used to call me her light. So I took Eliora, God my Light, as my name. And Lukio was always my most precious gift, so I named him Natan."

Still stunned from such a revelation, I remained silent. How strange that the same girl that had followed the Ark from Philistine territory would be here when I returned. Somehow, I was unsurprised that the boy had grown into a troubled young man. I well remembered the suspicious looks he'd leveled at me as we journeyed, even after I'd enticed him to take a closer look at my lion's claw necklace. It wasn't until I'd engaged him in a game of dice that he'd ceased to cast threatening looks at me behind his sister's back.

"I have you to thank," she said in a more mature version of the sweet voice I remembered from eight years ago. Then it had reminded me of a wounded bird, but now it was more like a gently plucked lyre, soft and melodic, the sound stirring a peculiar melancholy I'd not felt in years.

"If you did not find us," she said, "or bring us to Abinidab that day, we would have likely perished out there alone. And I certainly would not have the family I do now. When my father told me you were among the group of Levites coming to Kiryat-Yearim for the festivals, I was so glad that I would finally have the chance to express my gratitude."

Again her attention darted toward the forest, her expression shuttering. Whatever was going on with her brother must be more than just a young man avoiding a wedding feast, and the instinct to fix whatever might be broken welled up with surprising strength in me. Somehow, even after all this time, I felt responsible for the two young Philistines I'd found in a field.

But thoughts of that day near Beth Shemesh also reminded me of my purpose for following Eliora up here, and my hands clenched around the stone wall. My mission was vastly more important than contending with a boy's rebellious ways or a misplaced urge to soothe the pain I saw in his sister's deep green eyes. No, these plans had been in the works for an entire year, and I could not allow anything to take my focus from my duty to my family or my people.

Elazar had refused to listen to reason since Abinidab had died, obeying the commands of Samuel the Pretender instead of the priests who were the rightful authority over the holy implements—and who would soon return the center of worship where it belonged. And so, it did not—it could not—matter whether Arisa-turned-Eliora called the man who guarded this mountain *Father*.

The time had finally come to steal the Ark of the Covenant.

Fourteen

Eliora

Ronen had changed, although it had taken me no more than a few moments to recognize him when he'd arrived. His beard was thick and full now, and he'd added more breadth to his shoulders and a handspan of height, but those dark brown eyes that had been full of such mischief as he told Natan stories and indulged him in games of dice were still just as captivating, even more so now. I'd thought of him often over the years, every time I heard a pleasing melody plucked on a lyre or strummed on a lute, or whenever I'd sung with my sisters as we scrubbed laundry in the stream. I'd wondered where he was, whom he'd married, if he had children—silly thoughts of a girl who'd been enthralled with an older boy who had twice come to her rescue.

To avoid making a fool of myself any further, especially knowing that he'd watched me dance with all the grace of a camel, I put my eyes back on the path down below, praying for the thousandth time tonight that Natan would appear at the head of the trail.

"Much has changed here over the years," said Ronen, waving a hand toward the shared courtyard situated at the center of our compound. "I could not help but notice there are a number of new buildings."

"There are indeed," I responded, the sounds of joyful revelry below making my lips curve upward, in spite of how much Natan's absence weighed on me. "Not only has our family grown, but with the Levites who guard the Ark living here, along with a few of their families, there was a need for more rooms. Most of them live down in Kiryat-Yearim, though."

"How many are there?"

"Levites?" I paused, counting in my head. "There must be at least thirty or so who reside here full time."

His brows rose. "So many?"

"Although it's doubtful that anyone would be so foolish as to approach the Ark, my father wants to ensure that it is well guarded, day and night."

"A wise decision," he said, his eyes tracking off in the direction where the Ark was hidden—a coincidence, since only the Levites who had charge over the sacred vessel knew the exact location. With the exception of myself and a few other members of our family, of course.

In the silence that followed, I searched about for something to say, realizing that for as many years as I'd daydreamed about Ronen, I actually knew very little about his life other than that he was a Levite and had come to Kiryat-Yearim with his uncle.

"And your uncle, is he well?"

Ronen flinched at my question, perhaps startled by the abrupt change of subject. "Abiram? Oh . . . yes. He is fine. Busy with his duties as an elder of the Levites." His answer was strangely stilted. Perhaps there was some sort of rocky ground between them.

"And the rest of your family? Your wife? Children?" I asked, foolishly dreading the answers on both accounts. Ronen's eyes snapped to mine. Surely he could see the pool of embarrassment I'd had to swim through to even ask such a question.

"I am not married," he said. "I still live with my uncle's family."

"Oh . . . I did not know. . . ." Sensing there was pain beneath that statement, I fumbled about for a response, grateful that the twilight would hide the rush of heat to my cheeks. "I apologize for—"

"My father and brothers died in the war at Afek," he said, speaking over me. "And my mother remarried shortly after, so she and my younger siblings went north with her second husband's clan."

My heart flipped over in my chest, all mortification forgotten as I realized that when he'd found Natan and me in that field, he'd just lost one parent to death and the other had left him behind. He had been as much an orphan as we were back then. Yet he'd been so kind, so gentle, not displaying even a hint of resentment for the part that our own people had in the destruction of his family.

"Oh, Ronen, I am sorry. You must miss them so much."

He brushed away my concern with a swipe of his palm, affixing a smile to his lips that in no way reached his eyes. "My uncle's family has been more than generous. I owe them everything."

"Just as I owe Elazar and Yoela," I said. "Without their kindness to us, we would have had to return to Philistia and survive on our own. I thank Yahweh every day that Azuvah told us to follow the Ark." I repressed a shudder as the horrific moments following her command welled up in my mind.

"And what of the Ark? Have you seen it again since the day we—?"

His question was cut off by a strident call from Miri. "Eliora! You must come!" She bounded across the rooftop, one hand outstretched in supplication. The urgency in her tone made my stomach curl into itself. *Natan!*

"What is it?" I ran to her, heart pounding.

Miri's frown, and the way she gripped my arm, did nothing to quell my panic. "He's back, but he's not alone," she said. "Abba is speaking with the men who accompanied him here."

Without a thought I flew down the stairs, trying not to trip over my feet as I wound my way through the wedding guests and toward the back door to our home. When I arrived in the front room, my father and Gershom were standing with a filth-covered Natan, whose arms were crossed over his chest and who was glowering at the floor. Three strangers stood nearby with matching scowls on their faces as they regarded my brother with disdain. Two of the men sported darkening bruises on their jaws and looked nearly as grubby as Natan.

"This had better be the last time," said one of them. "I cannot be held responsible for what will happen if they go after our livestock again."

"It is only because he told us that he belongs to you that he is not in shackles," said the third man, who appeared unscathed by whatever tussle had taken place.

"I appreciate your grace in this instance, my friends," said my father, a deep pinch of frustration between his silvering brows as he spoke with firm authority. "I assure you, this matter will be dealt with immediately. Please, help yourself to food and drink. We are celebrating the marriage of one of my daughters." He laid a palm on Gershom's shoulder. "And my eldest here will ensure you have a place to pass the night so you may return to your village after you've rested."

The three men reluctantly accepted my father's offer without further argument, but all of them shot disgruntled looks at Natan as they trailed out behind Gershom.

My mother bustled into the room just as the door closed behind them. "What happened? Natan!" she exclaimed, rushing to examine him head to toe. "Where have you been? We've been so worried!"

Natan accepted her fussing for a moment, but when she started wiping the dirt from his face, he took a step backward, pulling away from her insistent hands. "I am fine. Just a misunderstanding."

"Misunderstanding?" said my father, incredulous. "How can theft be a misunderstanding?"

"We stole nothing," snapped Natan, stretching to his full height, which topped my father's by a full hand. It was no wonder it had taken three men to accompany him home when his height and bulk made him appear so much older than his years. It always had. "It was nothing more than a jest. Padi and Adnan thought it would be amusing to hide a few sheep in a cave. We had no intention of taking them for good. If those men hadn't appeared out of nowhere and wrestled us to the ground"—he gestured to the muck that stained his tunic from neck to knee with abraded knuckles—"it all would have ended harmlessly."

My father regarded Natan silently for a few very long moments, the silence in the room ripe with unease as my brother held his gaze with shocking audacity. Elazar was a fair man, but one who did not hesitate to discipline those under his command—or his children, when it was warranted. I knew this well because I'd dreaded such discipline since I'd stepped foot in his home eight years before, and I worked hard to avoid provoking the kind of intense expression he was leveling at my brother right now.

My stomach churned as I anticipated whatever well-deserved words of chastisement would soon follow. But to my surprise, instead of blistering Natan's ears, my father sighed, the sound weighted with disappointment. "We've all been very concerned for you, son. Your mother has been nearly ill with worry, and I don't think Eliora has slept for the past two nights. And, of course, you missed Safira's wedding. Your sister is wounded that you found other pursuits more interesting than joining with your family in this celebration. She's asked after you a number of times when she should instead be focusing on the joy of her new marriage."

Only a tiny twitch of his cheek hinted at Natan's guilt over hurting Safira, but then he pursed his lips and looked away, as if determined not to let it affect him. There was no contrition in his posture, but I knew Natan better than anyone and felt sure that he'd not meant to hurt Safira, even if his actions of late had become increasingly thoughtless and brazen.

"We'll discuss this tomorrow," said my father. "Now is not the time to deal with the consequences of your actions. Go wash yourself. And then apologize to Safira. She'll be relieved that you are safe."

Without a word, Natan left the room and with him the strong smell of animal waste. Whoever had discovered my brother and his unruly friends must have wrestled them right into a manure pile.

My mother went to my father's side, winding an arm about his waist. "This will pass, Elazar. You are doing your best with him."

"I cannot help but feel that my best efforts fall far short." He shook his head, then without another word or even a glance at me, turned and went back out into the courtyard, his shoulders slumped in a defeated way I'd never seen before.

"This is my fault," I mumbled, staring at the door he'd exited and feeling the weight of his disappointment in Natan on my own shoulders.

"Your fault?" exclaimed my mother, sounding scandalized. "Eliora, that is nonsense. You've been that boy's moon and stars since he was born. No one has loved him better than you, nor cared for him more selflessly."

"I cannot help but wonder . . ." I began, but my voice trailed off. Because although I'd asked myself many times what I could have done to keep Natan from becoming so bitter, I would not change a single decision I'd made from the moment Azuvah told us to flee. Everything I'd done had been only to protect him, and I desperately wished he could see it all through my eyes.

Sometimes Natan seemed to forget whatever burdens he carried. There had been years, even, when I'd felt like he'd finally allowed himself to be one with the family who'd embraced us so thoroughly. From the beginning, our older brothers had included him in all their romps through the woods and in every game and wood-sword fight and good-natured tease. For a long while, I'd been relieved when he seemed to transfer his affections from his distorted memory of Mataro to Gershom and Iyov. But with seven years between him and Iyov, and nine with Gershom, they'd grown out of boyish escapades far before Natan, and eventually he turned to boys outside our home to seek out adventures. And as each of our older brothers began training for their future Levitical duties, Natan slipped further into an attitude of belligerence, which seemed to only be worsening with time.

My mother reached up to cup my cheeks in her palms, her diminutive size no match for the large heart that lived inside her chest. "No more of this, Eliora. Natan makes his own choices. He is no little boy who you must protect anymore. You are not to blame for his actions, nor for whatever pain he is harboring deep in his soul. Besides, both Gershom and Iyov were no gentle lambs at that age either. He'll find his way to manhood, even if it is a rocky journey. We must trust Yahweh to watch over him along the way and guide his steps."

I let her pull me down for a kiss to my forehead, as usual feeling a tinge of embarrassment that I, too, towered over the women of my family. No matter how long we lived here and no matter how much Elazar and Yoela enfolded us into their clan, we would never look Hebrew. The golden-brown hair, pale skin, and peculiar height our birth father had passed to us from his far-northern ancestors would always make us stand out as different. It had done so even among our own people.

But my mother was right. I'd learned over these past years that it was the Eternal One who directed our path. He'd inspired Azuvah to teach us the ways of the Israelites and their language. He'd protected Natan and me as we walked through treacherous country unscathed. And it was he who led us to Elazar and Yoela's doorstep.

Therefore, tomorrow I would go to my special place and plead for my brother once again. For if there was one thing I knew after years of being witness to my parents' distress over Natan's increasingly volatile behavior, it was that only Yahweh could rescue my brother from whatever had such a grip on his troubled spirit.

Fifteen

Ronen

"Well, Ronen? What did you learn at the wedding?" demanded Machlon, the moment we were out of earshot of the camp. My cousin was impatient in the best of circumstances; he must have practically chewed his tongue to pieces as we lay in a tent last night surrounded by Levites who were not privy to our reasons for being among them.

Needing an opportunity to debrief and plan next steps with Osher and Shelah, the twin brothers my uncle had sent to help us with the mission, my cousin had approached Tuviyah, the leader of the musicians, and volunteered the four of us to fetch supplies this morning. Now with sunrise only a couple of hours behind us, the morning cacophony of birdsong was almost deafening in its exuberance, ensuring that nothing we said on the short walk down to Kiryat-Yearim would be overheard.

"I didn't learn much," I said with a shrug, my eyes trained on the shady trail ahead. "Everyone was occupied with talk of the wedding. There wasn't even a whisper about the Ark among the guests or the family."

"I heard nothing either," said Machlon, frustration thick in his tone. "Have they even forgotten the thing is up there? I tried every angle with those guards—carefully, so as not to provoke suspicion—but their lips were sealed. Even after a few cups of wine."

Machlon had undoubtedly done his best to wheedle information from the guards while making it seem as though he was completely disinterested in the answers they might give. He'd used the skill on me a time or two before, when we were younger, so I knew how effective it was. The men must truly be well trained to keep so close-lipped about their duties.

"While the two of you drank wine and feasted," said Osher, with a wry smile as he gestured to his twin brother beside him, "Shelah and I scouted the backside of the mountain again. But the trail has either been lost to the years or deliberately obscured."

Not for the first time, I wished that I'd paid more attention during the journey from Beth Shemesh eight years ago; but as I'd discovered yesterday as we took the long way around to Elazar's house, nothing up there was familiar to me other than the compound itself. I'd been far too distracted while carrying a Philistine girl on my back, keeping an eye on her energetic brother, and composing a new song in my head. Besides, as Osher indicated, many seasons of growth had passed between then and now, and unless the trail had been well used, it would have long since disappeared.

"We'll find it," he said with unswerving confidence. "Your uncle sent Shelah and me here for a reason."

I'd only met the men a few weeks before, when my uncle insisted that the strangers travel with us, saying they were sons of a friend who supported our cause. Shelah and Osher were also reputed as two of the best hunters in the territory, masters at tracking game across long distances. My uncle swore they were men of great loyalty and honor and assured me that if anyone could find the Ark on this thickly wooded mountain, it was the two of them. I'd had no choice but to believe him, and at his request, had talked Tuviyah into including the identical broad-shouldered men as extra guards for the journey from Beit El. Hopefully, I had not manipulated my father's closest friend for nothing.

"We only have a little over three weeks," said Machlon, as if we all had forgotten that Yom Teruah was the deadline for everything to be set in place. With Elazar's family distracted by celebrations that would follow the Shabbat rest of the Day of Shouting, the feasting and dancing late into the night, we would slip through the trees, subdue the guards, and make off with the Ark before the stars began to fade.

"Without a sure path to the Ark, and then back down the mountain," said my cousin, "this mission will fail."

Osher nodded in agreement. "If we have to search behind every bush and tree up on that mountain, that's what we will do."

"But we also must be careful as we search," I warned. "It will do us no good to alert Elazar and his men that anyone is poking about."

"That goes without saying," said Osher, his lips flattening with the barest hint of annoyance. "We'll complete the task we were sent to do." *And you tend to your own* was the silent implication.

"Are you sure you didn't find out anything at the wedding, Ronen?" With a grimace, my cousin paused to swipe at an enormous dew-lined cobweb that stretched from tree to tree before continuing on. "Anything interesting up on the roof?"

Stunned to realize he'd seen me ascending the stairs, I hesitated only for a moment, remembering Eliora's bowed shoulders as she searched the dark path below for her wayward brother and the flash of trust in her green eyes as she thanked me for rescuing her so long ago. "I figured during the day nothing much could be seen through the dense trees, but a torch might be spotted against the darkness."

"A good thought," Machlon admitted, and I breathed easier of the sweet morning air when he did not mention Eliora. "Did you see any lights?"

I shook my head as I stepped over a large snaking root across the path. No wonder Abinidab and Elazar had used an alternate route to transport the Ark; although well traveled, this steep and winding path would have been impassable for men carrying such a precious burden on their shoulders. "Either there were no torches lit around where the Ark is hidden, or the leaf cover is too thick between the compound and its location. They may even have it tucked away in a cave. If so, it'll be quite the challenge to evade all the guards Elazar has posted around the area."

"I doubt they have all that many up there at one time," said Osher. "We'll get past them."

"A rotation of thirty," I said, without thinking.

Machlon halted and turned to face me, brows high. "And you know this because . . . ?"

Trying not to grit my teeth, I attempted to sound unruffled by my slip. "I spoke to one of Elazar's daughters on the roof."

"Ah," he said, with a knowing grin. "I knew there was a reason you were flying up those stairs with your tzitzit on fire."

Determined to keep my face blank, since he was far too close to the mark, I shrugged. "I only happened across her while I was using the high vantage point to search for signs of the Ark."

"Why didn't you say something before?" He clapped me on the back and then directed a smirk at Osher and Shelah. "See, I told you he'd find an in with the family. I thought perhaps one of Elazar's sons might remember him from before. But a woman?" He barked out a laugh, startling a blackbird from its perch nearby as he shook my shoulder affectionately. "Even better, cousin!"

"What do you mean?"

"It's perfect, Ronen. Don't you see? That"—he made a circle in the air, indicating my face—"can be quite a weapon. One you can use to our advantage."

I flushed, annoyed with his mocking gesture. He and I were not that dissimilar in appearance after all, with the same hair color and general build, although I'd passed him in height by four fingers a few years ago. But he'd always made an issue back home of women staring at me, like I was purposefully drawing attention away from him.

"Elazar's daughters must know where the Ark is," he continued. "In fact, I would venture to guess that the women of that family are frequent visitors to the Levites who guard the thing, taking them food and provisions. There could be no better way to find out what we need to know. The guards might be suspicious of my sudden interest in friendship. But a woman on the prowl for a husband . . . ? Now there's an easy target."

My defenses flared. "I know why I am here, Machlon. And it's not to look for a wife."

"Of course not," he said, with a scoff. "My father would roast his own tongue and consume it whole before letting you marry a daughter of Elazar. But *she* doesn't know that. Flatter her. Woo her. She'll be wet clay in your hands, my brother."

Even though I'd had similar thoughts about Eliora's usefulness last night, the idea of manipulating her in such a potentially hurtful way set my teeth on edge. "She's a Philistine. Adopted by Elazar eight years ago. Perhaps she is not even privy to information about the Ark."

Machlon paused, brows lifted high. "The same one my father said you found behind a rock? The one who followed the Ark from Ashdod?"

"She is."

"Wasn't she enthralled with the box? Not wanting it out of her sight or some such thing?"

She had been singularly focused on the chest back then, her eyes latched to it almost the entire journey from Beth Shemesh to Kiryat-Yearim. "She was certainly determined to stay in its vicinity."

"Then don't you see? You've picked the very best of all the daughters to set your sights on!"

"I don't have my sights on anyone. She was barely more than a child when I met her."

He waved my argument away. "It makes no difference. I've seen you use that honey-coated tongue with both your mother and mine in many a prickly situation. I have no doubt you can work the same trickery on this girl."

"But you—"

He talked over me. "Since you'll be busy wooing Elazar's daughter, I'll search out musicians who might be amenable to joining our cause. I think that will be a better use of my time than trying to find weakness among the guards."

I did not like this change in the plans. We'd decided months ago that it was my job to befriend the musicians who would be joining us from among the rest of the tribes and determine who among them were loyal to the line of Eleazar ben Aharon and who pandered to the traitors who got my father and brothers killed. But I had to admit that Machlon was right. As much as the thought settled in my gut like unripe fruit, my connection to Eliora was more than advantageous.

This mission had been years in the making, and my uncle was counting on the four of us to smooth the way for it to be completed. Over the past few years, he and a few like-minded priests had gathered materials to restore the sanctuary, weaving cloth to replace the pieces that had deteriorated, repairing any implements that had been damaged during the hasty flight from Shiloh in advance of the Philistine attack, and guarding the dissembled Mishkan in a secret location. Now they were fully prepared to raise the holy sanctuary again at Nob, atop a high hill in the southeast that overlooked the city of Jebus and far from the borders of Philistia, in preparation for our arrival with the Ark.

Of course, this was merely the first step toward complete restoration of our ways and the return of the correct priestly line to the seat of power, but it was one of the most important. Not only did the misspent blood of my father and brothers demand it, but my mother would not return south until peace and safety could be assured in the region.

It had been over eight years since I'd seen my ima. Eight years since she'd married a man she barely knew in an act of desperation after being widowed with little ones to feed. She'd asked Abiram to take me in so I could continue in my Levitical training, then took my two younger sisters and my youngest brother—who'd been only a few months old then—to the most northern reaches in the territory of Naftali, as far away from the Philistine threat as they could go. My heart still ached from their loss.

If I failed now, it might take years to implement another plan for the Ark—decades, perhaps, before the priesthood was restored and a king with enough strength to defeat our enemies could be installed. And as my mother's new husband had told me before he'd left with what remained of my family, until our territories were no longer in danger of a Philistine takeover, he would not bring them back. I had to make certain this plan was successful, or it was likely that I might never see them again. Having my family restored to me was worth any cost.

"All right," I conceded. "She does seem to trust me already, because I was the one to find her and escort her here years ago. I am certain I can mine information without making her suspicious. But I also don't think it necessary to play with her affections."

"Use whatever persuasive arts you have at your disposal. We owe it to our people and to Yahweh to bring back the Ark." He gestured to the heavily wooded hillside around us. "This is no place for the holiest of objects. Hidden from the people and its supervision overseen by men who are not even sanctified kohanim. Such treachery is undermining the Covenant, tearing the tribes apart, and leaving us all vulnerable to invasion by the nations around us."

I could not agree more. The fissures between us had grown into chasms over these last eight years. The sons of Israel needed to unify, to be gathered beneath one banner. One High Priest. And then one king. But first, the Ark must be returned. And if I had to manipulate Eliora to accomplish that goal, then so be it. This mission was too important to let one lone woman stand in the way.

Kiryat-Yearim was well named. The city of forests was encircled by dense woods, and most of the town was not even visible from the valley floor through the trees. In fact, there was no way to know just how many homes were scattered all over these hills, hidden as they were in the shade of mighty oaks, majestic cedars, and sprawling sycamores that created a natural barrier to both invaders and storms that swept eastward from the coast. But from the number of people milling about, there were far more dwellings on this mountain than I had guessed.

Agreeing that we should remain as unobtrusive as possible as we gently prodded the townspeople for information, we split— Osher and Shelah going to find a butcher, while Machlon and I headed the other direction to seek out a produce supplier to keep our camp well-stocked over the next few weeks. But for as much as we'd hoped that our presence might go unnoticed, curious eyes followed us relentlessly. It had been nearly a decade since any sort of ingathering festival had taken place, and we were likely the first Levitical musicians anyone here had seen in many years. I pushed away the unease. Their attention was harmless, and none of them had any inclination about our true purpose in their town.

We passed by several shops—a carpenter, a potter, an olive oil vendor—before reaching the center of town, where Machlon headed for the first produce stall we came upon. As he chatted with the farmer who'd brought his goods up from the valley, I noticed two silver-haired women sitting in the shade of a small dwelling nearby. Both were spinning wool, yet their eyes were not on their hands as the drop-spindles spun around and around in swirls of deep indigo. Instead, their watchful gazes roved over every person who passed by, and every so often, they would lean close to whisper to each other. I had a sense that these two would be far more useful than the farmer Machlon was wasting his time with. I wandered over, feigning interest in the dance of the spinning threads.

"Shalom," I said, with a deferential nod of my head. "What a lovely color."

The first woman grinned up at me with open welcome, a multitude of wrinkles fanning out from eyes that sparkled with kindness, but the second pursed her mouth and continued spinning, still watching the street.

"That it is," said the first woman, without ceasing the rapid twirl of her spindle. "The secret of such a singular shade has been handed down from generation to generation in our family. You'll never see the likes of it anywhere else but here, young man, especially since the plant used in the dye is found only on this mountain."

"Bithya," murmured the other woman in warning. "Mind your tongue."

"I did not tell him which plant it *is*, Atara," said Bithya, with annoyance, "only that it is unique to this area." But then she leaned forward, causing her spindle to pause its movement. "Our Gibeonite ancestors were the first to discover it," she whispered loudly. "And now only my sister and I—and one other person in Kiryat-Yearim—know how to harvest it correctly."

Her sister sighed in exasperation. "If you keep talking, everyone will know by nightfall."

"Have no fear." I winked and pressed two fingers to my mouth. "My lips are sealed to the grave."

Bithya's dark eyes twinkled with mirth. "Oh, you're a charming one, aren't you?"

With a groan of annoyance, Atara shook her head, her mouth flattening into a line as her spindle flew impossibly fast. I suspected she was used to her sister chattering to anyone who bothered to stop and speak with two old women.

"So, the two of you are Gibeonite?" I asked Bithya, surprised that they would claim ties to the local Amorite tribe that lied their way into a peace accord with Yehoshua.

She nodded, lifting her spindle and, with an expert flick of her wrist, set it to spinning once again. "We are, although our great-grandfather married a Hebrew woman, and over time our clan became quite intermingled with the Yehudites. There are not many full-blooded Gibeonites in Kiryat-Yearim anymore, although a few live on the fringes, working as woodsmen."

There were so many Canaanites, Amorites, and Jebusites woven into the fabric of Israel that plucking one unadulterated thread from the rest was nearly impossible. All the more reason to ensure that our worship practices remained pure and holy, unsullied by men such as the sons of Eli, who'd turned the priesthood into a mockery.

"You know this used to be a holy hill for our pagan ancestors, don't you?" said Bithya. "There was a well-known high place up there where the baalim were worshiped under the trees. People came from all over this region to gather and perform their awful ceremonies."

My pulse flickered at the mention of a sacred grove in which Canaanite gods had been venerated. Could there be a connection to the current location of the Ark? Surely Abinidab would not hide our holiest relic in such a blasphemous place . . . would he?

"You've been up there?" I asked, valiantly keeping my tone smooth and even. It would not do for them to suspect just how interested I was in the answer.

A frown tugged at her lips. "Not since I was a small girl. I only remember trekking up there once when my grandfather was still alive. And there were so many trees and paths and so much overgrown brush that I was lost even then."

I held in a sigh of disappointment. Perhaps I had been wasting my time with her after all. Machlon had already moved down the street and was talking with a spice trader. I should catch up with him, or at least find someone else to coax information from besides an old woman who had not been atop the mountain in decades.

"And of course," she continued, oblivious to my frustration, "when Abinidab and his family moved up there, they knocked it all down anyhow, burned the idols and cleansed the place. To think that instead of all those pagan gods, the Ark presides over this mountain now. What a blessing that has been."

"How so?" I asked distractedly, my gaze on the crowd as I wondered who I might approach next.

"Ever since the sacred vessel arrived, the house of Abinidab has been mightily blessed," she said, with an almost reverent tone. "And that did not change with his death. Even though Yoela went for many years without a babe, all of a sudden her womb seemed to blossom. She birthed four more little ones—two of them twins! She may even be increasing again, if I'm not mistaken, and I'm rarely wrong on these sorts of things." The woman beamed as if it were her own daughter giving birth to so many.

"And the gardens—" She paused to place a gnarled hand on her heart. "Oh, you've never seen such extraordinary gardens, young man. The squash, the melons, every variety of vegetable and fruit and herb you ever could imagine grows in abundance up there. It is miraculous! There is so much they cannot use it all, so they share with us in town."

The idea that the presence of the Ark had in some mystifying way contributed to the expansion of both Elazar's brood and his prosperity amused me, but I squelched the smile that sprang to my lips. Perhaps if they could not provide me with the location of the Ark, they might at least inform me about the family that guarded it.

"Then Elazar is well respected in Kiryat-Yearim?" I asked.

"He is everything good and honorable," she said with a firm nod. "Just as Abinidab was before he went to his forefathers. It is no surprise that Yahweh led the Ark here. There could be no better man to watch over it."

"So Elazar's family stays up on the mountain, sending food down to you like they are kings and queens?" I asked, remembering that my uncle regularly accused them of acting as self-appointed royalty.

"Of course not!" Bithya sounded personally affronted by my assumption. "There is not a week that goes by that his daughters do not come down with basketfuls of food to hand out door to door to those of us who are in no shape to hike up the mountain and pick for ourselves. Such sweet children. They seem to revel in sharing their bounty. Even the neighboring towns have benefited from their generosity."

Her effusive praise had given me the perfect opportunity to slip in a question about the person I was most curious about. "And the Philistine girl they've adopted. What of her?"

138

"Eliora?" said Bithya. "Well now, when she and her brother first came to Kiryat-Yearim, we were all quite concerned, as you surely can understand, but by all accounts from those who've spent time in Elazar's home, she is a sweet young woman who barely speaks above a whisper and is always ready to serve. But we've only seen her a time or two in all these years. She very rarely ventures down the mountain. It's the other girls who deliver food to us. I wonder, now that two of them are married, if that will change—"

"The girl is not the problem," said Atara, speaking over her sister and surprising me with her sudden engagement in our conversation. "She keeps to herself, never creates any trouble. But that brother of hers . . ." The woman bunched her mouth into a scowl. "We've had more items go missing—"

"Atara! There is no proof at all that young Natan has had a hand in such mischief," said Bithya.

Her sister made a low noise in her throat. "And no proof that he has not. He's a wild one, and not to be trusted."

"He's as bad as all that?" I asked, dismayed that Eliora's concerns about her brother seemed to be founded on more than just avoiding familial responsibilities.

"Indeed," said Atara, with a huff of indignation. "If he's not instigating chaos, he's fighting. And as I said, there have been more than a few instances of stolen goods since that boy appeared in Kiryat-Yearim."

Bithya laid a hand on Atara's arm. "Now, sister. It could be any one of the wayward boys who run around this area. We must not bear false witness."

Atara frowned, unswayed by her sister's gentle rebuff. "Those eyes . . . I don't like the looks of them. It's not natural."

I'd forgotten that the boy I'd known as Lukio had two different colored eyes—which admittedly had been a small measure disconcerting at first—but I'd barely noticed them once he'd stopped glaring at me and gotten lost in the excitement of showing me how to play his dice game.

Bithya gave me a tilted smile, making it clear that the sisters had argued over all of this before. "Regardless of her brother's troubles, her heritage, and the fact that she's timid, Eliora is highly regarded in Kiryat-Yearim because it is she who tends those bounteous gardens up on the terraces. From what I hear, she is out there at first light every morning—weeding, watering, and who knows what else."

"Is that so?" My pulse flickered as the ladies unwittingly stumbled right onto the path I'd hoped to lead them down.

"At times I wonder if her hands themselves aren't blessed." Bithya's gaze drifted up the hillside, a bit of awe creeping into her tone. "Not only are the vegetables and fruit the largest and most flavorful you've ever had, but the flowers that young woman raises are beyond compare. Gan Eden could not have been lovelier."

"Tell me," I said, my warmest smile curving my lips. "If one desired to see these extraordinary gardens, how might he find them?"

Sixteen

Eliora

The rhythmic thwack of metal on wood drew me farther into the forest. It had not taken me long to find Natan once Gershom pointed me toward one of the smaller paths that snaked south of our home, saying he'd taken off just after dawn to cut up a fallen oak. The very one, I guessed, that he'd told me he was chopping up with his friends before he disappeared for more than three days.

"Tell him we need to depart soon or we won't make it down to Kesalon before dark," he'd said.

My father had determined that the best way for Natan to suffer the consequences of his actions was to have him rebuild the sheepfold he and his friends had partially destroyed and then help the shepherds with shearing the hundreds of sheep in the village of Kesalon.

To no one's surprise, Adnan and Padi's fathers were not interested in offering restitution for their sons' actions, saying they were too busy supplying logs for some urgent large-scale building project. My father had returned from his meeting with them greatly dismayed at their lack of concern, both for their sons' deviant behavior and for our relationship with our neighbors on the far side of the mountain.

I stepped into the clearing just as Natan swung the ax down on the fallen tree. Likely rotted at the core, it must have toppled during a recent storm, its top half sprawled across the ground like a fallen giant.

Unaware that I was watching, Natan again lifted the ax high above his head and let it drop with a grunt, sweat beading across his back and shoulders. It always surprised me when I saw him like this, engaged in tasks that required the strength of a grown man and wielding heavy tools like they were nothing more than the wooden swords he used to play with as a boy. In fact, if his curly golden-brown hair and broad-shouldered build were not so familiar, I might not even recognize him from this far away.

In my mind, he was still my little Lukio, the same boy who pleaded for me to carry him when his legs got too tired, who weaved his fingers into my hair as we slept snuggled together like kittens in a basket, and who placed his head on my shoulder as Azuvah told us her Hebrew stories. It seemed as though more and more traces of that little boy were fading away, swallowed up by the man he was growing into. However, if he continued on the path he'd been traveling, I worried just what sort of man he might become.

"I brought you some food," I called out before he could raise the ax again. He turned to watch me approach, leaning on the ax handle beside the surprisingly large stack of wood he'd accumulated in the past few hours. Wood shavings decorated his sodden curls and clung to the beard that was filling in more each day.

"You must be hungry. Gershom said you've been out here since dawn."

He shrugged, wiping the sweat from his brow with the back of his hand, and I passed him the basket, which included a few fresh rounds of bread, some fruit and olives from my garden, and a skin of cool spring water. "Abba will be grateful for the extra wood since we used so much during the wedding."

His expression darkened as he set aside the ax to accept my offerings. "He's too busy punishing me for something that was not my fault to even notice."

I lifted my brows, surprised that he'd brought up the altercation with the shepherds since he'd pointedly avoided discussing it with me the morning after the wedding. Settling myself on the intact portion of the fallen tree as he tipped the skin of water to his lips, I attempted to keep the accusation out of my tone as I responded. "You were there, Natan. How could it possibly not have been your fault?"

He scowled, speaking around the half-round of bread he'd stuffed in his mouth. "I already told you it wasn't my idea to let the sheep free."

"But you were still part of it. You were in the pen when the men came across you. Even I saw—and smelled—the filth on your tunic."

His jaw ticked, but he made no move to contradict me.

"Why do you insist on being friends with Adnan and Padi? They seem to do nothing but get you into trouble."

His eyes flared, a sneer on his lips. "Who else would I be friends with?"

I blinked at him in confusion. "There are plenty of young men down in Kiryat-Yearim near your age."

"Who want nothing to do with me," he mumbled as he bit into one of the red pears I'd harvested a week ago. The sweet smell made my own mouth water, so I reached into the basket and took one for myself.

"That's not true. Medad and his brothers were once your friends."

He scoffed, tossing the pear core into the brush. "Not anymore."

"Why not?" I pressed. "When you were younger, the four of you got along so well."

His lips pressed into a white line, and he would not meet my eye. "Leave it alone, Risi."

Natan still refused to use my new name, instead clinging to the nickname he'd given me when he was barely old enough to talk. Although at times it annoyed me since I wanted to leave Arisa far in my past, there was affection within the word, and I cherished any precious tendril between us. But his refusal to reveal whatever had passed between himself and the boys in Kiryat-Yearim disconcerted me.

However, my brother was anything but free with his thoughts these days, and I knew pushing him would only lead to more walls between us. I could only pray that someday soon he would lay down his defenses and share with me the way he used to.

Therefore, I went quiet, allowing him time to eat in peace and absorbing the vibrant hush of the forest around us, broken only by layers of birdsong and the chatter of tiny creatures in the brush.

Once the food basket was empty, Natan went back to his task at the far end of the log I was perched on, hefting the huge ax over his head. I felt the vibration of each strike and marveled at how far the chips of wood flew with every blow. When one of them landed in my lap, I stood and retreated a few paces to avoid being struck.

"Where did you get that ax?" I asked when he paused for a breath. The tool was larger than any I'd seen before, the iron head double-sided and glinting in the sunlight, reminding me briefly of the enormous man we'd seen march through Ekron so long ago.

"Adnan," he replied on a grunt.

"Why would he give you that? Doesn't he need it for his work logging the hills?"

"His family had an extra one, so he offered it to me."

I frowned, wondering why Adnan would share such a valuable asset with Natan. Iron itself was scarce among the tribes, since the Philistines had a stranglehold on the trade, and by the looks of the well-honed edges, the ax had been crafted by a master.

There was so much I didn't know about my brother anymore. When had he stopped viewing me as his confidant? Even when he'd run around with the boys in Ashdod, doing things I wasn't happy about, he'd always told me everything. Now he was secretive. Taking himself off into the woods whenever he could. Keeping even his joys to himself and rarely smiling anymore. He'd pulled so far away I feared at times that I would never get him back.

"Why would you go off with them like that during the wedding? I was so worried," I admitted. "I could not concentrate on my duties while you were gone."

"I knew it wouldn't take long for you to come after me," he said, huffing a sigh and then letting the ax fall again.

"Can you blame me? You were gone for three days! And all you'd told me was that you were going to cut up a tree. You could have been hurt, or worse, and none of us would have even known where to begin looking for you."

"I've heard all this from Gershom. I don't need it from you."

That constricted feeling in the center of my chest coiled even tighter. "Why do you insist on spending time with people who care little for you?"

"How do you know that?" he snapped. "You know nothing about my friends, or what they care for. Would someone who does not care about me give me such an expensive gift?" He lifted the ax in one hand, shaking it to prove his point. "And they are eager to help me learn their trade."

"Why?"

"What else do I have to do?" He threw his hands wide.

"Gershom and Iyov—"

"Are Levites. I am not," he stated, his narrowed gaze daring me to disagree. But he was right. No matter that Elazar's family had adopted us, nothing could ever make Natan a descendant of the sacred order of men dedicated to Yahweh's service.

"But they still have plenty to teach you, if you would just—"

"The only thing they are interested in telling me is what I do wrong and how disappointed they are. They want nothing to do with me."

"That's not true. They were both very worried when they heard you hadn't returned. They spent the entire day combing the forest and questioning everyone in Kiryat-Yearim. It wasn't until someone said you'd been seen down in the valley with those Gibeonite boys that they gave up the search, since you could have gone anywhere by then."

He blinked at me, seemingly taken aback by such a revelation. Then his lips flattened and he looked off into the trees, his jaw working as he thumbed the edge of the ax.

"If it had been you, they'd not have stopped looking," he said beneath his breath. "But then, I'm not nearly as perfect as you, *Eliora*."

The sardonic lilt of his tone stung, as did the pointed emphasis on my new name. "You are just as much a part of this family as I am," I said. "If you would only allow them to show you."

He shook his head, his brow wrinkled with mock sympathy. "You aren't Hebrew, Risi. And you never will be."

The blow hit me square in the chest, knocking the breath from my lungs. At the same moment, Gershom stepped into the clearing, a stern look on his face that made me think he'd heard more than enough of our conversation.

"Natan," he snapped. "We must depart. Now. I sent Eliora for you a long while ago. What is keeping you here?"

"Nothing." My brother gazed at me with an odd expression. "I'm ready to go." Then he slung the ax over his shoulder and followed Gershom back up the narrow path, not sparing me another glance as he walked away.

Seventeen

Months ago, messages had been sent to each of the tribes, calling for Levitical musicians and singers to join together as one for the first time since Shiloh had been laid low and celebrate the fall festivals. Although no one had been certain how many of the Levites scattered over the tribal territories would answer that summons, more sons of Levi had arrived in Kiryat-Yearim over the past few days, doubling the size of our camp and adding to the chaos. I did not envy Tuviyah, who had the enormous task of leading and organizing such a disparate group of men.

There were less than three weeks now to finalize the order of service for Yom Teruah—designated as the feast of shouting and trumpet blasts—and then only ten days past that to prepare for Yom Kippur, the day of fasting, repentance, and atonement. Sukkot, the Feast of Booths, would be the final convocation before the people tore down their *sukkahs* and dispersed back to their homes all over Israelite territory.

Although, if everything went according to plan, I would be leaving with the Ark the night after Yom Teruah, while the people were caught up in feasting and dancing after the sacred day of rest. What happened afterward made no difference to me. Abiram and his allies had called for the festivals to be held at Kiryat-Yearim solely for the purpose of retrieving the Ark.

"As you can see," said Tuviyah to the group of us gathered on a high ridge, his resonant voice echoing off the rocky outcropping above us, "this place will be the perfect area for the musicians and singers to be arranged." He waved a hand toward the valley below, where the people of Israel would soon gather. "They'll be able to hear quite clearly down there."

Surveying the way the hills curved to protect the area, I agreed. If worshipers gathered below this ridge, the sound of instruments and voices would reverberate across the expanse unobstructed. They should be able to hear even the smallest note with relative ease.

A far more difficult task would be to ensure that the musicians melded their various talents and instruments together in some semblance of order. As it was, the differences between our various traditions had already become such a source of tension in the camp that I wondered how Tuviyah would accomplish anything. He was a skilled leader, to be sure, but he was no Mosheh. Bringing together a group of men who had lately been acting more like squabbling children during practice sessions than consecrated musicians would more than likely require a miracle.

Too bad the time of signs and wonders was long over.

"How many people are we expecting?" asked one of the recent arrivals, a Levite from the southern territory of Simeon, as he peered over the edge at the eight or nine tents that had already been pitched at the foot of the mountain.

"There can be no way to know," replied Tuviyah with his palms spread wide. "Perhaps only a few more will travel here, or maybe thousands. But hopefully, with so many years between the last ingathering festivals and now, the people will be desperate to come."

"Desperate to come to this blasphemous mountain?" muttered Machlon next to me. We'd situated ourselves at the very back of the gathering, so I doubted anyone overheard him, but I kept an eye on the men in front of us just the same. Drawing too much attention would not be wise.

"With the Ark in such close proximity," continued Tuviyah, "we anticipate many will come simply out of curiosity, hoping to catch a glimpse of the vessel itself."

"But it won't be brought down from the heights, will it?" asked another Levite.

"No," said Tuviyah. "It is well ensconced up on the mountain, settled in a secret place and not to be moved until the correct time. But just as in the days when it sat at Shiloh, within the Holy of Holies and seen only by the High Priest, its nearness is a reminder of both our history and our future. And we as musicians have the opportunity to bring the people together in a way that has not been done in nearly a decade. With our songs, we will remind them of the beautiful and creative nature of the God we serve."

Something that had lain dormant inside me for a long while stirred at Tuviyah's speech. I well remembered the passion my father and brothers had for their duties at the Mishkan. Some of my most cherished memories as a boy were going up to Shiloh to see them play music during the festivals and lift their voices in worship to the Holy One. I had wanted nothing more than to be just like them one day.

But the music and lyrics that had once flowed like an everpresent wellspring inside me had slowed to a trickle. Few and far between were the times when unbidden inspiration kept me awake at night, demanding to be woven into song. In fact, it had been at least five years since I'd even had the time or the inclination to create something new. Of far greater necessity than composing songs was my skill in repairing and building instruments, which kept me close to Tuviyah and the other head musicians—connections that my uncle deemed far too precious to neglect for the sake of singing and composing with the other Levites.

"And who determines which songs we will play?" asked the first man, an edge of derision in his heavily accented voice.

Tuviyah's heavy brow creased. "Those of us who served at the

Mishkan in the years before the Ark was stolen are well trained in the old songs and the ceremonies that were conducted there."

"So the only songs allowed will be the same tired ones sung since Mosheh's time?" The question from somewhere in the crowd was thick with disdain. "Most of us have not sung those in a generation or more."

"I have no doubt that with such talented musicians, the old songs will become fresh again," said Tuviyah, remaining admirably calm in spite of the rising tension.

"And what of our own songs?" asked another man, whose brisk tones alluded to heritage in the Kinneret Valley. "Are they not worthy to be lifted up to Yahweh?"

Tuviyah's jaw ticked as if he were considering his words carefully before he spoke. "Many of our traditions go back to the time of Eleazar ben Aharon, or before. We must not discount the longevity and value of practices that were set in place by our forefathers."

"And yet it is not Eleazar ben Aharon's descendants who inhabit the seat of High Priest, but Itamar's," said another, whose brightly striped and fringed tunic was similar to the style worn by the Philistines. Another man from the territory of Simeon, I guessed. The intermingling there, as well as many of the western border towns, had been so prolific in the days before Samson provoked our enemies that many there counted themselves as much Philistine as they did Hebrew.

"Will the sacrifices be held?" interjected another voice. "As they were in Shiloh?"

"Yes," said Tuviyah. "The kohanim have determined that even though the altar at Shiloh was destroyed, the offerings prescribed by the Torah can be accomplished here on the mountain and an appropriate altar will be built on this ridge for that purpose."

"Under whose authority was this decision made?" said the man from the south, above the murmur of opinions that rose all around. "Ahituv? He is as much an interloper as his father, Pinchas, and his grandfather, Eli."

"This is not the time to discuss such matters," said Tuviyah, lifting his hands in supplication as the chatter intensified. "Ahituv is the acting High Priest, and we will leave any succession decisions to the elders of the kohanim. We are here only to perform our duty as musicians, nothing more."

However, his plea went unheeded, and soon arguments shifted from the priestly lineage into a heated discussion between those calling for a king to drive out the Philistines, those who touted Samuel's leadership as sufficient, and others who felt a peaceful compromise with our enemies was the wisest course of action.

"Adding to our numbers will be even easier than I thought," said my cousin, a note of delighted anticipation in his voice as he leaned closer to me. He gestured toward the brightly garbed men from Simeon's tribe with a subtle tilt of his bearded chin. "My father will be pleased."

Abiram would not be coming to Kiryat-Yearim himself, but instead would be waiting for us at Nob. But a number of priests who would be prepared ritually to carry the golden box on their shoulders and a small contingent of Levites who would serve as both our help in securing the Ark and as an armed guard during the midnight journey would arrive a couple of days before Yom Teruah as well. *No one wants a civil war,*" Abiram had told me, *"but we will not take any chances."*

Although most of Abiram's reasons for carrying out this plan resonated with me, the idea of Levites lifting swords against their brethren had caused my stomach to churn uneasily when he'd laid out his plans shortly after word of Abinidab's death reached Beit El. But I'd pressed those whispers of doubt aside, reminding myself that it was not my place to question my uncle, a man who was devoted in every way to Yahweh and far above reproach. Not to mention that I would never be able to repay him for taking me into his home when I had nowhere else to go.

To my surprise, Machlon added his voice to the rising tumult. "Why are these people hiding the Ark from us anyhow?" He'd spoken only just loud enough for the men in front of us to overhear, but the sly remark hit its target nonetheless.

"A very good question," replied someone else. "How do we know they even have it anymore?"

Within moments Machlon's seemingly innocent question had been multiplied tenfold, and Tuviyah lost complete control of the men he was supposed to be leading in joint worship. When Machlon chuckled under his breath, obviously enjoying the upheaval he'd fomented, the murky feeling of uncertainly in my gut returned.

I had only vague recollections of Elazar and Abinidab, but after the way the two old women in the market had spoken of their generosity with the people of Kiryat-Yearim, along with Elazar's willingness to adopt two orphaned Philistines, it made me question some of the more vehement claims my uncle had made about their nefarious motives.

It seemed to me that if Elazar meant to set himself up as some proxy High Priest, like Abiram accused, he would not hide the Ark away in a secret place; he would display it proudly and demand tribute for its protection in order to line his purse with silver. But so far, I'd not seen any indication that he was profiting from his association with the Ark. In fact, although the compound had doubled in the last eight years to accommodate the growing family and the Levites, Elazar's home itself remained as humble as it had been back then.

"Is this necessary?" I whispered, unsettled by the gleam of satisfaction in Machlon's eyes as he observed the increasingly heated volley of words. "Won't stirring these men up do more harm than good? Perhaps even bring undue attention?"

Machlon's gaze snapped to me, but his voice remained quiet. "I am no fool, Ronen. I know what I am doing. You just focus on the girl."

The reminder was in no way subtle. There was a distinctive bite to his words that I'd rarely heard from my cousin and closest friend. My hackles rose.

"I've not forgotten my mission," I responded. "In fact, I've discovered when and where to find her alone."

His brows went high, all sharp edges instantly smoothed away. "Have you?"

I nodded but remained quiet on the subject, wary even amongst the clamor that someone might overhear talk of Eliora's garden and her daily ritual there.

"Excellent," he said, a grin growing on his face as he nudged me with his elbow and leaned in close again. "Just think, cousin, when this is all over, you and I will be lauded for our part in this. If only your father and brothers were here to see what you are doing. Honoring their memory by making things right." He gripped my shoulder affectionately. "They would be so proud of you."

He was right. I may not be comfortable with Machlon's tactics, and perhaps Abiram had exaggerated Elazar's conceit, but when the priesthood was restored to its rightful heirs, the Ark stood once again in the holy sanctuary, and my family had been returned to me, how we got there would not make any difference.

Whether or not the thought of pursuing Eliora under false pretenses made my skin crawl, I knew my mission. And tomorrow morning I would seek her out and do my duty.

Eighteen

Eliora

I wrapped my hand around a frothy clump of stalks, enjoying the cool familiarity of the soil on my fingers as I drew a purple-and-white treasure from its secret place. *Such a gift*, I thought, as I lifted the turnip high and shook the dirt from its wispy roots. I inhaled its earthy scent, tinged with the hint of natural spice. This turnip was at least twice the size of any other down in the valley.

With my knee-high basket now overflowing with creamy white carrots, parsnips, onions, and a variety of herbs and roots, I stood and brushed the dirt from my tunic, making certain my headscarf was still wrapped tightly around my head before pushing back a few wayward tendrils. Although most of the townspeople did not come to the garden this early in the morning, I always kept my hair bound, unsettled by the scrutiny of those outside my family.

Having already collected more than enough produce and herbs to bring to Rina for the stew she planned to prepare for Shabbat, I determined that my flowers had been neglected long enough. Leaving the basket on the ground to retrieve later, since it would take all my strength to heft it back to the house, I made my way toward the other end of the terrace, the place I'd rather be more than anywhere else. And today, after Natan had returned from Kesalon even more sullen and belligerent, I ached to take solace amidst their vibrant beauty.

A sharp curve in the mountain's terrain secreted my varicolored treasures, tucking them away from damaging windstorms. The indulgent mixture of fragrances beckoned me forward, drawing me into the lush forest of blooms, vines, and greens like the crook of a lover's finger.

There was no place on the earth like this one, I was certain of it. And the profusion of colors that greeted me today was particularly brilliant beneath the golden spill of sunrise over the eastern hills.

Pausing at the center of the flower garden, I closed my eyes and breathed deeply, peace washing over me as I thanked the Creator for designing a sort of beauty that not only delighted my eyes and nose but that I could pull deeply into my lungs. The chirrup of myriad birds alighting in the trees mingled with the sensory feast, making me wish I could carry this quiet moment with me throughout the day.

If only Natan was drawn to this place like I was. He needed something to quiet his soul and to drain whatever poison had settled itself in his veins. All my hopes that he might reconnect with my father and brothers during the trip to Kesalon were dashed when Natan refused to speak to anyone during the evening meal and then snapped at our mother when she dared to ask him for help carrying a heavy jug of wine.

When I questioned my father about what had happened while they were gone, his weary sigh told it all. Natan had rebuilt the wall without complaint and took part in the shearing, but had refused any attempt at conversation until my father and brothers gave up trying.

This morning, as I slipped out of the house, I overheard my parents whispering together on their bed about what could be done to tame his volatile ways before someone got hurt. I could not help but wonder, for the hundredth time, if they regretted taking us in all those years ago. Perhaps if they'd known Natan would bring such chaos into their peaceful home, they might have made a different decision.

Sighing under the weight of such burdensome thoughts, I surveyed the weeds that had sprung up over the past few days, frowning at the insidious shoots of green that threatened to choke out the ones I'd worked so hard to nurture. Eyeing a particularly thick patch of weeds between two clumps of marigolds, I knelt to begin the never-ending task of pulling the invasive sprouts from around the flowers, so familiar with each variety of plant that it was simple to discern which did not belong. If only I could tend the rocky soil in Natan's heart in the same manner, cull the thorns and weeds that seemed to choke out any peace or joy that dared lift to the surface.

As I worked, memories of my sweet Lukio and his raspy laughter arose in my mind. One moment in particular stood out from the rest. After a few hours of playing together on the beach and digging for shells, he'd wrapped his spindly arms around me and told me he loved me most in all the world. I missed the sound of his laughter and the sight of amusement in his mismatched eyes and could not help but feel responsible for the loss of both.

Unable to contain the sorrow that I'd pressed down deep for the past few days, I bent my head to pray. When I'd first come to Kiryat-Yearim, my mother had told me that Yahweh would listen even to a Philistine if my heart was fixed on him, so I allowed my sorrows to flow quietly from my lips and my tears to spill down my cheeks.

When I'd exhausted my well of desperate entreaties to the Most High, I used the edge of my headscarf to wipe my eyes and delved back into my weeding. The sun was already far too high in the sky, and I needed to return with my goods and help with meal preparation. I could no longer wallow in my hurt over Natan.

I was so caught up in yanking a particularly well-entrenched thistle and whispering threats at it for encroaching on my beautiful garden, that it wasn't until I sat back on my haunches and swiped a palm across my brow that I noticed I was not alone. I let out a little bleat of surprised confusion when I saw Ronen standing a few paces away and bounded to my feet.

My free hand went immediately to my headscarf, ensuring it was still secure as my face flamed. How long had he been watching me?

"I did not mean to startle you," he said, palms uplifted. He remained where he was, but his eyes traveled from me to my flower garden, causing a flutter of unease in my stomach as he surveyed the work of my hands. Thank Adonai that Ronen had not arrived earlier to find me salting the soil with my tears. I could not imagine the humiliation of knowing he'd seen me in such a state.

"This place is . . ." His voice disappeared as he stepped forward, taking in one of the long-limbed explosions of vines that I'd twined around a tripod of sticks and now cascaded in a waterfall of spiky pink blossoms.

"I've never seen anything like this," he said as he leaned forward to smell the flowers, his eyelids dropping closed as he inhaled their delicate fragrance.

My heart was still galloping from the suddenness of his appearance, but his obvious appreciation of my cherished garden helped soothe a small measure of my agitation at being caught by surprise.

"How did you make all this?" He waved a hand at the groupings of flowers that I'd lined along the terrace. Those that seemed to need more sunlight were at the front and those that thrived in partial shade nearer to the trees—distinctions I'd made by trial and error over the years.

I shrugged, turning my face toward my flowers to avoid his scrutiny and praying he did not notice that my eyes were swollen and likely tinged with red. "I was told that some of the local flowers grew better up here on the mountain than down in the valley, their blooms larger and stalks taller. So I asked my father if I could use a small portion of the terrace to cultivate flowers instead of vegetables. None of us expected them to grow so prolifically.

Over time, I've expanded the flower garden to almost five times its original size."

"It *is* like a paradise here," he said, making me wonder what exactly he'd been told about my garden. He bent to brush his fingers over the blue petals of another cluster of blooms that bobbed and swayed in the breeze. "I've never seen this variety before. What is it called?"

"I do not know," I replied. "That is one someone brought me."

"From where?"

"Somewhere to the east. A few travelers who came to visit my father heard of my gardens, and now they bring me seeds, or even seedlings in some cases, whenever they trade in the area. Some have thrived, taking well to the soil here and the amount of rain the terraces retain, but others have barely sprouted, or withered the moment their shoots reach above the surface."

"The rumor is that your hands are blessed," he said, with a curious tilt to his chin.

I knew of these speculations—had been told by my sisters of whispers down in Kiryat-Yearim of some divine favor bestowed upon my ministrations—but the truth had nothing to do with me. I was only the keeper of the gardens, the one who took pleasure in removing the weeds that threatened their health, the one who ensured each plant was receiving its share of the rain and not being shaded by another. It was not my hands that made this garden what it was, but the golden chest that resided two-thousand cubits away in a grove of stately cedar trees.

"I am only a servant in these gardens. The real blessing flows from the presence of the Ark on the mountain."

He frowned, a disbelieving crease between his black brows. "You think the Ark of the Covenant is the reason for all this?"

I laughed softly. "The vitality of these plants has little to do with me. I merely tend to their needs and enjoy their offerings. This is why anyone from the town below is welcome to come here, harvest vegetables or fruit, collect herbs to spice their food, or even gather flowers to brighten their tables and homes. It may

158

be mostly my hands that work in these gardens, but they belong to all of us."

His gaze locked on my face, blinking at me like I was a stranger whose language he was attempting to decipher. Unsettled by the pointed scrutiny, I brushed dirt from my tunic, hoping to sway the subject away from myself.

"Is there some way I can be of service to you?" I asked, suddenly realizing that his presence here was odd. Everyone had so much to do to prepare for the upcoming celebrations, and the musicians would be no exception.

He cleared his throat, shaking his head as if loosening some thought that had taken hold. "I . . . I came to see if I can be of service to you."

"To me?" I asked incredulously.

"I've heard that your sisters deliver goods from your gardens down to the village on a regular basis, but that in all the upheaval with the wedding and the festival, it has been a couple of weeks since they've been able to do so."

A warm flush crept up my cheeks. "That is true. We've had such an abundance of melons and gourds recently that I'll need to find someone to make another trip down before they go to waste. As I said, many of the townspeople come to pick their own food, but there are a number of those who are elderly who cannot make the steep journey, so their deliveries are made first. I planned to send some down to your camp as well, since there is plenty to go around."

"And that is where I come in," he said, his arms stretched wide. "Think of me as your very humble servant." He bowed with a grin that belied his words.

Thrown by the unexpected offer, and the way my pulse stumbled whenever he directed that bright smile at me, I stuttered, "Don't you have things . . . plans to attend to? Songs to prepare?"

The amusement immediately faded from his face. "My part is minimal for now. I've already repaired the instruments that were damaged during the journey here, and I must be available in case anything else breaks during practices, but I'm certain I'll have a few hours of extra time each day."

"But don't you need to practice with the others? Will the choir be singing some of your compositions?"

Even though I'd understood little about the creation of music, I knew for certain that Ronen was a talented songwriter. He'd captured me with his voice that first day, as surely as if he'd tied me to that crumbling sheep pen. I'd been unable to move for fear of breaking the spell he'd woven within the space of only a few notes. I could only imagine that after all these years of training at the feet of master musicians, his music must be even more enthralling.

A shadow of something indecipherable moved across his face. "I have not composed in a very long time," he said, his tone clipped. "My skills as an instrument builder are far more necessary right now."

Bewildered by the terseness of his answer, and the surprising undertone of anger that lay beneath it, I dropped my eyes to the weeds still clutched in my dirty fist, feeling foolish. For as much as I'd held Ronen up in my mind as a savior, I really did not know him. He must think me ridiculous for my assumptions.

"Thank you for your offer." I tossed the thistle aside, suddenly eager for him to go. "But it is really not necessary. I'll manage."

Yet, in truth, I *was* in desperate need of help this week. The rest of my family had been busy lately, both with the wedding and with preparations for our many anticipated guests during the festivals. But perhaps I could talk Natan into helping me instead. Anything to keep him occupied and away from the Gibeonites would be worthwhile.

"Did your brother return unharmed the other night?" he asked, discerning my thoughts and ignoring my refusal of his offer. "After we spoke on the roof?"

I frowned, confused by the sudden turn of the conversation. "Other than a few bruises and scrapes—which he well deserved—and a foul-smelling tunic that took hours to scrub clean. Yes, he returned unscathed."

"What happened?" His voice was soft, sympathetic. But I was still unnerved from his earlier rebuff, so I settled for a brief explanation that would not press too hard into the tender spots left uncovered by my gut-wrenching prayers earlier.

"The same thing that has happened many times. He went off with friends, some Gibeonite boys, and they wreaked havoc on some poor shepherd's sheepfold. My father and brothers went back with him to rebuild the walls and make restitution for his folly."

He hummed in thought, his eyes skimming slowly over my flowers again before they came back to land on me. "Perhaps I can be of help in that regard as well?"

"How so?"

"He seemed to respond to me all those years ago," he said. "Perhaps he would again?"

I huffed a breathy laugh. "It would take more than a game of dice and a few stories to gain his trust now, I'm afraid. My father and both my brothers have tried and failed to draw him out. He refuses every attempt." I glanced away again, blinking my eyes against the renewed threat of tears.

"Then what would it hurt for me to try?"

I crouched down, turning my attention to an invasive patch of clover that encircled a densely blooming mallow bush. "I am certain you have far more important things to tend than my difficulties with Natan."

He did not respond, and I took his silence as agreement, allowing the quiet to fall softly between us as I continued to clear the soil around the prolific explosion of yellow blossoms. I was still at a loss as to why Ronen had even sought me out this morning. Something made me suspect that it was not simply to help me in the garden, but I did not have the courage to press the issue. When I was satisfied that the mallow was no longer under threat of suffocation, I plucked a handful of the edible leaves and then stood to brush the dirt from my tunic.

Ronen's attention was on some far point, as if he could see

through the dense forest to the other side of the mountain, and beyond it the sea beside which I used to live a very different life than the one I did now.

"I must be off," I said, forcing a smile. "Rina will be wondering why I've not returned with the bulk of the ingredients for her stew."

Ronen wrinkled his brow, taking in my small handful of leaves. "I certainly hope there will be more to this stew than that." The amused twitch of his lips grew into a wide grin that reminded me of the time he spent playing dice with Natan, and how he'd laughed with gusto as my seven-year-old brother beat him effortlessly.

"I've left my very full basket over there." I gestured toward the far end of the terrace, unable to restrain a responding grin to his tease. It seemed whatever cloud that had come over him when I asked about his songs had dissipated. Gone was the disconcerting flash of annoyance, replaced by the same warmth and confident ease that had made me trust him from the beginning.

"Then I will help you carry your very full basket back to the house," he said, waving a hand to usher me forward. "And tomorrow I, along with a couple of my friends, will be here early to help you harvest all those wonderful melons and gourds I've heard so much about. Perhaps I'll even get a chance to speak with this wayward brother of yours—see if I might offer a fresh voice of counsel on the type of company he's been keeping. I can be quite persuasive, I'm told." He winked, proving his own argument.

Obviously my refusal of help had been tacitly ignored. Although I wasn't certain that I welcomed other strange men disturbing my early mornings alone with my vegetables and flowers, I could use extra hands in the garden, and his concern for Natan did seem genuine. Perhaps Yahweh *had* answered my prayers for something to reach my brother's stony heart by bringing Ronen back to Kiryat-Yearim.

Nineteen

Relying on the familiar motions of slicing gourds from their vines to keep my attention away from Ronen, who'd indeed appeared this morning with his twin friends to help with the harvest, I startled when my name echoed across the garden, bouncing off the trees.

Before I could even determine which direction the sound was coming from, it repeated twice more, each time with more desperation. Bounding to my feet, I searched for the source of the frantic call as a girl appeared around a bend in the terrace, her long hair streaming out behind her like a brown ribbon and abject horror on her face. Realizing it was Shoshana, the daughter of Menash, one of the Levites who guarded the Ark, I dropped the yellow gourd I'd just picked, along with my knife, and jogged forward to meet her.

"You must come!" she called out as she stumbled to a halt in front of me. Her entire body was trembling, and her large hazel eyes were swimming in tears. "It's Lu . . . Natan. He'll be killed!"

My blood went still, and a faint ringing began in my ears.

"What do you mean? Where is he?" My own voice sounded distant as I gripped her arm.

"He and Medad are fighting, and it's so awful. Neither one of them will stop, they just keep pummeling each other. I tried—I tried so hard. I called his name and called his name, and he just refuses to listen. You have to come! He will listen to you, I know it!"

My chest pinched at the image her words created, one in which the Natan of the present was mingled with the Lukio of the past. The one whose bloody lip and black eye reminded me that I'd failed to keep my little brother safe.

"What is happening?" asked a deep voice that somehow cut through the pulsing chaos in my head.

Ronen was suddenly next to me, concern on his face.

"My brother has gotten into an altercation," I said, through the burn of tears in my throat. "I—I have to go."

Even as I spoke the words, panic began to well. It had been so long since I'd walked down the trail to Kiryat-Yearim, and even the idea of doing so made sweat break out on my forehead and my throat tight. But the thought of my brother in such danger was even more terrifying than leaving the only place I felt truly safe.

"I'm coming with you," Ronen said, his tone brooking no argument as he gestured for Osher and Shelah to follow. Although my heart thundered and jolted with every step away from the top of the mountain, I bounded down the jagged trail behind Shoshana, who'd not stopped weeping since she appeared in the garden.

When we were about halfway to the town, Shoshana suddenly dashed off the trail, pressing through the brush toward a small clearing up ahead. We heard the fight well before we saw it. The horrific sounds of flesh hitting flesh, along with a number of angry voices filtered through the trees as we neared the melee.

Medad's two brothers were on one side of the clearing, their faces twisted with menace as they screamed encouragement to their older brother. A few other young people from Kiryat-Yearim watched the chaos with varying shades of support for both opponents spewing from their lips. Adnan and Padi were there as well but spun around and left the moment they spotted me, belying Natan's assurances about their loyalty.

I heard the name "Demon Eyes" called out more than once, which I assumed was a spiteful moniker to mock Natan's mismatched eye color. But nothing prepared me for the sight of my brother straddling the other young man, his bloody fists swinging with such fury that they were nearly a blur.

I gasped his name on a sob, but his concentration was on his grim task.

Ronen charged forward, not hesitating to grab Natan by the tunic with both hands. But my brother would not be moved, ignoring Ronen's every attempt to pull him off Medad, unceasing in his relentless assault.

Blood was everywhere. On his knuckles, his face, his clothes. Both young men looked like they'd been to war.

I screamed my brother's name over and over, but he was deaf to me.

Ronen's friends joined the fray, and together the three of them used their joint strength to drag Natan backward, ignoring the vile curses that spewed from his mouth as they did so.

As soon as they gave him a bit of slack, Natan swung around, fist flying. Thankfully, Ronen anticipated the move, avoiding the blow with a surprisingly swift dodge. His friends regained their hold, one restraining his arms and the other latching on a choke-hold.

"Natan!" Ronen yelled, with a commanding edge in his voice that shocked me. "Your sister is watching! Stop this, now!"

Although his teeth were gritted and his face red, Natan's eyes wheeled toward where I stood with both hands over my mouth and tears soaking the sleeves of my tunic. He jerked his body, still fighting the hold the men had on him.

"Lukio!" bellowed Ronen. "Stop fighting them!"

Natan flinched at the sound of his birth name, his attention snapping back to Ronen. He gaped at the Levite, but then his eyes dropped to Ronen's neckline, where the lion claw necklace he'd been so enamored with as a child still hung on the same leather cord.

"You," he said, blinking rapidly. "You're that . . ."

Ronen nodded. "And just like that day, I am here to help. My friends and I mean you no harm."

My chest shuddered with trapped sobs, and, at my back, Shoshana trembled, her fingers clutching my tunic so tightly that I felt her fingernails digging into my skin.

Chest still heaving, Natan's body slowly relaxed, even if his jaw was still as tight as a bowstring. The Levites did not release him, rightly guessing that if let free my brother might re-engage with Medad.

However, a glance to my right showed that already the young man's brothers had him on his feet and slung between them as he limped off into the woods. The rest of the onlookers had already filtered away as well, uninterested once the fists stopped flying.

"You could have killed him," I said to Natan, my words a painful rasp against a throat aching from screaming his name.

"Given what he said, I had every right to," he spat out.

"What did he say?" I asked, taken aback by the vitriol in his tone.

He pressed his bloodied lips together, his nostrils flaring.

"Natan," I urged.

His brown and green eyes narrowed on me sharply. "He called you the product of a pagan and a temple whore at the foot of Dagon."

My mouth went dry as the blood seemed to drain from my face. I was not innocent to the ways my people worshiped their gods—little had been hidden even from my young eyes at the temple. Not only had my uncle been a High Priest of Dagon—to whom public fertility rites were performed without shame—but my aunt had been devoted to the Serpent Goddess, whose bare-breasted priestesses handled all manners of snakes in their rituals, some whose bites were known to cause the women to fall to the ground, bodies writhing and seizing as they divined all manner of prophecies. Nothing could wash away such disturbing images from my mind, but I'd hoped that Natan at least might be ignorant to some of the more lurid aspects of our past, since he'd been so young. However, it seemed I'd been the ignorant one.

"As vile an accusation as that is," said Ronen, "this could have been dealt with without bloodshed."

"What say do you have in any of it?" snarled Natan. "Whether or not you stumbled across us as children does not mean you have authority over me."

Ronen heaved an exasperated sigh. "Perhaps not. But your sister is right that you could have killed that boy if we had not arrived in time."

"He attacked me first," said Natan with a belligerent sneer.

"Doesn't matter. Anyone with eyes could see that you had no intention of stopping. And that would mean the penalty of death for you."

Natan jerked his head to the side, his jaw grinding as he glared off into the trees.

Ronen gestured to his friends, who slowly released my brother and then backed away. "If it had been my own sister, I might have been tempted to react in much the same way. But you lost that fight the moment you lost control."

"I knew what I was doing," Natan said, eyes now narrowed on Ronen and chin lifted. "He got what he deserved."

Ronen's answer was sharp as a blade. "Does your sister deserve to watch you be stoned to death?"

My brother's gaze slid back to me, and my heart squeezed between the equal weights of both my love and my worry for him. I stepped forward, the desire to embrace him nearly overwhelming. But he spun around, and after roughly brushing past Ronen's friends, bumping their shoulders unapologetically as he did so, strode up the trail.

"Let him go," said Ronen, his eyes on my brother's retreating back, but none of the edge leaving his voice. "He needs time to let his blood cool completely before anyone can reason with him."

Although it galled me to stop my feet from following, Ronen was right. Natan needed to uncoil himself first or he would hear no one.

I guessed where he might be headed—a cave he'd discovered on the west side of the mountain years ago. Although I'd once secretly followed him there, after an argument that left both of us tangled in frustration and hurt, I would never intrude on his secret refuge. I had my own place of retreat and understood the need for solitude when my soul was heavy.

"He's right that Medad instigated the fight." Shoshana released her grip on the back of my tunic and emerged with tearstains on her freckled cheeks. Distracted as I was, I'd forgotten that she'd been hiding behind me this entire time. "Medad has been pushing him for as far back as I can remember, insulting him, calling him 'Demon Eyes.' But I knew when he slandered you so terribly that Natan would not stand for it."

"How did you happen to witness all this?" I asked. "Were you with them?"

"No," she said. "I saw Natan and his friends leaving the marketplace and noticed Medad and his brothers follow them into the woods. I—I just knew something awful was afoot. So, I trailed them here." Her eyes filled with tears again as she looked at the empty trail where Natan had disappeared. "I couldn't bear to see him ambushed. I meant to warn him. But I was too late. . . ."

Something on her face told me she was more personally invested in Natan's safety than I had guessed, and I wondered what her father might think of such affection. She was nearly thirteen, not all that much younger than Natan. But even were he not Philistine, my brother had a few years before he'd be considered ready to sustain a wife and family. And perhaps the tenderness she harbored for him was only on her part, since I'd never heard Natan speak of her or noticed them together before.

"You did well," I said, pressing a kiss to the girl's forehead. "Thank you for alerting me. You may well have saved two lives today."

"I've never seen him like that," she half-whispered, then lifted a sad smile, her hazel eyes still shimmering. "I just wish I'd gotten to him sooner."

"He'll be fine," I said, my false assurance likely fooling no one.

"Osher. Shelah. Will you see this brave young woman home?" Ronen asked his friends. Although his tone was mild, I could tell that he was still shaken from confronting Natan. "I'll accompany Eliora back up the mountain and we'll finish in the garden when you return."

"It would be our honor," said Osher, gesturing for Shoshana to lead the way with a reassuring smile.

Shoshana looked up at me with a question between her brows. These men were as much strangers to her as they were to me—not to mention imposing with their large, identical builds. But as I had from nearly the beginning, I trusted Ronen. Even more so after what he'd done here today.

"Go on," I said. "They are consecrated Levites. They will keep you safe."

Satisfied with my endorsement, she took one more longing look toward the empty trail and walked away, leaving Ronen and me alone in the silent clearing.

"I can certainly see now why you've been so upset about your brother," Ronen said, a grim undercurrent to his tone. He ran a hand over his mouth and beard—a hand I noticed was trembling slightly. "He's not a little boy with a pouch full of dice anymore, is he?"

"No," I whispered. "No, he is not."

"Is your family not aware? Do they not see what a danger he is to himself? And others?" He swiped a palm in the direction Medad's brothers had led their bloodied sibling away from the clearing.

"They are worried for him, of course," I said, surprised that he was still so agitated. "Just as I am. But . . ."

He lifted his brows when my voice trailed away, waiting for me to finish my thought. But there were things I'd never spoken aloud, things that had remained between me, Yahweh, and the flowers in my garden, and I was uncertain whether I even knew how to say them, let alone reveal them to this man I barely knew. But then I remembered how he'd awakened Natan to his surroundings by reminding him that I was watching, somehow knowing that above anything else *that* was what my brother would respond to. He understood the bond the two of us shared, even if that once-strong connection had been corroded over the years.

I let out a shuddering sigh, keeping my gaze averted from Ronen, whose breaths were still rapid and whose fists were tightly clenched at his sides, almost making me wish I could reach out and lay a calming hand on his.

"Sometimes I still see that grinning little boy in my mind," I said. "Whenever he lets out a rare laugh, or when he calls me Risi. . . . There are glimpses of him there, deep inside. *My* Lukio is in there somewhere. . . . Yet I can't help but think that there is also quite a bit of our father inside him too."

"Elazar?"

"No," I said. "Our Philistine father."

Ronen remained silent, giving me space to explore the memories that swam in my mind, some of them sharp and clear and some of them blurred, like I was peering at them through murky water.

"Our mother died when my brother was born," I said. "I never understood exactly why, because I was so young when it happened. One day she was holding me on her lap and letting me feel for Lukio's kicks in her belly, and the next she was gone."

I paused, wishing I could forget the screams that echoed through our home that night and the horrible silence that followed.

"Afterward—the very next day, in fact—my father disappeared. He went to sea on one of his ships and was gone for months. When he came back, he was not the same man."

I lifted a small smile, skimming through a deep-seated memory, one that I'd clung to after he'd changed. "I remember riding on his shoulders during the festival of the new year, watching a parade of the gods through the city. And I even remember his laugh. . . . But after he returned from the sea, he did not smile, he did not laugh, and when I ran to him, excited that he was back, he pushed me away, saying he was tired from his journeys and to run along. He never asked to see Lukio, his firstborn son. Never even held him, as far as I know."

It had been during that time that my nightmares had been at their worst, those full-throated screams of my dying mother reverberating through my dreams until Azuvah's steady presence in

170

my bed, and the stories of Israel that she whispered each night in her soothing language, assuaged the terrors.

The titter of a wren on a branch nearby brought me back to the moment. Ronen's dark eyes were intent on me, but he'd calmed as I spoke, his jaw relaxed and his fists no longer clenched.

"That was one of the last times that I remember my father speaking directly to me. He would spend days locked in his chambers, not saying a word to anyone other than to demand the servants bring him fresh wine but refusing any food. Then, at times, he would go out and be gone all night, returning the next day bloodied and bruised from meeting opponents on the fighting grounds. And then there were the days he would rage—screaming at the servants, throwing furniture, cutting my mother's clothing to pieces, and shattering her cosmetics jars and accoutrements on the stone floor."

He'd worshiped her, Azuvah had told me. His heart had been broken into as many pieces as those pots and jars he destroyed.

"But then one day when Lukio was just over two years old, our father was brought back to our home, barely conscious and with a deep laceration on his face. And I overheard one of his friends tell a manservant that my father had beaten someone to death during a fight. It was not long after that that he took us to my aunt and uncle's house and left us there."

"He's your responsibility," he'd told me as I stood at the threshold of Jacame and Harrom's home, trembling as my father addressed me for the first time in months and for the last time ever. *"Keep him safe, or the last part of her will be gone."* Even though I knew he was speaking of Lukio, he'd not even glanced at the tiny boy sleeping on Azuvah's shoulder before he walked away, and I wondered now if the sight of him, of both of us, was too much a reminder of our mother, whose death had shattered him beyond repair.

"We never saw him again. He'd originally come to Philistia as a young man from a far northern country across the sea, but the moment he saw my mother in the market he vowed to remain. My aunt told me she suspected he'd returned to that distant country because nothing was ever heard of him after that."

He'd left behind his thriving trading business, his home, his wealth, and his children without ever looking back.

"I fear that within Natan lies the same demons my father seemed to battle," I said. "He is so much like him—his height, his strength, his coloring, even his voice. . . . And what if . . . ?" I pulled in a deep breath, blinking the blur of tears away. "What if next time, he doesn't stop? What if he ends up just like my father? As you said, Torah law does not allow a murderer to live, even if in Ashdod my father faced no such justice. In fact, he was undoubtedly lauded for slaying the other man and paid well for his victory."

"Have you told your parents this?" Ronen asked.

I shook my head, a wash of embarrassment warming my face.

"Perhaps it is time to do so?"

And perhaps it was. My fears had become a reality today. My brother was walking the edge of the same cliff my father had in his anger and bitterness, and I could not bear to see Natan topple into a similar abyss. But none of that involved Ronen.

"Thank you," I said in a rush, "for what you did here today. If I'd been alone . . ." I shook my head, trying to push aside the images such a thought conjured. "I am grateful that you stopped him when you did. You came to our rescue. Once again."

His gaze was intent on me but no longer edged with latent agitation over the fight, and even though I was thoroughly embarrassed over unburdening myself to a near-stranger, I was glad that he'd calmed in the meantime.

"We should head back up to the garden," I said, pulling a smile across my lips to cover my growing discomfort, both with the conversation and with being this far away from the summit of the mountain. "I don't want to keep you and your friends longer than necessary."

"We are at your service," he said, a spark of humor alighting in his dark brown eyes. "We'll not be missed among the growing number of Levites who have arrived over the past few days. And we are glad to be your pack mules for the day. There is nowhere else I would rather be."

Something about that statement, paired with the leisurely way his eyes traveled over my face, warmed my blood in a new way. I'd always thought Ronen handsome, even when I was only twelve, but his features had matured into strong, masculine lines that I was now hard-pressed to keep from dwelling upon too long. And the manner in which he was looking at me now reminded me that I was no longer a girl either.

He'd thrown himself between Natan and Medad without hesitation, for *my* sake, and instead of scorning me for being the daughter of a murderer or disparaging my Philistine heritage, he'd responded with a gentle tease and a genuine smile that caused my heartbeat to quicken.

"You must join me for a meal," I blurted out, to distract my own mind from going down paths that were better left unexplored. "My family . . . I mean. Tomorrow. On Shabbat. With all the extra produce we're harvesting today there will be plenty of food for you and your friends."

"Are you certain your parents will welcome our intrusion on your family gathering?"

"Without a doubt," I said. "Especially after they hear what happened here today, they will want to thank you in person."

"Not necessary," he said, with a dismissive wave. "But we will be more than happy to accept your invitation to enjoy the fruits of our heavy labors. After all, the Torah commands us not to muzzle the ox as he treads the corn, does it not?"

I laughed at his tease, relieved that he could not decipher the embarrassing notions that had been forcing their way to the surface. Ronen's time here in Kiryat-Yearim was temporary, and my attraction to him was futile. But I would always remember the way he'd dashed to my aid without question today, and I was glad that I'd trusted him with a small piece of my ugly past.

Twenty

I took advantage of my long-legged stride on the trail in order to be the first to arrive at the spring that gushed from a crack between two boulders not too far from our home. Still, I had only a few moments to bask in the quiet before my sisters joined me.

A multitude of birds filled the forest with song as a cool breeze whispered through the leaves and fluttered the edges of my head-scarf to tease the fine curls at my nape. I dipped my jug into the icy stream, filling the vessel with fresh, clean water before sitting back on my haunches to breathe deeply of the green-scented air and thank Yahweh for such extravagant provision.

Azuvah and the other servants in Ashdod had walked for hours back and forth from the well with their water jugs each day, and the labor took a heavy toll on their bodies. Yet I had only to walk about a thousand paces from our doorstep to find one of the many streams of clean water that bubbled up from deep in the earth, flowing down the mountainside in cascades that I'd been told had appeared only *after* the Ark rested at Kiryat-Yearim.

Miri appeared at my shoulder with her own empty jug, panting from her attempt to catch up to me. Rina and Safira would be along shortly, since the four of us had been asked to retrieve fresh water for our guests to wash their feet this evening.

"You always win," she pouted. "Your legs are far too long."

The comment was not meant to wound, but it stung nonetheless.

"You are the one who issued the challenge," I said. *And had you not been pressing me for information about Ronen earlier*, I thought, *I wouldn't have accepted.* I did not know how to talk about him without a flush coming to my cheeks. And I had no interest in explaining the unbidden reaction to my sisters.

She sighed and knelt beside me, dipping her jug into the water, and I prayed that our brief conversation back on the path was forgotten.

"Does Abba know Ronen and his friends are coming for Shabbat?" she asked, destroying my hopes.

"Of course," I said, holding back a groan of frustration. I should have known Miri would not let go of the subject. I willed my cheeks not to redden as her eyes sparkled at me. She was far too intuitive for a girl of thirteen.

Her lips curved into a demure smile that betrayed the mischief behind it. "Are his friends as handsome as he is? I only saw him for a moment when he carried your basket home from the garden, but I thought his appearance was quite pleasing."

My face blazed. "I invited them all out of gratitude, nothing else."

She raised a brow. "Are you certain of that?"

"We harvested more produce in those few hours yesterday than I did in all of the past two weeks alone. And they delivered three loads of food to the people down in the village," I said, then leveled my own teasing gaze at her. "If only I could have that much help every day. *You* were certainly nowhere to be found when I was asking for volunteers."

"I was helping Rina, Safira, and Ima with preparations for tonight's meal," she retorted. "Besides, I would much rather have my hands elbow-deep in dough than dirt."

I laughed, brushing my knuckles down her cheek. "I know, sister. I don't expect everyone to enjoy the lovely feel of dirt beneath their fingernails as much as I do."

She wrinkled her nose, and I laughed harder at her undisguised revulsion. She'd always been fastidious, barely tolerating any sort of stickiness on her hands or face when she was small and fuming whenever our brothers tracked mud across the woven rugs in our home. For as much as I loathed the tiresome job of scrubbing laundry until my knuckles were raw, Miri seemed to take pleasure in it, as if by cleansing the fabric her worries were washed away with the stains.

"I *might* be a small bit more amenable to digging around in your garden if Ronen and his friends continue to appear there," she said, an impish grin twisting her lips. "Even if it means dirt beneath my fingernails."

Rina and Safira joined us then, their own empty jugs perched on their hips. Although they were both now married, they'd been joined to Levite men who lived in the house next door and therefore hadn't been forced to move away from Kiryat-Yearim, like some of our cousins who married men from other towns. I was grateful our Shabbat gatherings still included my sisters and prayed it would always be so. I did not know what I would do without them.

When I'd first arrived in Kiryat-Yearim, I'd hoped to make friends with other girls my age, but it had not taken long to realize that my appearance made me stand out in town. Curious looks and whispers followed me everywhere, until it became much easier for me to stay on top of the mountain, where I was safe and secure. Up here, I could avoid reminders that, as Natan had said, I would never truly be one of them.

"And who is this Ronen?" Rina asked, deflating my hopes yet again that the subject would be dropped. "I heard we are to have visitors tonight."

I cleared my throat and looked down at my hands. "He is the same Levite who found Natan and me all those years ago. He returned with the musicians and has been helping me in the gardens."

Rina and Safira exchanged a look of surprise.

"And Abba approves?" asked Safira.

"Of course," I responded. "He is grateful the musicians have been aiding me with the harvest while everyone else is so busy."

I did not add that when he heard of Natan's altercation yesterday, and Ronen's part in stopping it, my father had immediately walked down the hill to personally thank them for their intervention and reaffirm the invitation. As far as I knew, my sisters had not heard of the fight, and I had no desire to discuss Natan's foolish behavior.

"I mean," said Safira, with a touch of amused condescension, "does he approve of a match between the two of you?"

My jaw dropped open as I blinked down at her, words refusing to slip easily past the confused knot in my throat. "No . . . it's . . . he is only coming for the meal. To thank him . . . it's not for me."

Rina's lips twitched. "It is far past the time when you should be joined with a good man, Eliora. And he is a Levite, after all. Of course Abba would approve of such a union."

I heard such statements many times from my eldest sister and from my mother: gentle reminders that I was older than Safira and not even betrothed, and that Abba would be thrilled to find a worthy husband for me. But I knew the way of things. I held no foolish notions in my head that one of the Hebrew men from our town might select me over all the young women whose family lines were drawn all the way back to Avraham. I may be joined in covenant with the Hebrews, but my blood was of the people of the sea.

"I am content as I am," I said, lifting my chin.

Rina set her water jug atop one of the flat boulders near the stream, then approached me with an expression that held both compassion and determination.

"We know you are content," she said. "You are the least greedy woman I've ever known, and even from the first day you came to us you were thankful for everything that was offered to you. You are eminently humble, and your dedication to serving both our family and the men who guard the Ark is unparalleled. But that doesn't mean you should push aside the desire to marry, Eliora."

Her words were kind and meant to be encouraging. But I could not help but wonder why they all continued to push so hard for me to marry. Would they be relieved when I no longer lived under Elazar and Yoela's roof? Were they disappointed that it had taken so long for me to leave?

I inhaled a sharp breath, disturbed that I was even entertaining such thoughts. But this conversation had dredged up fears I'd long thought buried.

"And you will be a wonderful mother," added Safira, oblivious to my silent distress. "You took care of Natan when he was small, protecting and guiding him after you lost your mother, and you will raise your own children with the same strength and dignity. It would be a tragedy if you did not have the chance to do so."

And yet Natan has become little more than a snarling, wounded animal, I thought. No matter how hard I tried, I was a poor stand-in for our mother.

Surrounded as I was by the three of them, I did not anticipate Miri snatching my loosening headscarf. My hair tumbled down, its length unwinding in a golden-brown spiral over my shoulder, the tail end of it dangling near my waist.

"If you would stop hiding all of this," she said, grinning, "Abba would not be able to decide between all the potential bridegrooms."

Face hot, I grabbed for the brown cloth, but Miri giggled and spun away, taunting me with the fluttering fabric. "If Ronen saw what was beneath these hideous headscarves you insist on wearing, he'd not be able to peel his eyes away."

Her laughter jangled my nerves, and a rush of aggravation barreled through me. Before I could think to stop myself, I used my long legs to dash over to her and snatched back the length of cloth.

"That is the last thing I want," I said, my words razor sharp and so loud that they echoed off the surrounding trees. "Why don't you all just leave me alone?"

Miri's jaw gaped at my cutting words and the force of my anger.

Hands shaking, I turned my back to her and rewrapped my hair in the cloth. I looped the fabric over the thick waves in the same fashion I had since I was younger than Miri, having found the attention unbearable whenever I left my head uncovered. As I did so, I worked to calm my breathing and willed my thundering pulse to slow.

My sisters said nothing, likely too shocked by my fit of temper to speak. Once my hair was wrangled into place, along with my unruly tongue, I entwined my still-trembling fingers at my waist and turned back to face the three of them. I'd never, in all the years I'd lived here, even raised my voice. They must be horrified by such awful behavior. I would not even blame them if they turned their backs and left me alone by the stream to drown in regret.

"I am so sorry, Miri," I said, shame flowing all the way down to my toes. "I should not have snapped at you. Please . . . please forgive me."

Rina and Safira stared at me with matching looks of confusion, but Miri rushed to me, throwing her arms around my waist, tears in her dark eyes. "Oh, Eliora, I am the one who should apologize. I did not mean to embarrass you."

"No. . . . It is I who am in the wrong," I stuttered as I returned the embrace. "I cannot believe that I yelled at you."

"I deserved it," she mumbled against my chest. "I pushed too hard. I am awful."

My own eyes blurred as I squeezed her tightly. "You are nothing of the sort."

Suddenly Rina and Safira were wrapped around Miri and me, the four of us locked in a joint embrace as they murmured assurances that my fit of temper was justified and that they would not shove me toward marriage again. My heart pulsed with love for my sisters, the ache of gratitude overcoming the embarrassment of my offense. How could I have believed for even a moment that they meant to push me into marriage to be rid of me? They'd never done or said anything that warranted such uncharitable notions.

And no matter that their harmless teasing had prodded the tender place inside me that wished Ronen would see me as someone other than the Philistine girl he found behind a rock wall, he was here only temporarily.

Once the festivals were complete, he would return to Beit El, and I would remain where I belonged. I had no interest in leaving the only place in the world I felt safe for even a day—let alone the rest of my life. I would control both my tongue and the foolish flutterings that winged around inside my chest whenever Ronen smiled at me, because I refused to live on the outside of Elazar's household ever again.

Twenty-One

The rains had come early, nearly undoing our plans for a large Shabbat gathering. But years ago, my father had commissioned an enormous tent for this very reason, since many were the days on this lush mountainside when the common courtyard became a muddy mess during the wet months. So, while my sisters and I had been hauling water from the stream, the men had raised the rainproof shelter fashioned from treated animal hides, stringing it between pillars and propping up the center with sturdy poles long before the first fat drops fell from the sky. With tightly woven goat-hair walls on each side and a thick hide roof, we would enjoy a warm and protected evening with our loved ones and guests.

I did my best to forget that Ronen would soon arrive, and the confusing emotions that thought inspired, as Miri and I gathered all the rugs from inside our home, and those of our neighbors, to spread upon the cold ground. In the very center of the tent, we prepared a fire, one that would lend light and heat, but whose smoke would drift upward through the hole in the roof created for that purpose.

When that task was finished and Miri had slipped out to help Rina with the food, I collected a few clay lamps and filled them with fresh oil from a stoppered jug. I'd only just laid one fresh wick of twisted linen in the first lamp when a sharp series of barks rang out in the courtyard. Then, to my shock, two furry blurs burst into the tent, one small one with a long bristling tail and the larger one with floppy ears, hackles raised, and teeth bared.

I cried out, dropping the clean wicks onto the packed dirt as I attempted to get out of the haphazard path of the dog and his prey, a gray squirrel that tried to take refuge behind one of the braziers I'd placed in the corner of the tent. The dog barked as he darted back and forth, trying to corner his quarry. Even though I knew this to be a pet of one of the Levite guards, the sound made the hair on my neck and arms rise, ushering me back to Ashdod in an instant, to my ninth year and the last time I'd been so close to a canine.

A little dog had followed me to Jacame's home after I'd delivered a message to her daughter-in-law across town. With her ribs showing beneath her mottled black-and-brown coat and her belly distended, it was plain that she was not only pregnant but starving. Wild dogs were common outside the city, scavenging among the refuse piles, some roaming in vicious packs to protect themselves from the humans that hunted them for meat, but I'd rarely seen one within the city walls, especially one that seemed in no way aggressive. Instead, she'd looked up at me with an almost audible plea for help that no nine-year-old girl could resist.

The moment I'd arrived back at the villa, I'd pilfered some pork trimmings from the kitchen refuse pot, wondering if the dog had waited near the back door. To my surprise not only was she there when I returned with the scraps, but once she devoured them, she rubbed her head against me and licked my hand before running off.

For the next two weeks, she appeared at the back door nearly every morning, lying low in a shady corner behind the house until I appeared with whatever remnant I could tuck away during meals. I was careful that no one might see me sneaking food to her. Jacame especially had a fear of dogs after some childhood incident, and I did not want one of her maidservants running off my little friend.

But all of my clandestine efforts were for naught because suddenly the dog stopped coming. And no matter that I wandered up and down the street for days, hoping she would appear, she seemed to be gone.

A week later, Harrom called the household to gather before the rubble of the small home next door, which he'd purchased from an indebted neighbor. He'd razed the home in order to expand his own villa, planning to construct an impressive vestibule that would display his wealth to visitors in grand fashion. With solemn ceremony befitting his priestly status, Harrom declared the expansion a gift from Dagon, and after pouring wine libations in a hole where the new entrance would be, called one of his servants to bring forward the threshold offering.

I heard none of what was said after that, too busy trying not to retch on the ground or sob, because I knew for certain that the tiny brindled pups squirming inside the clay pot the servant delivered to my uncle were those of the little dog I'd fed at the back door.

Although I kept my eyes pressed tightly closed, somehow I managed to remain standing through the grisly ceremony and the burial of the vessel beneath the new threshold, but the moment it was finished I dashed off without apology to hide beneath my bedcovers until Azuvah appeared to wipe my tears and whisper reassurances in her language until I finally fell asleep.

No matter how hungry I'd been after that, even when the city was overcome by plague and food was scarce, I'd never again eaten the flesh of a canine. In fact, when I'd come to Kiryat-Yearim and discovered that, unlike my people, the Hebrews found dog and pig meat to be abhorrent, I'd been beyond relieved.

I swallowed down the nausea such memories invoked and fled, leaving the dog to continue her fruitless search for the squirrel, who'd most likely slithered beneath the tent wall and escaped.

The rain had slowed for now, leaving the air replete with mist and the trees all around our home dripping. Glad for the cool air, I inhaled deeply, once again giving thanks that there were no terrible threshold offerings with the community of Israel, that human infants were not buried in pots beneath their floors, and that fertility and divination rituals were seen as the height of repugnance. Worship of Yahweh was a stark contrast to that of my people, and I would ever be grateful that I'd been invited into Avraham's covenant.

Pushing the macabre images from my mind, I focused instead on all that remained to be done and headed out of the courtyard toward the side of the house. We would need at least a few more logs to keep the fire going, since our Shabbat gatherings usually lasted long into the night, especially when my father got lost in telling stories of the ancients, as he frequently did.

To my surprise, Natan was at the wood shelter, unloading logs from large leather packs strapped to one of our sturdy donkeys, whom Miri had named Kalanit for the reddish hue of its coat. The sodden and bedraggled animal looked nothing like the graceful poppy flower she was named for as she patiently awaited her un-burdening, shifting foot to foot while her long ears twitched and her white-rimmed eyes blinked away the rain droplets.

My brother had returned from his sulk in his cave last night, bruised and battered but much calmer than when we'd parted ways in the clearing. It seemed Ronen's suggestion to allow him room to settle had been a wise one. To my great surprise, he'd not balked when our father asked to speak with him alone upon his return and had followed him to the roof to accept his chastisement with silent resignation. In fact, when I'd been asked to join them there, in order to answer my father's questions about what I'd witnessed, Natan had already informed Elazar of Ronen's intervention. And by the contrite set of his swollen and split lips, something Ronen had said after the altercation must have gotten through to him.

"How much more of that tree is left out there?" I asked, choosing to ignore the enormous purple-and-green bruise that encom-passed his eye, cheek, and a large portion of his forehead.

"I've managed to cut up most of the branches, but the trunk will take me quite a few more days. Of course, it's soaked now and won't be useable until it dries out for a few weeks."

"Haven't your friends been helping?" I asked. "I would guess it would be a three- or four-person job."

"I don't need them," he said, a sharp edge to his tone. "I can handle it on my own." He stared off into the distance, silent yet full of thoughts that I desperately wished he would share. But Ronen had taught me that it was better not to push. Natan would speak when he was ready to, and not before.

So, I waited, my gaze on the misty woods before us but watching from the corner of my eye as my brother scratched at his stubbled jaw. He looked more like our father every day, but there were also hints of our mother in his features, something I'd neglected to tell him and wondered if I'd been wrong to do so.

"I am sorry you saw me like that," he said, scrubbing Kalanit between the eyes. "I didn't mean for it to go as far as it did."

I repressed a smile of triumph that my patience had been rewarded so soon. "Did you not?"

"I only meant to stop him from slandering you," he said, glancing up and then away again. "Not . . . well, I didn't like that you saw the two of us."

"Nor did I. It . . . it frightened me, Natan. Ronen is right that if you'd kept going, I would have had to watch you be sentenced as a murderer. And I could not bear—" My words were choked off by a glut of emotion in my throat. "I can't lose you."

His chin jerked up, his brown and green irises finally meeting mine, something he'd not allowed for weeks, if not months. "I know, Risi. I'm sorry."

Losing all restraint at the sincerity in his tone, I threw my arms around his waist and planted my forehead against his shoulder, vaguely noting that he'd grown since the last time he'd allowed me to embrace him.

"Please," I said. "Please. Walk away next time. I can bear to be called names. But if something happened to you . . ."

He patted my shoulder, clearing his throat. "Risi. That Levite is back."

Dropping my arms from around his waist, I whirled about to find Ronen coming up the trail, followed by another man who looked very similar to him. Their mantles were soaked and their hair was dripping, but Ronen's eyes were on the two of us as they came closer, a faint curve of amusement on his lips.

I glanced up at Natan, realizing I'd not told him that Ronen and the others would be joining us for the meal and fearing that leftover emotions from yesterday would erupt again. But although Natan's posture was rigid, he simply watched in silence as the men came nearer.

"Natan!" exclaimed Ronen, as if he'd not just yesterday nearly come to blows with him. "I've told my cousin here"—he gestured toward the other man—"of the game you taught me when you were small. Perhaps you'll give him a demonstration?"

Natan sniffed, taciturn as he met Ronen's eye. A few long moments ambled by as they held each other's gaze, some sort of silent exchange passing between them that I did not grasp.

"I lost those dice long ago," said my brother, shocking me with the admission. But now that I considered it, he had stopped wearing the little leather pouch around his neck in the early months after we'd arrived in Kiryat-Yearim.

"Ah. Just as well. You'd likely trounce me as you did when you were a boy." Ronen laughed, the rich sound doing something strange to my insides. "Although, since it took three of us to wrench you off that young man yesterday, I'd guess you would trounce me in most things."

My heart stuttered, and I restrained a gasp of shock that he would bring up the fight before he'd even set foot inside our home. Natan was as stiff as a stone column beside me while I blinked at Ronen, horrified by his audacity. What had I been thinking of inviting him here so soon after such a heated confrontation?

"I'm certain we can find something you might have a better chance at besting me in," replied my brother evenly, and I braced myself against whatever sharp-tongued insult he might lash at Ronen. "Those soft hands must be useful for something. Milking goats, perhaps?"

Ronen paused only two breaths before he burst into laughter, tilting his head back as the sound of his amusement echoed off the surrounding trees. "That they might," he said, stretching his long fingers in the air. "Although I can't say that I'm adept at milking either. Somehow I always seem to get kicked."

Utterly bewildered by this exchange, I divided glances between Natan, who now seemed to be fighting his own smile, and Ronen, whose dark eyes glittered with mirth. Less than one day ago, I thought the two of them might tear each other apart, and now they seemed to be sharing some sort of joke that I did not understand.

"That you do," interjected Ronen's cousin, with a laugh that was a poor imitation of Ronen's rich and deep one. "His mother gave up asking him to help with the livestock when we were boys because he always managed to end up pinned in a corner, bleating for help."

"Not true. It was only that one evil ram who had an unnatural hatred of me." Ronen elbowed him with a mocking scowl, then turned to address me. "This is my cousin, Machlon. Osher and Shelah had other duties to attend to this evening, so I invited him to come with me. I hope that is not too presumptuous."

"Of course not," I replied, smiling at Machlon. "We are delighted to have you join us for Shabbat. With all the produce your cousin and his friends helped harvest yesterday, there is more than enough."

He bowed his head in response, a palm to his heart. "It is my honor," he said, then lifted his brows as his dark eyes swept over me, head to toe. "I've been eager to put a face to everything Ronen has told me about you."

My cheeks went hot, and without forethought, I reached up to ensure my head covering was secure. What had Ronen told his cousin that would cause him to scrutinize me so openly? Although a smile remained on Machlon's lips, something in his perusal unsettled me, reminding me of the way the people of Kiryat-Yearim watched me when I first arrived. The two men might be cousins and similar in appearance, but I had the sense that they were very different in ways that mattered much more than looks.

Even when Ronen had found me behind the sheepfold, dressed in Philistine clothes and my speech thickly accented by my mother tongue, he had never made me feel like a foreigner. But the assessing look his cousin gave me now made me acutely aware of my heritage, even though my hair was hidden from view.

I was rescued from responding to Machlon's unnerving statement when my father came around the side of the house, his smile lighting up at the sight of Ronen.

"Shalom!" he called out. "I am so glad you've braved the rain to join us!"

"A little water would not stop me from accepting such gracious hospitality," Ronen said, before again introducing his cousin.

"Abiram's son?" my father asked.

"That I am," said Machlon with a firm nod. However, his smile was tight, and I wondered if there must be some sort of strain between him and his father.

"A man of great honor," said my father. "Even if we've had our differences in the past, his leadership among the Levites is to be commended."

A barely perceptible glance passed between the cousins, one that further solidified my feeling that there was contention within their family.

Oblivious to the undercurrent, my father gestured toward the open courtyard gate. "We have fresh water to wash the mud from your feet, and Eliora here will make sure you have something with which to dry your heads. She's already prepared a lovely fire to warm your bones."

Ronen turned his dark eyes to me as water dripped from his hair and trailed down his high-cut cheekbones. "From all I have seen and heard, your daughter is the very embodiment of generosity, Elazar."

My father too turned to look at me, a twitch of amusement on his normally solemn mouth. "That she is. There is no one like our Eliora."

"Indeed," said Ronen, so softly that I barely heard the word.

My face blazed at the pointed attention on me. It took everything I had not to spin around and run into the house, away from both the scrutiny and the unexpected pleasure of that one word from Ronen's lips.

But then, perhaps sensing how close I was to bolting, my father clapped a large hand on Ronen's shoulder. "And we have you to thank for her presence in our lives, as well as Natan's. The day they joined our family was a joyful one. One meal will not be sufficient to convey my gratitude for finding them, and for your help yesterday, both in the gardens and with my son."

At the mention of my brother, I realized that he and the donkey were no longer standing beside us. I leaned to peer around Ronen and Machlon, catching a glimpse of him leading Kalanit into the house, where she would be tucked into the warm stable on the lower level.

For as surly and snappish as Natan was with most people around him, he treated animals with the utmost care, something he'd done even when he was a small boy. In fact, I'd even overheard him talking quietly to the donkeys in our native language a time or two at night, when everyone else was asleep upstairs. Although I remembered much of the Philistine tongue, I'd refused to speak it out loud since I'd adopted Hebrew ways as my own, so he must have decided to keep his knowledge of the words alive in a different way.

"Come, my friends." My father gestured for the men to follow him into the courtyard. "We will fill your bellies with the best food and wine on the mountain and then you must tell me news of Abiram and the other Levites in Beit El."

The rain picked up again as I watched them go, droplets sliding down my face and soaking my headscarf. Regardless of the disquiet Machlon stirred up and the strange draw Ronen had on me, there was food to carry, fires to tend, people to serve. So, although there was still much to discuss with my brother, I ran to fetch towels, determined to extend the full measure of my family's generosity. The thought of shaming my mother and father by allowing any important detail to fall by the wayside tonight was too humiliating to even consider, especially when I had the disconcerting feeling that Ronen's cousin might be watching my every move.

Twenty-Two

Trying to ignore how stiff my fingers were, I shifted my weight as I crouched in the wet brush and tugged my woolen mantle closer around my body. I breathed out slowly, listening for the scuffle of footsteps, the rasp of a body moving through the woods, or even just a change in the air.

"See anything?" Machlon whispered near my shoulder.

"No," I replied, keeping my voice low as well.

"They have to be here somewhere," he mumbled. "They said they'd meet us here when the moon was high."

While Machlon and I ate with Eliora's family, Osher and Shelah had been scouting the area, trying to pinpoint exactly how many guards were positioned around the top of the mountain and where they were stationed.

Since Tuviyah and the other musicians would assume Machlon and I had been invited to stay the night with Elazar's family after the meal, we took advantage of the freedom it gave us to do some exploration of our own after we left. So far we'd seen four armed Levite guards, men who were surprisingly alert as they paced back and forth in the moonlight, eyes roving the trees. As I'd noticed during the wedding celebration, there were no torches lit to mark the resting place of the sacred vessel, but if the guards were here, then it could not be too far away; within a thousand cubits, I ventured to guess.

Nothing more than a few night birds trading stories and the whisper of the frigid breeze in the trees broke the silence around us. Perhaps Osher and Shelah had returned to camp after all, leaving the two of us here in the woods, waiting for no one.

I began to get drowsy, my belly overly full from the feast Elazar's wife and daughters prepared. I had to admit that the two old weavers had been correct to say that the fruits and vegetables harvested from Eliora's garden were second to none—the flavors richer and deeper, or sweeter and more delicate, than I'd ever tasted before. I'd been helpless against Yoela's continued insistence that I pile more food into my bowl, especially when every bite I scooped into my mouth seemed more delicious than the last.

Although Eliora's mother in no way resembled my own—her diminutive size and overabundance of black curls the opposite of my mother's willowy build and sleek brown hair—they were both generous in their affection for their families, and I could not help but be assailed by memories of my ima as I watched Yoela interact with her youngest children. They adored her, ever clamoring for her attention and never being turned away. Even when she was deep in conversation with one of the other women, she was stroking one of their heads with gentle fingers, or tugging one onto her lap, or pulling another tight to her side.

It had been nearly nine years since I'd seen my mother, and I could still feel the distinct sensation of her lips pressed to my forehead, as if the last kiss she gave me before her new husband drove away was permanently tattooed onto my skin.

Even worse than the dredging up of the pain of her loss was the twist in my gut as I watched Gershom and Iyov laugh with Yonah. Seated between his oldest brothers, the boy who walked with a distinct limp due to a deformed foot beamed with all the brightness of the sun at their focused attention. Not only did the sight stir up longings for my own younger brother, who'd only been an infant when he left, but it also called up memories of my older brothers and the way they always spoke to me like I was a man, even though I was over a decade younger than either of them.

Along with evoking deep yearnings for the return of my family, sharing a meal with Eliora's family made me admit that my uncle's home was not nearly as warm and loving. Abiram and his wife had given me a roof over my head and food in my belly, but there was none of the overt affection or the animated chatter that characterized Elazar's household and, indeed, had been the norm in my own. I missed it, more than I'd even realized, and found myself envying Eliora and Natan's adoption into such a welcoming clan.

I shifted again in place, unsettled by my own musings, and very glad that my cousin could not hear such traitorous thoughts. Even if my uncle was unbending and rarely spoke to me about anything other than his plans for the Ark, he had invited me to stay when my mother left and had told me many times that one of his goals in all of this was to avenge my father's and brothers' deaths by removing the descendants of Itamar from the seat of High Priest. I owed him my loyalty.

Besides, half of my family was dead and the other half gone, so without Abiram and Machlon, I had nowhere else to go.

"I met with the men from Be'er Sheva while you were digging in the garden," whispered Machlon, the sound seeming too loud in the stillness.

My response was barely above a breath. "And were they receptive?"

"I think so. Of course, I said little, only asked questions and let them speak. After a few cups of beer, I did not even have to guide the conversation; it flowed easily into the exact stream I expected. I have no doubt we'll have plenty of men to overtake these guards when the time is right."

Remembering the way the Levites from the territory of Simeon had so brazenly called out Tuviyah, I was not surprised that they were of like mind with us, but I still could not understand why Machlon was so eager to trust men he'd only met. This entire mission was too precarious to place faith in the wrong people. We only had a narrow window of time to recover the Ark and could not afford a mishap.

"Excellent work on the Philistine girl, my brother. She is smitten with you."

A jolt of panic seized hold of me at his assertion.

I'd suspected that she'd begun to trust me the moment she told me of her fear that Natan was following in his birthfather's dangerous footsteps, but instead of feeling pleased that I'd already maneuvered myself into her confidence, I found myself second-guessing my plans.

And tonight, instead of simply considering her a source of information on the Ark, I'd found myself fascinated as I watched her move about the tent filling cups, delivering baskets of bread, and bending low to look each of her young siblings in the eye while she spoke to them in calm and patient tones. Ever in motion, she was like a gentle gust of wind flowing about, unseen except for the effects of her silent, selfless service to all those around her.

As I'd allowed my curious gaze to follow her while Elazar recounted a story about Samuel the Pretender that I'd only been half-listening to, I found that what truly amazed me was that I was the only one who seemed to be watching her.

As full as that tent had been with people, a number of them unmarried men, everyone else fell prey to her skillful knack for disappearing among the crowd, regardless that she stood nearly a head taller than most of the women. And although many of those other women wore scarves on their heads, none wrapped their hair so diligently that even the color was a mystery—a mystery that, for some reason, I was desperate to solve.

Eight years ago, her hair had been braided and wound into a knot, and it was dirty from her long trek from Ashdod, but I remembered it was lighter than anything I'd ever seen and guessed that now it was similar in color to Natan's. As foolish as I felt even admitting it to myself, I could not stop wondering how long it was, or what it might look like in the sunlight, unfettered.

"Ronen?" Machlon prodded, dragging me out of my musings over a woman. I was glad it was too dark for him to see the flush that crept up my neck or I'd never hear the end of it. I hoped he would assume I was only pausing to listen for evidence of more guards.

"I believe I've won her trust," I said, ignoring his earlier provocation, "but it's done me little good. There was no talk of the Ark during the meal. Elazar was too busy extolling your father to say anything of note."

Eliora's father had indeed spoken of Abiram with admiration, which surprised me since my uncle practically snarled and spat whenever he mentioned Elazar, or his late father, all too quick to expound on their faults.

Yet, after spending a few hours with Elazar, listening to him unspool the ancient and tragic story of Yaakov and Esau to a captivated audience in the flicker of firelight, and hearing the bone-deep sincerity in his voice when he lifted a blessing over the heads of the people at the conclusion of the Shabbat gathering, I'd begun to wonder whether Abiram's perspective might be somewhat skewed.

"Do not let that snake fool you, cousin," said Machlon. "He knows exactly what he is doing. His father was in league with Eli and his wicked offspring from the start and fell in with Samuel and his unsanctioned babblings years ago. We must expose the Pretender for who he truly is before he digs his claws any deeper into the people."

Most of what I knew of Samuel had been from the lips of Abiram, other than the ridiculous story of Yahweh talking to him as a boy inside the Mishkan, which was an oft-told tale. Many among the tribes believed him to be a prophet, the mouthpiece of Adonai himself, and his supporters among the priesthood were strong in number.

But the idea that a child of tender years and untrained in the ways of Mosheh was a conduit by which the Almighty One spoke to his people was laughable. How his fame had continued to grow among Israel since then—as if he were on equal footing with Mosheh himself—was beyond my comprehension. Until I heard a prophecy from his mouth being confirmed with my own ears, I would never believe such stories were anything more than exaggerations or outright lies. Lies like the ones that led to my father and brothers being slaughtered on a field in Afek and the rest of my family being stripped from me.

"And just as you must be wary of Elazar's treachery," Machlon said, "you must remember that it was a Philistine beauty who was Samson's ultimate downfall. Don't let Eliora beguile you. Too many are counting on us to deliver the Ark into the right hands. We cannot afford to be distracted from our purpose. The future of all Israel is at stake."

Although I could not see my cousin's face in the darkness, the censure in his voice was as clear as midday. Perhaps I'd been the only one watching Eliora, but Machlon had been watching me.

I inhaled a sharp draft of air through my nose, meaning to refute him or offer an excuse for why my eyes seemed compelled to follow her whenever she was near, but we'd been careless as we whispered, growing complacent the longer we'd crouched in the brush under the full moon.

Just off to our left, and far too close to be coincidental, a twig snapped.

Twenty-Three

Eliora

White light spilled through the window, beckoning me to slip quietly from the bed I shared with Miri and Amina and pad across the room to peer up at the sky. Round and full, the moon cast its gaze in such a familiar way that I could almost understand why so many of my ancestors revered it as a god. But knowing what I did now, that Yahweh spoke the heavenly lights into existence and placed them there to remind us of signs and seasons and mark time with perfect consistency, I pitied those ancient ones who worshiped the created thing instead of the Creator.

It had been hours since the last guest departed, every bowl and pot had been cleaned, and the little ones had fallen into dreams, but no matter how hard I'd tried, I could not sleep.

Tonight had been a disaster.

Although all of our guests, including Ronen and his cousin Machlon, seemed to enjoy the food and drink, eating to their hearts' content, I had made an enormous mistake.

When the dog and its prey had burst in on me, I'd been so startled and disoriented by the ruckus that I'd dropped the fresh wicks for our oil lamps on the ground and then ran from the memories the animals had provoked.

But apparently the squirrel had not escaped like I'd thought, and it seemed that a violent chase had ensued inside the tent after I'd left. Pillows had been gutted, lamps broken, and one of the tall ceramic braziers I'd lit beforehand had been knocked over, setting coals flying and one wall of the tent alight. Thankfully, not only was the outside of the tent still damp from all the rain, but someone in the courtyard smelled the acrid scent of smoldering goat hair and doused the fire with a nearby pot of rainwater.

I'd been horrified when I'd returned with towels for Ronen and Machlon and realized what had happened. Not only were our guests forced to endure the odor of burnt hair throughout their meal, but the new wicks I'd prepared for the lamps were also soaked and muddy, so old ones had to be scrounged up from the houses while everyone waited in the dimly lit tent.

Even though the images of Harrom's terrible threshold sacrifice had reared up with such force and vivacity that I'd been engulfed in a flood of emotions, I should have locked them away like I normally did whenever thoughts of Ashdod nagged at me. It was almost like Ronen's appearance in Kiryat-Yearim had broken the latch on the box where I usually kept them.

If only I had not let myself get so caught up in memories that were better left buried in the past, or let my anxiety over both Natan's behavior and Machlon's subtle disdain for me distract me from my responsibilities.

It did not matter that my mother brushed aside my profuse apologies, nor that no one else mentioned the lingering odor of charred wool. I'd been devastated. Only the certainty that my parents would be even more shamed if I fled the courtyard kept me from running out into the woods and secreting myself away in my special place.

I'd not even had the courage to look Ronen in the eye after that. What a clumsy fool he must think me. I was so grateful that the men had congregated on one side of the tent and the women on the other so I'd had every excuse to stay far away.

Only one time had our gazes tangled. Halfway through the meal, my sisters fussed at me to stop serving and sit down to eat, and I'd finally given in to their persistent coaxing. The moment I folded myself onto a cushion, my youngest sister, Dafna, toddled over and plopped down in my lap, filling my ears with some unintelligible story full of sweet giggles and waves of her chubby arms. Suddenly feeling as though I was being watched, I allowed myself the briefest glance toward the other side of the tent and found Ronen's attention on me, one side of his mouth tilted upward. Struck by embarrassment, and the way my pulse tripped over itself under his attention, I'd immediately dropped my gaze, shifted Dafna to my mother's lap, and returned to filling wine cups and replenishing bread baskets. As for the warm curl of pleasure I'd felt in my belly when he'd met my eyes for those fleeting moments, I'd pushed it aside. If anything, he was simply noticing just how different I was from my tiny black-haired sister, or noting how awkward I was around the Levite wives.

It did not matter that I'd known most of them for eight years now; I'd never felt comfortable among them. There were times I'd tried to relax, allowing myself to laugh just a little bit louder at some amusing tale or to interject a comment or two, but somehow I always left feeling as though I'd pushed too hard, forced myself into their circle uninvited, and annoyed people who were too kind to tell me so. I was much better off serving silently and staying in the shadows, more than content to allow Miri and my other sisters to shine like the beautiful lights they were. Hopefully my glaring blunder hadn't ruined the night for them as well.

Tomorrow I would make it up to all of them by harvesting a few baskets of my most profuse blooms in the garden. It had been so gloomy lately, with the weather a near-constant drizzle, so I knew a variety of colorful flowers inside everyone's home this week would be welcome.

Bolstered by my idea, and knowing I really should try to sleep, I inhaled deeply of the night air, glad that the rain had stopped for at least a little while. When I looked up again at the moon, a strange shadow had eclipsed its fullness, transforming it into an unnatural shape.

My breath caught. I'd only seen an occurrence like this one time before, just before the Ark of the Hebrews had been brought to Ashdod. The moon had turned a strange reddish color, like blood in the water, and my uncle had woken us all in the middle of the night to beg Dagon for mercy against whatever evil had come over Philistia. At the time I'd cared little for Harrom's hysterical ravings and had only wanted to go back to sleep. Little did I know how much would change soon after that sign appeared in the sky.

Wanting to get a closer look, I carefully made my way down the stairs and through the house, then tied my sandals to my feet and crept out the door, careful to pull the latch tightly behind me without making a sound.

Leaning my back against the side of the house, I watched the moon for a long while, tracking the movement of the cloud across its surface, wondering how such a thing was even possible, and what it might mean. But before I could slide back inside once the moon returned to its full brilliance, a shadow flickered in the corner of my sight.

I peered into the darkness, wondering if it might be a deer dashing through the clearing, but instead, Natan's distinctive form was outlined by the moonlight, his long legs taking him away from our home and into the woods.

What could he possibly be doing out here so late? I suspected it must have something to do with Adnan and Padi.

Before I could even pause to consider the wisdom of following him past the dark tree line, my feet were moving in that direction. I considered calling out his name but worried it might wake someone. *Best to simply catch up with him*, I thought, frustration welling up, *and drag him back home by the ear.* There was no use alerting everyone in our home and the others nearby that, once again, Natan was up to something.

However, I underestimated my brother's ability to outpace me, especially when the thick tree cover blotted out the sky and left me with only miserly shafts of moonlight by which to navigate.

I found myself alone in the woods, my brother nowhere to be seen, and with no idea of where I was or how to get back home. Knowing that the Levites were out here patrolling this area gave me a small measure of comfort. From what my father said, they rarely reported spotting any dangerous animals, only a few small bears in the early months and a pack of jackals from time to time. Both could be easily scared away by loud noises that I was more than prepared to make if necessary.

Knowing that trying to find Natan now was futile, I walked on a bit farther, hoping I might stumble across one of the guardsmen who would certainly lead me home. Although they were all trained never to take the same path twice through the woods, a safeguard against inadvertently making trails that would lead enemies to the Ark, all of them were experts at finding their way on this mountain, and, as my father had bragged many times, could practically do so with their eyes closed.

The longer I walked, the angrier I grew. Natan had no business sneaking about in the woods at night, especially with such worthless friends leading him about by the nose. I'd been so hopeful earlier when I'd caught sight of Ronen and Natan talking together after the meal. Ronen had been grinning as he spoke, his palm curved over my brother's shoulder in an affectionate manner. Losing the fight against whatever humorous thing Ronen was saying, Natan's mouth had twitched with an almost-smile. My heart had leapt into my throat at the sight, tears filling my eyes. No matter what Ronen thought of me or how I'd ruined his Shabbat meal with my carelessness, at least he'd stood by his promise to attempt a connection with Natan. And for a few moments tonight, it seemed as though they had indeed found common ground, since they continued to talk until Machlon made it clear he was ready to make his way back to camp.

I'd been relieved when they left, both because I worried that I would do something else to prove myself awkward in Ronen's presence and because an eerie sense of discomfort enveloped me whenever Machlon looked at me. How two men from the same family could be so very different—

Something slammed into me, knocking every thought from my head as my skull crashed into a tree trunk and then my body hit the ground. With my mind swirling, I lay twisted in the underbrush as two blurry shadows hovered over me. A man cursed, only his lips visible in the weak moonlight. His face looked to be covered with mud, or perhaps the darkening haze across my vision had caused such a strange illusion.

"We need to go," rasped the other shadow. "Leave her."

Something about the voice seemed familiar, but before I could organize my jumbled thoughts, a shofar sounded close by.

The shadows dashed away without another word, gone so quickly that I wondered if I'd imagined them in the first place. But the pounding in my head and the sting on both my palms and knees gave testimony to the fact that someone had indeed collided with me.

Shofar calls repeated, this time much closer, and then the crash of multiple footfalls approached. Terrified that the men who'd attacked me had returned to finish the job, I held myself still, trying to be invisible, even though I was trembling violently on the inside.

"Eliora?" said a familiar voice. "Is that you?"

I peered through the mess of my hair, which had somehow come loose from my sleeping braid, and saw three sets of sandals near me. I whimpered and tried to shrink back, but when one of the men knelt beside me, there was just enough moonlight to see that it was Rami, one of the older Levite guards.

"Go on," he ordered with a quick jerk of his head. "Don't let those two get away. I'll get her back home."

Without another word, the other Levites dashed off into the brush in the direction my attackers had gone. And then, with quiet words of reassurance that I would be all right and that I was safe, the broad-shouldered Levite carefully scooped me off the ground and lifted me in his arms as if I weighed no more than Miri.

"Let's get you back to your father."

Twenty-Four

"Then tell me, Menash. How did they get so close? Especially when you were right there?" demanded my father, his resonant voice rolling through the window like thunder as he questioned Shoshana's father. I'd not meant to overhear him interrogating the guards first thing this morning, but since my mother insisted I stay abed until my head stopped pounding, I'd been an uninvited audience to the meeting happening in the courtyard just outside. I could not hear the mumbled response but imagined that whatever excuse Menash might have to offer would not satisfy my father in the slightest.

He'd been livid when Rami brought me home, bleeding from the head and still disoriented from my collision with an oak tree. I'd been horrified that his blustering woke everyone in the household, except for little Dafna, who slept blissfully unaware through the entire ruckus. Between my father ordering Rami to wake the other Levites and join the search for the perpetrators, my mother fluttering about treating my wounds, the twins' loud tears over my injuries, and my tangled hair spilling all over the place in full view of everyone, I'd been utterly mortified.

The fact that Natan also appeared in the main room while I'd been explaining my reason for going outside to look at the moon in the first place had only added another layer of confusion to the embarrassing situation. Had I conjured the image of my brother wandering about in the night? Perhaps whatever mystical occurrence had happened in the heavens tonight had caused me to see things that were not there.

"You were *asleep*?" bellowed my father. "A highly trained Levitical guard charged with protecting our most holy object would endanger it by *sleeping* during his patrol?"

I cringed, feeling mortified on behalf of Shoshana's father. I'd never spoken with the man, but I had recently overheard my parents talking about how changed he was after the death of his wife and how Shoshana had been forced to shoulder the burden of care for her little brothers in spite of her tender age.

Menash must have shifted closer to the window because I was finally able to hear his response. "I have no excuse, Elazar. None." He cleared his throat. "I grew complacent after so long without even a hint of danger. That is my only explanation. I accept full responsibility for my actions."

Everything was silent for a long while. I could only imagine how anxious the man must be. My father was never unkind, but he could be stern and unbending if the situation warranted.

"You are off the rotation, Menash," said my father, and the iron undergirding his words was enough to make me certain that the man would never again stand guard on this mountain.

"No. Please, Elazar. My family—"

My father spoke over his useless pleas. "Your children will not go hungry. There are other ways you can serve your brothers." The statement was as much a command as a reminder of whom he had betrayed with his careless behavior. "The elders will decide what will be best for you in the long term, but for now I cannot have an unfit man guarding the Ark."

There was no response from Menash. What else could he do but accept his punishment? My father's word was law atop this mountain.

"You are dismissed," said my father, as unrelenting as I'd ever heard him. "Send Rami over to me before you head home."

I considered making a noise, alerting my father to the fact that I was within hearing of his conversation, but Rami spoke before I could do anything, and curiosity won over my pangs of conscience.

"Menash is done?"

"He is," replied my father. "Find him some work to do in town. He has no one else but us, after all. What did you find in the woods?"

"Nothing," said Rami. "There was no trace this morning, except for some trampled brush, where it looks as though a couple of them were hiding. We think there must have been at least three men, possibly four. Maybe even more, there's no way to know. We think they went in different directions once the shofarim blew. It just took too long for our men to respond once Menash finally blew his horn, and there was some confusion about who should remain in position after the alarm sounded. Running across Eliora didn't help either. Oren and Eli couldn't catch up after that."

My stomach seemed to make an entire rotation in my gut. Obviously I should not have been out there in the first place, since I'd been dreaming up Natan's presence in the shadows, but to hear that the men had missed out on catching whomever had been trying to get to the Ark made me ill. How could I have been so foolhardy?

"She could have been killed," said my father, his tone as icy as the streams that flowed from the foundations of this mountain.

"I thought she had been," said Rami, with a bleak note in his voice. "She was so still there on the ground when we approached. But I don't think they meant her harm. She said one of them just barreled into her, perhaps even by accident."

A low sound of disagreement emanated from my father's throat. "That makes no difference."

"Do you think this was a Philistine scouting party?" asked Rami.

"They learned their lesson the last time they came near the Ark. Even they wouldn't be so foolish. And they wouldn't have left witnesses alive. No, I think these were some of our own."

I could not fathom the thought that a Hebrew could have been behind this.

"Do you suppose Menash was involved?"

My father paused. "No. He seemed genuinely remorseful. But he will need to be questioned more, just to be certain."

"Agreed. And we should regroup," said Rami. "Add more guards. A double layer of security."

"If not more," said my father. "Tell the men not currently on watch to gather at midday. I'll speak with the others this morning. Whomever did this is likely still in the area, and we cannot take any chances. There will be no more complacency."

Before Rami had even left the courtyard, I was off my bed and moving toward the door, regardless that my skull was vibrating with pain and my eyes went a bit hazy if I turned my head too fast. Thankfully, no one was in the front room when I came down the stairs, and I was able to slip outside without notice and catch my father before he left the courtyard.

"Eliora," he said, his silver-threaded brows furrowed deeply. "What are you doing out of bed?"

"I am fine," I lied, blinking away the blurred spot in my vision. "I needed to speak with you."

"I must deal with my men."

"Please," I said, "it will only take a moment. I must apologize."

"Apologize?"

"For being out there. It was so foolish. I don't even know what I was thinking."

Unless I had proof that Natan had been sneaking off in the night, I did not want to make things worse by revealing it to my father. My brother was barely speaking to any of us as it was.

"It was *very* foolish, Eliora. It would have been a simple thing for you to wake me, or one of your brothers, to accompany you if you were so desirous of seeing the moon."

"I know, Abba. Please forgive me." My hands trembled as I awaited his censure.

His mouth was set in a tight line and his expression severe, but he placed a hand beneath my chin, forcing me to look into his eyes. "If those men had meant to hurt you, you would not be alive right now."

I shivered, remembering the force of the shadowed man's enormous body as he hit me like a runaway chariot. "Do you really think it was Hebrews?"

His brows went high, and then his gaze flicked up toward the window where I'd been listening. My face flushed. "I didn't mean to—"

He held up a palm. "It's fine. I should have chosen a more private place to deal with Menash."

"If it wasn't Philistines, then is the Ark in danger?" I blurted, the worry in my gut boiling over.

"Eliora," he said, his expression softening somewhat. "You were there in that valley eight years ago. You know who protects the Ark."

Indeed I did. For the rest of my days I would always remember the prickling sensation that lifted the hair on my neck and arms as the clouds swirled over the valley of Beth Shemesh, and then the horrific clap of thunder and the smell of charred flesh.

"But it is my duty to guard this area," my father continued, "and to ensure that unsanctified men remain far enough away that they do not suffer the consequences. Those men last night were taking their own lives in their hands—especially if they were Levites."

"Why would Levities be more at risk than others?"

He contemplated for a few moments before speaking. "You told me once of the disrespectful way the Philistines treated the Ark when they brought it into Ashdod. Do you remember?"

The memory arose clearly: the sounds of the crowds screaming in vicious glee, my first glimpse of the fascinating golden box, and the feel of Azuvah's reassuring presence at my side as she mourned the desecration and mockery of the sacred vessel. An unexpected swell of latent grief over her loss welled up, something I thought had been buried alongside my other memories of Philistia.

"Nothing happened to those Philistines that day," he said, "even though they offered up the very seat of Yahweh to their pagan god."

"Was it only because they did not open the box?"

"We don't know if they did or not," he replied.

"Then why?" I asked, finally able to articulate the question that had always niggled at my mind. "Why would Levites be struck down immediately when the uncircumcised men who stole the Ark off the battlefield and tossed it at the foot of Dagon were not?"

"I wondered that myself," he said, "especially after the tragedy at Afek. I even discussed it with your grandfather a few times."

He went silent for a few moments, and I thought perhaps he would simply excuse himself and leave me without an answer. He had much more important tasks to attend to right now, after all. But instead he surprised me by continuing.

"Let me ask you this," he said. "When you lived in Ashdod you were subject to the laws of your seren, correct?"

I nodded, remembering well the horrifying sight of soldiers dragging thieves through the street and men hung on the city walls for unknown offenses, left to be picked over by the birds until only their bones remained as a warning.

"But when you came here," he continued, "you were no longer under the jurisdiction of the kings of Philistia. You accepted the offer to become a part of our family, and in doing so, placed yourself not only under my authority, but also the authority of the Covenant."

I nodded. Being washed in the cold stream and then speaking aloud my intentions to be part of Israel in front of Elazar's family would always be one of my most cherished memories. The fact that Natan agreed to observe the Torah laws, yet refused to undergo the rite of circumcision, still bothered me, but did not lessen the joy I'd felt that day.

"You became a daughter of Avraham, just as much as those

born of his lineage, and are therefore subject to the entirety of the covenant Adonai cut with him—both its blessings and its curses."

"Curses?"

"Yes. Disobedience always has consequences. Which brings me back to the Levites. You remember the story of the golden bull in the wilderness, and how the Levites were the only tribe willing to mete out justice against those who worshiped the blasphemous idol?"

"I do." The stories of the multitude at the foot of the mountain of Adonai, along with their escape from Egypt, were among the many Azuvah had told Natan and me when we were young. But it wasn't until I heard them from the lips of my grandfather in the first months of our arrival that I truly understood their significance and how they displayed the power and might of the God who plucked his people from Pharaoh's grasp and deigned to speak his commands directly to them from the fiery cloud atop the summit.

"After that day, the sons of Levi were given a special role among the tribes. We alone hold the responsibilities of caring for the Ark, the Mishkan, and the holy implements for the sacrifices. Not all of us are born of Aharon's priestly line, but we are all set apart for a holy purpose. And because of that separateness and high responsibility, we must be careful to uphold every aspect of Mosheh's commands with regard to the sacrifices and the implements—to the very letter."

"So, because the men at Beth Shemesh were Levites," I concluded, "they are held to a higher standard?"

"Exactly. Beth Shemesh is a Levitical town, designated as such by Mosheh himself. They disregarded the Torah—either willfully, or because the knowledge of the laws regarding handling of the Ark was not properly taught generation to generation. They suffered the consequences for such disobedience. The Philistines are not beholden to our laws. They have no such sacred responsibility. However, they still were cursed because of their foolish boast that they'd been victorious over Yahweh—a notion that the Pharaoh in Mosheh's day learned by suffering his own plagues."

Even after all these years, the memory of the horrific black boils on Harrom's face managed to send a shiver across my shoulders. And the sound of Jacame pleading for Beelzebub, her Mother Goddess, and all the rest of her menagerie of sightless gods to heal her weeping sores and spare her children and grandchildren still rang in my ears with near-perfect clarity, as did the sounds of suffering that had echoed across our city as I lay beside my brother, shivering and weak. All because the seren of Ashdod, along with my uncle, thought they'd bested the Almighty.

"Ah. It looks as though you have a visitor," said my father. Startled, I followed his gaze to where Ronen stood fidgeting at the entrance to the courtyard, hesitant to disturb our discussion. My head swam briefly; whether from surprise at his appearance or my injury, I wasn't certain.

"He does seem eager to help you in the gardens," my father said, with the barest hint of amusement in his voice.

"He and his friends are merely being kind," I said. "They are grateful we've been sharing food with their camp while they prepare for the festivals."

He hummed, sounding unconvinced. "I've now given two daughters away in marriage, Eliora, and arranged matches for Gershom and Iyov as well. I know a concealed motive when I see one."

A rush of heat washed through my limbs. My father must be mistaken.

He chuckled softly, gesturing for Ronen to join us. "Perhaps we will be celebrating your own wedding soon." He dropped his tone as Ronen approached. "His uncle is as surly as a cat in a rainstorm these days, but young Ronen seems to be honorable."

"But . . ." I choked on my raspy whisper. "I don't want . . ." My tongue seemed to fill my mouth as all my fears welled up and my mind raced at full gallop. The idea that my father might actually be considering Ronen as a match, as Rina had implied, was as thrilling as it was terrifying.

By the time Ronen stood before us, I could barely control the instinct to run to my secret place and plead with Yahweh for the privilege of remaining on this mountain for the rest of my days, and to beg him to take away any desire for a man who would take me from this blessed place.

"Shalom," Ronen said. He gave my father a deferential nod of his head but seemed uneasy. A spear of panic went through me. Surely he was not here for the reasons my father had hinted at. Not this soon. Not when I hadn't even allowed myself to consider the impossibility of a betrothal. My knees wobbled, and my head felt light again.

"I'm glad you are here," my father said to Ronen, even as he reached out to steady me. "Eliora needs to go back to the house to lie down. Will you escort her?"

Ronen looked bewildered by the request. "What is wrong?"

"She was attacked in the woods last night and injured by the brute who slammed her into a tree."

"A tree?" Ronen's jaw went slack as his eyes darted to my forehead. My mother had wrapped a linen bandage over the bruised gash there, but by the way Ronen paled at the sight, I knew it must be peeking out from beneath my headscarf.

"She'll tell you what happened. I need to go deal with my men." My father turned his eyes back to me, a glint of iron determination in their depths. "But rest assured, I *will* find out who did this. And when I do, they will not go unpunished."

Twenty-Five

Ronen

Elazar's declaration made my stomach roil and pitch long after he walked away and left Eliora and me alone. Clearly he had no notion that I was in any way involved with the goings-on last night or he would not have entrusted me with his daughter.

I'd climbed up the hill this morning after only a few hours of fitful rest, both to allay any hint of suspicion by my appearance and to reassure myself that Eliora was safe. Osher and Shelah had sworn she was uninjured, but the bandage on her head belied their account.

"How were you wounded?" I asked, barely able to look her in the eye for the guilt coating my insides.

Her hand went to her forehead for a swift moment and then back down to her side, seeming embarrassed that she'd drawn any attention to it. "It was foolish. I should not have gone out there. But I thought . . ." She chewed her lip, glancing around before she told me of how her restlessness led to thinking she'd seen her brother out in the dark under a strange moon, before getting lost and run over by a shadowy figure.

For as much as I was relieved that she seemed not to have recognized Osher, I was horrified she'd endured any of it. In addition to the wound at her temple, there was also a faint bruise on her cheekbone and more than a few scratches on her arms and legs, causing the images of Osher and Shelah plowing over her like a team of runaway oxen to circle in my mind over and over. If they knew what was best for them, they'd stay far away from me for the next day or two.

"Please don't say anything to anyone," Eliora said, breaking into my thoughts. "I don't know if I actually did see Natan, or if I was mistaken. He was back at the house by the time I returned with Rami."

As usual, Eliora was protecting her brother, even if he did not deserve it. I wondered if he had any idea the danger he'd put her in with his skulking about. What if it hadn't been Osher and Shelah out there in the woods last night, but an actual enemy?

Another wash of guilt came over me. Who was I to cast blame on the boy when I had been part of the disaster that led to her injuries in the first place?

When the twins came flying toward Machlon and me, crashing through the underbrush with less stealth than a herd of boars, we'd scattered in four directions like we'd planned. The flight down the mountain had been harrowing, since I'd had no other direction to aim than downhill. In the near blackness of the tree cover, my sandals skidding on sodden ground and decaying leaves, I prayed I would not fly over the edge of a cliff or pitch headfirst into a ravine. I nearly had been caught, but somehow I'd heard my pursuer and flattened myself beneath a bush, narrowly avoiding detection. I'd emerged from my hiding place well after the guard disappeared into the woods—soaked through, shivering, and livid.

After wandering for what seemed like hours through the forest, when I'd finally joined Machlon and the others at our agreed-upon meeting point, I'd not held back my frustrations.

"This entire night was a waste," I spat, anger alone warming my bones. "Now the guards suspect something is going on, and the mission is likely compromised because of your carelessness."

"Relax, Ronen," said Machlon. "She didn't see their faces. We are safe."

"She?" I whipped my head around to glare at my cousin.

"Your Philistine." He waved a dismissive hand at Osher. "Somehow this big ox plowed over her up there. Who knows what she was doing wandering around in the middle of the night. Maybe you aren't the only man she has dangling from her claws."

It took every thread of restraint inside me to keep from slamming my fist into his lascivious grin, but I knew if I reacted to his goad then he would only mock me further. For as much as he'd been the one to push me toward manipulating Eliora in the first place, Machlon had been almost hostile at every mention of her name since then.

Osher launched into his account of nearly being caught by one of the guards who'd been dozing against a tree. But after listening to his tale, as well as his paltry assurances that Eliora had only been bumped to the ground, I was only more furious. My uncle had sworn the two were the best trackers in the territory and yet they'd done nothing more than bring down Elazar's guard on our heads and attack an innocent woman.

I'd thrown my hands in the air and headed back toward camp, having nothing more to say to the two fools who'd nearly undone everything we'd planned for so long, put an innocent woman in danger, and possibly ruined the only chance I had to reclaim all that I had lost.

"What I don't understand," mused Eliora, drawing me back to the present, "is why any Hebrew would chance going near the Ark. Its power is nothing to take lightly."

I held back a scoff, but something in my expression must have given away my doubts. She shifted her gaze on the forest beyond the compound to study my face intently. "You don't agree?"

I considered keeping my lips sealed, but after such a long and sleepless night, my inhibitions had crumbled to pieces. "All I know is that my father and brothers are dead because of that golden box."

Her lips parted on a silent gasp. "What do you mean?"

"They were loyal Levites, Eliora. Among the first to volunteer to accompany the Ark to Afek under the leadership of the High Priest Eli's worthless sons. They were given every assurance by Eli himself and the other elders of Israel that the sacred vessel would not only protect them in battle but would also annihilate our enemies without a sword being lifted. Instead . . ."

"My people killed them," she finished for me on a whisper, tears glinting in her deep-forest eyes.

I flinched at the reminder, but it was true. Soldiers from her city—perhaps even some of her own relatives—had been on that battlefield. They'd slaughtered my father and brothers without remorse, and if some of the accounts I'd been told later were true, encouraged their packs of war dogs to desecrate the bodies while they plundered the fallen.

"The presence of the Holy One may have once resided on that vessel," I said, "and of course it is still sacred and an important focus of our worship, but it's just a box now."

"Oh, Ronen," she said as a tear spilled down her bruised cheek and over her jaw. Somehow, even in my agitated state, my eyes were drawn to the trail of it, and a strange compulsion to catch the precious thing with my finger gripped me. "I remember you said they'd been lost that day, but I had no idea they were so close to the Ark. No wonder you doubt its power."

I suddenly hated the way she was looking at me, like I was some-one to be pitied. I much preferred the way she'd flushed and darted her eyes away the other night when she caught me watching her, trying to conceal the way my attention affected her. "As I said, I don't dispute its importance to our priesthood. Without the Ark re-turned to the Mishkan, proper worship cannot be conducted the way Mosheh ordained, but there's no actual danger from the relic itself."

"But you were there at Beth Shemesh," she said. "You saw the aftermath."

"Of the lightning, yes. But that had less to do with the Ark and more to do with the fools who left it atop a boulder in a flat valley and gathered around it during a storm."

"There was no storm, Ronen. The sky was clear that night. Don't you remember that I was there? I may have only been a girl, but I will never forget the moments after those men opened the Ark." She paused and shuddered slightly. "The sound was deafening and the light so brilliant I thought perhaps the world had ended in a flash. But it did not come from above, even though a swirl of colorful cloud appeared directly overhead. The light came from between the wings of the creatures and split into as many shards of fire as there were men in that valley. I hid my face after that, terrified that the light would seek my brother and me out too, but somehow we were spared such an awful fate."

I'd never actually heard her firsthand account of the events at Beth Shemesh, only a few minor details from my uncle, who'd brushed her story off as nothing more than the imagination of a child desperate for attention. But hearing it now, I wondered if my convictions on the matter might not be so well defined, had I been privy to such a vivid description. It was more than obvious that Eliora believed that what she saw was an act of divine judgment.

But the fact remained that the Ark had been impotent on that battlefield. And my father and brothers had been destroyed because Eli and his sons convinced them that it would protect them from harm.

Even as much as I'd come to crave Eliora's timid little smiles and despite the fact that the sight of her bruised face made me want to tear Osher and Shelah limb from limb, I still had a job to do on this mountain, and we were running out of time. I couldn't let my draw toward this woman preclude the justice my father and brothers deserved.

However, no matter if Machlon protested, I was done using Eliora in this quest for information. Spending time with her had yielded nothing more than an increasingly desperate desire to know what she looked like with her hair unbound and an impossible yearning to be part of the family that had invited her into its warm embrace. It was more than evident that I would not learn the location of the Ark by indulging in the pleasure of her company or basking in the generosity of her compassion.

"I came to tell you that I'm not able to help you in the gardens today," I said, ignoring the confusion in her expression as I suddenly changed the subject. But I needed to make certain she was no longer involved and had already come up with a plan before I'd even known the extent of her injuries.

"One of the lutes we brought has a deep crack down the center of its neck," I said. "I need to replace it and require a long stretch of olive wood to do so. From what I understand, Natan knows where to find such material."

It had occurred to me as I'd spooled and unspooled the problem while I lay unsleeping that it would be far better to find out what a young man who spent his days tromping around the woods knew about the Ark's location, rather than his sister, who spent most of her time in a garden far from the area guarded by Elazar's men.

Surprised delight flashed across her face. She likely assumed my only motive was to befriend her brother for her sake. "Of course. If there is any gain he's made from passing time with those Gibeonite boys, it's knowing the trees on this mountain like the lines on his own palm. I'm certain he could help you."

A shaft of sunlight broke through a part in the clouds at that moment, illuminating the side of her face and painting her pale skin with a golden glow. The urge to curve my palm over that smooth cheek, absorb the warmth that had nothing to do with the sun and everything to do with Eliora was nearly uncontrollable. The name she'd taken fit her so well. Regardless that she kept all that light hidden beneath an ugly brown scarf, a tucked chin, and the inclination to blend into the background, it shined from within like a house lit with a thousand lamps, spilling brilliance from every window.

She was lovely, kind, and generous, everything I could want in a wife, but once I finished my job here in Kiryat-Yearim, I would not be returning.

And when she realized my duplicity, she'd not want me to anyhow.

By the time I walked her back to her door, made her promise to go rest, and set off to find her brother so I could achieve what I'd set out to accomplish, I already felt the loss of her like a knife between my ribs. But it was time to keep my distance.

Twenty-Six

With a crack the olive tree fell, its gnarled trunk bouncing twice before settling precariously on its splayed branches. Natan swung the double-edged ax up to rest on his shoulder with a self-satisfied grin. He'd chopped it down with the ease of a man ten years his senior and he knew it.

"Are you certain the wood will be of the right quality?" I asked. "I need the best to repair this instrument. It's been handed down for two generations."

"It will," he said. "A few of these olive trees were struck with some sort of disease a few months ago, but it seems to only infect the leaves, not the heartwood. I don't know that any of them will survive the cold months, let alone bloom again. And not even Adnan and Padi could tell me if the disease will spread to the other trees. So it's probably best that we take them all down."

It was the most I'd heard the boy say since my arrival, but something about sharing his knowledge of trees seemed to cut through his guardedness, so I took advantage of the opportunity.

"Your Gibeonite friends seem quite knowledgeable about these woods," I said, using my own smaller ax to chop the branches. "How did you meet them?"

He went stiff for a moment, but I kept my expression bland

and my ax at work so he would not ascribe nefarious motives to the question.

Something must have assuaged his defensiveness, however, because he began to tell me about how one day he'd been exploring the southwestern slope and happened across the two Gibeonites.

"They didn't care where I was from," he said with a shrug. "They simply invited me to help them cut up a tree they'd felled and taught me about all the different varieties and best uses for each type of wood."

"Valuable information," I admitted.

"It is. And I hope to join their endeavors soon. They're getting rich off the Philistines."

"How so?"

"Iron forges need wood," he said, "and lots of it. It's one of the reasons the serens of Philistia want this land so badly. The shephelah contains some of the thickest forests south of Tyre."

"And we control most of the shephelah."

"Yes. So, for now, the Gibeonites are profiting from the Hebrew domination of this area by logging and transporting the wood to the coast. Although if my ancestors get their wish, they'll overrun these hills and do their own clear-cutting."

I paused at his blasé statement.

"Doesn't that upset you? That many of your heritage want to subjugate the people who've adopted you?"

"I suppose so," he said, and although conflict raged in his dual-colored eyes, his tone was dismissive. That he even tolerated the idea of the Philistines overtaking us deeply unsettled me, so I allowed silence to drape over us as we stripped the trunk of branches. But soon the quiet became burdensome, causing my bones to buzz and my skin to prickle with unease, so I made another attempt to draw him out.

"I enjoyed the Shabbat gathering the other night," I said. "Your family's reputation for hospitality is well deserved."

He grunted a non-response. Then, coming at the log from two different directions, he created a notch in the wood before using his whole upper body to come down on the trunk. Sooner than I expected, he'd split the roots of the olive tree from the upper half.

"Your brothers must be impressed with your ability," I said.

He huffed a mirthless laugh. "They are only glad they don't have to waste their precious time cutting wood."

His tone was so derisive that I felt a sharp pang of defensiveness for Gershom and Iyov, whom I'd found to be nothing but welcoming. Although their presence at the meal had caused me a small amount of discomfort, since their tendency to poke at each other good-naturedly and their obvious affection for their siblings, including Eliora and Natan, reminded me so much of my older brothers that I'd avoided looking their way.

"I am certain that is not the case," I said. "Levitical training can be intensive. Learning the statutes of the Torah from the elders and painstakingly memorizing the words of Mosheh is no easy task. There is a reason it takes years to accomplish. Gershom and Iyov are doing what their heritage demands, but that does not change their regard for you."

"They are not even my real brothers," he said, propping a foot on the trunk of the tree as his eyes rolled skyward.

Somehow the snide gesture snapped something inside me, but I did my best to rein in the anger that lapped at my restraint. "I'd do anything to have my own brothers alive again, Natan. Do not belittle the worth of good men who've called you brother and treated you as equal to their blood kin since you came to this mountain."

His nostrils flared as he glared back at me. "I did not ask to come to this mountain."

His harsh words startled me. "Perhaps not. But you cannot argue the fact that Elazar's family has been far better to you than any Philistine would a Hebrew. If it were the other way around, you would be a slave. Not a son. Or a brother."

His chin jerked as if he'd been slapped, brows coming together as he stared at me. Although a hundred other admonishments sprang to my lips, not the least being the way his wayward behavior wounded his sister, I held my tongue, allowing him time to consider the weight of my words. As I did so, I realized that Natan and I had much in common. Both of us had lost fathers. Both of us had been embraced by families not our own.

Although Abiram was nothing like my father, who'd been far less openly opinionated than his older brother, and twice as compassionate, he still had taken me in when my mother had turned her back on me. And Machlon had filled a large part of the void my brothers had left behind. No matter that I was becoming increasingly unsettled by the idea of betraying Elazar and his family, I could not fail the men who'd given me so much and who were the only family I had left. Nor could I fail my people by letting my heart rule over my head.

When the silence again filled with that same buzzing from before, I decided to shift away from such a fraught conversation, sensing that if I pushed him any further today, I would lose any chance that he might eventually confide in me.

"I need an arm-length piece," I said, gesturing to the trunk under his foot and forcibly clearing my expression of frustration. "And about as thick as a man's wrist." I wrapped my fingers around my own to demonstrate.

Natan's eyes narrowed slightly, perhaps suspicious of the change in subject. But then his features relaxed, and the corner of his mouth tipped up.

"Your arm? Or mine?" he said, stretching his hands far to the side, his huge ax still clutched in his fist. The boy did have an impressive wingspan, and he knew it, if the edge of mockery in the question was any indication.

I was glad for the slight dig, however. It gave me leave to nudge him in more profitable directions. "If we made the neck for the lute as long as your arm no one would be able to play it but you. And I don't think we have time to teach you before Yom Teruah."

His brows rose, a hint of amusement pulling at his lips. Then he set about splitting the log lengthwise, as I considered how best to bring up the Ark and stealthily ask about his midnight activities.

"I saw Eliora's face this morning," I said, deciding to aim two stones with one hand. "It's fortunate she wasn't hurt worse. I still don't understand what she was doing out there in the first place, though."

Natan's ax paused at the top of his swing as he darted a glance at me. "It's just like my sister to chase after the moon without thinking." He let the ax-head drop with a heavy crack.

"What do your brothers have to say?" I cringed at being forced to use my own culpability, but I could think of no other way to steer the conversation. "Do they think whomever ran into her was after the Ark?"

"I couldn't say," he replied, swinging the ax down again on the log. "They don't tell me much."

"Have you seen it?" I asked, doing my best to sound disinterested. "Since we brought it up here?"

"The Ark? Of course not. Have you forgotten I'm not one of you?"

"Hebrew?"

"No. Levite. I'm not to even approach the guards when they are on duty, in case I should accidentally step over some invisible line and burn to ash." He scoffed.

"So, you don't believe the Ark is dangerous? Even after Beth Shemesh?"

"I was seven." He shrugged. "All I remember is a storm and lightning. Besides, Arisa covered my eyes after that and wouldn't let me look over the wall, saying that it was too horrible to see. She may be blinded by devotion to your Yahweh, but I'm not convinced."

The scornful way he spoke of Eliora's faith in the One True God gave me pause. I wondered what had convinced her so thoroughly that Yahweh was the God above all gods. Had it been the old Hebrew slave who taught her to speak our language? Or had it been whatever she imagined happened during that storm in the valley? I'd accidentally overheard her tearful pleas to Adonai in the garden and felt certain she believed that he heard every word, as if he were a friend meeting with her, like Adam in Gan Eden.

"Were you serious before?" asked Natan, the expression on his face suddenly boyish. "About the lute?"

I unrolled the words we'd spoken over this past hour and remembered that I'd teased him about learning to play. "Do you *want* to learn?"

His man-size hands twisted back and forth on the handle of his ax, and a faint blush pinked his thinly bearded cheeks. "Shoshana enjoys music."

Understanding dawned almost immediately, but I refused to embarrass the young man. "Shoshana? The girl from the other day?"

Natan cleared his throat and nodded. "She and I . . . are friends. We have an understanding of sorts."

"Is that so?"

"Please—you can't—don't say anything to Elazar," he said, his words tripping over themselves.

"I would never betray a confidence," I said, placing a hand on my heart to display my sincerity. "You have no cause to worry."

His shoulders relaxed, but he seemed to be having trouble looking me in the eye. How quickly he vacillated between boyhood and manhood. I wondered if my brothers had seen the same double-mindedness in me when I was fifteen.

"But I will say this—" I waited until he finally lifted his curious gaze—"one day she will make a lovely bride."

He smiled the first true, genuine smile I'd ever seen on his lips. "She has always been kind to me," he said quickly, as if he were desperate for my approval. "Even when many of the other Hebrew children were not."

The sorrow within that statement reminded me once again that inside Natan the near-man was Lukio, the orphan whose foreign looks and manner must have made him an outcast of sorts among the children of Kiryat-Yearim. I wondered how much of that painful history played into the fight I'd broken up between him and one of the locals near his age.

"One day I will be ready to provide for her." Natan held up the ax, his meaning clear. His drive to become a woodcutter like the Gibeonites had less to do with a desire for riches and more to do with the young woman he'd set his future hopes on. "And then I will ask Elazar to arrange a match."

I studied the piece of olive wood that he'd expertly cut to give myself time to arrange my thoughts. Although he'd given me very little indication that he knew the location of the Ark, I suspected he might know more than he let on. "Unfortunately, it will take a day or two to carve and sand down this piece of wood into a serviceable neck for the lute, and then the musicians will be using it for practice, so I won't be able to teach you how to play."

His shoulders slumped, his countenance falling.

"However . . ." I grinned, enjoying the way his face lit with anticipation as I teasingly drew out the word. "I brought another instrument with me from home, one that is easier to learn than the lute. Perhaps I can bring it up with me in the morning and I'll teach you a song or two?"

"Truly?" He sounded incredulous. "You'd do that for me?"

"Of course! Besides, I still owe you a debt after you beat me so handily at dice all those years ago. I'll teach you and we can call it even. Yes?"

He laughed, shaking his head. But then his grin faltered. "Eliora made me promise to help with the apple harvest tomorrow. With all the fruit on those trees of hers, the work will probably take up the next couple of days."

Time was not my friend. Yom Teruah was only a couple of days away, and I was no closer to pinpointing the location of the Ark than I had been when I came. I had to figure out if Natan knew something, anything, that might point me in the right direction.

"How about if I work extra hard repairing the lute this afternoon and then I come up and help with the apples tomorrow? That way the harvesting will go a little faster and you and I can work in some music lessons during breaks."

That honest smile appeared on his face again, and I wished

Eliora were here now to see the miracle of it. "Shoshana will be pleased."

"Nothing better to win the heart of a beautiful woman than a song from your own heart." My father had told me the same thing, speaking of the way he'd wooed my mother when he was only a little older than Natan. But as I spoke his words, it was not Natan's Shoshana I was thinking of, but rather a green-eyed woman whose sweet voice was an intoxicating melody all on its own.

It seemed the resolve to keep my distance was a weak one indeed.

Twenty-Seven

Eliora

Reaching for the golden fruit at the very top of the tree, my fingertips barely brushed the sun-warmed skin of the apple as it slipped from my grasp yet again. Annoyed, I pushed upward on my toes, determined to conquer the very last holdout on the tree I'd been harvesting, but the ladder beneath me juddered and my footing slipped. I gasped loudly, desperately grabbing for a nearby limb, but in the same moment, Ronen appeared beneath the trembling ladder, his long fingers wrapping around the sides to steady its wooden frame.

Natan had told me Ronen was coming to help today, but I'd been doing my best not to look over my shoulder every so often, anticipating his arrival. However, I'd been failing miserably, so his sudden appearance had come as a surprise.

"I guessed that might happen," he said, a mischievous glint in his dark eyes that made me think he must have been watching me for a while. "The ground is still soggy from last night's rains. And I also knew you could not ignore that one at the top."

Frowning, I glared up at the offending apple, which mocked me from its unreachable perch among the dew-laden leaves. "I cannot just leave it," I said, eyes narrowing, "or it will have won this battle."

He laughed, mouth wide and shoulders shaking. "Eliora, slayer of apples and all manner of wayward fruits. Perhaps you'll let me be your champion?"

I looked down at him, making a quick study of the shoulder-length hair swept into a dark knot at the back of his neck and the way the deep brown of his irises looked like well-polished mahogany in the sunlight, before glancing back up at the apple.

"What is the use of being the tallest woman in Kiryat-Yearim if I cannot reach the top branches?" I grumbled, but descended the rungs of the ladder and traded places with him.

Of course, he climbed the tree like a bushy-tailed squirrel and snagged the golden apple with ease, but instead of handing me the trophy, he put it to his mouth and took an enormous bite.

"Ronen! What happened to acting as my champion?"

He shrugged a shoulder, then descended with his ill-gotten gains. "It was worth the deception. This is the best apple I've ever tasted."

He took another bite, grinning at me as he chewed.

I shook my head, feigning annoyance, but truly he seemed to be so lighthearted this morning, and my own spirits echoed the levity. Even the morning had been bright and the rains had ceased for a few hours, and I was grateful for the sun warming my back as I worked.

"It should be the best apple you've had. It came all the way from Naftali territory."

"That far north?" he said incredulously.

"Yes. One of the Levites who came to guard the mountain four years ago originated in Kedesh. He brought cuttings from some of the local trees with him, having heard that plants grew in this area with extraordinary abundance. He was curious to see if this variety might thrive here."

He tipped his head back to take in the height of the branches. "This tree grew so tall from a cutting in only four years?"

"Oh no, it was joined with the root of another tree, one that was well-established but only produced bitter fruit."

"But how . . . ?" His forehead wrinkled. "I don't understand."

"Come," I said. "I'll show you."

Ducking under the lowest branches, whose leafy fingertips nearly brushed the ground, I led him in a crouch through the dappled shade to the trunk.

"This"—I pointed to the crotch between limbs—"is where the new portion was joined to the original tree. The Levite taught me how to cut the bark and attach the cutting with the trunk, then bind the wound with wax and cord until the two became one. We added seven branches to this tree, all of the Naftali variety he'd so carefully transported, wrapped in damp rags." I pointed to the intersection of each one. "So now, instead of bitter fruit, this tree now bears apples that are sweeter than date honey."

"And this works with all trees?" His tone was incredulous.

"Some better than others," I replied with a shrug. "Many times well-cultivated olive branches are grafted onto wild trees, which produces an abundance of fruit in a shorter amount of time and higher quality oil. We aren't certain why, but two of the branches we tried to affix to this tree did not actually take hold, although they were treated with the very same care. The Levite who brought these cuttings to Kiryat-Yearim insisted that the apples tasted even better than they had where he came from and wondered if something in the soil affected the flavor."

He reached a hand out to shake one of the branches, testing its integrity. "Foreign branches joined to an established tree," he said, tilting his head back to gaze up through the leaves. "I've never heard of such a thing."

A strange thought rooted itself in my head as he spoke. "Just like me."

"What's that?" he asked, his attention back on me.

"The branches were brought from far away and joined to this tree. Just like Natan and I came from Ashdod"—I touched two of the solid connections I'd wrapped with my own hands under the Levite's guidance—"and became part of Elazar's family." I slid my hand down the trunk of the tree and then pointed at one of the curving roots that disappeared into the soil. "And now I am rooted on this mountain, as firmly as if I were born here."

How marvelous that two enemy children, wild branches by any measure, could—like my father had said—become one with the sons of Avraham. Just as if we were born of the same blood.

The choice Elazar had given me eight years ago had been a gift of immeasurable mercy. He could have sent us back like Abinidab had offered to do. Or he could have simply left us there in the field to perish. But instead, he'd offered not just food and shelter, but a family whose love far outshined that of the one I'd been born into.

"Risi! Where are you?" Natan's voice filtered through the canopy of branches under which Ronen and I had been talking, bringing me back from the wandering path my thoughts had been traveling.

I flushed, realizing how it might look that we'd been secreting away alone and slipped out from under the tree, doing my best to appear unruffled as I brushed a few stray leaves from my tunic. Hopefully, Ronen would pause before emerging as well.

Thankfully, Natan's back was to me as he called my name again, so I slipped around a neighboring tree, coming from an entirely different direction.

"There you are. Iyov just came to collect me. An oak fell across the main path up from Kiryat-Yearim. With the ground so soft after the rains, he said it just toppled over, roots and all. I need to go help clear it."

I put my fists on my hips, peering at him with pursed lips. "I think you are just trying to avoid picking more apples."

His brown and green eyes sparkled, the sight causing a small bubble of hope to burst open inside my chest. "It could be," he said. "I am certainly not brokenhearted to trade my harvesting basket for my ax."

I chuckled. "Go on, then. At least I have a few others to help me today. But do not think that you've escaped the harvest completely." I pinned a playful gaze on him.

"Nor your music lesson," said Ronen, who'd appeared at my

side. He gestured to a leather pack on the ground nearby. "I hefted my lyre all the way up the mountain just so I could teach you a few notes."

"Why don't you teach Risi instead?" said Natan. "She'd probably learn it so fast she'd outshine you in a day or two. It's her way."

An odd statement. He'd never said anything so generous about me before, at least in my hearing. Ronen turned to me with brows raised, and I recognized challenge in his expression. I took all too much pleasure in the teasing grin.

"I have far too much to do today," I said, sweeping my hand in a half-circle.

"No one will perish if you take a few moments to rest," said Natan. "You work harder than practically anyone else on this mountain."

I was stunned. This was the second time my brother had praised me this morning. Had his brief time with Ronen out at the olive grove yesterday had such an effect on him already?

"I agree," said Ronen. "I'll help you finish up the tree you are working on, and then we'll find some shade, sample a few more of these delicious Naftali apples, and I'll teach you to play."

With a wave, Natan walked off, and I watched him go, noting the way his shoulders did not seem to droop as much as they had before Ronen took an interest in him. How would I ever repay this man for his kindness?

"All right," I said, resigning myself for Natan's sake. "But we cannot waste too much time." I pointed to the twelve other trees that made up my small apple orchard. "We have all those to harvest before it rains again." They were finally bearing fruit after years of failing to bloom, following their grafting. They were so prolific, in fact, that some of the boughs dragged on the ground. I could not wait to send basketfuls of this bounty down to the people in Kiryat-Yearim.

"I am ever at your service," said Ronen, with a little bow and a palm to his heart. "Let's finish your tree, and then I'll show you my most treasured possession."

Twenty-Eight

Ronen

We sat in the shade of a sprawling oak, and I slid the lyre from the leather satchel that had been specifically crafted by my great-grandfather to replace the one that had disintegrated over time. I unwrapped the thick layers of linen and wool, holding my breath as I briefly inspected the wood to ensure no cracks marred the priceless instrument. Satisfied that it remained intact, I exhaled in relief.

"This," I said, as I smoothed my hand over the body of the seven-stringed lyre, "is nearly four hundred years old."

Eliora's eyes went wide as she took in the shine of the well-oiled rosewood on the ancient lyre. "How?" she breathed out in amazement.

"It has been passed down, generation to generation, since the time of Mosheh. And in fact, if the stories are true, it was actually built during the flight from Egypt."

"How is that possible? Wasn't it too chaotic then, to craft such an instrument? Azuvah told me about the way Pharaoh pursued your people and the crossing of the Red Sea."

"I don't know. But the legend that has been passed along with the lyre is that one of my distant Levite ancestors made this for the woman he married, an Egyptian."

It had been years since I'd thought of the way my father had told me stories of the Great Exodus, his knack for describing detail so enthralling that I could envision myself traveling along with the slaves of Egypt, cowering with the Red Sea at my back, my tongue clinging to the roof of my mouth while standing before the bitter waters at Meribah, and falling to my knees before the shekinah that engulfed the Mountain of Adonai in flames and swirling smoke of every color.

"An Egyptian?" Eliora repeated, studying my face so closely that I wondered whether she was searching for distant echoes of Egypt in the shape of my face. My mother had told me many times that there was a regal cut to my cheekbones that whispered of my father's ancient heritage.

"Indeed. The woman was a slave who went with the Hebrews when they escaped after the night of firstborn deaths. She turned her back on her Pharaoh and her gods to follow Mosheh, and therefore Yahweh, into the desert."

"What inspired her to do that?"

"Many of the details of who they were and how they came to be joined along the way have been lost, along with their names, but this remains as a lasting testament to his love for her." I slid my fingers over the goat-gut strings. As an instrument builder myself, I knew the mastery involved in designing one that had lasted so long. My forefather had known his craft well, and even now the detail was exquisite.

"Look here," I said, my finger tracing down the length of one arm of the lyre. "Time has softened the once sharp etchings, and after so many years of oiling and polishing, most of the paint that once covered the surface is gone, but you can still see the original design."

On the body of the instrument there were two birds, swallows with their beaks parted in song, and down both arms of the instrument were long vines entwined with lotus blooms. About half of the lotus flowers retained blue paint in their deepest grooves, and one of the sparrows looked to have once been painted black or brown, perhaps with hints of yellow and red. I could imagine how vibrant it all must have been when the artist had only just completed the masterpiece.

Eliora scooted closer to examine the instrument. The sweet apple fragrance of her breath filled the space between us, and my pulse reacted to her nearness.

I'd chosen to stay when Natan left, knowing that the decision was born purely of the desire to be close to her for just a little while longer. Listening to her explain about grafting wild branches had been fascinating enough, but when she connected the process to her own adoption into Elazar's family and being joined to the established root of Avraham, I'd realized just how ensnared I was by everything about her. The temptation to collapse the remaining distance between us now and see if she might allow me to taste her lips was undeniable. However, I did not want to frighten her. This quiet moment alone—no family, no mission, no Ark—was too precious to endanger.

So, for now, and if only for today, I would pretend that I was here in Kiryat-Yearim solely for her. Pretend that when I left, she wouldn't still be here on the mountain, mourning my betrayal. Pretend that the declaration of love carved into this lyre was made by my own hands and not those of my distant forefather.

"May I?" she asked, her fingers hovering over the lyre.

"Of course," I said, then shifted the instrument to her lap with the same care as I might transfer a newborn babe to her arms—a thought I forced away as suddenly as it came to me. She would be a mother someday, and a perfect one at that, but there was no use in imagining a future for the two of us that would never be.

With gentle reverence, Eliora's finger barely touched the silken surface, one that I had spent many hours polishing with a soft oiled cloth to maintain its sheen. "Why bring it with you," she asked, "when it surely would be safer at your home in Beit El?"

"It was always my father's greatest joy to play this lyre during worship at the Mishkan." I paused to take a deep breath and swallow the pain of the memories. "Even if I am not playing with the others during the ceremony, I just could not leave it behind. Besides, when it is not with me, it is kept under guard with the rest of the priceless instruments we brought with us."

Perhaps it had been foolish to bring it all the way here to Kiryat-Yearim when my job was to maintain the Levitical instruments, not play them. And my true purpose here had nothing at all to do with music, but the compulsion to keep it with me had been too overwhelming to ignore.

She held out the lyre to me. "Will you play me something?"

A discordant pang hit my chest, and I lifted my palms. "No, I'm here to teach you."

She looked stricken by my refusal. "But why not?"

"It has been a long time," I said, scrambling for an excuse. "My fingers have lost their calluses."

"Please," she said, the arch of her delicate brows pleading. "I remember the song you sang at Beth Shemesh about the shepherd boy and the stars. It was so lovely. I . . ." She paused, her lashes fluttering. "Whenever I've thought of you since then, I always imagined you playing music and singing. . . ." Her voice dissipated as a flush of pink rose on her cheeks.

My chest expanded with almost painful swiftness. She'd thought of me over these years? Held on to the words of a song that I could not even remember myself?

When she pressed the lyre into my hands a second time, I did not refuse. How could I after such a revelation, especially when she was looking at me with such wide-eyed anticipation?

I was not lying when I said that it had been a long time since I'd played with any frequency. I taught the younger Levites, of course, demonstrating correct techniques or musical patterns, and strumming various chords to ensure that strings were properly adjusted whenever I was conducting repairs, but taking the time to simply lose myself in the interplay of notes and words . . . it had been years. My palms began to sweat as I fiddled with the knobs drilled into the crossbar for a few moments, plucking strings and tuning them to my satisfaction, while I wondered if my rusty skills would compare to whatever she'd built up in her mind.

Left without any further excuse for delay, I strummed my fingers across all seven strings, the action so evocative of memories of my father that I knew exactly which song I would play for her—one he'd composed when I was just a boy and that I'd begged to hear nearly every evening.

Although I did not sing as I played, the words moved through my mind like the unwinding of a scroll. Many of the songs the Levites had sung in the Mishkan had been written by my father, his adoration of Yahweh so consuming that lyrics extolling his greatness poured from his soul like a constant stream. In fact, part of the reason I'd avoided joining in the practices for the Yom Teruah ceremony was because it hurt too much.

But as I played for Eliora, the edges weren't as jagged as they'd been in the past. Instead of focusing on the loss of my father, I concentrated on the melody he'd created, letting my fingers pull the beauty from the lyre purely for the sake of pleasing her.

When the last note trembled away, I realized that I'd closed my eyes at some point, my hands knowing their duty even after all this time, and I lifted my gaze to find Eliora's palm over her mouth and tears on her cheeks.

"Ronen . . ." she whispered.

Overcome by her reaction, I gave in to the compulsion to share the truth with her. "My father wrote it."

She nodded slowly, seeming to understand every emotion such a simple statement stirred within me, then lifted a gentle smile that was like a healing balm over the raw places in my heart. "Play me another. One you wrote."

I could deny her nothing.

This time I pushed aside my trepidations and sang as well, letting my voice fill in the gaps where my fingers were inadequate and finding a fresh burst of inspiration from the presence of the green-

234

eyed woman at my side to add another few lines about Yahweh's glory illuminating the canopy of leaves above us. By the time I finished, all the sorrow dredged up by the first song had been laid to rest, and my fingers itched to continue. A compulsion I'd not experienced in a very, very long time.

"Yahweh has given you a gift like nothing I've ever heard," she said. "How can you have gone so long without using it? If I could play like you, or sing like that, I would never stop lifting my voice to the Most High."

The answer was a complicated one. I'd never consciously stopped playing, or even creating new songs, but over time the desire had simply withered away. The longer I'd lived with Abiram and his family, and the more entangled I'd gotten with his plans for the Ark and the priesthood, the less compelled I'd felt to indulge in such pursuits.

"Were your brothers songwriters too?" she asked, then flinched, no doubt realizing that such a question might reopen wounds.

But I answered without hesitation. "No. The eldest, Yehud, was a leader of the percussionists. He loved banging on drums." I smiled, remembering how he used to pound away during celebrations until sweat coated his face and the dancers could barely keep up with his rhythms. "And Michael was the one who taught me instrument building, a skill he'd learned directly from our grandfather. He could play many instruments with dexterity but had little interest in performing."

"So you alone followed in the footsteps of your father," she said. "He must have been so proud."

The stark realization landed on me like a boulder from the sky. *No*. He would not be proud. I'd not spent the last eight years crafting new songs to praise Yahweh as he had, nor lifting my voice in worship. I'd done little more than my duty with woodworking tools and teaching Levite boys simple tunes, but my entire focus lately had been to rescue the Ark from the clutches of Elazar. A plan I knew deep in my gut my father would abhor.

He'd respected his older brother and never spoke an unkind

word against him, but he did not believe that Itamar's descendants had stolen the priesthood. He felt Eli had been granted the seat of High Priest for a specific reason and that if the honor was to pass back to the line of Eleazar ben Aharon, it would be at a time of Yahweh's choosing, not Abiram's.

Something of the turmoil inside me must have shown on my face. Eliora reached out a hand and placed it on my wrist. "Play more. I want to hear another."

Needing the distraction, and desperate to please her, I complied. Then I followed up the lively tune about Yosef's triumphs in Egypt with a ridiculous one about four goats repeatedly slipping away from a shepherdess. Her laughter chased the remainder of my shadows away.

"Music fills your soul," she said as my fingers strummed a gentle melody. "You must not neglect it anymore, Ronen."

She was right. The passion that I'd once had for singing and playing used to be so fervent, so all-encompassing. But over the years, I'd allowed layers of pain and bitterness to snuff out the joy and then gradually shifted all my focus to Abiram's plan instead. Until one afternoon with Eliora brought it gushing back to the surface.

"I cannot write beautiful songs like you, but I have a place that fills me up in much the same way." Her words were soft and hesitant. "I go there when my spirit is troubled."

Intrigued, I cut off my playing to study her face. "Your garden?"

"Well, yes. My garden is a comfort to me." She bit her bottom lip as if considering whether to reveal more. "But there is a quiet place I go to talk to Adonai."

"Show me," I challenged, enticed by the idea of knowing more of her.

"Oh . . . I couldn't," she stammered. Back at the orchard, a few townspeople had appeared with their own baskets to fill. Natan and Iyov must have finally cleared the tree from the path. "It's very . . . high. And we have work to do."

I gave her my most enticing smile. If this was my last day with her, I'd steal every moment I could. "Come, show me. I promise to keep your secret."

Succumbing with a shy smile that made me want to lean forward and press my lips to her poor bruised cheek, she stood up before I could fall prey to the instinct. Then, to my astonishment, she slipped off her sandals, darted around the side of the very tree we'd been sitting under, and reached for the lowest branch. After a sly glance at me that had me bounding to my feet and removing my own sandals, she placed her bare sole on the trunk and began climbing.

Twenty-Nine

Eliora

I pulled myself onto a higher branch, the bark pressing into the skin of my palms and the sharp smell of sap soothing in its familiarity. I still could hear the voices of the townspeople who'd come to harvest from my apple trees, but the sound was merely a distant murmur below.

"How far do we go?" asked Ronen, who'd taken another route up the tree and was nearly even with me as I climbed the sprawling oak that towered above all the others around it.

"Just a few more branches," I said, then found myself grinning at him. "Unless this is too high for you. You are welcome to stay where you are."

His eyes narrowed at my tease, and he reached for the next limb. "When I found a trembling little waif behind that wall all those years ago, I never imagined she might one day be the death of me."

I laughed and stretched my foot to the next branch, boosting myself upward.

"Why this tree?" he asked. "What makes it different from any other in this forest?"

"You'll see," I replied. "I found this spot only a year or so after I came to the mountain. The forest has grown since then, the leaves fuller and the trees taller, but the view is unparalleled."

We finished our climb in silence, Ronen keeping pace with me, and then as I perched on my usual branch and he stood on the one almost directly below me, his long arm wrapped around the trunk so that his head was a handspan from my knee, I pointed to the west. "There, do you see the strip of blue along the horizon? In that gap between the hills?"

"I do. Is that the sea?"

"It is. Sometimes it's almost like I can hear the sound of the waves crashing against the rocks near Ashdod," I said. "And the creak of the boats bobbing up and down in the port."

He was silent, wordlessly urging me to continue.

"My people have been seafarers for as long as anyone remembers," I said. "Even before we left our homeland in Caphtor to come here. Our boats are built like none other, with birds adorning both the prow and the stern. Once, just before my brother was born, my father took me on a voyage. Not a far one—only up the coast to Acco to pick up a shipment of purple dye and fine cloth. But I will never forget the way my stomach pitched and roiled when the wind picked up and blew us a small bit off-course."

My father had been so gentle, pulling me close and whispering assurances to me that day. The last day, in fact, that he'd ever shown such tenderness, since only a few months later he disappeared for the first time. The disquieting memory reminded me why I'd brought Ronen up here in the first place.

"But as lovely as the sight of the sea is, especially when the sun sets that patch of blue aflame, that is not why I come here."

"It's not?" He shifted his perch and peered up at me, the breeze fingering the dark hair that had slipped from the knot at the back of his neck. I'd been drawn to this man eight years ago, when he was not that much older than Natan was now and I was nothing more than a terrified Philistine girl. But nothing had prepared me for the strong attraction that had only deepened since he'd reappeared in my life.

Spending this last hour with him had done nothing to dispel that draw either. His singing voice had only become richer and more soul-stirring since the last time I'd heard it, and the way his fingers drew music from that ancient lyre had been nothing less than awe-inspiring. I'd been so captivated as he sang that I'd found myself leaning closer and closer, helpless to take my eyes away from his beautiful mouth. I'd barely managed to pull back before he opened his eyes and nearly caught me a handbreadth away.

It was evident from the way he'd pulled that first lament from the hollow heart of the lyre that his own was still grieving the loss of his family. I'd felt a kinship with Ronen from the first time he'd mentioned losing his father to death and his mother to a new marriage, and I felt it only more deeply now that he'd given me a glimpse into how much he'd adored his older brothers as well. I could not imagine losing Gershom, Iyov, Yonah, or Shai to death—let alone my precious Natan. And even though there was something about Ronen's cousin Machlon that made me apprehensive, I was glad that at least he'd had someone to walk beside him in the place where his brothers should have been.

I realized that instead of finishing my thought, I'd been staring at him, all the reasons I'd had for arguing against the idea of marriage suddenly seeming insignificant. He'd come to my rescue a number of times, been extraordinarily kind to Natan, and understood what it was like to be grafted into a new family. And in addition to being remarkably talented, he made me feel like a new fountain of hope had broken through the protective layer I'd built around my heart.

Pulse thumping so hard Ronen likely could see it fluttering in my throat, I broke the eye contact and had to remind myself what I'd been about to show him. With a deep breath to collect myself before I spoke, I lifted my hand to gesture south.

"You'll have to look closely," I said, proud that my voice did not warble. "As I said, the leaf cover up here has grown thicker and the trees much taller since I found this place. But there is a grove of six cedars on that ridge. Do you see them? They stand taller than the rest."

"I do," he said, shifting close enough that his shoulder now rested against my leg, sending my heartbeat into a dangerous gallop. "They must be very old from the reach of their branches."

"They are. From what my grandfather said, the Gibeonites who first settled this town named it Kiryat Ba'al in honor of their primary god. Some of their elders traveled north all the way to Sidon and collected saplings from an ancient cedar forest that, by their legends, had been sown by the gods at the beginning of time. They brought those trees here and planted a circular grove around the high place that was dedicated to the deities they revered."

"But why should ancient cedar trees, especially ones meant for such detestable purposes, give you a sense of peace?"

"It's not the trees," I said, "although their presence is a good reminder of the reason why I am here on this mountain. It's the tent that sits at the center of their circle." I lowered my hand, pointing at the barest hint of brown and black that could be sighted through the branches. "And the golden box that resides within it."

A strangled gasp came from Ronen's lips, and his face paled.

"Don't worry," I said, remembering he would be aware of the boundaries preventing anyone from getting too close. "We are plenty far enough away. I've climbed this tree a thousand times over the years. Nothing has ever happened to me, other than a few splinters."

I did not mention that being able to see the resting place of the Ark with my own eyes gave me such a deep sense of security that I rarely went more than a day or two without coming up here, just to remind myself that I had no need to fear, that it was still there and had not been moved away.

"Have you seen it?" he asked, his voice barely above a whisper.

"Not since that day," I said, my cheeks heating, "when you carried me up the mountain on your back. My grandfather had the Ark put inside his own home until an appropriate covering could be prepared and a worthy platform built where, long ago, pagan worship was conducted on the high place."

"Why?" asked Ronen, a sharp edge to his voice. "Why would he put our most holy object on such defiled ground?"

"He'd cleansed that place long ago, when he first came to this mountain and my father was young. Instead of a place of horrific sacrifices and disgusting rites, that ridge became a place where he would go alone to worship the One True God. It was bathed in the outpouring of his heart to Yahweh and consecrated by the words of Torah he recited aloud to keep his memory of the sacred truths fresh. But most of all, the reason he placed the Ark there was because of me."

Confusion swept over his features.

"You see, Azuvah, the Hebrew slave who raised Natan and me, said only one thing the night that we fled Ashdod, just before she was murdered by my cousin because she refused to allow him to sell me to be used in the temple of Dagon."

His mouth went slack, and I knew he had questions, but I continued. "Knowing that she would not be able to follow us out the window, Azuvah told me that I must follow the Ark, without turning from the path, until it rested beneath the cedars and I was sheltered in perfect peace. The night you found me and I told Abinidab what she'd said, he knew exactly what Yahweh wanted: for the Ark to be taken to Kiryat-Yearim and to be placed within that grove of ancient cedars."

I turned my eyes back toward the place where only a glimpse of the tent could be seen through the trees. When I'd first found this place, I'd been able to see the entire outline of the shelter, woven with the finest wool and underlined with treated hides to ensure that the precious treasure would not be touched by the near-constant rains that characterized this time of year.

"Why did Abinidab not keep it in his house?" Ronen asked. "Where it would be more protected?"

"In addition to the words he took as a prophecy, he felt that it was too dangerous to live in such close proximity to the Ark—

especially after what happened to the Levites of Beth Shemesh. So, he charged my father with guarding over it out here, where the trees themselves surround the tent with protection from the elements and the thick underbrush keeps its location hidden. Even the Levites who are consecrated to guard the tent itself are told to take a different route every time they approach, so their feet do not press a path into the ground."

"Does your father know that you come here? To this tree?"

I shook my head. "He knows I spend most of my time in the gardens, and that I enjoy my time alone there among the plants and flowers, but this is my own holy sanctuary where I come to speak to the God who led me to this mountain and to the shelter of peace and safety that is my family's household. You . . ." I paused, my voice dropping into a near-whisper as embarrassment rolled over me like a wave. "You are the only person I've ever shared this secret place with."

Ronen did not respond, his eyes latched on the tent, and I cursed myself for revealing too much. He was probably overwhelmed by the torrent of revealing words that had gushed from my mouth—or annoyed by my obvious affection for him.

The wind picked up, ruffling his hair again, and in the distance, I saw the flap of the tent part and for the space of only a heartbeat the sunlight reached inside and glinted against gold. He turned back to look up at me and, to my horror, all the earlier levity in his expression had been washed away by the overflow of my foolish heart.

"We should go back down," he said abruptly. "I promised I would help you finish those trees, and I have a few other things to attend to before evening falls."

"Of course. I should not have . . ." I stammered, then gave up attempting to smooth over my humiliation as I began my descent from the place that had always been my respite from tumultuous emotions before today.

Once we were on the ground, Ronen picked up the satchel containing his precious lyre, slipped it over his shoulder, and walked back toward the garden, taking his lovely music and any absurd notions I'd briefly entertained with him.

After one last glance over my shoulder in the direction of the cedar grove to remind myself that this mountain was indeed where I belonged for the rest of my days, I followed, my mind already back on my apple trees and all the work I had left to do before the sun went down. Ronen would leave soon, and eventually the memory of him and his beautiful voice would fade, but today, my family and the people of Kiryat-Yearim were counting on me.

Thirty

I strode off the ridge where the Levitical musicians had assembled to rehearse for Yom Teruah. A thunderstorm was building in the west, and Tuviyah had sent us to get the instruments under cover. Already the wind had picked up, but my own lyre was well protected by layers of oiled hide within my pack. I'd split away from the others and taken a roundabout path, needing to compose myself before heading back down to camp. A little cool rain might even do me some good. Finding a boulder to perch on that overlooked the valley, I heaved a sigh and scrubbed at my face.

I had not felt so alive in years. Everything around me seemed brighter and fresher, and my blood was still singing after fully immersing myself in worship alongside my Levitical brethren for the very first time.

And it was all thanks to Eliora.

Although I'd still been reeling from her revelation—and what to do with the knowledge—the moment I'd returned to camp after finishing the apple harvest, I'd sought out Tuviyah.

I thought perhaps he might turn me away, saying I'd waited

too long to be included with the other lyre players during the ceremony tomorrow night. But instead, he'd accepted my offer with tears in his eyes.

"I understood your grief, Ronen," he'd said, "I loved your father like a brother. But I always knew one day you'd allow the music to flow again. It is too much a part of you to keep hidden. He would be so pleased."

And this morning, the music had indeed flowed from me. Although arguments over song selections, struggles over which instruments should lead, and quarrels over lyrics due to vastly divergent tribal dialects had led more than a few Levites from other territories to pack up their instruments and leave the mountain. But those who remained seemed to truly want to worship. Perhaps Tuviyah had performed a miracle after all.

I knew the songs we were playing. Those that weren't ancient had been composed by my own father, so instead of worrying about notes or timing, I'd closed my eyes and let the sounds of a hundred voices lifted in praise envelop me. I pressed into the words of adoration and supplication and found myself marveling over Yahweh's goodness as I did so. My abba had once told me how when he was deep in the throes of composing a song he felt a sense of oneness with the Creator of words and music itself, and somehow today, in the midst of a hundred Levite voices with his words on my lips, I'd felt that same sense of wonder.

However, the moment I'd seen Machlon peering at me from the other side of the choir, a frown on his face as he pounded out a simple rhythm on a hand drum, the euphoria brought on by my renewed passion for worship had been tarnished a small measure.

Even though the words had been heavy on my tongue for the past few days, I still had not told him what Eliora had revealed. Each time I'd been close to sharing what I'd discovered, feeling guilt-ridden for withholding the very information I'd been sent to uncover, I saw her face. I heard the depth of compassion in her voice as she empathized with my grief. I saw the trust in her beautiful green eyes as she revealed her secret place to me and poured out her heart. And my resolve failed, over and over.

Moving my attention to the north, where I had a fairly clear view of the place where her gardens were terraced on the mountainside, I searched for that oak tree we'd climbed. Just before she'd inadvertently spilled her secret in our hidden perch among those branches, I'd been wondering if there would ever be a way that Elazar might consider a potential match between myself and his daughter, regardless of my uncle's opinion on the matter. But the moment she revealed the truth, I was reminded how futile such thoughts were, because I was in Kiryat-Yearim not just for the festival. I was there to lie, to steal, and to betray the woman who had given me back my love of music through nothing more than a listening ear and a few gentle words.

In spite of the way my heart had soared during the rehearsal earlier, I was teetering over an abyss. On one side were my obligations to my uncle and my cousin, along with my desire for my mother and siblings to come home. And on the other, a woman I'd come to care for deeply in spite of everything and whose warm and welcoming family I'd secretly found myself wishing could be my own by marriage—yet another betrayal of my uncle's trust in me.

I shifted my seat on the rock and fixed my eyes near the summit of the mountain, in the place where Eliora had inadvertently delivered the Ark directly into my hands. Although I could not see the tops of the cedar trees from this distance, blending as they did with the rest of the thick woods, I was certain that were I in her garden I'd be able to walk straight to them. With only a few words I would accomplish my part of the mission and could leave the rest in the hands of the priests whose job it was to carry the Ark away. My uncle would be satisfied, my cousin would be proud, and events would be set in motion that would bring about justice for my father and brothers and open the way for the rest of my family to return.

And I would leave behind a woman who never would know how close I'd been to choosing her instead.

As if my divided thoughts had conjured him, Machlon appeared at my side.

"There you are," he said. "I thought I saw you wander off this way after the rehearsal ended. We need to go meet with the others."

"Who? Osher and Shelah?"

"Yes, and a few more I've recruited over the past few days. Now that we have more men to help during the mission, we'll need to adjust our strategy."

"How many more?" I asked.

"A dozen or so, perhaps more," he replied. "The musicians from Simeon and a few others who are disillusioned with the leadership in Kiryat-Yearim."

"And you trust these men?"

"We have a common goal," he said, his lips hardening into a flat line. "My father entrusted this mission to me, Ronen. I won't jeopardize it by placing my trust in an unworthy man."

Again, that disquieting roiling in my stomach returned, making me feel like I was balancing on the edge of a cliff with a boulder in each hand.

"No matter who is part of this, we must make certain the plan remains the same," I said. "We tie and gag the guards while we move the Ark. No one gets hurt."

"Of course not," he said, with a dismissive swipe of his palm.

"Because after what happened to Eliora—"

"And Osher feels terrible for that," he said, his tone sincere as he placed his hand on my shoulder. "It was an accident. She was simply in their path at the wrong moment."

I had to admit that after hearing Eliora's account of the night, it seemed it had only been unfortunate timing, but I still did not fully trust Osher or Shelah to remain levelheaded if plans went awry.

"Speaking of being in the wrong place at the wrong time," Machlon said, his face brightening suddenly, "do you remember just after you came to live with us and we snuck out of the house to follow my older brothers to that wedding banquet?"

"Of course." I laughed, remembering how stealthy we'd imagined ourselves, sneaking about in the shadows along the road. "Getting caught only an hour out of Beit El and being sent back by your irate brothers was certainly not among our finer moments."

"Too true," he said, his brown eyes crinkling as he shook his head. "But you remember, don't you, that I took the blame that day. Insisted it was entirely my idea to tag along with them."

"I do."

I'd been terrified of what Abiram might do when we'd shuffled back in the door with our tails tucked, since it had only been a few weeks since my mother had left me behind. But even though I'd been equally responsible for the ill-fated excursion, and just as curious about the banquet Machlon's older brothers had been invited to by friendly Amorites in a neighboring village, Machlon had insisted that he'd practically dragged me with him and accepted the punishment for both of us that day.

"I will always have your back, cousin." He pinned me with a look of determined sincerity. "We may have different fathers, Ronen, but you are a brother to me all the same. We are joined by blood, by purpose, and by shared devotion to our God, and I would lay down my life for you if necessary."

Without forethought, my eyes darted in the direction of the cedar grove, every muscle in my body taut as I realized that somehow he knew I was wavering and was reminding me where my loyalties should lie.

"I think I know where to find it," I said, almost immediately wishing I could spool the words back in again.

"The Ark? You know where it is?" His eyes were wide, excitement flaring brightly in them.

Willfully swallowing the rock that seemed to be lodged in my throat, I nodded. A sudden rumble of thunder behind me caused me to flinch, and I glanced up at the sky, which had darkened drastically. Tuviyah had been right to dismiss the musicians. The clouds promised a deluge.

249

"How? Where is it?" pressed Machlon, heedless of the second clap of thunder that seemed much closer than the first.

I sprang to my feet, snatching up my pack from the ground and slinging it over my shoulder. "We should head down."

Machlon grabbed my arm, his fingers clamping hard to hold me in place. "Ronen, where is the Ark?"

There was nothing I could do now but tell the truth.

"In a certain grove of trees. Eliora said the guards are trained to never take the same path there. But I saw the tent with my own eyes."

My cousin let out a whoop of joy that was nearly swallowed up by yet another boom from the sky. "I knew it! I knew you'd wheedle it out of that Philistine. She was practically slavering over you the other night."

Bristling at both the derisive Philistine comment and his crass insinuations, I opened my mouth to challenge him, but a brilliant flash of lightning coincided with the next crash of thunder, blinding me and causing my bones to rattle and the soles of my feet to vibrate. Instinctively, I dropped to the ground.

When my sight cleared, both of us were crouched alongside the rock.

"That was close," said Machlon, looking nearly as shaken as I felt. "We'd best get off this ridge."

"Agreed. Let's head that way." I gestured toward the tree line, but before I pushed myself to standing, a glow up on the mountainside in the same area as Eliora's terraced gardens caught my attention. "There's a tree on fire up there."

"I wouldn't doubt it," he replied as both of us got to our feet. "That strike was close."

"It won't spread, will it? It's been raining all week." Flames were slowly overtaking the upper branches of the majestic oak. Surely not the same one I'd climbed with Eliora two days ago . . .

Machlon shrugged, tipping his chin up to watch the fast-moving clouds swirl across the sky. "Likely not. But you never know, the forest is dense here. Perhaps the underbrush isn't quite so saturated."

A few drops of rain hit my skin, but it was nowhere near enough to put out a fire. A fire that was adjacent to the gardens Eliora had spent the last few years cultivating and which fed not only her family but many of the families in Kiryat-Yearim.

My decision was made before I took another breath. But just as my feet began to move in the opposite direction of camp and toward Elazar's home, Machlon pulled me to a halt.

"It's perfect," he said, renewed excitement in his voice.

"What is?" I barely restrained the urge to throw off his arm and tear up the mountain.

"As soon as that fire spreads, everyone up on that mountain will be frantic to put it out."

"Of course they will. Their homes are not that far from Eliora's gardens." I tugged my arm, but he did not release me. "Let me go, Machlon, I need to warn them."

"Let it burn," he said. "No one will be on the lookout for us with such chaos happening. Elazar and his guards won't be thinking about anything but keeping the fire contained. You can lead me right to it."

I blinked at him, mind whirling with frustration and confusion. "We can't go after the Ark now. We aren't prepared. The kohanim aren't even here yet."

"I know that," he scoffed. "But we can see the area with our own eyes and plot out exactly how to extract it and how best to get it down the mountain. Also, we'll take note of how many guards are at the actual site, since they will likely not leave their posts, even for a fire."

"No." I yanked my arm from his grip, my frustration hardening into astonished anger. "This isn't the time for that. I need to warn them. Now! Lives could be at stake."

My cousin bellowed my name as I sprinted away, heading for the path up the mountain, but I ignored the call. *She's lost too much already*, I thought, as the memory of our afternoon in the tree came to mind, along with the way I'd found myself wishing there were not so many obstacles between us.

I could not make Machlon forget that I knew where the Ark was hidden, and I wasn't certain I even wanted to, but at least I could try to save the gardens for the sake of the woman who loved them so much.

Thirty-One

Chest heaving, I banged on the door with the side of my fist, feeling the hinges shudder at the force. I'd spent the entire climb up to Elazar's home praying that not only would the heavens open up, but I would make it here in time to prevent a catastrophe. So far, my prayers had been answered with nothing more than a few sprinkles of rain.

I'd never forget the sight of the rampaging fire that devastated Shiloh after the Philistines set their crops ablaze nine years ago. Machlon and I had climbed the highest hill near Beit El to see it with our own eyes, shortly after a messenger arrived with news of the invasion, along with the devastating report of my father's and brothers' deaths. Smoke had blanketed the entire northern horizon as everyone in Beit El packed belongings and readied animals in case we too were forced to flee. The fact that we did so with hearts already burdened with sorrow had made the entire process even more agonizing.

Neither Philistines nor flames came south that day, but the memory of that terror was still fresh in my mind, even after all this time. I couldn't bear for Eliora or her family to suffer in such a way, especially after I'd already betrayed them. Although thunder still echoed around the hills and the clouds continued to flare brightly within their swirling depths, I'd seen no more bolts streak toward the mountain. One fire would be enough to deal with tonight.

Gershom opened the door, a dagger in hand and his eyes wide, making me realize that I'd likely frightened them all with my insistent pounding. Thunder rumbled at my back, and another flash of lightning lit up his shocked expression.

Taking in my wild appearance, his face contorted with confusion. "Ronen, what are—?"

"A fire! A tree was struck near the gardens. We need to get it down and douse the flames or it will spread—if it hasn't already!"

Gasps and exclamations behind him made me realize that the entire family was gathered in the front room, partaking of a midday meal. Within moments, Iyov and Gershom had pushed past me heading for the Levite quarters to alert the others. Natan strode from the room, heading toward the lower level, where I assumed he kept his ax. We would certainly have need of his skill tonight.

Elazar too was on his feet, strangely calm as he ordered the women to grab as many empty jugs and pots as they could and head for the nearest stream. But when his wife pushed to her own feet, preparing to comply with his command, he pulled her close, kissed her forehead, and told her that her part would be to protect their unborn baby and keep the little ones inside until the danger was past. The rare show of affection from Elazar to his wife caused a pang of longing to hit me directly in the chest, something I'd never experienced before I'd come to Kiryat-Yearim, before I'd reacquainted myself with the girl I'd found in a field, who'd grown into the woman who approached me now with tears in her eyes as her sisters bustled out of the room to fetch vessels.

"Where is it?" she asked, her expression begging me to calm her worst fears, but she would know the truth of it soon enough.

"I could see it clearly from the ridge I was on," I said, then lowered my voice. "I would guess that it is near the tree you showed me the other day . . . if not the very one."

Her hand flew to her mouth just as Natan appeared at her side. With one ax slung over his shoulder, he held out the smaller one

254

I'd used on the olive tree. I accepted it with a nod of gratitude and then stepped back as Elazar came to the doorway.

"Don't worry, Risi," Natan said, putting a palm on her shoulder as he passed on his own way out the door. "Your gardens will be safe." Eliora looked nearly as shocked by his concern as she did the physical contact, and her eyes welled again.

As compelled as I was to reach out my own hand to comfort her, Gershom called my name. The rest of the men were already assembled, some with axes, some with wooden buckets, and all practically vibrating with urgency. The sky was still dark, the clouds overhead roiling as they hovered over the mountain, but thankfully nightfall was still many hours away, or this task would be even more dangerous than it was.

Realizing that I still had my pack slung over my shoulder, I slipped the strap over my head and held it out to Eliora. "Find a safe place for my lyre before you head to the stream with the others."

She accepted, pulling the pack close to her chest as I spun away with another glare at the miserly sky. *Where are you?* I found myself muttering to Adonai as I strode toward the men, a prayer I'd uttered many times since the battle at Afek.

And one to which I still had no answer.

My heart sank as the tree came into view. It was indeed Eliora's giant oak that had been set aflame by the bolt of lightning. But instead of the entire crown being engulfed, as I'd expected, it seemed that the very heart of the tree was burning instead. The trunk remained standing, but the inside was glowing, orange-red flames bursting from a few gaps near the top, as if the heat inside had hollowed out the center but left most of the outer bark intact.

"How could this happen?" asked Iyov, his mouth gaping. "Why is the whole thing not on fire?"

"The outside must have been wet enough from these past few days of rain that the inside is burning first," said Natan. "Adnan told me that this happens from time to time when conditions are just right."

"What do we do?" I asked.

"Take it down," he said, his mismatched eyes traveling the length of the tree. "We'll take turns chopping until it falls, and then we can put out the fire. We'll have to let it fall in the garden, in the open area, because the other direction will only send it into the other trees." He glanced over at his sister, who was watching us with the group of about ten women, who stood a good distance away with full jugs of water in hand. "The ground is still soggy there, so it won't spread." His mouth pulled into a grim curve. "But many of her flowers will be ruined."

As I'd feared. Gershom and Iyov looked at each other, silently deciding whether to follow the advice of a fifteen-year-old boy.

"We have no choice," I said, wishing Eliora was not here to see her hard work destroyed. "He's right. Natan, show me what to do."

Although his solemn expression did not change, his shoulders straightened ever so slightly at my confidence in him. "Everyone stand far back," he shouted, his raspy tone more man than boy at the moment. "And be ready with the water as soon as it falls."

He strode forward, his ax in hand, and swung a few times until he'd cut a large notch in the side nearest the garden. Smoke poured from the wound. The tree was burning much more slowly than I'd anticipated, but we did not have much time before the heartwood was consumed top to bottom.

"Ronen," Natan said, with a jerky gesture as he flanked the tree. "You take that side and I'll take the other. Don't stand anywhere near that notch I made. We chop in one spot until this thing goes down. It should go down fast with that hinge I made."

For what seemed like an hour, he and I swung our axes, wood chips flying and the both of us grunting like boars. Above us, the fire inside the tree continued to crackle and moan. Once, after a loud pop, sparks singed the skin on my arms and burned a few tiny holes in my tunic before I could brush away the embers.

When my arms felt like worn leather, I passed the ax to Iyov and backed up a few paces. But Natan was still steadily chopping away at the cut we'd made, determination on his face as his ax moved easily into rhythm with his older brother's.

He may be an obstinate youth right now, and his immaturity a frustration to his family, but I had the distinct sense that one day Eliora's brother would prove to be a man whose relentless determination would keep him and those he loved alive in dire circumstances. In fact, the impression of his future course was so clear and firm in my mind that it seemed someone had whispered it into my ear—or shouted it, perhaps.

I flinched at the notion, my gaze flying upward where the clouds had darkened even further while we worked at the burning tree.

Then Natan shouted for us to get back. A loud crack split the air as the tree bowed beneath its own weight and fell, smoke and fire exploding outward as it slammed to the ground in the very center of Eliora's beautiful flower garden. But then, Yahweh decided to answer my faithless pleas, and the floodgates of heaven opened.

After the fire had been doused by a sudden deluge while we all took cover beneath the trees, Elazar had insisted that I pass the night in their home and allow them to offer gratitude in the form of a meal. Although I'd ultimately had nothing to do with keeping the fire from spreading—something Adonai himself had accomplished—I'd been only too grateful to accept, if only to stave off explaining to Machlon why I'd walked away from him on that ridge.

As Shai and Amina squabbled loudly over who'd received the larger portion of bread, their voices overriding the boisterous conversations of Elazar's gathered friends and family in the full room, he leaned close to me, his expression solemn. "I remember your father well, Ronen."

I nearly choked on my wine. "You do?"

"We served together at the Mishkan a time or two when our designated rotations overlapped. He was an honorable man. I was grieved to hear that he'd been lost at Afek."

My chest flamed with pain. "My two brothers were slain that day as well."

"May their souls be at rest," he murmured, compassion etched into every line of his face. Then he sighed, shaking his head. "If only the Ark had been left in its place."

"Or if the claims about its power were true," I muttered, before realizing I'd spoken my doubts aloud. My prayer that my comment would be swallowed up in the chaos went unanswered.

"You doubt the stories of the Ark?"

I shrugged, taking another draft of wine to collect my thoughts before replying. "I don't disbelieve that during Mosheh and Ye-hoshua's day, miracles occurred. But it's been hundreds of years since then, and obviously, by the way the Ark was captured by our unconsecrated enemies, whatever power it may have had is long since departed."

Elazar's response was incredulous. "You were there, Ronen. You saw the bodies of the Levites in Beth Shemesh who approached it without the proper reverence."

"A bolt of lightning, just like this storm."

"And the plagues in Ashdod? You discount those as well?" His silver-threaded brows furrowed.

"As Abiram says, disease and famine happen, especially among those who discount Torah law and eat the flesh of swine, rats, and dogs."

To avoid his pointed scrutiny and the deep frown on his mouth, my eyes moved to Eliora across the room, where she was carrying little Dafna on her hip as she finished peacemaking between the twins, refilled their stew bowls, and then retrieved another basket of bread to distribute. As I watched with increasing frustration, her mother made an attempt to get her to sit down and eat, but Eliora shook her head and continued to tend to everyone's needs but her own.

"Ronen," said Elazar, his voice soft but firm as he reclaimed my attention from his daughter. "The Ark was not taken at Afek be-cause it was powerless—although the power is not in the box itself but the indwelling of the *Ruach Ha'Kodesh*, which was clearly not present on the battlefield that day. The Ark was taken as punishment for our disobedience and to sever the chains we've allowed the Philistines to wrap around our necks. The loss of the Ark is nothing in comparison to what will happen if we don't turn our faces back to Adonai."

"They shouldn't have died," I said, hackles rising. "They revered Yahweh and were on that battlefield because they believed the stories of old, of the Ark going before the army in triumph."

"No, they should not have died," said Elazar, "because the elders and priests who made that decision did so without consulting Yahweh. They made their own plans and expected him to submit to their will. They tried to force the hand of the Almighty. And thirty thousand Hebrews suffered for their folly, including your father and brothers. We cannot make the same mistake again. We must wait. Be patient. And listen to the man who speaks for him."

"Samuel?" I asked, knowing immediately who he was speaking of, since far too many of the Levites were of the same mind. "You truly believe he speaks with the mouth of the Holy One?"

"I do. Not only was I there when he publicly admonished Eli for his sons' repugnant behavior and predicted their demise after hearing the voice of Yahweh in the Mishkan, but I saw that prophecy proven correct when word arrived that they'd been destroyed on the battlefield and Eli's neck was broken when he fell from his stone chair at the news. Since then, Samuel's words have been consistently in line with the laws of Mosheh. He may be a little over thirty years old, but his wisdom far exceeds any man I've ever known—my own father included, and he spent hours every day on the rooftop beseeching Adonai for understanding. Samuel's devotion to prayer is unrivaled, and his depth of knowledge beyond explanation. Indeed, I have a feeling that the years to come will prove Samuel to be the type of leader who might even rival Mosheh himself."

I was stunned speechless at such a comparison and grateful that

Abiram was not here to hear it. He might suffer a fit of apoplexy from such a bold statement.

"And I am determined that until Yahweh commands the move of the sacred vessel, either through Samuel's mouth or other divine means, it will remain upon this hill. Anyone who ignores the lesson of Pinchas and Hofni's arrogance will undoubtedly suffer the same demise, and I will do everything I can to prevent such a tragedy."

Thirty-Two

Eliora

With Ronen's lyre secure in the cradle of my arms, I headed for the stairway that led to the upper room, where he'd passed the night with my older brothers and Natan. It had taken them until after dark to ensure that the fallen tree was no longer smoldering after the cloudburst passed over, so he'd been invited to stay. Assuming he might want to leave first thing this morning to head down to the musicians' camp, I'd woken before dawn, anxious to return his instrument before I left to survey the damage to my flowers.

But just as I lifted my foot to the first step, my mother called my name across the courtyard. I paused, waiting as she bounded across the space toward me as if she were not well into her third decade and carrying a babe within her womb. Her coils of dark hair, like Miri's, framed her round face as she reached for me, tugging me down to kiss my cheeks.

"Shalom, my lovely," she said. "Did you sleep well?"

I tried to smile, but it fell flat. "Truthfully, no. It was difficult to see exactly what was ruined last night after twilight fell, and I've been dreading what might greet me. But I could not remain abed any longer. I have to see."

With her brown eyes full of compassion, she reached up to place her palms on my cheeks. "I know it hurts, daughter. You have put so much of yourself into that garden these past years. But it will grow again. And perhaps you will be surprised at not only what survived such a devastating blow but what beauty will be born from the destruction."

I sighed. "I do hope so, but I am preparing myself for the worst."

She winced, her hand dropping to her belly. "This one afforded me little sleep last night either. I have a feeling this will be another boy to add to our family, if the early movement is any indication. Although Dafna was almost as lively." Her attention dropped to the burden in my hands. "What is that?"

"Ronen's lyre," I said. "He asked me to keep it safe while the men tended to the tree."

Her brows lifted. "Did he now?"

Something in her tone made heat rush to my cheeks, and I cursed my too-pale skin when she grinned at me. "He seemed to be greatly concerned for your gardens last night."

"He is kind. I am grateful that he saw the lightning strike in the first place, or the orchard may have met the same fate as that oak."

She peered up at me, maternal knowing in her gaze. "It seems to me that it was more than kindness, Eliora. Should your father and I expect a visit from him sometime soon?"

Seized with strongly competing emotions at the idea of my parents arranging a match with Ronen, I insisted that nothing was going on between us, but she talked over my spluttering response.

"And why not?" she said. "Not only has he proven himself to be honorable and concerned for the well-being of others, but if I am not mistaken, he is quite enamored of you. None of us are blind, daughter, and that man follows you with his eyes."

"He . . . he does?" I choked out, pulling Ronen's lyre tight against the place where my heart seemed to be squeezing into a tight fist.

"Indeed." Her gaze turned questioning. "But do you feel the

same? I thought perhaps you might, but I cannot quite decide if I am correct, since you treat him with the same kindness you do everyone else. If you were Miri, I'd have no such trouble, since she withholds nothing, but you keep your emotions pressed down so deeply that I cannot discern the truth."

Memories of the woman who'd given birth to me seemed almost transparent now, and for as much as I still loved my Philistine mother, it was Yoela who'd chosen me, who'd taken me into her brood with no thought for my enemy heritage, and whose warm and loving home had offered me the peace I'd been promised by Azuvah that last night in Ashdod.

And now, with her gentle prodding into places that I'd not truly even allowed myself to dwell in too long, especially after the abrupt shift in Ronen's demeanor in the tree, I barely suppressed the urge to throw myself into her arms and let everything pour free the way Miri was prone to do.

"I don't know," I admitted, dropping my gaze to my sandals. "With all he's done for Natan . . . and then with the tree last night . . . I cannot help but be drawn to him. If I am honest," I said, my cheeks flaming, "I've thought of him many times over these past years, even before he returned."

She placed her fingers under my chin, nudging me until I met her eyes. "Then why are you so hesitant about entertaining a betrothal?"

"I can't leave here," I blurted out. "I can't. This is where I belong."

"Oh, my precious girl, of course you belong here. Yahweh brought you to us in his marvelous generosity, and I cannot thank him enough for doing so. But for as much as I selfishly would love for you to remain here, he may have plans for you beyond this mountain, whether that is with Ronen or with another man who will see the great worth in you and plead with us to make you his wife and the mother of his children."

Every bone in my body recoiled at the suggestion of leaving Kiryat-Yearim. "But I must stay. This is where the Ark is."

She tilted her head, studying my face intently. "And why must you be where the Ark is?"

I chewed on my lip, gripping Ronen's lyre even closer to my chest. "Because . . ." My voice dropped. "Because I feel safe here, in the place Azuvah told me I would find peace. And because it is nearby, I am at rest and know that Yahweh hears my prayers. When I go too far away, even down into town, I am . . . uneasy."

"Oh but, daughter, do you not remember that Yahweh is not a regional god like those of your people? He does not live on this mountain, or even within the Ark, although there have been times when the indwelling has resided upon its throne. The Ark itself is just a thing, fashioned by the hands of men, even though it was commissioned by Yahweh himself. But the Eternal One was not made by man; there is no place you can go that he will not be with you. Whether that is here, or Beit El, or Ashdod, or any other place. He is the God Who Sees. There is no place you can go to escape his vigilant watch over you. If it were not so, then he would not have heard our ancestors cry out to him from Egypt or see our sufferings there."

"But what about Natan?" I sputtered. "I could not abandon him, especially when he seems so lost. And you'll have another little one soon. I need to help you and Rina too—"

"Eliora," she interrupted, "do you remember the story of Sarah? The wife of Avraham?"

I blinked at her abrupt question. "Of course. Grandfather told us the story of her life many times."

"She was not perfect, by any measure. And neither was her husband, for that matter. But one thing is clear: when Avraham was told to pack up all he owned and leave his country for this one, she went too. She left all she knew back in Ur. Family. Friends. Her home. And although she did not even know her destination, and even though there were many pitfalls along the way, she trusted Elohim enough to go. And look at the blessings that came from her obedience. She is the mother of Yitzhak. The grandmother of Yaakov. The great-grandmother of the tribes of

Israel, and therefore, by rights of adoption and covenant, your own ancestor."

Although I'd been coming to a deeper understanding of what my joining with the people of Israel meant, I'd not considered that their forefathers were now my own as well.

"And what if she had refused?" my mother continued. "What if she had planted her sandals on the ground and refused to go with her husband? Refused the call of a God she could neither see nor hear? We can never guess what may come of our obedience, Eliora, but that is not for us to know anyhow. We are not the All-Knowing One. We are simply called to 'hear and obey' and to love Adonai our God with all our hearts, all our minds, and all our strength. I do not know what good things he has in store for you, but I will say this: if Ronen is one of those gifts, it would be disobedience to turn it away, even if that means leaving Kiryat-Yearim. It is not the Ark you must follow, my precious child. It is the God who made you."

Tears blurred my vision as she laid bare all my fears with the gentlest of chastisements.

"I have prayed for you to be married to not just a good and kind man, but one who sees you for who you truly are and appreciates every part of you, even the parts you do not count as valuable. If that is Ronen, then your father and I will be pleased to see you joined with him, even if it will pain us to let you go. And as for Natan—" She sighed, her palm swirling over her belly in a sooth-ing gesture. "I know you love him, and that your heart is just as burdened as ours over his brokenness. But you are not his God, Eliora. You cannot save him from himself. That task is Yahweh's alone. Remember, you were not the only orphan who was led to Kiryat-Yearim that day. He too followed the Ark, even if he did not understand the reasons for it. And I hope . . . no, I believe that there is a reason for it all. Just like Sarah and Avraham, our path is not always straight, and at times we may lose our way, but somehow Yahweh's good will always prevails."

She gripped my wrist, lifting it and turning my hand upward

so my palm lay open, fingers splayed wide. "Let go of the firm grip you have on Natan. Release him to the care of the God Who Sees, and have faith that no matter what may happen to that boy, and no matter how far he may stray, Yahweh still holds him in the palm of his hand. And then be still, my daughter, and know that he is God, no matter where he leads you."

Before I could gather my thoughts enough to respond, she pressed a kiss to that palm, smiled up at me with the same generous affection that she'd offered since the first day I'd met her, and sent me on my way up the stairs. With my mind in turmoil, I obeyed, and nearly collided with Gershom as he and Iyov met me at the top.

"Shalom," he said. "I thought you might already be in the garden, surveying the damage."

"I am heading that way," I said, then patted Ronen's pack, and I hoped that the confusion and upheaval I felt after my conversation with our mother was not written all over my face. "I just need to give Ronen his lyre before he leaves."

"Ah. He did say he would be expected down in camp first thing this morning." Gershom's expression turned compassionate. "I am sorry, sister, about your flowers. We will all do our best to save what we can."

Iyov nodded in agreement. "Abba has given us both leave from our training to help chop up the tree. Natan says he'll build a charcoal mound with the remains."

"I am just glad that no one was injured, and that the fire did not spread."

"We have Ronen to thank for it," said Gershom. "We owe him a great debt."

"That we do. He is a good man." Iyov grinned at me as he moved to follow Gershom, who was already halfway down the stairs. "The kind I might not mind having for a brother someday." He winked as he passed by, leaving me blushing. Was I truly so transparent?

When I turned around and found Ronen himself leaning against the parapet a few paces away, watching me, I nearly bolted from the roof. But instead, I prayed that he'd not heard Iyov's comment and composed a smile on my face.

"Shalom," I said, holding out his instrument as I approached. "I brought this for you. I knew you would need it this morning."

"Thank you," he said, accepting the pack. "I appreciate you keeping it safe for me."

"And I am so grateful that you came to our door when you did."

His gaze moved to the portion of the terraces that could be seen from the rooftop. "I only wish your oak hadn't been destroyed. Along with your beautiful flowers."

Turning to the parapet, I leaned forward, placing my folded arms on the stone ledge, and allowed myself to look in the same direction. Even from here I could see the gap where my special tree used to stand, and the sight gutted me.

"They were only flowers. I am just thankful that the vegetable garden and the orchards were spared," I said. Then, hit with a wave of exhaustion that had followed me through a restless night of worrying over what I might find on those terraces in the daylight, I scrubbed at my eyes with my fingertips.

"Have you slept at all?" he asked. He was no longer staring out at the vista, but instead scrutinizing my face, a pinch of concern between his brows.

"Of course," I said.

"The shadows beneath your eyes tell another story."

Without thinking, I pressed my fingers to the place he'd spoken of, as if I could hide the telltale signs of a night spent tossing and turning.

"When your brothers and I went to bed last night, you were still awake, scrubbing pots and cleaning, and that was after you helped herd all the little ones to bed and served a meal in which you barely took three bites for yourself. Yet here you are, barely after dawn, delivering my lyre before you scamper off to tend that huge garden by yourself."

Bewildered by his obvious frustration, I stared back, slack-jawed for a few heartbeats. "I could not leave all the work for my mother and sister. And I love working in the gardens, you know this."

"I do, but rarely do I see you rest, Eliora. If you are not in the gardens, plucking every weed that dares mar its perfection and harvesting bushels and bushels of produce to deliver to others, you are in this house, serving your family from the rising of the sun until well after nightfall."

"It is my pleasure to serve my loved ones."

"And rightly so. Your family. . . ." He paused, swallowing hard. "They are wonderful, Eliora. Your brothers remind me so much of my own. And your parents, your siblings, they plainly adore you. So why do you work so hard for a place at their table when you already have one?"

Speechless, I blinked at him in confusion.

"I have watched you these past weeks, and at first I thought perhaps you were just as the people of Kiryat-Yearim told me: an extraordinarily kind woman whose good deeds had no deeper motive. But I was wrong."

Stung, I backed up a step. "I have no motive other than love for my family and love for the people on this mountain."

"No," he said, meeting my retreat with his own step forward. "You misunderstand me. I do not mean to insinuate that your reasons for such self-sacrifice are anything but honorable, only that you do not allow yourself to relax and enjoy what you have, because you are working so hard to earn something you've already been given."

I had no ready response to such an accusation. Already this morning I'd been told by my mother that I was holding too tightly to Natan and now here was the man who'd come to mean so much to me, the one man for whom I'd considered the unthinkable— leaving Kiryat-Yearim—saying that I was trying to earn my family's love?

"You told me that day in the orchard that you were like those foreign branches, grafted into a new tree. Do you remember?"

I nodded, jarred by the shift in subject.

"And yet I think that maybe you've not truly accepted that you are indeed bonded permanently to the root. I wonder if you so fear being rejected by them—that someone will come along, think that you don't belong, and cut you off again—that you cannot embrace who you are now."

"I don't . . . I don't understand."

"This," he said, pointing at my tightly wrapped headscarf. "Why do you wear this thing?"

My hand instinctively went to my crown, and my hackles rose. "Many women wear head coverings."

"They do, but not every moment of every day. I would venture to guess that even your family does not see you without it."

He would be right. The habit of wrapping my head every morning was deeply ingrained after so many years.

"So why?" he pressed. "Why cover your hair? From what I remember, it is a striking color, like liquid gold."

His choice of words made my heart thump unevenly. "People stared," I said, the admission coming out on a soft breath. "I didn't like it."

"Being admired?" he asked, looking shocked that I'd reject such attention. "Being beautiful?"

"Being Philistine!" The words spilled from my mouth, unbidden and unrestrained. "I hate that I stand a head taller than my mother and sisters. I hate that my hair is garish instead of dark and lovely. I hate that my veins flow with enemy blood. I wish I'd been born on this mountain. That I'd known nothing but Kiryat-Yearim and did not remember awful things from Ashdod that I can never wash from my mind."

"But that is who you are! And just like those cuttings from Naftali territory that produce distinctly flavored apples because they are now nourished by roots established on this mountain, you bring your own uniqueness with you from Ashdod. Revealing your hair, standing at your full height, or displaying any other markers of your heritage will not cause the people you love to cast you out, Eliora. They adopted you. Made a binding covenant with you. And anyone else who does not see the beauty in the incredible story of your grafting into Israel or misses the brilliant light that shines from the very center of your being does not matter."

I stared in disbelief at his outburst, along with the realization that Ronen had been much more observant that I'd thought. I felt exposed like never before, but at the same time, understood in a way I'd never experienced. My mother's words from earlier came back to me: "*I have prayed for you to be married to not just a good and kind man, but one who sees you for who you truly are and appreciates every part of you, even the parts you do not count as valuable.*"

Could it be that Ronen was that man?

When he spoke again, his tone was gentle. "May I see?"

"See?"

"Your hair." His expression was meek, almost pleading. "You don't have to, of course. I understand if it makes you uncomfortable. It is just . . . I have been going out of my head imagining what you look like without the scarf."

My pulse took flight as I weighed his words, searching for the truth of their meaning on his face and finding only sincerity there. Something told me this moment would change all the others to come, but I lifted my hands, slipped my fingers beneath the tucked-in end of my scarf and loosened its tight hold.

With my eyes averted, I unwrapped my hair, allowing its heavy bulk to unfurl, the thick spill of it cascading over my shoulder, then held my breath as I allowed him to look his fill.

"You are . . ." He paused, then, to my astonishment, he reached out and drew one of the golden waves between his fingers, slowly sliding down its length in the same reverent way he played his lyre. "You are the most beautiful woman I've ever known," he whispered. "But I thought that even before you removed the covering. I would think that even if I was blind."

Astonished by his bold declaration, I jerked my chin up and met his eyes. "Even though I am a Philistine?"

He took a step closer, his gaze traveling over my face in a leisurely way that made my palms go damp and my bones numb. "Because you are the woman the Creator made you to be, no matter where you come from or what you look like. I could never have guessed eight years ago, when I found you trembling behind that rock wall in the middle of a field, that I would want so badly to make you—"

The clearing of a throat interrupted whatever Ronen was about to say, and both of us turned our heads to find Natan standing a few paces away, hands on his hips and wicked amusement in his eyes.

"Not interrupting anything," he said, flashing a grin of pure younger-brother mischief, "am I?"

Thirty-Three

Ronen

For the first time since I'd known him, Natan had sought out my company of his own volition, asking me to help him build a charcoal mound, which told me that somehow I'd actually broken through some of his more stony defenses. It was a victory that was worth putting off everything else for another hour or two. Including the inevitable confrontation with my cousin.

But even as I followed Natan on the muddy path toward the burned-out tree, my blood was still humming from my conversation on the roof with Eliora. I'd not meant to speak so boldly to her, nor to reveal myself quite so thoroughly, but last night had opened my eyes to more than just my lack of faith in the God Who Hears.

I'd always known Eliora was devoted to her family, but I'd watched her rush about the household all evening, tending to everyone's needs with downcast eyes, as if she were some sort of servant who might be whipped if she did not perform.

When I'd realized that her determination to refuse help and to carry everyone else's burdens upon her own back was more about fear than anything, I had not been able to control my mouth, desperate to make her see herself as I did and to stop pushing herself to exhaustion in the quest to prove her worth. When she'd surprised me by complying with my presumptuous request to uncover her hair, it had been all I could do to not drag her into my arms, regardless of what I'd been sent here to do.

I'd spent many hours last night battling my rapidly escalating guilt over deceiving her family, which had been exacerbated by the quiet but unsettling conversation I'd had with her father. Tangled up with what Elazar had said about Samuel was the way my half-hearted prayer for rain had been answered so clearly, along with the soul-whisper I'd had about Natan's future. And I could not stop thinking about how Eliora said her Hebrew slave in Ashdod had somehow known the Ark would one day rest within a grove of cedar trees.

Had Abiram's insistence that signs and wonders were a thing of the past—and therefore only the priests must be the source of guidance and wisdom—been based on faulty assumptions? Or worse, had my uncle deliberately misguided me for some reason?

I'd been so wrapped up inside my divided mind as Natan and I made our way to the remains of Eliora's oak tree that I was stunned to find myself standing in front of its carcass. My stomach twisted at the sight, and I was glad that she was not here to view the wreckage in full daylight. Years of her work undone in one night and all by the blackened husk of the enormous tree that had been such a refuge and comfort to her.

"Where do we start?" I asked Natan, in order to distract myself from thoughts of his sister's beautiful green eyes overflowing with grief at the damage.

"Let's cut up as much as we can before I start building the mound. Shouldn't take long since much of the center burned away already." Natan kicked at the charred trunk, and the bark promptly collapsed inward. "It'll take me a few hours to build the mound, but I'd like to have the fire burning before nightfall."

I slipped my lyre from my shoulder to place it atop a nearby boulder and off the sodden ground. "I'll help as long as I can, but I need to go rehearse with the others and then make sure all the instruments are ready for the ceremony tonight. Besides, my cousin will be wondering where I am."

"Are you avoiding him for some reason?"

It was the first time Natan had asked something personal of me, and I was so shocked by the novelty of it that I answered without forethought. "I'm deliberating something that I'm not quite prepared to discuss with him."

He fidgeted with the ax in his hand, running a finger along one of its edges. "Risi?"

"What about her?"

He pinned me with a sardonic look. "I'm not a fool, Ronen."

I thought of the way he'd come upon us on the roof, and the knowing amusement in his mismatched eyes as he'd interrupted the moment in which I'd nearly lost my head and begged her to be mine, regardless of the cost.

"No," I said, acknowledging the truth. "No, you are not."

"Are you planning to approach Elazar soon?" He seemed to be gritting his teeth, bracing for the answer.

"It may not be as simple as that," I murmured, looking down at the crushed remains of Eliora's flowers beneath the burned-out tree. She would be devastated when she saw how it had cut a path of destruction that may take years to restore to its former glory. Would my deceit cause the same sort of damage to the fragile thing that had been blooming between us?

"What is difficult? You want her as a wife, do you not?"

I did, even if I hadn't fully admitted the truth to myself before now. The draw she'd had on me, even from the first time I'd seen her dancing at the wedding, was undeniable. And every moment I'd spent with her since then had felt like the unfurling of something far more precious and rare than the most exotic bloom Eliora had cultivated on this mountain—even when my intentions had been less than honorable.

But how could I reconcile all that stood in our way? I could not possibly walk away from this mission. Not when Abiram had been planning all of this for so long. Not when doing so would mean letting go of both justice for my father and brothers and the return of the rest of my family. And yet the conversation I'd had with Elazar last night during the meal had made me question everything in a way I hadn't before.

It made me wonder for the very first time if perhaps I was on the wrong side.

"There's no need to worry," said Natan. "It's plain she would welcome the match."

"And how would you feel," I asked, hesitantly, "if Elazar did accept my offer?"

"I have no say over her decisions," he said, his tone as severe as the edge of his ax. "And you certainly don't need my blessing, so there's no need to waste your time with me."

I flinched, taking a step backward. "What makes you think I'm wasting my time with you?"

He huffed a laugh. "Again, Ronen, I am no fool. I thought perhaps . . ." He paused and pressed his lips in a tight line for a moment before he continued. "Feigning friendship with me won't change how she sees you, and Elazar and Yoela think you're some gift sent from the sky for their beloved daughter. What is the point in waiting?"

"Where did you get the idea that my regard for you is anything but genuine, Natan?"

He replied with nothing more than a grunt as he crouched to untangle two limbs, cursing when they refused to submit to his harsh and jerky movements. I nudged Natan's shin with my foot in a half-teasing, brotherly gesture. Scowling, he swiped at my sandal, but I would not let him get away with saying what he did and then shrugging me off.

"Tell me, Natan," I ordered. "What have I done to give you such a ridiculous notion?"

"Nothing," he said, aggravation practically spewing from his mouth as he pushed to his feet. "Nothing at all. But I know what comes next."

"Next?"

"Gershom and Iyov moved on. Medad and his brothers moved on. Adnan and Padi have moved on. Even my own father . . ." He stopped, glaring at the dirt by my feet. "You're no different. And I don't expect you to be."

The words sounded as hollow as the gutted tree laying before us. Natan may look like a man, with muscled shoulders from hefting his ax, but he was still a boy who'd been left behind, tossed aside, and forgotten. I knew the feeling all too well.

"I want your sister as my wife, Natan. It's becoming more and more clear by the moment that she's everything—" I cleared my throat—"that there is no one else like her in all the world. But that has no bearing on our friendship. I was impressed with you eight years ago, with the way you fearlessly took me on to protect her, even though back then I was the one who towered over you. And even though you are as prickly as a thistle more often than not, I see myself in you."

His brow furrowed, the ire seeming to drain from him.

"I am just as much an orphan as you. My father is dead, my brothers are dead, and my mother took the rest of my siblings off to Naftali territory to live with her new husband. I understand what it's like to feel untethered. Like you're unsure if anyone truly cares whether you live or die. But this family . . ." I paused to take a breath and steady myself before saying more.

"Elazar's family truly loves you, Natan. They invited you and Eliora in without precondition. There is no hidden motive. No merit to be earned. And they certainly won't cut you off if you step over the line—or they would have already. Gershom and Iyov may be busy with their training, but no matter how much grief you've given them—and I'm certain I only know a portion of it—they speak of you with affection that cannot be contrived. I would venture the two of them would go to the ends of the earth for you if necessary. And any so-called friend who cannot remain loyal in trial or pushes you to become something you are not was never a friend at all. And if miracles actually do happen and Eliora becomes mine, then I will be proud to call you my brother."

Both of us were stunned by my outburst. And I realized at that moment that I'd made a decision without even knowing it. How I would possibly explain that decision to my uncle, and what it all meant for the future, I couldn't begin to consider. But I needed her. I'd been empty for so long that the only thing seeming to fill that void had been thoughts of restoring what had been lost to me—until Eliora reappeared in my life and made me hope for something I'd not even cared about before now. I wanted to know more of her, to build a future with her, to hold a life in my hands that we'd created together.

I could see the skepticism on Natan's face and knew he didn't quite believe that I meant what I said. Remembering how we first connected all those years ago, I made yet another decision.

Lifting my hand to my neck, I gripped the lion claw one last time as I thought of the moment my father had given it to me. He'd pressed a kiss to my forehead, reminded me that Yahweh was with me, and strode off to do the duty that would lead to his death, because he'd followed the leadership of men who claimed they spoke for Yahweh but actually spoke for themselves.

"Here," I said, slipping the necklace over my head. "I want you to have this."

He raised his palms in refusal as I held it out to him, eyes wide with surprise. Although my heart ached at letting it go, I knew for certain it was time. My father would approve. And Natan needed the reassurance.

"You know what this means to me," I said, shaking it so that the claw clattered against the wooden beads that were strung on either side of it. "I do not give it to you lightly."

He must have finally accepted my sincerity, because he turned his hand over and allowed me to lay it in his palm. I hoped he understood that I was not offering a charm against calamity but a vow of brotherhood.

With a solemn nod, he slipped the necklace over his head and settled it in the center of his chest carefully, as if it were just as precious to him as it was to me. Then he folded his arms as he glanced away and cleared his throat, twice. My own was choked with emotion as well, so I decided to give both of us some relief by shifting the subject.

"Now," I said, deciding to test whether our unspoken vow would hold, "when are you going to tell me what you were doing out there in the dark that night Eliora was injured?"

He blew out a hefty sigh, his chin dropping. "She saw me?"

"Do you really think your sister would be off chasing the moon? As usual, she protected you by saying nothing."

My admonishment did not go unnoticed. Natan grimaced, hooking a hand around the back of his neck. "I . . ." He cleared his throat again. "I went to meet someone, but she wasn't there, so I went back. I didn't know Risi was behind me."

"She?" I pressed.

He scratched at his scraggly beard, a tinge of pink on his cheeks. "Shoshana. She said she needed to tell me something, but she must not have been able to get out of the house undetected."

I gave him a warning look. "Careful, young Natan. Angry fathers are not to be trifled with. And neither are innocent maidens."

"I mean to marry her someday," he said, squaring his shoulders with a defiant lift to his chin. "I'd only planned to meet her for a few moments, hear what she had to say, and then escort her back home. I'd never put her in danger. Or Risi, for that matter."

"I believe you," I said. "Your protective instinct was one of the first things I ever noticed about you. I know you wouldn't do so purposefully."

"I haven't seen her since then, so I still don't know what she wanted to speak to me about. But with strangers wandering about up here, I won't chance meeting her alone until I know for certain it's safe again."

I tensed. "You mean whoever hurt Eliora?"

He shook his head. "I went to pick a few more apples for Risi yesterday, and there was some man I'd never seen before in her orchard."

"Was he aggressive in some way?"

"No," he said, "nothing like that. He looked like perhaps he'd slept up there. And from the dusty pack he was carrying and the state of his clothes, he had to have traveled some distance. Mostly he was just . . . odd."

"How so?"

"His hair was very long. Like nothing I've ever seen on a man before; his braid was even longer than Eliora's, and she has not cut her hair for as long as we've lived here."

"A Nazirite, perhaps?"

"What's that?"

"Someone who makes a special vow to Yahweh. They do not cut their hair, drink wine, or touch the dead. Usually it's just for a period of time, but a few have been known to take a Nazirite vow for life. Like Samson, the shofet who was killed at the temple in Gaza."

He hummed absently, pondering the information. "Well, Nazirite or not, the man peered at me in such a strange way, like he was seeing me through a haze or looking straight through me to the other side. When I asked him who he was and what he was doing in the orchard, he was silent at first, acting as though he hadn't heard me and gazing off toward the east, like he was watching the sunrise. When he did finally speak, he made little sense."

"What did he say?"

"He said I was a wild branch. And that I shouldn't fear the fetters that carry me off to sea, or some such nonsense." He waved off the idea with a huff of laughter, brushing aside the statement.

But all the blood seemed to drain from me as he spoke. I'd heard those words before—just two days ago, in the very same orchard—from Eliora. "He said . . . he said you were a wild branch?"

He nodded, with an amused tilt of his lips. "Yes. He also said that when I stand at the watchtower and hear thunder from on high, my knee would bow to the true king." He shook his head and chuckled.

"What else? Was there more?" I pressed, my mind whirling, grasping for meaning.

He huffed in annoyance and scratched his head in thought. "Something about my roots growing deep in the shadow of cedars?"

"Which tree?" I asked, my breaths coming faster. Had someone heard Eliora and me talking about wild branches? But weren't we in the tree when she spoke of living in peace in the shadow of cedars? No one could have possibly overheard that conversation so high up in the boughs. "Which tree was he standing beside when he spoke to you?"

"I don't know," Natan responded with a shrug. "The sweet one, I think, with the yellow skin. The Naftali apple."

My jaw went slack as a number of things clicked into place, like a key turned in an iron lock.

Although I'd never seen him in person, it was widely known that Samuel ben Elkanah was a lifelong Nazirite, a result of the vow taken by his mother even before his conception. Elazar had insisted to me last night that Samuel was a prophet of Yahweh, possessing a depth of knowledge that defied explanation, and here was Natan telling me that this stranger had spoken of wild branches and cedar trees in the same place Eliora had made the connections between her adoption and the process of tree grafting.

What other explanation could there be for such a remarkable coincidence, aside from Samuel being exactly who Elazar said he was: a man who spoke for the Most High?

"I have to go," I told Natan. "I'm sorry. . . . I wanted to help today, but I have to . . . I have to go." I ignored the confusion on his face and spun around to grab my lyre as the implications from my revelation became very clear.

If a Hebrew woman enslaved in Ashdod, an old Levite who lived on a mountain, and a confirmed prophet of Yahweh were all in such perfect and inexplicable accord as to where the Ark's resting place should be, then I could no longer ignore the truth: Adonai had placed the Ark in Kiryat-Yearim for a purpose, and until that purpose was complete, it should remain among the cedars where Abinidab had hidden it.

I was on the wrong side of this fight after all.

Thirty-Four

Even with mud clinging to my sandals as I navigated the path littered with a multitude of downed branches from the storm, the trek back down the mountain was far too short. I dreaded the last few steps, knowing that by the time I arrived at our camp, I must have a clear and formidable response for Machlon about why I'd left after the lighting strike and why I believed that we should abandon our mission. But my thoughts were nearly as slippery as the trail that descended through the sodden forest.

From the moment I'd entered Abiram's home, I'd never questioned his wisdom, never doubted his authority or that of the well-respected priests and Levites who'd concocted this scheme in secret. But if the men clamoring for the return of the Ark, and also the restoration of Eleazar ben Aharon's line, were running ahead of Yahweh's plans, then I had been blindly obeying leaders who were placing their own desires above the Almighty's.

I would never know why my father made the choice to go to Afek that day, or if he'd had doubts about the validity of the claims made by Eli's sons that the Ark would win the battle for them. But that last memory I'd had of him, as I'd placed the lion claw necklace in Natan's hand, had reminded me that I'd had the distinct impression at that moment that something was very wrong. Perhaps it was the expression on his face, the way his hands gripped my shoulders so tightly, the sheen of tears in his eyes, or maybe even a whisper from the Ruach Ha'Kodesh, but I'd felt a bone-deep certainty that he should not go.

Yet I'd said nothing. I'd watched him and my brothers walk away and kept my mouth tightly closed. Of course, had I relayed my concerns, it was doubtful any of them would have listened to me, but at least I could have tried.

I would not make the same mistake again. No matter Machlon's failings, he was my cousin—and as much a brother to me as my own had been—and I would do anything to stop him from ending up like Hofni and Pinchas, or worse, the Levites in Beth Shemesh, whom I was beginning to believe had actually been struck down by fire from Yahweh, just as Eliora had said.

I was only grateful I'd stumbled over the truth before Yom Teruah began. At least I had an entire night and day to convince Machlon that his father's plan was not only flawed at its foundation but eminently dangerous.

The closer I came to camp, the clearer my plan became for how I could persuade my cousin of the truth. I would tell him everything—from the brief glimpses I'd had of the charred bodies in the valley of Beth Shemesh to Natan's encounter with Samuel and the impossible connections between Eliora's Hebrew slave and the man who'd heard the voice of Yahweh with his own ears when he was only a child.

Machlon knew me. He knew that I would not be swayed by trivialities and that I would not dare to go against his father unless I was firmly convinced. We could stop this, together. Even if Abiram would be angry when he discovered what had happened later, I hoped he might eventually accept that I had only my cousin's well-being in mind.

But all my hopes of persuading Machlon withered to nothing when I stepped into the clearing and was almost immediately greeted by none other than Abiram himself.

"There you are!" said my uncle, a wide smile on his face as he approached. He embraced me and kissed my cheeks. "Machlon said you've been chasing down lightning strikes."

Stricken mute by the surprise of seeing him, since he had left to make preparation at Nob at the same time Machlon and I departed Beit El, I could do little more than stare at him with my jaw slack.

The plan had been clear from the beginning: Machlon, Osher, Shelah, and I would spy out the location of the Ark and would bring it to Nob, where my uncle and his cohorts would install a man from Eleazar ben Aharon's line on the seat of High Priest at the rebuilt Mishkan. What possible reason would he have for being here now?

"Did you save the gardens?" he asked, clearly having been informed of my insistence to warn Elazar's family after the lightning strike.

"Most of them," I replied, distracted as I tried to make sense of his appearance. "The tree fell on the flower garden, so not all of it went unscathed, but at least the fire did not spread."

"How fortunate you arrived in time. I'm certain Elazar—and his daughter—were grateful for your intervention." My uncle's statement was appropriately sympathetic, if pointed, in its delivery. "Indeed," he continued, leaning in and lowering his voice. "It sounds as though they've become quite indebted to you, my boy. Well done." He squeezed my shoulder. "Very well done."

For all the years I'd been a part of his household, I'd craved affirmations such as this. But instead of the triumph I'd expected to feel upon such long-desired validation, nausea flamed at the base of my throat, and I had the urge to flee. Had his eyes always had such a scrutinizing quality? Suddenly the palm on my shoulder seemed a bit too heavy, and the pressure of his fingers far too tight.

With another glance around to ensure that none of the musicians who were milling about the camp might be listening, Abiram dropped his voice lower. "Ingratiating yourself into that pit of vipers was a shrewd tactic, son. I will ensure that the kohanim are fully aware of your sacrifice once the reins are restored to the correct hands. I can only imagine how appreciative they will be when they hear of your part in this mission—and how generous, once the full tithe is restored. Your dedication to Yahweh is to be commended, my boy."

The insinuation was plain. The rewards for betraying Elazar and Eliora would be great; I'd be lauded and compensated well for slithering my way into their regard. After all his years of railing about Eli's sons and their corrupt ways, Abiram himself was walking the very same path, calling it a righteous one, and in doing so, was taking the name of Adonai in vain.

The truth of it all settled into my bones, as did the realization that the very thing I'd called out in Eliora I was guilty of as well.

After losing both of my parents and all of my siblings, I'd been desperate to please Abiram and his family. I'd set aside my desire to play music with the Levitical musicians because Abiram told me that my skills as an instrument builder were much more profitable than singing and playing a lyre. I'd gone along with every scheme Machlon dreamed up, no matter how ill advised, out of fear of being set aside or left behind. And I'd sat at Abiram's feet and soaked up every word of his bitter rants against Elazar without questioning his motives.

In a way, I too had been grafted into a new family like Eliora, but it was becoming clearer by the moment that Abiram's root may be rotten at the core. And no matter how much I'd ached to be accepted by my uncle, to be loved the way Eliora and Natan were by the family that had welcomed them without condition, I'd been little more than a token Abiram had been moving around a game board from the beginning. And nothing I could say to him would assuage his determination to finish what he'd started. I had to find my cousin. It was my only chance to stop this before it all began.

"Where is Machlon?" I asked, attempting to keep the panic from my voice as I surveyed the bustling campsite. The Levitical musicians were well occupied with preparing for this evening's ceremonies, a few of them already wearing their white garments after having washed in the clear, sweet water that flowed in mysterious abundance from the heart of this mountain. Yet another miracle I'd discounted in my arrogance.

"He's meeting with a few more men interested in joining with us," he said. "He's been quite successful in gathering supporters."

"We're bringing in *more* men? Is that wise at this point?"

Abiram's eyes narrowed slightly. "As I told him in my final message a few days ago, any man who is willing and *loyal* to our cause is welcome."

I did not miss the emphasis. Nor did it escape my notice that I had not been told that Machlon was in contact with his father while we were in Kiryat-Yearim. And why exactly, if he was so pleased with Machlon's efforts in recruiting new men, was Abiram here now?

I had the very strong impression that it had something to do with me but had no idea how to ask such a question without making my suspicions known. It was plain that Machlon had been less than forthcoming with me.

"Then I should acquaint myself with these men as well," I said, "if you'll point me in the direction of their meeting."

He waved a dismissive hand in the air. "Machlon will find you later. I know he is eager to continue your conversation from last night."

Eager was likely a vast understatement. Machlon would be furious with me for refusing to lead him directly to the Ark, and the way Abiram was looking at me now made me suspect that my every move for the past weeks had been reported to him in detail.

"Ronen!"

I startled at the sound of my name and turned to find a visibly panicked Tuviyah striding toward me, the fringes of his Levitical garment fluttering in the breeze. "There you are! Where have you been all night? We've been looking all over. There's been a disaster with the harps!"

"I'm sorry, Tuviyah, there was a fire up—"

He brushed away my explanation. "It's no matter now. You must repair the standing harps. Someone cut all of the strings, and

I don't know if we have enough goat-gut or even enough time to get them back in working order! And the foundation of the entire first song is those harps—"

I interrupted his rant, pained to see my father's friend so dis-composed. "I will go repair them immediately," I said. "Have no fear, we have plenty of replacement strings, and it won't take me long if I recruit a couple of the apprentices to help me."

With the load of responsibility Tuviyah had been carrying on his shoulders these past weeks, along with the frustrations of deal-ing with a group that had as many opinions as musicians, it was no wonder that this setback would push him over the edge.

"How did this happen?" I asked. "Who would cut the strings?"

"I don't know. It makes no sense," he said as he scrubbed at his forehead with white-knuckled fingers. "They've been under guard. Some of those harps are from the first years in Shiloh—they are irreplaceable. My only guess is that some of the local townspeople are unhappy about the festivals being celebrated here. But with all the goods we've been purchasing, I'd hoped to inspire goodwill, not frustration."

A sick feeling began to wind its way through me. Although there was a rotation of men watching over the priceless instruments in the tent we'd raised to shelter them, Osher and Shelah were among that number. I wondered if perhaps this had nothing at all to do with disgruntled locals.

"You go on with Tuviyah and do what you must," said my uncle. "I need to prepare for my own role tonight and make cer-tain everyone understands their duties. We don't want any more surprises, after all. I will see you later. And then you, Machlon, and I will talk. We have much to discuss, and I've missed you both these past weeks." He gave me a benevolent smile that I in no way believed was sincere.

Tuviyah thanked Abiram and spun away, but before I could take a step to follow him, my uncle gripped my wrist, an intense look pinning me in place.

"I can't tell you how glad I am that I took you in all those years ago, son, when your mother turned her back on you. It would have been . . . unfortunate"—he frowned, silver brows drawing together in the semblance of regret—"had you been lost to us forever."

The warning could not have been clearer had he pointed a dagger at my chest. My indecision had not gone unnoticed. If I tried to dissuade Machlon from going after the Ark of the Covenant, my uncle would not forgive me. And, if I succeeded in stopping him, that would mean my mother and siblings would not be returning south any time soon either, so I would lose the only family I had left. No matter what decision I made, the cost would be great. But as my father and brothers had learned the hard way on the field at Afek, the cost of going against the will of the Eternal One was greater by far.

I finally caught sight of Machlon ahead of me as all the musicians made their way up the steep path toward the ridge, most with instruments in hand, and some carrying unlit torches that would guide our way back down later tonight. Repairs had taken longer than I'd hoped, since in addition to slicing through the goat-gut strings on the harps, the vandals had also broken the heads of three drums.

I'd prayed that somehow I would find my cousin before the ceremony, and away from any place that Abiram might see us talking, and was beyond relieved that I'd succeeded. We would not have much time to speak now, since we musicians were expected to assemble on the ridge well before the sun met the western horizon, but at least I could ask him to meet privately with me as soon as the service ended and the day of Shabbat rest began. Without my knowledge of where the Ark was, the entire mission would be impossible, and I needed to make it clear that I would not be leading him to the cedar grove tomorrow night.

With many apologies to the Levites I jostled as I pushed my way past them on the narrow trail, I finally reached my cousin and grabbed his arm.

288

"Machlon!" I said, tugging him off to the side of the path and into the brush.

"What are you doing, Ronen?" he snapped, settling the drum he was carrying onto his hip.

"We need to talk," I said. "I've discovered something"—I lowered my voice as the stream of white-clad Levites continued by, a few grumbling about us blocking the way—"about the Ark."

His brows rose. "Have you learned more from your Philistine?"

My teeth ground at the flippant way he spoke of the woman I desperately wanted to call my own. "No. But perhaps we need to rethink this plan."

He scowled. "There is no rethinking. Everything is in place. Tomorrow night during the feasting you'll lead us to the location and the kohanim will take it from there."

"But—"

"This is neither the time nor the place to discuss this," he said, his gaze darting back over his shoulder. "We will have plenty of time after the ceremonies. Then you can tell me why you are all of a sudden turning into a coward."

"It's not cowardice—"

"Later, Ronen. The sacrifices will begin soon. We need to go."

Stomach churning, I acquiesced, and he strode away to catch up with the rest of the drummers. He was right that anyone on this path could overhear our discussion and even though he was in the wrong, I had no desire for Abiram to be publicly branded a traitor. I only wanted to convince Machlon to call off the mission. The ceremony would be complete after the sighting of the new moon, and then I could share my concerns. I could only pray that he would hear me and not cut me out like Abiram had hinted, because my only other option was to go to Elazar and warn him what was to come, and admitting my betrayal would mean losing Eliora forever too.

As for now, all I could do was to take my father's precious lyre to the ridge and play the songs he'd composed in adoration of the Most High. Singing those words in his memory was far more honoring to him than trying to claim justice for his death by lying and stealing in his name. The reminder that I'd been planning to do exactly that shamed me as I followed my Levitical brethren and took my place among them, where I should have been all along.

Somehow, through all the disorder of the past weeks—the arguments, the frustration, the vandalized instruments, and the significant number of Levites who'd abandoned the entire ceremony—the first song avoided being a complete disaster.

The relief on Tuviyah's face was immense as we finished the last verse of the song written by Mosheh himself; a reminder from the time in the wilderness that Yahweh was our Rock of Salvation, and it was to him we would be lifting our voices, and that he would hear our shouts as we called out for rescue from our enemies.

Just as I'd anticipated, the sound of hundreds of Levite voices melding with the lyres, harps, pipes, and drums was nothing less than majestic. My skin was awash with gooseflesh as the final notes echoed over the valley and the next song began. I'd seen Elazar, along with the rest of his clan, on a bluff across the way and imagined Eliora among them, the same rapture on her lovely face as when I'd played for her in the orchard. The thought of admitting the truth to her was almost as terrifying as facing Abiram's wrath, but I hoped that I could head off his plans without her ever knowing just how close I'd come to divulging her secret.

The sky had already begun to flare orange in the west, and torches were being lit both on the ridge and among the many tents and bodies gathered down below. There were not nearly as many worshipers in the valley as had been expected, something I knew many of the priests were lamenting. Additionally, a rumor was going around camp that two parties of travelers had actually been waylaid on their way here by Philistines, with many of them killed and a large number taken prisoner—an occurrence that had become more frequent over the past few years. It seemed our enemies had already forgotten their losses at the hands of Yahweh in Ashdod and Gath and were gradually rebuilding their campaign to overtake the hill country.

An altar of uncut stones had been built in the center of the ridge, and I watched in fascination as a number of animals were slaughtered and prepared for the sacrifices. My uncle, dressed in white like the rest of us, was assisting with the gruesome under-taking, his years of working in the Mishkan evident by the way his knife expertly butchered a goat. A discomfiting thought struck me as I watched him strip flesh from bone: if I was not successful in convincing Machlon to halt those plans, it was conceivable that a war could break out between many of the priests now working alongside him on this ridge. And the divisions between the Levites that I'd witnessed during the past few weeks would be nothing if Abiram was successful in deposing Ahituv and replacing him with a successor from the line of Eleazar ben Aharon.

The true weight of my conviction and its implications settled over me, just as a man holding a torch strode across the ridge and silently planted himself in front of the altar. Gradually, those working on the sacrifices halted in their work to gape at the inter-loper.

It took less than three breaths for me to realize that my guess earlier was correct, Samuel ben Elkanah—once assistant to Eli the High Priest and a man who, since the destruction of Shiloh, was known to wander the length and breadth of the Land prophesy-ing and exhorting the tribes to repent—was on the mountain of Kiryat-Yearim.

"People of Yahweh," he called out, his voice echoing across the valley with surprising strength, "you gather here this day to shout to the Most High. You come before him with sacrifices"—he ges-tured toward the smoking altar—"and with glorious songs that lift high his name above all other gods. You claim him as your Rock of Salvation with the words of Mosheh and plead with him to rescue you from your oppressors. Yet I have been walking among you today." He pointed his flaming torch at the crowd below. "There are heathen votives in your tents, graven images of false gods around your necks, and the flesh of swine in your stewpots."

All around me, Levites shifted, craning their necks to see the speaker and murmuring about his identity, but otherwise the congregation was quiet, both in the valley and on the ridge, all of us seeming to hold our collective breath to hear what Samuel might say next. There was nothing extraordinary in his appearance, other than the long, dark braid that dangled to the bottom of his spine, and he wore simple clothing that gave no indication to his unique, divinely appointed status among the Levites. But every eye in the valley was trained on him, and the authority in his voice was unmistakable. I briefly wondered if this was what it might have felt like for the distant ancestor who'd made my lyre to watch Mosheh speak on the Mountain of Adonai in the wilderness.

After a taut silence in which I glanced over at my uncle, who was glowering at the prophet, with his bloody knife still clutched in his hand, Samuel began to speak again, his voice strengthening as he called on the *am segula*, Yahweh's beloved people, to repent of whoring after the gods of the Philistines, the Canaanites, and the Amorites. He told us to break down the high places and cleanse the Land, instead of inviting the repugnant practices into our homes and convocations and calling them holy. He implored us to get on our faces and repent, to burn the idols and images and amulets. He declared that until we turned our faces to the Most High, our calls for rescue would not be heard, our holy sanctuary not restored. He spoke of how entwined we'd become with the enemies among us and that the process of untangling ourselves from them would be a difficult and painful one—one that would divide fathers and sons, brothers and friends, tribes and clans—but one that was necessary if we desired to be a light to the nations as Mosheh had challenged us to be.

"Yahweh is a jealous God," he shouted. "He will not tolerate your detestable idols. Do not rely on your own strength for your salvation, nor on the wicked plans of those who claim to know his will but speak with the tongues of vipers for their own gain. You are the beloved of the Most High, and it is he alone you must obey. So, as the sacrifices are being made here on this altar, throw your amulets into your fires. Smash your idols and burn your graven images. And when the first sliver of the moon is seen in the sky, shout to Adonai, lift your trumpets to the Holy One as our ancestors did at Jericho, and cry out in his name as you repent and plead mercy for the wayward tribes of Israel."

The moment Samuel began to speak of wicked plans, my attention had gone back to Abiram. No longer was he glowering at the prophet; instead, he and his friend, Bezor, were standing together, still covered in the blood of sacrifices, but both with expressions of satisfaction on their faces.

Stricken at the sight of their arrogant display during a call for repentance, I turned to look over my shoulder, searching for Machlon. When we'd lined up earlier on the ridge, he'd been three rows behind me, with the other drummers. Now he was nowhere to be seen, and I had no idea how long he'd been missing. For all I knew, he'd left before we played our first note. Another quick overview of the men gathered on the ridge told me that Osher and Shelah were not here either.

There could be only one reason as to why none of them were here right now.

"There is no rethinking. Everything is in place," Machlon had said on the path. It seemed as though he hadn't needed me to lead them to the Ark after all. No wonder Osher and Shelah had sabotaged the instruments today; they'd wanted me occupied so I didn't realize I'd been entirely cut from the plans.

With my heartbeat thundering in my ears, I vaguely noticed that Samuel had stopped talking. After a lengthy moment in which he stared out at the people, he turned to cast his gaze our way, his eyes traveling over the musicians with the same scrutiny he'd given the congregation below. For the briefest of moments, his attention fixed on me, and a flood of regret and foreboding rushed through my limbs—as if the man of Yahweh could see all the way down to my guilty bones.

The moment he released his stare and continued his perusal of the rest of the Levites, I leaned over to the musician standing next to me, a man I barely knew.

"Take my lyre back to camp," I whispered. "I need to go."

"What?" he hissed, as I pressed my priceless instrument into his hands. "Where are you—? You can't leave!"

But I'd already turned away, slithering through the rows behind me and considering how fast I could reach the summit. I had to reach my cousin before he did something that could not be undone.

Thirty-Five

Eliora

I caught up to Natan at the remains of my tree, just as the sun began to sink behind the western hills. Although he'd ignored me the whole way, he'd known I was behind him on the trail or he would have far outpaced me and left me to find my way through the woods alone. I knew my way fairly well on this part of the mountain, even at dusk, but after my run-in with those men the other night, I'd been much more cautious about returning to the house well before dark.

Although my father reminded me that I would be missing my very first ingathering festival, I could not leave Natan alone, not after he'd come home this afternoon with bloodied knuckles and a thunderstorm on his face, refusing to say what had happened to him. In fact, the only words he'd uttered since then had been a vehement refusal to go with the family down to the bluff to watch the Yom Teruah ceremony and sacrifices. I'd been so excited to see Ronen play his lyre alongside his fellow musicians and to take part in the Hebrew tradition, but I had the very deep conviction that my brother needed me right now.

I surveyed the mess of mud and shattered logs and sticks that must have once been a charcoal mound in the center of the clearing. It likely had taken Natan hours to build this, and now it was as destroyed as my oak tree, looking like it had been hacked to pieces by an ax.

"What happened?" I asked.

His jaw ticked, as if he were grinding his teeth together.

"Was it . . ." I paused, bracing myself for the answer. "Was it Adnan and Padi?"

He shook his head, his eyes traveling over the mess dispassionately, his lips pressed tightly together. Remembering again how Ronen had said that my brother needed time to let his emotions settle before he could discuss whatever was on his mind, I remained quiet.

Natan was wearing something around his neck that looked suspiciously like Ronen's lion claw. It took everything in me to not ask him why he had it, since I remembered the story of the treasured possession being passed down generation to generation within Ronen's family. But instead of falling prey to my curiosity, I forced myself to stay silent, giving Natan all the time he needed to calm his soul.

I peered up at the slowly dimming heavens to distract myself, searching for the faint crescent that would herald the beginning of the seventh month. Seeing nothing more than one lone star just over the eastern horizon, I dropped my gaze to the treetops. Although I could not see the cedar grove from this vantage point, and perhaps never would again now that my oak was gone, I turned my face in the direction of the Ark and prayed that somehow, someday, my brother's troubled heart would be mended and that he would find true joy.

"She doesn't want me," Natan said, his sudden statement nearly startling a squeak out of me.

"Who?"

"Shoshana," he replied, his tone dry and flat and completely at odds with the abrasions on his knuckles. Remembering the way the girl had looked at my brother the day of the fight with Medad and how shaken she'd been as she'd called my name in the garden, I doubted such a statement but did not want to contradict him when he was finally talking to me. It seemed that Shoshana's affection had not been one-sided after all.

"What happened?"

"She's betrothed to someone else."

I barely stifled my gasp. "Betrothed?"

He nodded. "To Medad."

I let my eyes drop closed, my head tipping forward. No wonder he was so devastated. The girl he'd set his hopes on would marry the friend who'd betrayed him. "Oh, Natan, I'm so sorry."

He shrugged. "It is done. Their fathers already drew up the *ketubah*. In two years' time, she will be taken as my worst enemy's wife. I tried . . ." He paused, took a breath. "I tried to convince her to plead my case, or even to leave with me instead. To choose me. We are young, and I have nothing to offer as *mohar*, but I said I would work with Adnan cutting wood, or perhaps find work as a farmhand down in the valley. But she . . . she said that she could not go against her father's wishes. And that it was too late to undo anyhow."

"And your hands?" I asked, keeping my tone as gentle as possible.

He lifted them, turning them back and forth to examine the knuckles with detached curiosity. Then he gestured behind him at the woods. "A tree."

I breathed a sigh of relief. At least Medad had not been the recipient of whatever blows he'd inflicted on some unsuspecting oak. After what had happened last time Natan lost his control with his former friend, I feared that losing Shoshana to him might push my brother over a line he could not step back over, just like our father.

"Why did you make me go?" he asked.

I furrowed my brow in confusion.

"I would have been better off in Ashdod, among my own people."

297

I stiffened, struck by the defeat in his voice. "That's not true. And they are not your people anymore."

He stretched his neck and straightened his shoulders. "Yes, they are. We were born Philistine. No matter that you refuse to speak our language or how much you hide yourself away and pretend, you do not truly belong here."

I flinched at the stinging attack. "We are part of this family—"

"I'm not. I'll never be."

Anger began to simmer beneath my breastbone. "Of course you are. Abba and Ima have been nothing but kind to you. Our siblings treat you as one of them. They have never done anything but love you. I don't understand why you refuse to see this!"

"They pretend just as much as you do," he said. "But it's not real. We already have a family, in Ashdod."

"They're dead, Natan. All of them. There was nothing left for us there but misery." *And something worse than slavery for me.*

"We have Mataro."

My jaw dropped open. "Mataro?"

He folded his arms across his chest, his jaw going hard. How could he even suggest that our cousin was in any way a better choice?

"I know you were young when we left, but don't you remember what he tried to do to you?" I asked.

"He was going to make me famous."

"No, Natan. He was using you. Planning to throw a seven-year-old boy out onto the fighting grounds to pummel other children in order to make himself rich."

"Perhaps so, but I too would have become rich in the process. And powerful and admired. I may have only been seven, but I bested two boys older than me that day. Mataro was going to teach me to become the greatest fighter in all of the Five Cities. Instead, you dragged me away, made me come to this place where everyone hates me."

"You don't remember the danger we were in that night. There was a reason Azuvah sent us away—"

"She just wanted us gone. Like everyone else."

I blinked, his statement so utterly untrue that I could not wrap my mind around it. "No, she loved us—"

"She was a slave, Risi. Nothing but a slave obligated to care for two children. And when she tired of dealing with us, she tricked us into climbing out a window and running off."

I curved a hand over my wrist, gripping the old, tattered tzitzit there that still reminded me of that slave's love. "You are wrong. Have you forgotten how she sang to us? How she told us stories of the Hebrews? How she called us her lights?"

He shrugged a shoulder.

I had to tell him. I don't know why I'd waited so long to do so. When he'd been a boy, I'd wanted to keep the horror—all the horrors—away from him. Protect what innocence remained in him. And then, over the years, I'd convinced myself that dredging it all up again wouldn't profit him, or me. "He killed her, Natan. Our cousin killed Azuvah that night."

His eyes narrowed at me. "That's a lie."

"As soon as we left that room, he broke in and murdered her."

"How would you know? We were gone."

"I—" My throat closed, and I choked out the words. "I heard him . . . and her screams as he beat her."

"But you didn't actually see her dead, did you?"

"No, but I know—"

"Why would he destroy his property? What use would he have for a dead slave?" His voice sounded so cold that I shivered. "But instead of finding out what happened, or giving me a choice, you forced me to leave my people. To follow a magical box to this place where I am nothing but a pariah."

Frustration ground at my bones, and I grit my teeth. "They aren't our people anymore, Natan. And I am glad. The Philistines are cruel. They worship bloodthirsty and depraved gods. They want nothing more than to steal this beautiful land from those Yahweh gave it to."

He shook his head. "You are blinded by your devotion to the Hebrews. You don't even know what you are talking about."

"Natan, please—"

"Lukio!" he snapped. "My. Name. Is. Lukio!"

The sound of shofarim and loud shouts from down in the valley jerked my attention to the sky, where the barest sliver of the new moon was now visible on the horizon. The piercing blasts continued on and on to herald the beginning of Yom Teruah.

At nearly the same moment, a shofar sounded in the other direction. My head whipped around to search out the origin. This blast did not sound like the long, drawn-out ones down in the valley.

It sounded more like an alarm.

"The Ark," I breathed out.

Another shofar bleated, this time from a little farther away but was quickly broken off. Knowing the summit of this mountain the way that I did, I felt certain that the Levite guards had blown those rams' horns not to celebrate the day of shouting, but as a call for help. Immediately, I was back in those terrifying moments when those two enormous shadows flew at me in the darkness. Had those same men returned tonight while everyone was occupied with the ceremony? I knew my father had added another layer of guards after he'd dismissed Menash, but something deep inside me whispered that perhaps it was not enough.

With my heart pounding, I turned back to tell Natan we should go find our father but discovered he was gone. I shouted his name three times, but he'd disappeared into the deep-shadowed forest, leaving me behind to find my way alone.

Torn between the instinct to follow my brother and the urgency in those shofar blasts, I wavered. Natan was so confused. So lost. And I had no idea how to convince him of the contrast between the life we would have had in Ashdod among the Philistines and this peaceful and safe one with the Hebrews.

But for as much as I was compelled to fix whatever was broken in him, I had to remember that just like my mother had said, I was not his God and I could not save him from himself. The alarms had sounded during all the noise of Yom Teruah, and if something had happened out there with the guards, no one else may have heard it but me. I had to leave behind the brother only Yahweh could heal and run for my father.

Thankful that there was still enough light remaining to find my way through the woods, I left the usual path and headed in the direction of the ridge, where the Yom Teruah ceremony was being held, all unease at going down the mountain swallowed up in panic that I might be too late for whatever had happened with the guards. I knew the exact bluff where my family planned to watch the festivities and was glad I would not have to search them out among the hundreds gathered in the valley below.

However, just as I neared the head of the trail that would take me down to my father, I noticed a flash of movement about forty paces down the hill and coming up the path directly toward me. Stumbling to a stop, I dashed behind a nearby tree, crouching as my pulse galloped wildly. I prayed that it was only one of the Levite guards making his way toward whatever emergency had arisen, but after what had happened to me before, I would not take any chances.

I held my breath and peered slowly around the tree trunk, glad that my brown headscarf would camouflage my hair. The color of my tunic was nearly indistinguishable from the bark, and the brush in this area was thick. I was certain no one would see me here if I held still enough.

Again, I saw movement down below—a tall body dressed in pure white and striding quickly up the rough path. When he was about twenty paces away, he lifted his chin to survey the trail ahead of him and even though the light was dim, my heart leapt into my throat as I recognized the shape of the handsome face that had become so familiar and dear to me these past few weeks.

Ronen!

Relief sluiced through me. Perhaps he too had heard the guard's shofar calls and was coming to help. I pressed to my feet and opened my mouth to call his name just as four men barreled out of the woods and surrounded him, swords and knives drawn.

Ronen's empty hands flew into the air. I'd never once seen him wear a weapon, and it seemed today was no exception. I dropped back down in the brush behind the tree, my body shaking as I watched the men close in on him.

As far away as they were, I could not hear what they were saying, only that their voices were agitated. Ronen shook his head, and they searched him for weapons, finding nothing. One of the men pressed his knife to the center of Ronen's chest, barking out an indecipherable command. My trembling hand flew to my mouth to restrain the cry that burned up my throat. Surely they wouldn't kill him, would they? They looked to be Hebrew, but their clothing resembled that of the Philistines instead. Perhaps these were the very men who had assaulted me in the woods a few days before.

Two of the men grabbed Ronen's arms and yanked him forward, driving him up the hill toward me. I sank down farther, holding my breath and willing the gathering darkness to hide me in its embrace.

In answer to my prayer, they passed by my hiding spot without seeing me, a silent Ronen between them. His features were shadowed, but the resignation on his face was unmistakable. For some inexplicable reason, he did not even seem shocked that he'd been taken captive.

I had to do something. I could not just watch these strangers march Ronen off into the woods. He was no weak man by any measure, but he was not a warrior; he was a musician and, as a Levite, not even allowed to train with a sword. But I certainly could do nothing to save him. I could run fast and could climb trees like a squirrel, but I could not overpower anyone. I must go get help.

But even as I considered the distance between myself and the bluff where I knew my father was, I realized the other two men who had surprised Ronen had remained on the trail. Their backs were to me, but there was no possible way for me to get around them undetected unless I backtracked a good distance, forged my own path through the woods in the dark, and then looped back around to the path farther down the slope. And who was to say that there weren't more of these men, whoever they were, guarding the trail farther down?

I was trapped. Either I could take my chances in the dark and attempt to find my way down to my father, which might take me three times as long if I got lost, or I could follow the men who took Ronen and perhaps create some sort of distraction. Even if something terrible had happened to cause the alarms to be blown, there were sixteen Levites guarding the area around the Ark, and four stationed at the tent itself. Surely one of them had to already be on his way down to the bluff to retrieve the rest of the guard. I had absolute faith that my father would come.

In the meantime, I would keep my eyes on Ronen and think of some way to help him. I could not bear to lose anyone else I loved.

Thirty-Six

I'd known that Machlon had gathered more supporters for this effort and had not imagined a warm welcome when I came barreling up the mountain looking for my cousin, but I'd not expected to find myself taken captive by men with swords.

I was only thankful that they'd given me enough time to explain who I was before slaughtering me. And by the menacing expressions on their faces, I'd been moments away from that fate before I invoked Machlon's name.

As they silently herded me through the forest, one on either side of me and their weapons at the ready, one thing was very clear. I'd been woefully ignorant to the true scope of my cousin's plans.

The men who had greeted me on the trail with threats of impaling me from all sides if I so much as cried out were the very same Levitical musicians from Simeonite territory who had been so vocal during that first gathering with Tuviyah. I had to wonder whether they'd ever planned to join in the ceremonies, or if the event had simply been an excuse to come north and foment division. But I did not fight them, knowing that my best course of action was simply to allow them to take me to Machlon so I could plead with him face-to-face.

I knew where we were going, but still, the shock of being led into a small clearing, completely encircled by the six enormous cedar trees Eliora had pointed out from the boughs of her oak, was enough to make my breath catch. At least thirty armed men were spread around the perimeter of the clearing beneath the outstretched boughs of the cedars, including Osher, Shelah, and Machlon, who'd not yet noticed me with my captors. A few torches lit the clearing, allowing me to see the large stone platform at the center, upon which stood a small but sturdy tent.

There was nothing in its appearance that gave a hint as to its priceless contents. It was simply a humble black-and-brown goat-hair shelter, indistinguishable from those the Hebrews had been residing within down in the valley for the past week. But beneath the deceivingly ordinary covering lay the most sacred treasure of my people. And although I'd spent the last few years denying that that box had any real power, I now knew the truth. The Ark of the Covenant was more than a golden vessel that contained a few relics of the past; it was the physical reminder that the Creator of the universe himself had deigned to dwell among his people. He'd chosen to come down and reside between the outstretched wings of the cherubim atop the lid. He'd chosen to fill the Mishkan with the same brilliant shekinah that had led our people all the way from Egypt to Canaan. And he'd chosen to allow the blood of sacrifices to be sprinkled on the mercy seat in order that our sins might be covered by his grace. He'd chosen us and asked us to choose him back.

All of these truths that I'd learned at my father's feet flooded my mind as I gaped at the tent opening, where four white-clad priests had emerged, carrying the linen-covered Ark. I could see nothing more of the vessel than the golden poles resting on the shoulders of the kohanim, who obviously had been ritually prepared for that purpose, but there was no mistaking the silhouette of such a revered object.

The urge to drop to my face and worship was nearly overpowering. I could practically feel the song of adoration weaving itself together at the very core of my being and pressing into my throat with a surge of overwhelming emotion, but before I could give in to the instinct, Machlon was in front of me.

"Why are you here, Ronen?" he said on a sigh. "You should be down on the ridge with the musicians." He waved the two men who'd detained me away. They acquiesced, letting go of my arms and sheathing their weapons, but stepping back only a couple of paces.

I looked at him in astonishment. I'd expected frustration at my intervention, perhaps even anger for my failure to disclose the location of this place, but his tone was more annoyed than aggravated. "I came to tell you that you cannot go through with this."

A gleam of amusement came into his eyes. "I think you are a little too late."

"No. Listen to me. This is dangerous. We have been wrong about all of this. You need to put the Ark back and leave it alone."

Across the clearing, the priests were now carefully descending the stone ramp, their steps slow and measured as they balanced the vessel between them. Abiram had at least recruited men who respected the Ark and treated it with due reverence.

"That is not happening, and you know it. My father has spent the last year planning every step of this day, and years before hoping for just such an opportunity, and there is no abandoning the mission he gave me."

"But you don't understand what you are stirring up. Not only is the Ark supremely dangerous, it is not meant to leave this place."

He huffed a laugh. "Says who? You?" Then his brows lowered, his lips going flat. "Or the traitor and his Philistine daughter who has turned your head?"

"This has nothing at all to do with Eliora," I said. "And Elazar is not the man your father accuses him of being. He is not arrogant and driven by greed or lust for power. He has simply been tending his sacred duty with integrity and honor and patiently awaiting Yahweh's direction with regard to the Ark. His only goal has always been to protect the holy vessel until the proper time to remove it from the mountain."

"It *is* the proper time. The Mishkan is rebuilt at Nob. The priests are ready to receive it. And there is nothing you can do to stop what must be done."

Osher approached, his features solemn as he glanced between us. "We need to be on our way, Machlon. This is taking far too long. The others are getting restless."

"We will wait for our guides," snapped Machlon. "They will be here at any moment."

"Please," I said, ignoring Osher altogether, "all of this will only end in bloodshed. There is no chance that stealing the Ark will not further aggravate the conflict that is already between us."

I gestured back at the Levites who'd snatched me from the trail. "Those men had no problem brandishing swords at me, and I have no doubt they would have killed me had I not identified myself as your cousin. Levites are made to be set apart for holy service, Machlon, not to fight their brethren!"

"We will do what is necessary to ensure that our priesthood is pure and the Ark is in the right hands. Our nation will never be strong otherwise." He turned to Osher, telling him to let the others know to prepare for departure at his signal.

I was running out of time. Whatever sign they were waiting for was imminent, but I had to make him understand, to second-guess everything I myself had been convinced of for so long.

"Do you think that fomenting hostilities between the tribes is what Yahweh would have for us?" I asked. "We are already at each other's throats, even among the musicians. It will not take much for those embers of resentment to spark into a civil war, and then no king or priest or shofet will be able to repair the once-strong bonds between the sons of Yaakov."

Machlon's features went hard, all appearance of patience gone. "This is the way it must be. If Elazar and his father had listened to reason eight years ago, this wouldn't even be an issue. They will be the ones to blame if it does come to war. We have no choice but to take the Ark by force."

"*Of course* you have a choice! What is being done here is not in alignment with the way Yahweh moves among his people. Does our God carry out nefarious plans under cover of night? Does he lie and steal and betray and encourage his people to do so as well?" I knew I was speaking my own guilt aloud, but I had to give Machlon cause to doubt, give him a reason to hesitate.

"So, you speak for our God now, do you?" said Machlon.

"No. But Samuel does."

"I should have guessed," he said, visibly exasperated. "I should have guessed that your infatuation with the Philistine would lead to falling in with her so-called father and therefore the Pretender."

"He's not a pretender, Machlon. I've heard the proof of his foreknowledge with my own ears."

"Stop this! I knew you were wavering from the beginning, which is why I kept the changes in the plans from you. And the moment you ran off to warn Elazar of the fire without telling me the truth, I knew I'd made the right choice."

"The *beginning*?"

"You've never had the stomach to do what is necessary here, Ronen. My father told me months ago that I was foolish to think you did. If you didn't have the connection to Tuviyah through your father, he never would have included you in the first place."

I could do nothing but stare at him in astonishment. "It was all a lie? I was only ever a tool to be used and then discarded?"

"Of course not. You are my cousin, and I was not lying when I said I would have your back. Why do you think I let you believe that this mission would not be happening until tomorrow night? That I cut you from the plans? I did not want you to get hurt. And if things went badly, you would have been safely down at the ridge, away from all of this. Now you are right back in the middle."

"Because I had to stop you!"

He shook his head. "I told you, there is nothing to stop this now. The Gibeonites have already set fire to the town and will be here any moment to lead us off the mountain. By morning the Ark will be in Nob and within its rightful place inside the Mishkan."

All the breath rushed from my lungs. "Fire? Machlon. What have you done?"

He shrugged. "What was necessary."

"Why would destroying Kiryat-Yearim be necessary? What if someone is hurt or killed?"

"The Gibeonites were only willing to take part in this if we make it possible for them to take back their town. They settled it, after all, hundreds of years ago. It's not that great of a sacrifice; there are plenty of other Hebrew towns in the valley where the people can flee. And the Gibeonites have sworn by their gods that they will not kill anyone. They've set fire to a few unoccupied buildings, merely as a show of force. They've even promised to allow the Hebrews to retrieve their belongings before they go."

The enormity of all that I had been blind to these past weeks settled on my shoulders like the weight of the entire mountain. I'd been so wrapped up in Eliora and my own doubts and hurts to realize that Machlon was planning not just the theft of the Ark but the overthrow of Kiryat-Yearim.

"There was no other way, cousin," he continued. "You failed to bring us the location of the Ark, and Osher and Shelah could not get close enough to determine the correct route to evacuate it. We needed men to show us the way and found some who were also willing to create a big enough diversion during the ceremony that Elazar and the rest of his guards would be preoccupied. We were fortunate Osher and Shelah ran across two Gibeonite boys in the woods one day. Their elders were only too happy to make an agreement benefiting both our sides."

I had the awful feeling that I knew exactly which two Gibeonite boys had been at the center of these negotiations: Adnan and Padi, the same ones Natan counted as his only friends.

"Listen to me, Ronen." Machlon came close, his hands gripping my shoulders and his eyes full of sincerity. "We are family. The same blood flows in our veins. You've been twisted up by Elazar's lies and that foreign girl's wiles, but you can redeem yourself now. My father will forgive you. And as I said before, you and I will be hailed as heroes when Eleazar ben Aharon's line is back in power. I know you want our nation to be united and strong. I know you want your mother and your siblings to come back home to enjoy peace and security." He gestured toward the linen-covered Ark. "*This* is how we accomplish that. Do not throw away your family for a woman. Especially a Philistine one."

The dilemma he laid out before me was clear. But even if he thought my indecision was about Eliora, it was not. It was the choice between my family and my God. If I turned my back on Abiram and Machlon, I was also ending any hope for my mother's return. But as I wavered one last time, Samuel's admonition to disentangle ourselves from false gods arose in my mind. He'd said that choosing truth over comfort was never easy. That it would mean division between clans, between families, between brothers. And suddenly there was no more wavering. All of the doubts I'd entertained, the lies I'd told myself, and the stubborn rebellion that I'd clung to dissolved like ash in the rain.

"No," I said. "We may have the same blood, and I may have revered your father to the point of blind obedience, but he is not Yahweh and neither are you. And until the King of the universe gives clear indication that the Ark should be moved, it must remain on this mountain."

I took a deep breath and chose Yahweh over everything. "And I am willing to die to stop you."

I grabbed for the sheathed sword of the Simeonite man next to me, who'd been distracted by some sort of commotion across the clearing. I dashed toward the Ark, a foolishly desperate plan forming in my head.

There were four sanctified kohanim with poles on their shoulders. If one of them was injured and unable to walk, the vessel could not be moved safely. And for as much as Machlon seemed to be taking the danger lightly—he and the other Levites who were coming so close to the Ark—it was clear that Abiram had insisted that the commands regarding the transportation of the holy object be observed, even if he'd always denied that the men at Beth Shemesh had been slain for ignoring them.

I made it only five steps before I was tackled to the ground and my pilfered weapon stripped from my hand. At least three bodies lay atop me, one man's hand gripping my hair and smashing my face into the dirt with a curse, while the others jerked my arms painfully behind my back. Before I could come fully to my senses, I was hauled back to standing, blood trickling from my nose and my chin abraded.

Machlon stood about five paces away, his expression blank as he stared at me wordlessly. Osher approached him again, followed by a few other men I'd never seen before, all red-faced and out of breath. They must have run into the clearing during my futile attempt at attacking a priest.

"We have a problem," Osher told my cousin. "The Gibeonites failed. They set fire to the butcher's shop, but somehow an alert went up before they could do more damage. The two boys who were supposed to lead us down the mountain were caught on their way up here as well."

"We need to go—now," said one of the men. "Before Elazar realizes that something is amiss up here too. He was well occupied when we slipped away, but we can't take any chances."

"Even if he does," said another, "he is down to ten men and we are thirty. What can he do?"

A curl of dread wound its way up my spine as I looked around the clearing. I'd been so focused on speaking to Machlon that I'd not noticed that the guards who'd once stood watch over the tent were nowhere to be seen. My cousin had sworn to me time and again that no one would be killed during this mission, that the Levites would be subdued and then bound and gagged so they could not raise any alarms. But had those promises been lies as well?

"Osher, Shelah. Can you get us off this mountain?" asked Machlon.

"It won't be the fastest, or even the easiest of routes, especially in the dark," replied Osher. "But once we get past the eastern ridge, my brother and I know the way."

"What do we do with him?" asked the brute who still had me by the hair.

My cousin looked at me without even a flicker of recognition for the blood-bond he'd earlier sworn we shared. "Make certain he doesn't follow."

Thirty-Seven

Eliora

A creeping sense of dread came over me as I followed Ronen's captors. Even without the high vantage point of my oak tree, the distinctive shape of the cedars up ahead announced their destination long before they even reached the clearing.

The trees were even more massive than I'd anticipated, their furthermost branches seeming to reach for the stars and each trunk so wide I guessed four men could not encircle it with fingers touching. These trees were centuries younger than the famed ones they'd sprouted from in the ancient forest of Sidon—some perhaps even dating to the rebirth of the world after the flood, if my grandfather's stories were to be believed. I could easily understand why cedars such as these were coveted for ship masts and soaring temple roofs.

The flicker of torchlight glowed between the trees up ahead, confirming my escalating fears. The men who guarded the Ark were forbidden from lighting any flame at night, to avoid announcing its location. Somehow they must have been overtaken or the clearing would not now be glowing like a signal fire.

Since my attention was pinned to Ronen's white garments, determined as I was not to take my eyes from him until my father arrived, I stumbled over something in my path and fell to my knees.

With my shin smarting from scraping it against a pinecone, I twisted around to see what had tripped me and gasped far too loudly before slapping my hand over my mouth.

I'd stumbled over a man's leg. And not just any man lay unmoving on the forest floor with a dark stream of blood trickling from his mouth. Rami, my father's second in command, had been slain. Tears blurred the horrific scene before me into a pool of grief. Rami had been one of the first men outside my family who I'd learned to trust in the days following my arrival at Kiryat-Yearim. He was kindness personified and a man of unwavering loyalty.

A low moan drew my eyes to another body a few paces away, and I shuffled over to find Nahor, another of the Levitical guards, lying on his side, breathing in shallow spurts.

"Nahor," I whispered, "can you hear me?"

Another rasping moan came from his mouth.

"You will be all right," I said, choking on the lie, since the awful rattle in his chest suggested otherwise. "My father will come soon."

I held his hand, determined that the poor man would not take his last breaths alone and prayed that my father would indeed arrive with more men to put to rights whatever horror had transpired here tonight.

Sooner than I expected, Nahor's labored breaths ceased, the night going terribly still around me.

If these two men, trained to defend the Ark at any cost, had been killed, then what of the rest? The shofar blasts I'd heard back at the charcoal mound had lasted for only a short time and had been few in number. Something, or someone, had cut them short, and my guess was that the men who'd taken Ronen into the clearing up ahead were part of a much larger group. They had to be in order to overpower all sixteen men out here at once. The attackers must have been lying in wait, holding off on their strike until the noise of Yom Teruah began.

A plan that was as sinister as it was well coordinated.

Had I erred in not taking the long way down to the bluff to find my father? I'd thought one of his guards might do so, but Rami and Nahor's deaths made me abandon the hope. And now Ronen was at the mercy of men who'd committed such awful deeds, and I was torn all over again. Should I run back down the mountain? Or check on Ronen and be patient?

Please, Yahweh, I breathed. *Give me wisdom.*

Shouts in the clearing made the decision for me. I bounded to my feet and headed for the cedar grove. Dodging behind the nearest tree, I peered around the enormous trunk and nearly cried out to see the man I loved being dragged to the ground by three rough-hewn men. He tried to fight them off, twisting his lithe body until one of them grabbed ahold of his hair and slammed his face into the ground. A sword was snatched from Ronen's hand, making me wonder how he'd gotten ahold of a weapon and why it looked as though he'd been headed toward the linen-swathed Ark of the Covenant at the center of the clearing and the white-clad priests who held it aloft.

Even in my distress over Ronen, the shock of being so close to the precious box I'd not seen in so long caused a bevy of memories to rise up: the moment I'd first seen it being jostled down the street on the back of a wagon, the soldiers hefting it on their shoulders with such lack of care and dropping it in front of Dagon, the way it shimmered after the earth shook and the idol fell at its feet, and finally the thundering booms and flash of light that cut down the men of Beth Shemesh as they gathered around to peer at the sacred objects inside.

My attention was pulled back to Ronen as the men hauled him to his feet, his once pure-white garments covered in dirt. And standing in front of him, seemingly uncaring that Ronen had been assaulted by brigands, was his cousin Machlon.

My confusion only grew as Machlon and the man I'd known

as Ronen's friend, Osher, stood calmly discussing some sort of failed Gibeonite plot and then how best to remove the Ark from the mountain.

No, came a whisper from deep within my soul. *You cannot allow this to happen.*

But I'd waited too long. I would never reach my father in time if I ran now. I had no weapon to fight them. No shofar to call for help. I was all alone, a Philistine woman with only words to wage battle against all these men. Men who'd already killed two of their tribal brethren, perhaps more, and held their own cousin and friend captive.

But even as I mourned my powerlessness and considered what I could possibly say to convince them, Azuvah's words from so long ago rose in my mind: *"You will never be alone, lior."*

I wrapped my hand around my wrist, feeling the knotted cords of Azuvah's tzitzit under my palm, knowing exactly what I had to do.

I leaned my back against the mighty cedar tree, hands shaking and breathing out a prayer that I would not meet the same fate as my father's men before I could speak. Although my heart crashed against my ribs so violently it felt bruised, I could no longer hide in the shadows. Both Ronen and the Ark were at stake, so the only thing I could do was make a scene, stall for time, and pray that my father would appear.

I bolted from my hiding spot and shouted, "You cannot move the Ark!"

To both my relief and horror, the entire company of men turned to face me. I'd hoped that the sight of a woman in the clearing might give me enough time to speak before they realized I was defenseless, and by the shocked confusion on their faces, I'd calculated correctly.

Ronen surged forward, calling my name and trying to get to me, but the men who had ahold of him threw him back to the ground, piling atop his struggling body without mercy even as he pleaded with Machlon to leave me alone. One man untied his belt and gagged Ronen with it. Tears filled my eyes as I watched him slump to the ground helplessly.

"My dear Eliora," said Machlon with false affection, "I am so glad you've joined us. You seem a bit confused. But perhaps this is because my cousin neglected to mention his true purpose for being here in Kiryat-Yearim." He spread his arms wide, his raised brows and haughty smirk implying that the man I'd come to admire so much over these past weeks was part of this plot.

I dropped my gaze to Ronen, every part of me screaming that it could not be true, but the guilt on his face telling me it was indeed.

"Oh yes," Machlon said. "And I thank you for revealing the exact location of the Ark to him."

An exclamation of dismay burst from my mouth as our time at the oak tree came to mind, when I'd felt I could trust him with the deep things in my heart—and with my secret place. Shame flooded through me. I'd done this. My foolishness over a man had made the Ark of the Covenant vulnerable to these thieves.

From his place on the ground, Ronen shook his head vehemently, silently denying his cousin's accusation. But it had to be true, otherwise, they would not have known how to find this well-hidden place. Yet, if he was part of this plot, then why had he been dragged here and then subdued? None of it made any sense.

But I did not have time to wallow in my guilt, Ronen's betrayal, or the confusing circumstances of his capture. I had no idea what these men had planned for the Ark of the Covenant, but I had to do anything I could to keep them from removing it from Kiryat-Yearim. And even if they were nothing but thieves and liars, their own lives were at stake here as well, and I could not stomach watching more men be struck down like those at Beth Shemesh.

"You will never be alone, lior."

"If you are part of this, then you have blood on your hands," I said, praying that Yahweh would make my spine as strong and tall as one of the mighty cedars, even though my hands and knees were shaking. "And you must be brought to justice under Torah law."

One of the white-clad priests addressed Machlon, even as he held aloft the Ark. "What does she mean?"

Machlon scoffed. "We don't have time for this. Osher. Shelah. Tie her—"

"Two of the Levite guards were killed tonight," I yelled, which somehow halted the two men who'd been coming for me. "For the crime of protecting our most holy object."

"Is that true?" the priest snapped at Machlon. "Your father assured us that there would be no bloodshed."

Machlon waved the man's concerns away. "She knows nothing. No one is hurt." Then, in three strides, Ronen's cousin was directly in front of me, his gaze penetrating and his expression menacing. "Say one more word and Ronen pays the price."

"You would kill him?" I said.

"He betrayed you, foolish girl. It's true. But he also betrayed me, my father, and the rest of the righteous priests who were counting on him. It is my duty to remove this box from Kiryat-Yearim by any means necessary, and Ronen is merely an obstacle at this point." His gaze traveled over my face in that strange scrutinizing way I'd noticed the night he came to our home. "And no matter that he abused your trust and ran to me as soon as he discovered this location, I can tell you still care for him. You don't want to watch him suffer. Do you?"

I swallowed hard, my eyes blurring. Everything he said was true. Even if Ronen had revealed every one of my secrets to his horrible cousin, there had to have been a reason. Those moments under the oak tree were too real, his emotions too raw to feign. Perhaps Machlon and his father had manipulated him in some way. But regardless of his guilt or innocence, I did not want him to die.

"What do you want?" I whispered.

He smiled, the haughty movement of his lips highlighting the differences between himself and his cousin. "Unfortunately, we've lost our guides. But you know this mountain, don't you? In fact, I'll wager that, smart girl that you are, you remember the exact way Abinidab transported this thing up here."

318

I let my eyes close and my chin drop forward. I did know the path. Natan and I had explored every part of the mountain together in the early months of our life here, and I'd noted the route we'd taken followed a narrow stream of water that flowed from a cracked boulder just outside the perimeter the Levite guards kept around the cedar grove. It was easy enough to head east from this place and cross paths with that stream. Although the trail was long obscured with vegetation, I was certain I could find it, even in the dark.

Letting out a shuddering breath, I looked over at Ronen, whose penetrating gaze was on me. I loved him. His deception did not change that fact, and somehow I was convinced that there was more to the story than what Machlon had revealed.

I had to trust that the same God who directed those two milk cows to Beth Shemesh, returning the Ark directly back into the hands of the people he'd gifted it to in the first place, was still in control.

"You will never be alone, lior."

Keeping my gaze on Ronen, who returned my stare with a heart-rending blend of guilt and confusion in his dark eyes, I told his cousin that I would do whatever was necessary to save his life.

Thirty-Eight

It was simple enough to find the stream, which had only grown in the years since I'd noticed its path. The water shushed its way along the slope through the trees, and I followed its course, leading the small procession down the hill with the precious vessel they had stolen.

Other than the crunch of our footsteps on dried leaves and pine needles, the night was still, although a few night birds startled into the sky as we descended on the opposite side of the mountain from Kiryat-Yearim, moving farther and farther away from anyone who might be able to stop this before it was too late.

Next to me, Machlon held a torch high to light my way. He'd said little as we walked but had, to my relief, ordered someone to remove Ronen's gag and bonds. He'd threatened to allow the men who'd beaten Ronen to do as they pleased with me once we reached the valley if he spoke a word or made any attempt to come within ten paces of me.

How Ronen could be related to such a man, I could not fathom. Ronen may have lied to me and even betrayed me and my family, but in Ashdod, I'd lived with men who'd relished violence—on the fighting grounds, the battlefield, and even in the temples—and Ronen was nothing like them. If anything, the remorse all over his bruised and bloodied face gave testimony to that, along with the way he'd pleaded with his cousin to let me go free before he was silenced.

The closer we came to the bottom of the mountain, the less hope I had that my father would find us before we came out of the trees. Once there, it would be simple for Machlon and his men to swiftly cross the valley. It would not be long before my help was unnecessary.

What would my father do when all was revealed about my part in this travesty? Not only had my misplaced trust in Ronen led these men directly to the Ark, but I'd chosen to lead them down the mountain to save a traitor's life. Elazar had been only too swift to relieve Menash of his duties for the sin of sleeping during his watch. How much more would I be punished for mistakes that had actually caused the holy vessel to be stolen?

We reached the farthest ridge, marked by an enormous flat boulder silhouetted against the starry sky and past which it would be simple for Machlon to navigate the final slope into the valley. I knew that it was time for me to make one last attempt to stop these men. But sensing that any appeal to Machlon would go unheeded, as focused as he was on what he considered his duty, I decided my best course of action would be to speak directly to the men upon whose shoulders the golden box rested.

Given courage by the flicker of indecision I'd seen in the priest's eyes when I announced Rami and Nahor's deaths, and hoping that Ronen would take my distraction as an opportunity to escape, I lunged for the torch in Machlon's hand. He was so taken off-guard by my sudden movement that I'd already darted away by the time he recovered enough to grab for me.

Glad for my many years of shimmying up trees, I scrambled atop the slick boulder and lifted the torch high. Inspired by Ronen's admonition to embrace my unique appearance as a testimony to Yahweh's goodness, I yanked my headscarf off my head, tossed it to the ground, and shook out my hair so that it flowed in golden-brown waves around my shoulders and to my waist.

"I am Philistine," I called out, swallowing the instinctual shame that went along with that statement and forcing myself to stand at my full height. I pushed past the discomfort, aimed my gaze at the priests, and pointed at the burden they carried on their shoulders with a trembling finger.

"I was there when the Ark of the Covenant was brought into Ashdod," I continued, my voice growing louder in spite of the burn in my throat. "I watched it be offered to Dagon as a war trophy. And I also saw it sitting on the temple porch, unmoved after the earth shook violently, while the god of Ashdod fell before it. I heard the terror of the priests the next day when it fell again before the Ark, breaking to pieces even when the earth was still. Moving it now from this place would be disastrous."

"We are priests, not pagan Philistines," said the man whose voice I recognized as the one who'd reacted to my announcement back in the clearing.

"This woman is the daughter of Elazar," said Machlon, his finger jabbing up at me with frustrated accusation, "who is in league with both Ahituv ben Pinchas and the Pretender Samuel. Do not listen to her."

"I thought you said you were Philistine," said the priest.

"I am," I said, "but I am also the adopted daughter of the man who has watched over the Ark for the past eight years. And it was he who told me of the peculiar responsibility you priests and Levites have to uphold the statutes regarding the handling of this sacred object and the dire consequences for ignoring them. Even though I was a child when I followed the cow-drawn wagon to Beth Shemesh, along with the five lords of Philistia, I vividly remember the sights, the sounds, and the smell when the Levites' bones burned before they hit the ground because they mishandled the Ark. Those men too were of the sanctified line of Levi, and their grave miscalculation cost them their lives."

I let my gaze travel over the men gathered below, some who glared back with malice, and some whose brows were furrowed with curiosity. "So you must ask yourself, are you truly convinced of the righteousness of your mission here—this clandestine plot carried out under cover of night, which already cost two Levites their lives—and are you willing to die an excruciating death if you are wrong?" I braced my feet on the boulder, spread my arms wide as the torch fluttered in the breeze, and met Machlon's infuriated glare with the most determined stare I could muster.

"Just as my people learned the hard way, you cannot control Yahweh. And the Ark he gave to your ancestors is a gift. A reminder of his justice, his mercy, and his provision. It's not a weapon to be wielded, or even an instrument to elevate the power and status of Israel among the nations."

"She's right," said Ronen, from beside me. I'd not even seen him approach or climb atop the boulder as I'd made my impassioned speech.

"I was just as convinced as you that Abiram's and Bezor's motives for doing this were pure," he said. "But if that is true, then where are they now?" He gestured wide. "It is all of us who are in danger here, being this close to the Ark—not the men who planned it. Even Pinchas and Hofni believed in their faulty judgment enough that they walked onto the battlefield with everyone else."

He continued, his voice growing stronger. "We have learned this lesson time and again from stories of Adam, Avraham, Mosheh, and Yehoshua: when we run ahead of Yahweh's will, men die needlessly. We must be patient and wait for clear direction, not trust men whose motives are obscure, to say the least. What *is* clear, from the supernatural blessing bestowed on both this mountain and the clan that protects it, is that Yahweh has chosen this place for the Ark to remain, for however long he deems it necessary. If we drag it to places it should not go for our own gain, how does that make us any different from Eli's corrupt sons, or from the rest of the men who died for their folly?"

"What shall we wait for then, cousin?" asked Machlon, a heavy note of mockery in his voice. "A pillar of smoke to lead the way?"

"Perhaps," Ronen said, in all sincerity. "I've spent the last eight years closing my eyes to the miraculous ways of Yahweh, thinking that times of such inexplicable wonders had long since passed, but I now believe that it was only my stubborn blindness that kept me from seeing marvelous things that were right in front of me all along."

"What if they are right?" said one of the other priests. "And this move isn't sanctioned by Yahweh?"

"These two know nothing," replied another. "And they need to be dealt with."

"You mean like our Levite brethren who were murdered tonight for doing their duty?" said someone else.

When I sought out the owner of the voice, I was shocked to see it was Shelah, the twin whom I'd never heard say a word.

"I did not volunteer for this mission to have bloodshed on my soul," he said, "nor to be struck down myself if this entire thing is only about power and influence for Abiram and his cohorts." Without further comment, he turned and strode away, followed quickly by his brother, who glanced up at me with a remorseful look on his face before he disappeared into the trees.

Chaos erupted after that, with at least five more Levites following after Osher and Shelah, and the rest of the men voicing their conflicting opinions about whether our warnings were valid. Machlon was in the center of it all, the men around him demanding an answer to Ronen's question about why Abiram and Bezor were safely down in Kiryat-Yearim while all of them shouldered the risk, quite literally.

As the men he'd been in league with argued, Ronen turned to me, his face a swollen, bloodied mess and his once-pure tunic soiled and torn. "I must beg your forgiveness. Eliora . . ." His dark eyes shimmered in the reflection of the torch. "I was wrong. I cannot even begin to tell you how sorry I am for all of this."

I swallowed hard. "You used me, Ronen. You must have known that I felt . . ." I stopped, unwilling to reveal my heart to him now.

"My excuses don't matter now," he said. "I can only pray that you will give me the chance to explain later. But know this: even if I came here for all the wrong reasons, my feelings for you have been entirely genuine." His gaze traveled over my face, as if he was memorizing the sight for the last time. His expression was so pained as his eyes followed the cascade of my hair down over my shoulder that I felt the longing in it like a physical touch. "I am so proud of you. For standing here as your true self without apology. No matter what happens now, promise me you won't hide your light anymore. There is no song more beautiful than the one the Creator is composing with every single note of your life, one he's been weaving together even before your first breath."

Stunned by his exquisite words but still so conflicted over his deception, I could do nothing more than stare at him with tears rolling down my face.

"Look!" cried one of the men, dragging my attention away from Ronen and toward the fog that was seeping out of the forest and curling around the base of the boulder under our feet.

"We will be trapped here," said another man. "It's too thick!"

Indeed, the mist was rising swiftly, swallowing the trees around us with surprising speed.

And then, I felt it.

My skin prickled, making me shiver as my scalp tingled and my bones suddenly went heavy, the weight pressing me down, down, down. It was the same bewildering sensation I remembered from the valley of Beth Shemesh.

"Get off the rock," I said to Ronen as I tossed the torch away. "Now."

Without argument, he obeyed, both of us scrambling off the boulder. Heedless of the fog that enveloped us, we dropped to the ground behind it. As we did so, fearful cries to Yahweh went up from the men who'd only just been shouting at one another. Some of the voices were coming from farther away. It seemed some men were fleeing blindly into the fog, and the rest were sobbing, repenting, and pleading for mercy.

"Take off your sandals," I rasped, suddenly recalling the story Azuvah told me of Mosheh and the bush that burned without ceasing.

Since I could not see Ronen in the eerie blackness, I did not know if he'd complied with my strange order, but as soon as my own feet were bare I pressed my face into the rocky dirt, trembling just as violently as I had in the valley of Beth Shemesh. And then Ronen was there, his warm body pressed up against me. His hand somehow found its way to mine, his long fingers securely entwined with my own. Regardless of everything that had been revealed, his presence beside me felt right, and I was grateful he was there.

Although my eyes were pressed tightly shut, a blue-white glow flashed against my lids, and the faces of my family, Natan, and even Azuvah went through my mind. We were too close to the Ark. Too vulnerable to the terrible glory. We would not survive.

And yet somehow, no consuming fire swallowed me whole, and my lungs continued to draw breath after panicked breath. Even though I'd braced for all the horrors I'd experienced eight years ago, there were no booms of thunder or indications that the others had been burned like at Beth Shemesh.

I had no idea how long Ronen and I remained facedown in the dirt and was too terrified to peel my eyes open to see if the brilliant light and fog had dissipated, until an unfamiliar voice spoke from above us.

"Well. That was certainly exhilarating, wasn't it?"

Blinking in confusion, Ronen and I raised our heads to find a stranger standing atop the boulder, blazing torch in hand, gazing down on us with a glint of humor in his light brown eyes and a long, thick braid trailing over one shoulder.

"It's all right, the danger has passed now," he said with a comforting smile. "You can come out from behind the rock. The rest of those fools have fled, and it seems the three of us need to have a conversation."

Thirty-Nine

Ronen stood alone, his head bowed in submission, and his open hands still at his sides. The courtyard was full of curious onlookers, including all of my family members and those of the Levites who guarded this mountain. Only Rami and Nahor had been killed during the attack, with the rest of the guards either tied and gagged or knocked unconscious, so many of them stood witness to Ronen's confession as well.

He had explained everything, going as far back as the day he'd found Natan and me up until the moment the prophet Samuel came for us last night. He'd left out our tender moments under the oak tree and within its branches, much to my relief, but had made it clear that he'd taken every opportunity to mislead me, my brother, and the rest of our family as to the true nature of his presence in Kiryat-Yearim.

"I can only plead for your mercy," he said to the elders— including my father, Ahituv the High Priest, and Samuel himself— who were gathered to hear Ronen's testimony. "Although it is not a sufficient excuse for all my choices, I was blinded by my loyalty to my uncle, who I now believe preyed on my lack of maturity and my longing for a father's guidance, and kept secret both the actual scope of his plans and his reasons for the deception in the first place."

Abiram and Bezor had fled Kiryat-Yearim, along with a number of other men who had been involved in the scheme. Osher and Shelah too had disappeared. But Machlon, along with a few other Levites and priests, had been arrested before they got off the mountain. Already Machlon had testified that Ronen was ignorant to much of the plan, that he'd had no involvement with the Gibeonites, and was innocent of bloodshed.

From what my father said, Ronen's cousin had been altogether altered by his close encounter with the terrifying glory of Yahweh, and truly repentant for his part in everything, including duping Ronen, manipulating him into using me, and threatening both our lives—something he swore was only a ruse to force our hands. He now stood off to the side of the courtyard, under guard, looking pale and humble as the elders conferred privately.

I had not spoken to Ronen since last night. After Samuel had arrived and heard our explanation of what had transpired, my father and his men appeared to take Ronen into custody, and with the help of some of the priests who'd not been involved with the plot, returned the Ark back to its tent within the cedar grove. The cowards who'd stolen it had left it sitting on the ground in their hasty flight for their lives.

But Ronen looked so lonely standing there in the courtyard and drained of spirit after his confession that it was all I could do to remain in my place and not run to him and wrap him in my arms. Yes, he'd been wrong, but I, out of everyone, understood the desire to belong, the drive to prove worthiness, and the feeling of indebtedness to a family whose generosity had rescued you.

My father turned to face the crowd, his intense discussion with the other leaders now complete.

"The charges against all involved in this plot are serious. It is only by Yahweh's extraordinary mercy that those who were there last night still live and breathe. We have determined through extensive interrogations that two of the Levites from Simeonite territory are guilty of manslaughter and will be sent north to Shechem to live out their lives in the city of refuge. The rest will be banned from participating in any Levitical duty for an indefinite period and are ordered to pay restitution in the form of forced labor here in Kiryat-Yearim, with the exception of Ronen, who is released into the custody of Samuel ben Elkanah."

Ronen's chin jerked upward, and he stared at my father in bewilderment, likely expecting his punishment to be the same as the others.

"This entire event has been eye-opening for all of us," said my father. "I knew Abiram was bitter that the Ark was left in the care of my father and me here in Kiryat-Yearim instead of being transported to Beit El under his own authority. But I never imagined he would go to such lengths to undermine that decision and then leave his son and nephew to suffer the aftermath of his plot. He and the rest involved in this scheme will not go unpunished, I assure you. An extensive investigation will be undertaken by the Levitical elders, and justice will be done."

Ronen did not react in any visible way to this pronouncement, so I wondered if my father had already discussed it all with him before now. It certainly explained why Abiram had been so cut-throat in his determination to move the Ark. I was so grateful that he'd been thwarted and hoped that anyone else who might be tempted to do so in the future, without clear direction from Yahweh, would remember the outcome of his failed coup.

Living in Kiryat-Yearim had insulated me from so much, including the friction between the priestly lines of Aharon's two sons, something I'd only learned about last night as Ronen told Samuel some of the underlying reasons for the plot. Samuel had not responded to the revelation in any way, merely nodding his head as he acknowledged Ronen's explanation, and I could not help but wonder if he had some sort of insight into how it all would turn out in the end. After all, it was his childhood prophecy that had forewarned Eli about his own sons' corruption and predicted that the line of Itamar would be cursed. But I suspected that whatever Samuel knew, or didn't know, would be revealed in Yahweh's perfect timing.

"I can only pray that Samuel's admonitions during the Yom Teruah ceremony are heeded," continued my father. "We must, as a people, repent for our arrogant and idolatrous ways and turn our faces to Yahweh. Possession of the Ark, the Mishkan, or any of the holy implements is not what guarantees the promises of this nation. It is the eternal covenant they symbolize. We must stop fighting among ourselves over man-made traditions and power struggles and submit ourselves to Yahweh's commands alone. I shudder to think what horrors Israel might be subject to if we do not remember the lessons of the past. Let us spend these next days leading up to Yom Kippur meditating on all these things and preparing to plead for Adonai's mercy on the Day of Atonement."

On that solemn note, the gathering was dismissed, and Machlon and his men led away. As I watched in fascination, Samuel approached Ronen, who had not yet moved from his place at the center of the courtyard, and placed his hand on his shoulder, speaking in low tones that I wished I could discern. Ronen nodded, lifted his chin to look into Samuel's eyes, and then followed the man of Adonai as he walked away.

Just before he turned out of the courtyard, Ronen glanced back over his shoulder to meet my eyes. A vast and fathomless ocean of regret stretched between us. And then, just as suddenly as he'd appeared in my life, both times, he was gone.

The little ones had been clinging to me all afternoon. Shai and Amina followed me around the house, showing me a variety of treasures and innocently asking questions about last night. Dafna, who knew nothing of what had transpired, had insisted that I carry her practically everywhere since the trial in our courtyard disbanded. It was almost as if they sensed I needed distraction from both the ache in my chest after Ronen's departure and the confrontation I knew was coming as soon as my father returned home.

He'd been so focused on dealing with the perpetrators of last night's events that he'd only spoken to me for a few moments this morning, just long enough to hear my side of the story before he strode out the door. But I was under no illusion that the one conversation was sufficient to cover all that needed to be said.

And so, I kept busy. I swept the house top to bottom. I helped my mother and Miri prepare the evening meal. I tended the donkeys that Natan had neglected today after disappearing early this morning. I helped Yonah restack the end of one of the woodpiles that had toppled. I let Amina and Dafna braid and unbraid my hair a number of times. They'd been fascinated with the color of it, now that I'd finally put aside my headscarf and allowed my hair to fall down my back unfettered. I'd made a silent promise to Ronen that I would let my light shine, and even if he'd left me without even a good-bye, and with a thousand questions I would never have answers for, I was determined to keep it.

By the time my mother sent Yonah to call the men to the meal, I was exhausted from being in constant motion but found a new burst of energy the moment my father, Gershom, and Iyov came through the door. To my surprise, Rina and Safira followed them, saying their husbands were busy tending to the prisoners, so they'd decided to join us.

More often than not, we had extra guests at meals—the single Levites, one of the neighbor families, and sometimes people from down in Kiryat-Yearim. But tonight, only my mother, father, and siblings sat together on the floor of our home. Natan had apparently refused Yonah's call to eat, too busy repairing the charcoal mound that had been destroyed, so I set about filling an extra bowl of vegetable and barley stew for him to eat later.

"Sit down, Eliora," said my father, when I'd sprung up to place the bowl on a shelf. I startled at his demanding tone, tears immediately springing to my eyes and the memory of Menash's dismissal heavy on my heart. Would this be the last time I was allowed to partake of a meal with this family I adored?

I obeyed, my pulse racing as I fidgeted with the bowl on my lap. "I cannot begin to tell you how sorry I am, Abba. You welcomed

Natan and me into your home, treated us as your own, and I repaid your generosity with betrayal. I deserve whatever punishment you deem fitting."

The room was silent as I remained with my head down, my eyes on the stew but seeing only every single mistake I'd made since Ronen had appeared in Kiryat-Yearim.

"Eliora," he snapped, the uncharacteristic edge in his voice making me flinch and nearly spill the bowl. "What are you talking about?"

I lifted my gaze to find him staring at me, wide-eyed and jaw agape.

"It is my fault. I showed Ronen where the Ark was. I did not even stop to consider . . ." I swallowed against the hot lump in my throat. "And then instead of running for you that night, I followed after him instead, which of course led to being coerced into leading Machlon and the others down the mountain. There is no excuse for my actions, other than profound foolishness."

"You *are* foolish," he said, the words striking hard at the very center of my chest. "Foolish for blaming yourself for something that was in no way your fault. Foolish for thinking that I would be angry with you for being tricked by a man who deceived me as well. And foolish for imagining that I would punish you for trying to save the life of someone you care about and for risking your own life for Israel's holiest treasure."

Speechless, I sat with my mouth hanging open and my eyes streaming.

"It is not you who must apologize, my precious daughter. But I do. We all do."

"I . . . I don't understand." I blinked, my gaze moving around the room in bewilderment at my siblings and my mother—all who looked regretful—and then landed back on him.

"When you came to our home," he said, his tone now infinitely more gentle, "you were so eager to be a part of us. You dove into everything with both hands and seemed so cheerful to be involved with our household, always serving everyone in that sweet, quiet way of yours, without a hint of discontent. Somehow, without meaning to, I think we gave you the impression that was what we expected of you. That you had to earn our affection by carrying everything on your shoulders, especially Natan's troubles. Your mother warned me something was wrong, months ago, but I was too busy with my responsibilities to truly listen. If Ronen had not opened my eyes to all of this earlier, made me see how deeply you were hurting, I think perhaps you would have pushed yourself to illness after this incident, especially carrying this load of needless guilt."

"*Ronen* told you this?" I asked, my mind whirring like a spindle.

"Indeed he did. The boy may have much to atone for, but there is no denying his deep affection for you."

A thrill pulsed through my limbs at the same time my cheeks heated, since all eyes in the room were still on me.

"You know you were adopted into our family, Eliora. But I think perhaps you have not truly accepted what that means. You are not an outsider who is only allowed to stay because you work your fingers to the bone or because of some level of perfection you maintain. You are our daughter—no different than Rina, or Safira, or Miri, or Amina, or Dafna. When you accepted the invitation to join our family, that was permanent. Unbreakable. Irreversible. We will never ask you to leave or turn our backs on you. There is nothing you can do, or fail to do, that will make us stop loving you."

My hands flew to my face, sobs breaking free, and the bowl in my lap clattered to the ground. And then, before I knew what was happening, I was being pulled to my feet, my father's strong arms wrapped around me as he held me tight and reassured me that I was his own. That his love was without condition and without end. My mother's voice joined in, her own arms slipping around my waist as she told me that the day Natan and I agreed to stay was just as thrilling and joyful as the days each of our siblings was born. And then I was surrounded by the rest of my family, each of them whispering words of love and apology, kissing my wet cheeks, or in the case of Dafna, demanding to be lifted into my arms for a tight embrace. For the first time, I allowed myself to bask in the sweetness of their affection and acceptance, letting it soak down to the marrow of my bones and set me free.

The only thing missing from this overflowing moment of joy and peace was Natan.

Forty

Natan had done a thorough job of removing the fallen oak tree from my flower garden. All that was left were ashes and charred leaves atop the squashed and burned remains of my once-vibrant blooms. I pressed my sharp-edged wooden shovel into the earth and turned over a scoop of dark soil, knowing from experience that the ash would nourish the earth and provide an even richer bed to establish new plants in place of those that had been ruined.

It had been three and a half days since the shocking events in the woods, and in each moment I felt freer than the last. Every breath I took was deeper and more refreshing, every birdsong in the trees sweeter, and instead of feeling like everyone was staring at my hair or my height or labeling me a foreigner, I'd found myself thanking Yahweh for the tangible reminders that I'd been grafted into a deep-rooted family who did not count my Philistine heritage as something shameful. They saw my past as something that made me unique and gave testimony to the greatness and mercy of the God who'd drawn me out of Ashdod and led me to dwell among his covenant people in a house devoted to his ways. No longer was I uneasy about accompanying my sisters down to Kiryat-Yearim to deliver baskets of food to the residents there. I knew for certain now that it was as my mother had said: it was Yahweh I must cling to, and in him I found my peace, not my proximity to the Ark or even my continued presence on the mountain. And where Yahweh led me, I was determined to follow.

Hearing that the whole reason for the Yom Teruah gathering had been a ruse to cover the theft of the Ark was disheartening, and I wondered how long it would be before another ingathering festival would be called, especially since according to Gershom, a surprising number of the congregation in the valley had packed up their tents and disappeared the morning after the trumpets sounded, most likely because of Samuel's insistence that they turn away from mixing pagan worship with that of Yahweh.

Thankfully, those who remained had obeyed the call. Hundreds of unholy objects had been engulfed in cook-fires that night and a spirit of solemn repentance now hovered over the valley as the people prepared for Yom Kippur, when sacrifices would be offered for the atonement of the entirety of Israel.

I, however, found myself anticipating the day of fasting and reflection in an entirely new light. After letting go of my fears that Elazar and Yoela might someday turn me out, either because of my own failings or Natan's, I looked forward to spending that day thanking Adonai for removing me from a people whose gods demanded everything and gave nothing back, and placing me among those whose God lavished blessings on his own and asked only that they love him with all their heart, mind, soul, and strength.

Neither Ronen, nor Samuel, had been seen since the trial, and I did not anticipate that I would see him again soon, if ever. But I wished I could thank him for telling my father what I hadn't had to courage to say, and express my gratitude for challenging me to consider myself an ongoing work of the Creator, which had shifted my perspective of myself and my past so completely.

In the days since he'd been gone, I'd called up his words time and time again about Yahweh composing a beautiful song with every note of my life. I missed him so much and could only pray that he might enjoy a fraction of the peace that he had given me.

Also missing lately was Natan, who'd made only rare appearances at home to eat, sleep, or tend to the animals. I'd attempted to talk with him a few times, but it seemed that the revelation of both Shoshana's betrothal and Ronen's betrayal had erased any progress he'd made in reopening his heart to me, or anyone else. But I would not wait much longer to search him out and try again; he needed me and I needed him. We had a bond I refused to relinquish, no matter how hard he tried to push me away or how much distance he put between the two of us.

I glanced back at the place where my oak used to stand, where now only a stump remained, longing for that place of refuge high up in the branches that I'd only ever shared with one person.

"I'm sorry I wasn't able to save it," said a deep and lovely voice that made my heart leap into my throat. Before I turned to look at him, I took a few slow, measured breaths, so my own voice would not betray the bone-melting relief that threatened to bring me to my knees. He hadn't left for good after all.

"It was not your fault," I said, finally meeting Ronen's eyes. "You came as fast as you could." He looked tired and gaunt, like he'd spent the last three days not sleeping or eating.

"It wasn't fast enough," he said, and I knew that he was speaking of more than the fiery destruction of my tree. "I did not discern the danger, and when I did, I took far too long to gather the courage to open my mouth."

I paused before responding, searching the features that had become so familiar during these few weeks: the mahogany-dark eyes that had sparkled with mischief and affection, the lips that had sung me songs of immeasurable beauty, the hands that stroked the lyre with such tenderness as he told me the story of enduring love between his ancestors. He'd asked me for forgiveness as we'd stood on the boulder before the Ark, and I had yet to offer it.

"Where have you been?" I asked, peeling my gaze away to resume shoveling the ash-laden dirt.

"In the olive grove on the eastern slope," he said. "I needed a place to be alone with my thoughts. To fast and pray. To truly seek Yahweh's council on something Samuel proposed."

Burning curiosity over my father's decision to release Ronen into Samuel's hands had been a constant these past three days. But when I'd asked him to explain, he'd only smiled enigmatically and told me that I would understand in due time. He must have known all along that Ronen would return.

I lifted my brows, silently demanding explanation. But instead of telling me what I wanted so desperately to know, Ronen was staring at my hair with a distracted smile.

"*Ronen.*"

His attention snapped back to my face, but his smile only grew. "You uncovered it."

A warm flutter winged its way around my stomach as he waited on my response. "You asked me to," I whispered, knowing I was revealing far too much.

He stepped closer, and it was all I could do to remain in my place and not throw myself into his arms, seek out the rightness I'd felt when we lay side by side behind that boulder with our hands entwined. But first there were questions to ask, answers I required, and things I needed to say.

I cleared my throat and asked the most pressing question first. "What has Samuel asked of you?"

"He has begun to assemble a group of young people in his hometown of Ramah who desire to study the Torah of Mosheh and to explore the mysteries of prayer and prophecy by learning from Samuel himself. He says that the next few years will be decisive for Israel, and he needs disciples who are ready to stand firmly for truth in spite of severe opposition, bold enough to call for repentance no matter the cost, and fearless enough to join with him in the effort to tear down the ancient Canaanite high places all over the Land."

My mouth had gone slack as he'd spoken. From the astonishment on Ronen's face, he too was still in awe over the invitation.

"But . . . how? Why?" I stuttered. "After what happened?"

He huffed a laugh and ran his fingers through his hair. "That's just it. He was there, Eliora. He heard everything you and I said to Machlon and the priests. He said that anyone who was willing to sacrifice his family, his livelihood, and everything he loved in order to speak such bold truth was the sort of person who Yahweh could use in this endeavor. And he had already spoken to Tuviyah about me; he knows that my strengths lie in composing songs and says that it is a skill that will be of utmost importance in the days to come. I have no idea what that means or how writing songs will have any impact on Israel's future, but how could I possibly refuse such an honor? Especially when I do not deserve it after all I have done."

"You can't," I replied, smiling widely even as my heart splintered in two. "You must go. This is a gift to you from Yahweh because of *his* goodness. Just like I've learned that my failures do not lessen my family's love for me, yours do not change the character of the God who offers grace for all of us through the blood of the sacrifice on the mercy seat. I know Abiram turned his back on you, Ronen, but Adonai vowed to never leave or forsake us. We both must hold tight to that promise and find peace in it."

Ronen's eyes dropped closed, his lips pressed together as if he were restraining deep emotion. For a few moments, I just watched him, breathing in tandem with him as he collected himself enough to speak. When he did lift his lashes to meet my gaze, they were wet.

"How are you so good?" he asked. "Why are you not railing at me? Screaming at me for my lies and foolishness? Cursing my name for taking advantage of your kindness and generosity? I do not deserve your compassion. I do not deserve your forgiveness."

He sank to the ashy ground in front of me, looking up at me with pleading eyes. "And yet even though I know I am not worthy of that forgiveness, and far from worthy of your love, I cannot help but beg of you to listen, to hear me when I say that although Machlon made it sound as though I was playing a game with your heart, it is not the truth. I was so relieved when you didn't seem to know exactly where the Ark was and thrilled when Natan too, revealed nothing, and then so very devastated when you showed me your secret refuge.

"I hated that knowledge and wished so much that I had never climbed into that oak tree with you, or that in your innocence you hadn't shown me the location. In a moment of weakness, I did tell him the Ark was in a cedar grove—I confess that freely and with deep regret—but it was the Gibeonites who gave him the exact location. I did not want to betray you, Eliora, even if that's what I was sent here to do. From the moment I found you in your garden, crying out to Yahweh on your brother's behalf, I struggled between what I thought was my sacred duty to my God and my family, and the draw your sweet and generous spirit has had on my tortured one."

I had no time to wallow in embarrassment that he had indeed heard me pour out my heart to Adonai that day, because he was not finished.

"And it was a priceless gift that you gave me, showing me that it was not by taking vengeance that I would honor my father and brothers, but by lifting up my voice in adoration and glorifying Yahweh with the same devotion they did. Even for those few moments I played my lyre and sang with the other Levites on the ridge, I was overcome with the sense that I was finally where I was meant to be and doing exactly what I was supposed to do. All because of you, Eliora. Your kindness, your strength, your loyalty, your patience, everything about your beautiful heart makes me want to be the man who might one day deserve you.

"And it was not just you who I came to esteem either," he continued, barely taking a breath. "But your father, your brothers, and your entire family. The accusations my uncle spewed about them were proved utterly false during that first meal. I could not help but immediately see the contrast between the family that took you in with such openness and unconditional love and the one that manipulated and used me, and I wished that—" He stopped, swallowed hard, and then half-whispered, "I wished that you would consent to be my wife, so they could be my family as well."

Everything seemed to stand still as he looked up at me with such hopeful apprehension, including my breath, the birds in the trees, even the whisper of the breeze in the orchard nearby, or perhaps the thundering of my heartbeat drowned it all out.

"I know I have much to prove," he said, the words toppling over themselves. "And I vow to you that I will do everything in my power to show you that I am, in fact, a man of integrity. A man who can be trusted with both your heart and your future. I have already spoken to your father, told him I plan to travel with Samuel for the next few months as he goes town to town, seeking out others he means to invite to Ramah, and calling for repentance along the way."

"So, you have decided to go?"

He nodded. "After three days of fasting and prayer, I truly believe it is what I've been called to do."

"And what did my father have to say about all of this?"

His lips quirked, a small measure of that mischief I so enjoyed creeping back into his countenance. "He said to ask you."

I trusted my father implicitly in all things, even more than I had before he'd asked my forgiveness and expressed his deep love for me. If he had given leave for Ronen to even hint at a betrothal, then he must believe this man was sincere in his repentance and his regard for me.

"And what will happen when you return?" I asked, doing my best to temper the excitement building in my chest.

"That depends upon you, my love," he said, his tone solemn but expectant. "Are you willing to go with me to Ramah? Samuel assures me that there will be plenty of other women living in the new community he calls Naioth, including his own wife, whom he says would both welcome your arrival and be thrilled to share her own knowledge of the Torah with you."

I blinked down at him, trying to focus on everything he'd said instead of just the way his endearment seeped deep beneath my skin and made my mind a little hazy. "But . . . but I am Philistine."

"That you are," he said, with a gentle smile, "and Avraham was an Amorite. Rahab was of Canaan. Calev was a Kenite. And many who entered this land with Yehoshua were of Egyptian and other foreign descent. As I said on the rooftop that morning, I think your heritage only makes your witness more powerful. And Samuel agrees with me."

"He does?"

"Didn't you hear what I told you? He heard *everything* you and I said to the priests. The invitation to Ramah is not just for me. It is for both of us. Together."

I thought of Azuvah, and how she'd repeated the stories of her people to herself so she would not forget them even in the dark misery of slavery. How she spent night after night telling two Philistine children those same stories in her tongue without knowing how important such knowledge would one day be for us. How she sacrificed her life for our freedom so I might one day be offered the opportunity to know more about the God she clung to even in her forced exile. I curved my hand over the tzitzit she'd given me and blessed her memory before I gave my answer.

"I have not been away from this mountain since you brought me up here on your back," I said, remembering how thrilled I'd been to be so close to him even then. "And for all these years I've been terrified of being away from the Ark. Its nearness has given me peace, made me feel safe."

"We can stay," he said. "I am willing to remain in Kiryat-Yearim and guard the—"

I placed a hand over his mouth, his warm breath on my palm causing a small shiver.

"Let me finish," I said, and at his nod—complete with a smile in his mahogany eyes—I dropped my hand. "As I was saying, my mother reminded me that it is not the Ark that watches over me and protects me, but the God Who Sees. The God who led Natan and me to a house where I entered into covenant with his beloved people and have enjoyed such peace and blessing. And since I've now truly come to see myself as one of those beloved people, I have full confidence that no matter where I go, Yahweh's peace and protection will go with me." I moved forward, placing my hands on either side of his face, reveling in the softness of his beard as

I stroked his cheekbones with my thumbs. "To Ramah, or to the ends of the earth, if that is where you ask me to go."

"I don't deserve—" he began, but I cut off his words by bending forward and pressing my lips to the ones that I hoped would sing me many, many more beautiful songs.

"You hurt me," I said, looking into his eyes, which were so luminous and full of remorse. "You lied. You deceived. But I also empathize with your justifications for doing so. If I would have been taken in by someone like Abiram, I might have made the very same choices. I can only be grateful that it was Elazar who adopted me and afforded us *both* grace for our mistakes."

A shudder went through his body as I placed my forehead on his. "I forgive you, Ronen," I whispered. "And I would be honored to be your wife. To be your family."

With a smile that outshone the sun and moon and all the stars, he surged to his feet, pulling me into his arms and making the gentle, sweet kiss I'd given him a distant memory.

Forty-One

Once the two of us floated back down to earth, Ronen reluctantly released me to slide the strap of his satchel over his head.

"This is my pledge to you," he said, pressing the familiar bag into my hands and then another soft kiss to my lips. "So that you know I will return in a few months for my bride."

"I believe you, Ronen. You do not have to give me anything, let alone your most valuable treasure." I tried to shift it back into his arms, but he resisted with a shake of his head, curling his hands around mine so that we both had a firm grip on the lyre.

"It is not my greatest treasure anymore, Eliora." He delivered another brush of his lips to my cheek and then my forehead. "You are. And have you forgotten the story of its origins? There can be no greater mohar than an instrument made by a man who adored his foreign bride beyond all description.

"You keep it safe while I am away. And when I return to you, I will write new songs about how much I cherish you. About these green eyes that remind me of a sunlit wood . . ." He pressed a feather-light kiss to each of my eyelids. "About this golden hair that has been taunting me for so long . . ." He reached up to run his hands through my locks and then bent forward to bury his nose in my neck, inhaling deeply. "And about a Philistine woman who I would gladly shave my own head for."

I laughed loudly at his sly mention of Delilah, feeling his body vibrate against mine as he chuckled at his own jest. "I wouldn't sharpen your razor just yet, though I'm glad your strength is not dependent on it. I like your hair." I tugged at the portion that had slipped free of the knot at his neck and tucked it behind his ear.

"Do you?" He grinned.

"I always have found your appearance . . . how did Miri say it? Oh yes . . . pleasing." I matched his mischievous grin. "In fact, I used to—" I stopped, realizing how ridiculous my admission would seem.

His brows lifted high as he held me closer. "You used to what?"

I dropped my eyes, my cheeks blooming with heat. "I used to think about you when I was younger. . . . I used to dream that you would come back to Kiryat-Yearim and see me as more than a terrified orphan hidden behind a wall."

"You can be assured, my love, that I in no way see you as a girl anymore." He pulled me in for another kiss, then whispered in my ear. "And these months apart will be the longest of my life."

They would be the same for me as well, but knowing that soon we would be together in Ramah and be part of a community of people under Samuel's tutelage would make the wait a little more bearable. And at least I would have some time to adjust to the idea of leaving my family before he came for me. Thankfully, Ramah was less than a day's walk from Kiryat-Yearim, and I knew my separation from them would not be a permanent one.

"Oh!" I said, pulling back from him. I'd been so absorbed in joy that I'd nearly forgotten there was one more person who would need to be consulted about our plans. "Natan! I cannot leave him behind, especially now that Shoshana is betrothed and his Gibeon-ite friends have been arrested. I wonder if he might benefit from coming to Ramah as well. It may give him a chance to heal. To learn more about Yahweh."

Ronen nodded. "Of course. Perhaps Samuel might allow him to take part in studies as well."

His easy acceptance of my idea made hope take flight in my

chest. "Yes! And I am certain my father will agree. He and my mother love him dearly, but they have been bereft of ideas for breaking through to him. Perhaps a fresh start in a new city might help him to see things in a different light. I know he is restless here on the mountain and desires to see other places."

"Convincing him to go may not be as simple as you hope. I have some groveling to do with your brother," he said with a sardonic smile. "You are not the only one whose trust I abused."

"He'll forgive you," I said, fully convinced. Natan had been at the trial after all and heard the entirety of Ronen's contrite explanation. Even if he might struggle with it at first, eventually my brother would not be able to deny Ronen's remorse, nor the sincerity of his love for me.

I slipped the strap of the lyre Ronen had given me as a betrothal promise over my head. Someday we would pass this treasure on to our own firstborn child, along with the story of how we'd found our way to each other because of a golden box on the back of a cow-drawn wagon and the prophetic words of a Hebrew slave who gave her life for mine. Then I tangled my fingers with his and gave his hand a tug. "Let's go talk with him now. I know just where to find him."

It had been a long time since I'd been to this side of the mountain, but once I found the trail along the southwestern ridge, slithering back and forth like a serpent, it was fairly easy to make my way to Natan's cave. As we hiked, Ronen told me more about his revelations regarding his father and brothers, his answered prayer for rain as my tree burned, and how Azuvah's words had agreed so perfectly with Samuel's that he could do nothing but believe the truth. He even told me what Samuel had said to Natan, about being a wild branch and being carried away by the sea. Stricken by the confusing and foreboding prophecy, I'd kept quiet for the rest of the walk, pondering what it all might mean.

The mouth of the cave was a gaping black maw in the hillside, but I knew it was the same one I'd found him in before because it faced the gap between hills in the distance and the narrow line of sea-blue that edged the horizon. I wondered how much of Ashdod Natan even remembered after so long. I still needed to talk to him more about Azuvah and help him understand why exactly our father had left and how it had nothing to do with him. And also to explain how I'd learned to embrace my past, instead of despise it.

"Natan?" I called out, stepping into the mouth of the cave, with Ronen right behind me. I blinked my eyes, hoping they would adjust quickly. I would not put it past my brother to be hiding here in some niche and jump out just to hear me squeal. In fact, after all that had happened, I almost wished he would. At least it would be something affectionate and teasing between us.

I called his name again, threatening to make him pick the rest of the peas in the garden by himself if he did not answer me. But instead of his ever-deepening voice responding to my jest, a small sob reached my ears.

Gut clenching, I rushed forward into the cave, searching out the origin of the muffled cry and found Yonah sitting with his back against the far wall, hands over his face as he wept.

"Yonah!" I knelt and wrapped my arms around his small body. "What happened?"

"I tried," he said, shuddering as he attempted to drag in a breath. "I tried to follow him, but my leg . . ." He huffed out a tearful growl through his teeth as he slammed his twisted foot against the stone floor. "I hate it." His face was mottled red as he dissolved into tears again, pressing his forehead into my chest.

"I don't understand. Where did Natan go? Is he back at the house?"

He shook his head, his voice small. "He hates it when I follow him, but I wanted to help. He went to the charcoal mound, and you were there"—he looked up at Ronen, his eyes red-rimmed—"both of you. And then he was so mad and he told me not to follow him, but I did, and when I got here, he had his ax and his pack and then

I couldn't keep up—" He pressed his face against my shoulder, grabbing my tunic with both hands. "I tried, Eliora. I'm sorry!"

I rocked him back and forth, pressing kisses into his sweaty hair. "It's all right, Yonah. You know Natan loses his temper and stomps off, but he'll come back. He loves you, even if he's not so good about showing it."

He just shook his head, weeping as though his little heart was in a thousand pieces on the floor.

"Eliora," said Ronen, from the side of the cave where he'd been looking around as I comforted Yonah. His expression was so troubled that I pressed one last kiss to my brother's forehead, told him I'd be right back, and disentangled myself in order to join Ronen.

"What is it?" I asked.

With a frown, he took my hand in his and filled it with a handful of pebbles. Confused, I took a step back toward the mouth of the cave, shifting my hand so the sunlight would illuminate whatever he'd found. But what lay in my palm was not pebbles at all. It was Ronen's lion-claw necklace, smashed to pieces. And among the fragments of his family heirloom lay another familiar trinket. A six-sided piece of bone, once smoothed into a soft patina by years and years of handling and being carried in a pouch around a young boy's neck, now gouged deeply by what looked to be the sharp edge of an ax. It was a miracle that it was still in one piece. I fingered the remaining holes on one side of the die, tears pricking my eyes as I remembered the day I'd found it in a drain by the road and the smile on my brother's face when I tipped it into his small palm.

"What does this mean?" I whispered. "Why would he do this?"

Ronen's arm came around my waist, holding me tightly to him, and perhaps bracing me against whatever he might have to say. "Look over there," he said, gesturing toward a spot a few paces away. "It looks like he's been storing provisions in here. Stockpiling food and such."

Curling my fist around what remained of the gifts both Ronen and I had given him, I held my breath as I pulled myself from

Ronen's hold and went to examine the pots and baskets he'd indicated. They were empty. Only a few crumbs of salted meat and a trace of roasted barley remained in the pots. With my heart throbbing, I estimated that if he was carrying with him all the provisions that had been in these vessels, he would have enough food to last him for a good many days, perhaps even weeks. Also missing was the large pack that he used to haul wood, and as Yonah had indicated, the double-edged ax he carried practically everywhere was gone too.

"It looks like there was a pallet laid out here," said Ronen, brushing a foot over the dusty cave floor. His tone was gentle and hesitant. "He likely rolled it up and took it with him as well."

No. No, he couldn't. He wouldn't do this to me.

"Natan!" I yelled, gripping his once-treasured possessions so tightly in my hand that I felt something pierce my skin.

"Natan!" I shouted from the mouth of the cave, again and again, hearing my voice echo down into the valley while tears burned my cheeks and my throat went raw from the force of my desperate calls. Ronen's strong arms slipped around my waist from behind, his own body shaking as he pulled me into himself while uttering promises that my dazed mind could not comprehend. My knees buckled as I let out one last agonized cry.

"Lukio!"

Epilogue

Lukio

ASHDOD, PHILISTIA

Everything looked smaller, and yet in some ways, the city of my birth was far grander than I remembered. Or perhaps they'd rebuilt it in these past years with even more splendor than before. As a boy, I'd been much more concerned with running about with my friends, playing dice games, tossing stuffed goat bladders in the dusty street, or snatching fruit off of traders' tables when their backs were turned.

With their impressive façades facing outward, stately white-plastered homes lined the roads in well-disciplined grandeur, nothing like the rough-hewn stone Hebrew dwellings whose function was far more important than their form. This cultured and prosperous city put to shame the tired little town among the trees where I'd been living.

Most of the buildings had two, or even three, stories of tiered rooms, with open-air colonnades or canopies from which all sorts

350

of fabrics and ribbons fluttered in the sea breeze. The columns themselves were painted with bright reds, yellows, and blues, and intricate carvings and carefully designed swirls, birds, gods, or animals decorated the archways and doorways of each shop and home. The enormous variety of colors and shapes were so dazzling that my eyes barely knew where to land.

A group of four wealthy women passed by, and unlike the drab, earth-toned tunics the Hebrews wore, these women were attired even more vibrantly than the buildings. Their skirts were multilayered and tasseled, a style I vaguely remembered my aunt Jacame wearing, and instead of the demure braids most Hebrew girls tucked beneath headscarves, these women seemed to be competing with one another for the most complicated hairstyle. Tiny shells and gold or silver beads were woven among their oiled and curled strands, and in the case of one of them, gemstones sparkled among her deep black tresses. Most shocking was that their torsos were covered only by the sheerest of linen fabric, and I was helpless to peel my eyes away.

One of the women lifted a brow as she caught me gawking at her brazen nakedness, and my face blazed with embarrassing heat. She returned my stare with an obvious perusal at my own form and offered me an enticing smile that caused me to stumble in surprise. She laughed and passed me by, but not before dropping a small wink and making a comment to her friend that I could not discern but made it clear that she appreciated what she saw.

Immediately Shoshana came to mind, her wide and fathomless hazel eyes looking up at me with innocent admiration, but I pushed away the uneasy feelings of guilt by reminding myself that she'd chosen Medad. She would be *his* wife. She would bear *his* children someday. I was less than nothing to her anymore, no matter how many pretty lies she once told. The excuses she'd given me when she found me at the charcoal mound meant nothing. If she'd truly cared for me like she said she did, then she would have let nothing come between us, not even her father's demands. If the women of Ashdod found my appearance pleasing, then I would take pride in it and not allow myself to be drawn back into regret over a girl who did not want me.

Even Risi didn't want me anymore. She'd made that abundantly clear with her decision in the garden, while wrapped in Ronen's arms. I hadn't meant to spy on them, only to finish rebuilding the charcoal mound.

But there she and her lover had been, entwined in each other, making plans to abandon me like everyone else had. I had no idea how she could possibly even forgive that traitor after what he'd done to her. I cared nothing for the Ark and had in fact laughed when I'd heard that something as silly as fog—a common occurrence during the rainy months—had scared away the thieves. But the fact that Ronen had slithered his way into Risi's favor and pretended to care for me was far more damning than his machinations to steal a box.

I'd thought perhaps he truly had cared for me, especially after the night we'd worked together side by side with the burning tree. He'd treated me like a man then, not some throwaway child. But he'd gotten what he wanted and would have given up the pretense of friendship eventually. That's what liars did, after all.

So, of course I'd not waited around to hear Risi justify marrying such a deceiver. There would have been no reason to do so. She'd made her choice, and I made mine. But I could not lie, even to myself, and say that I did not miss her. Even ten days later, I still felt as though someone had taken my ax to the center of my chest in the same indiscriminate way I'd destroyed the charcoal mound the moment Shoshana left me. I rubbed at the ache, wondering how long it would take to go away.

I wandered through the town, passing by the temple of Dagon, where a new and larger image of the god I remembered had been erected. I had a vague recollection of thinking that the original one was frightening when I was young, but now it only reminded me of when Adnan and Padi had taken me up to one of their ancestral high places the night after my fight.

When I'd been hesitant to accept their invitation, my Gibeonite friends had told me that my own people worshiped in a similar manner, that they had seen it with their own eyes when they'd recently traveled to Ekron with a load of timber. Both my pride and my curiosity had finally won out as they described all the fearsome Philistine warriors they'd met while they were there and the cultured and sophisticated ways of my countrymen. What I had seen on that mountaintop had shocked, fascinated, and disgusted me all at once. However, I'd fled like a coward when I thought of my sister knowing what I was standing witness to, and how disappointed she would be.

Afterwards, Adnan and Padi proved to be just as loyal as everyone else. They'd had nothing to do with me since that night and had only been too quick to get involved with the scheme that put Risi in so much danger. Their betrayal mattered little, though. I'd only began associating with them as a means to provide for Shoshana and a future that now would never be.

I glanced back at the temple one more time before turning away, remembering the sick feeling in my gut as I'd observed the proceedings on that supposedly sacred high place. I had no desire to set foot in *any* place of worship ever again. My choices were my own. My destiny a path only I could determine. No god, Philistine or Hebrew, had any sort of appeal to me.

My feet found their way to the front of the first house I ever remembered living in. As I stood at the door, I wondered if this place too would spit me out the way Elazar's had done.

I took a few long moments to battle the indecision that tugged at me, whispering in my ear that it was not too late to go back, to beg Shoshana to change her mind, and to plead with Risi not to leave me behind.

But I knew those were futile hopes. Shoshana was forever lost to me, and Risi planned to go up to Ramah with the betrayer and that madman I'd come across in the orchard, the one who'd called me a wild branch. She'd not even stopped to think about me while she'd skimmed over all Ronen's sins and then threw herself into his arms just as I walked away.

With Risi gone, I doubted my welcome in Elazar's house would have continued had I remained, but along with the pangs of grief at losing my sister, I could not help but miss Yoela as well. Even if she wasn't truly my mother, she'd been kind to me, fussing over me just like with her own sons, but I knew I disappointed her just like I did the rest of them.

No longer would they have to tolerate my presence. They would forget me soon enough. And I would forget them. I had to. It hurt too much otherwise.

My long hesitation on the doorstep must have alerted someone inside to a visitor because the door swung open, and to my surprise, my cousin Mataro himself stood in the doorway, a deep frown on his face as he looked up at me. A good bit heavier than I remembered, his skin was still marked from the boils he'd suffered when his parents died during the plagues, and his hair was stringy and thinning on top.

"Who are you?" he said, voice gruff and eyes bleary, as if he'd just awoken from sleep at midday. The gust of wine-laden breath that accompanied the question made it clear why he seemed so unsteady on his feet.

It had been a very long time since I'd spoken my mother tongue, other than a few words here and there to the animals, since my sister adamantly refused to speak it with me once she decided she wanted to be a Hebrew. But I hoped I remembered enough to make myself understood.

"Hello, Mataro," I said. "I have come back."

With his brow furrowed in confusion, he scrutinized my face, and by the scowl he gave me, I fully expected to be turned away. But then I saw the moment he recognized my two-colored eyes. His own went wider, and his jaw slackened.

"Lukio?"

I nodded.

"How are you here?" He bent his head forward, gaze moving up and down the busy street, expecting Risi to be with me, no doubt. "And where have you been all this time?"

"With the Hebrews," I said, working hard to quell the images of Elazar's home and the faces of each of the people I'd lived with on the mountain of Kiryat-Yearim. *They don't want you*, I reminded myself.

"The Hebrews?" He laughed, the sound rusty and followed by a phlegmy cough. "Well now, isn't that an interesting turn of events?"

Before I could ask him to clarify his statement, he folded his arms across his chest, and for the first time really looked me up and down, his gaze becoming more sober with every moment.

"You've grown up! Nearly as big as your father, I would guess. And I'm certain your days of growing are far from over." He reached out and clamped a sweaty palm on my shoulder, eyes flaring a bit when he gripped the hardened muscle I'd earned from all my months of woodcutting. Then a sly smile spread across his face, and I swore I saw a glitter of silver in his dark brown eyes as his fingers gripped even tighter.

"It's good to have you back where you belong, Lukio. Welcome home."

A Note from the Author

After digging around in the book of Samuel, I found myself wondering, what was life like for the tribes of Israel during this time and what made them later demand a king so vehemently? Why did the Ark of the Covenant get left on the mountain of Kiryat-Yearim for seventy years until King David "discovered" where it was and brought it to Jerusalem, even though the Mishkan (Tabernacle) had actually been rebuilt at Nob (which is near Jerusalem) sometime in the interim? And what did the contentious relationship between the Hebrews and Philistines look like during this period in history?

Also during that time I had the opportunity to travel to Israel. When we drove up the coast and through the hills just west of Jerusalem, our tour guide said, "This is precisely the area through which the cow-drawn cart carrying the Ark of the Covenant traveled on its way from Ekron to Beth Shemesh." And right then, I had a flash of inspiration and wondered, what if someone other than the kings of Philistia followed that strange parade? And what if it was two children? And even more interesting, what if it was two *Philistine* children? As an adoptee myself and the mother of adopted children, I was intrigued with the idea of a Hebrew family bringing these two enemy orphans into their home and showing them the beauty of living in Covenant with Yahweh. Of course, as we have seen in *To Dwell among Cedars*, those two "wild branches" had very different reactions to their new life.

But who were the Philistines? Where did they come from, and why did they feature so prominently in the Old Testament? Most of us know them as "bad guys of the Bible," or perhaps we only remember the story of Samson and that awful Delilah who cut his hair. Once I began doing research for this series, I was shocked to find that until fairly recently there was not a whole lot known about them or their culture, and, like as with all archeology, there are a lot of disagreements, conjectures, and sometimes just plain fictions built around the scanty (in relation to other ancient cultures) material evidence of their existence along the coast of Israel.

Fortunately, in the past few years, some really exciting discoveries have been made in what was once Gath, Ashdod, and Ashkelon, and some of the pottery and other materials pulled from the ground over the past few decades have been making the case for proving what the Bible always said—that the Philistines were an Aegean people who arrived by ship on the coast of Canaan. Recently released DNA evidence (taken from Philistine cemeteries) has proved that they most likely came from the island of Crete, which is called Caphtor in the Bible (Jeremiah 47:4; Amos 9:7). How exciting that we live in a time that even the bones of the long dead can speak truth to us and prove the historicity of the Word!

Since during the latter Bronze Age the residents of Crete were the Mycenaeans (and before them the Minoans), both of whom left some fairly strong evidence of their own surprisingly advanced and distinctive cultures, I used some of their histories and language (known as Linear B), along with the Egyptian mentions of conflicts with the Sea Peoples and references in the Bible to their national character, in order to piece together an idea of what this enigmatic group might have been like. And as usual, all inaccuracies are a product of my own overactive imagination.

Unfortunately, the practice of puppy threshold sacrifice is a real one, proven by excavations in ancient Philistine cities (as hard as it is to read), and it is possible that babies also might have sacrificed in this way, according to similar burial practices under Philistine homes. Also, Lukio's favorite pastime with his friends was a common game, since dice from that period (with the exact number of dots as on our modern dice!) have been found in Philistine cities as well. One of the few words we know for sure are Philistine is *seren* which means *lord*, and is seems to be interchangeable with the designation *king* used in the Old Testament for the rulers of the five city-states collectively known by us as Philistia.

The other interesting aspect of this time period for me was the line of succession for the seat of High Priest, which had originally been designated as that of Aaron's son Eleazar (yes, the same one from *Shelter of the Most High*). Somehow, and no one knows why, that honor moved to the line of Itamar, who was another son of Aaron, and continued to be passed down through Itamar's lineage until the time of David, when he reappointed a descendant of Eleazar as High Priest.

When I stumbled over ancient writings by the Samaritans that said that a civil war broke out between the priests who supported Itamar's line and priests who supported Eleazar's (of which there is no evidence either way), my imagination was sparked. I wondered, what if there were a group of priests who were so upset about this shift in the succession of the High Priesthood that they were willing to set off a war with their tribal brethren for the sake of getting their hands on the Ark and rebuilding the Tabernacle in a new place?

The Bible is silent on what—if any—struggles happened after the destruction of Shiloh (which has been proven by recent evidence of devastating fires in the exact time period in which the Bible places these events), but as history shows us time and time again, human beings are prone to power struggles, especially when issues of religion and politics are at the center of those conflicts.

I find it very doubtful that everyone was happy with the shift in succession and that everyone believed Samuel truly spoke for God. Even Jesus says that a prophet is not honored in his own country

(John 4:44). Just ask the rest of the prophets, both Old Testament and New, who endured all sorts of persecution and, often, horrific deaths for speaking the truth. The tribes of Israel during this time were nothing close to a unified nation, were regularly at each other's throats, and were so influenced by the nations around them that Samuel had a hard road to climb as the final Judge of Israel in getting them to repent, throw off their idolatrous ways, and bow their knees to Yahweh at Mizpah (1 Samuel 7:5–6).

Kiryat-Yearim (which literally means "the city of forests") is a fascinating place, and one in which recent excavations have given us tantalizing clues as to its importance in the history of Israel. For example, a platform was discovered near the summit where some have conjectured that the Ark may have stood at one point (although that is highly contested, but still intriguing). And yes, ancient thick forests once stood in this region, most of which were destroyed either by Philistine demand for timber for their iron forges, numerous invading armies that used the trees for their voracious war machines, or by shifts in climate and/or devastating erosion over the past few thousand years. Thank the Lord that the people of Israel have been gradually replanting those beautiful forests and the Land is indeed blooming like a rose again (Isaiah 35:1).

As one will note by reading 1 Samuel 5–7:2, there is no mention of a special blessing on the household of Abinadab and his son Elazar for guarding the Ark, but I took a bit of artistic license and conjectured that if Yahweh blessed Obed-Edom during the three months the Ark resided in his household (2 Samuel 6:11), then perhaps Abinidab's clan and even the ground upon which the Ark stood might have been affected in a similar way over a seventy-year period. I also took some artistic license with the earthquake at the beginning of the story, since the Bible says nothing about the ground shaking to cause Dagon to fall. This was purely for dramatic effect and to sow some doubt in the minds of the people as to the cause of the destruction of their god. But who knows exactly how it all came about, especially since the coastal region of Israel is highly prone to seismic activity. However it happened, it certainly scared the Philistines out of their wits and showed them that their sightless god was without power.

It's certainly been fun to dig into a different era of history, study some fascinating cultures, and discover new characters, and I hope you have enjoyed the beginning of this journey to ancient Israel with a brief stopover in ancient Philistia and that you are eager to find out how Lukio's story will resolve in *Between the Wild Branches*.

I'd like to first thank my family. Chad, for carrying a lot of the burden for our cross-country move, which, of course, happened to coincide with the week before the deadline for this book, and also for always being my hero. For Collin, for being such an encourager, and for putting up with having to cook his own food to feed his teenage appetite many nights. For Corrie, who listened to me read this book out loud and who is always so quick with both much-needed hugs during times of overwhelm and generosity with her time and assistance while I work.

Denise Thayne, thank you for giving me some extra space to focus during some of those difficult deadline-crunching days by inviting my kids to your house and blessing them with your time and attention, and also for your continuous prayer support and encouragement.

Joanie Shultz, I cannot begin to thank you enough for reading this entire manuscript not just once but twice during my editing overhaul and for such helpful critiques on both passes. Tina Chen and Ashley Espinoza, thank you both as well for your beta reads of this book and for your helpful comments that give me objective insight when there are things I don't see because I'm too close to the project.

Rel Mollet, there are no words to describe the incredible help you have been to me over these past couple of book launches. Your attention to detail, your creative and insightful suggestions, and your willingness to handle some of the tasks that drain me most during my busiest seasons has been a game changer. Tamela Hancock Murray, I am so grateful for your support and encouragement, as always, along with that of the rest of the Steve Laube Agency. I am so honored to be called one of your authors.

Raela Schoenherr and Jen Veilleux, I can never thank you ladies enough for your editing expertise, for your fantastic suggestions that sometimes take my stories in wonderful new directions I hadn't expected, and for being such enthusiastic supporters of both me and my work. (And special thanks to Jen for working through my edits while serving as a volunteer firefighter in the midst of the COVID-19 pandemic—you awe me, gal!) I cannot express how grateful I am to work with you both and all the wonderful people at Bethany House Publishers who take my stories from early manuscript to a gorgeous book that readers cannot wait to get their hands on. Jennifer Parker, thank you for creating such a unique and eye-catching cover for Eliora's story that is the perfect blend of ancient and modern.

Finally, thank you to my team of Wanderers who are my first-line cheerleaders and are so faithful to read my books and share their enthusiasm with others. And thank you to every single reader who spends their precious time reading my stories, sending me sweet notes of encouragement, and writing reviews to help other readers discover my books as well.

> May the Lord bless you and keep you. May he make his face to shine upon you and be gracious to you. May he lift up his countenance upon you and give you peace. (cf. Numbers 6:24–26)

Questions for Conversation

1. What understanding did you have, if any, about the Philistines before reading this book? Did your perception of them change in any way? What contrasts do you see between their culture and the Hebrews' way of life?

2. Do you know anyone who has been either adopted from another culture as an older child or perhaps has immigrated from another cultural background? What challenges do you think are inherent in such drastic changes in life circumstances?

3. In the eight years since we first encounter Ronen, he becomes so caught up in his uncle's political beliefs that he loses much of his passion for music. Are there ways in which you have allowed distractions to creep in and undermine your own desire to worship the Most High?

4. Eliora and Lukio (Natan) have a special relationship rooted in common loss and history. Do you have a special bond with your own sibling(s)? If not, does this story make you yearn for a deeper connection?

5. For readers of Connilyn's previous series, did you catch

the subtle connection to another of her books? Did that tie-in surprise you?

6. Ronen struggles with his decision to not only go against his family, but also against men who he has always considered godly authorities. What circumstances might cause you to question or even stand up to those who are in authority within the body of Christ?

7. What parallels do you see between the Ark of the Covenant and our Messiah Yeshua? Especially in relation to this story, have you observed ways his name is misused or wielded improperly by those either within the church or outside of it?

8. In the Bible we encounter Samuel as a child (1 Samuel 1–3) and then we more or less don't hear much about him until he is an old man (1 Samuel 7). What new insights did you glean about him here during these interim years?

9. Are there ways that you, like Eliora, find yourself trying to work harder to "make a place for yourself at the table" instead of relying on Yeshua's finished work at the cross to seal your adoption into the family of God?

10. What do you anticipate Lukio's journey will look like in *Between the Wild Branches*? What do you hope will have occurred in Ronen's and Eliora's lives in the meantime?

Connilyn Cossette is a Christy Award and Carol Award winner, whose books have been found on ECPA and CBA bestseller lists. When she is not engulfed in the happy chaos of homeschooling two teenagers, devouring books whole, or avoiding housework, she can be found digging into the rich ancient world of the Bible to discover gems of grace that point to Jesus and weaving them into an immersive fiction experience. Although she and her husband have lived all over the country in their twenty-plus years of marriage, they currently call a little town south of Dallas, Texas, their home. Connect with her at ConnilynCossette.com.

Sign Up for Connilyn's Newsletter

Keep up to date with Connilyn's news on book releases and events by signing up for her email list at connilyncossette.com.

More from Connilyn Cossette

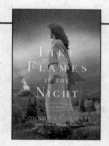

On a hunt for his daughter's killer, Liyam's last hope is a bargain to rescue a strong-willed woman who refuses to leave her mission uncompleted. Can Tirzah convince him to fight alongside her in the refuge city of her birth? Or will his thirst for vengeance outweigh his duty to his people, God, and the woman he's come to love?

Like Flames in the Night
CITIES OF REFUGE #4

You May Also Like . . .

Egyptian slave Kiya leads a miserable life. When terrifying plagues strike Egypt, she chooses to flee with the Hebrews. Soon she finds herself reliant on a strange God and falling for a man who despises her people. Will she turn back toward Egypt or find a new place to belong?

Counted with the Stars by Connilyn Cossette
OUT FROM EGYPT #1
connilyncossette.com

Yeshua has two sisters: Damaris and Pheodora. When Damaris's husband is invited to join the Pharisees, she is excited even though some aspects of the lifestyle seem contrary to what she was taught. After Pheodora's husband is thrown into debtors' prison, she must struggle to keep her family alive. Calling on their wits, their family, and their God, can they trust that He will hear?

The Shepherd's Wife by Angela Hunt
JERUSALEM ROAD #2
angelahuntbooks.com

In her wildest dreams, Esther could never have imagined that she would end up as queen of Persia. But when she's caught in the middle of palace politics and finds herself in an impossible position while relying on a fragile trust in a silent God, can she pit her wisdom against a vicious enemy and win?

Star of Persia by Jill Eileen Smith
jilleileensmith.com